THE GRAND GAME
BOOK 4: HOUSE WOLF

THE GRAND GAME
BOOK 4: HOUSE WOLF

TOM ELLIOT

COPYRIGHT

The Grand Game

Still Hunted.
Still Alone.
But many times stronger.
Can Michael survive the Game?

Months have passed since Michael first entered the Forever Kingdom, and while a great deal of the Game remains a mystery, his own place in it grows surer. Yet, survival—much less success—is by no means assured, and Michael will have to tread a delicate path to forge a place for himself.

Ancient mysteries resurface. And long-buried truths are uncovered.
The Forever Kingdom's past is as murky as the Game, and there are nearly as many truths as factions. But if Michael is to emerge victorious, he must separate fact from fiction.

Will House Wolf rise again?
Will the ancient bloodlines be restored? Can Michael find trustworthy allies? And what price will he have to pay to secure House and allies?

Follow Michael on his epic journey and find out!

PRAISE FOR THE GRAND GAME:

"Interesting portal litrpg. Well-paced and the start of a new series. Curious to see where it goes..." —**Tao Wong on goodreads.com.**

"... Great action, great storyline and I honestly binge read it, start to end..." —**Alex Kozlowski on goodreads.com.**

"Smart MC. Great Tension. Full of Action." —**CookieCrumble on RoyalRoad.com.**

"Everything I look for in a LitRPG." —**CosmereCradleChris on RoyalRoad.com.**

"Oh I liked this very much!" —**The Enlightened Beard on amazon.com.**

"One of the best in this category this year." —**kindle customer on amazon.com.**

Author's Note

Dear Readers,

Thank you for reading the Grand Game. This is a self-published book. Even though care has been given to the review and editing of this novel, some mistakes may have slipped through. If you spot any grammatical errors or typos, please get in touch with me via email.

This book also contains game-like elements. They are generally unintrusive and integrated into the story, but beware, they exist. Otherwise, I hope you enjoy Michael's story.

Happy reading!
Tom (**TomLitRPG.com**)
Support me on PATREON[1]

---

[1] https://www.patreon.com/grandgame

CONTENTS

Michael's Evolutionary Path

Level	Primary Class	Secondary Class	Tertiary Class	Wolf Marks	House Rank	Class Rank
80	**MINDSLAYER II** [M] Slayer's heritage, Nightwalker, Slaysight, **Mental Focus**			new class trait		II
95	**MINDSLAYER III** [M] Slayer's heritage, Nightwalker, **Slaysight II**, Mental Focus			upgrade class ability		III
104	**MINDSLAYER VI** [M] Slayer's heritage, Nightwalker, Slaysight II, **Mental Focus IV**			upgrade class trait		VI
125	**MINDSLAYER VI** [M] Slayer's heritage, **Wolfwalker**, Slaysight II, Mental Focus IV		evolve trait	PACK HUNTER		
	MINDSLAYER VI [M] Slayer's heritage, Wolfwalker, Slaysight II, Mental Focus IV, **Arctic wolf**		new trait	PACK ALPHA		
129			**VOID MAGE** [M] Void touched, Spell illiterate, Void armor			

BOOK THREE

As always, Michael continues to grow during his adventures in the Forever Kingdom. The chart above only illustrates his latest achievements (as accomplished over the course of the last book). If you wish to view Michael's earlier evolutionary charts, please visit my site at the link below.

tomlitrpg.com/michael

THE SYSTEM OF THE GRAND GAME

The universe of the Grand Game continues to expand with every book in the series, and at this point, it no longer makes sense to include all the maps, charts, and diagrams in each new book.

If you wish to learn more about the world of the Forever Kingdom or understand the system of the Grand Game better, please visit my site at one of the links below.

tomlitrpg.com/game-lore
tomlitrpg.com/world-lore
tomlitrpg.com/glossary

Player Profile: Michael

Level: 129. Rank: 12. Current Health: 100%.
Stamina: 100%. Mana: 100%. Psi: 100%.
Species: Human. Lives Remaining: 3.
True Marks (hidden): pack-alpha.
False Marks (fabricated): Lesser Shadow, Lesser Light, Lesser Dark.

Attributes

Available: 0 points.
Strength: 13. Constitution: 19. Dexterity: 33. Perception: 25. Mind: 71.
Magic: 21. Faith: 0.

Classes

Available: 1 point.
Primary-Secondary Bi-blend: mindstalker (fabricated). mindslayer VI (hidden).
Tertiary Class: void mage.

Traits

slayer's heritage (hidden): +2 Dexterity, +2 Strength, +4 Mind, +4 Perception.
beast tongue: can speak to beastkin.
Marked: can see spirit signatures.
wolfwalker (hidden): improved senses in all conditions.
anointed scion (hidden): bound to House Wolf.
inscrutable mind: +8 Mind.
secret blood (hidden): conceals bloodline.
mental focus IV: increases effectiveness of Mind skills by 40%.
budding explorer: all key points in newly discovered sectors logged.
arctic wolf (hidden): +5 Constitution, +2 Mind, +3 Strength.
void touched: +6 Magic.
spell illiterate: cannot cast mana-based spells.

Skills

Available skill slots: 3.
dodging (current: 107. max: 330. Dexterity, basic).
sneaking (current: 103. max: 330. Dexterity, basic).
shortswords (current: 113. max: 330. Dexterity, basic).
two weapon fighting (current: 104. max: 330. Dexterity, advanced).
light armor (current: 107. max: 190. Constitution, basic).
thieving (current: 78. max: 330. Dexterity, basic).
chi (current: 105. max: 710. Mind, advanced).
meditation (current: 131. max: 710. Mind, basic).
telekinesis (current: 109. max: 710. Mind, advanced).

telepathy (current: 104. max: 710. Mind, advanced).
insight (current: 124. max: 250. Perception, basic).
deception (current: 106. max: 250. Perception, master).
channeling (current: 10. max: 210. Magic, basic).
elemental absorption (current: 10. max: 210. Magic, master).
null force (current: 10. max: 210. Magic, master).

Abilities

<u>Constitution ability slots used:</u> **5 / 19.**
minor lighten load (5 Constitution, advanced, light armor).

<u>Dexterity ability slots used:</u> **27 / 33.**
crippling blow (Dexterity, basic, shortswords).
minor piercing strike (5 Dexterity, advanced, shortswords).
lesser backstab (5 Dexterity, advanced, sneaking).
improved trap disarm (5 Dexterity, advanced, thieving).
superior lockpicking (5 Dexterity, advanced, thieving).
set trap (Dexterity, basic, thieving).
whirlwind (5 Dexterity, advanced, two weapon fighting).

<u>Mind ability slots used:</u> **24 / 71.**
simple mass charm (5 Mind, advanced, telepathy).
stunning slap (Mind, basic, chi).
two-step (5 Mind, advanced, telekinesis).
simple reaction buff (5 Mind, advanced, chi).
simple astral blade (Mind, basic, telepathy).
medium shadow blink (5 Mind, advanced, telekinesis).
minor chi heal (Mind, basic, chi).
simple mind shield (Mind, basic, meditation).

<u>Perception ability slots used:</u> **22 / 25.**
improved analyze (5 Perception, advanced, insight).
improved trap detect (5 Perception, advanced, thieving).
conceal small weapon (Perception, basic, deception).
facial disguise (Perception, basic, deception).
superior ventro (5 Perception, advanced, deception).
lesser imitate (5 Perception, advanced, deception).

<u>Other abilities:</u>
improved slaysight (hidden) (Class, advanced, telepathy).
basic void armor (Class, basic, any void skill).

Known Key Points

Dungeon Sector 14,913 exit portal and safe zone.
Kingdom Sector 12,560 nether portal and safe zone.
Kingdom Sector 1 safe zone.
Dungeon Sector 101 exit portal and safe zone (scorching dunes).

Dungeon Sector 102, 103, and 104 exit portals and safe zones (haunted catacombs).
Dungeon Sector 105, 106, 107, 108, and 109 exit portals (guardian tower).
Kingdom Sector 18,240 nether portal 1 (guardian tower), and nether portal 2 (Draven's reach).

<u>Equipped</u>

ebonheart (+30% damage), concealed.
winter bone-hide armor (+10% damage reduction, -70% Dexterity and Magic, +5 stealth in snow).
shortsword, +1 (+15% damage, +10 shortswords), blunt!
slim dagger.

<u>Backpack Contents</u>

<u>**Money**</u>: 0 gold, 5 silver, and 3 copper coins.
snow-cone map of the tundra.
leopard cloak (-20% movement speed).
tavern bill of ownership.
Tartan token.
Viviane token.
BHG ID.

<u>Miscellaneous Loot</u>

None.

<u>Bank Contents</u>

<u>**Money**</u>: 0 gold, 0 silver, and 0 copper coins.
2 x full healing potions.
2 x full mana potions.

<u>Open Tasks</u>

Find the Last Wolf Envoy (hidden) (find Ceruvax).
Heist in the Dark (steal chalice from the Power, Paya).
Probie (complete two tier 4 bounties).
Preying Mantises (stop the assassins hunting you).

If you wish to view Michael's earlier player profiles, please visit my site at the link below.

<u>tomlitrpg.com/michael</u>

Chapter 242: The Guardian

Awakening guardian...

Alone in the final chamber of the guardian tower, and with only the savant boss' corpse for company, I stared at the Game message.

The dungeon was complete. My work in it, finished. I had what I'd come for—a new Class and two powerful skills. All I had to do was leave. So, why had I been so foolish as to tamper with long-buried things best left alone?

The Game message flashed again.

Awakening guardian...

It was not the sort of response I'd been expecting. My head swiveled left and right, searching the walled compound for the promised 'guardian.' The long grass was still, the mounds of white powder sat unmoving, and the crystal gate remained open.

Nothing stirred.

Nothing *except* the statue.

My gaze returned to the giant figure of a human man looming over me. It had begun to shake, causing slivers of marble to break off. It was a safe bet that the statue was the waking guardian.

I'd hoped that relinquishing the amulet would earn me a powerful artifact or reveal another secret nether portal or, better yet, grant me access to a second Wolf trial.

What I'd *not* bargained on was awakening a sleeping giant.

Scrambling out of the hole I'd dug around the statue's base, I drew ebonheart. There was no telling how the 'guardian' would react. But while I was wary, I was not overly concerned.

The drawing at the base of the carving made it obvious the statue was connected with the Primes. As was I. As a scion of House Wolf, I should have nothing to fear from the guardian. Then again... there was still much about the ancients I didn't know.

The revival is complete. Guardian awoken.

Here we go.

The crystal gate into the compound slammed shut. An ominous sign, but I ignored it and fixed my gaze on the statue. Its—*his?*—shaking intensified, causing more stones to fall free. *Is he going to crumble?*

The guardian's trembling stopped, and his eyes snapped open. *Guess not.*

Two marble eyes, shining with an inner fire, roved over the ground. They passed over me twice but failed to see me. "*W-w-h-hoo... has... awoken... me?*"

The voice brushed the edges of my mind, sad and forlorn. My trepidation eased. Whatever the guardian was, he didn't appear a threat. Sheathing my blade, I addressed the statue. "I did."

The searching eyes did not react.

I frowned. *"I did,"* I repeated, using mindspeech this time.

The statue's eyes snapped to me. *"You? Who are—?"* The guardian broke off, and when he resumed, his voice thrummed with new energy. *"I know you."*

I blinked. *"You do?"*

"Your mind... it tastes of Wolf. You are of his House."

How had the guardian figured that out? My bloodline was supposed to be concealed, but I could see no benefit in attempting to deceive him. *"I am."*

The statue's brows twitched. *"You are young. Barely more than a babe. Why have your elders allowed you to contact me?"*

Elders? I scratched my head. Was the guardian referring to the pack council? But I was an alpha in my own right and didn't need the council's permission. *"I have no elders,"* I said, straightening.

My response only seemed to confuse the guardian further. *"Where is your Prime?"*

I stared at him. How could the guardian know about the Primes but be ignorant of their fate? *"Wolf is dead."*

The guardian's head creaked from left to right, releasing another puff of dust. The movement was tiny, barely more than a fraction of an inch. Nonetheless, the denial was emphatic. *"That cannot be. The Primes are eternal. When one falls, another rises. Always."*

"Uhm..."

Nothing about this encounter was going in the manner I expected. The guardian had plied me with question after question, leaving me no space to voice any of my own, and I was tempted to let his latest utterance go unchallenged. But I couldn't stay quiet—the statue's unblinking stare demanded the truth.

I sighed. *"House Wolf has not had a Prime in centuries, perhaps even longer."*

"Impossible!"

I winced as the guardian's retort rolled across my mind like thunder.

"Why have the other Houses let this stand?" he demanded. *"What of Wolf's allies?"*

I rubbed my temples, feeling the onset of a pounding headache. It was finally dawning on me that the guardian had been asleep for longer than I'd thought—placing me in the unenviable position of educating him. *"They're all dead, too,"* I said tiredly. *"The Primes are no more."*

"You lie!"

"I do not," I said softly.

The statue shook again, releasing a violent shower of rocks. I was tempted to retreat but stayed where I was, afraid the guardian might interpret it as a sign of fear or guilt. Finally, he quietened.

"We shall see," he pronounced ominously.

My brows creased in confusion. What did that mean?

The light in the statue's eyes dimmed. Sensing an opportunity, I asked, *"Will you tell me what you are?"*

There was no response.

"Guardian?"

Still nothing. My frown deepened. Had he fallen asleep again? The statue's cold, inert surface gave me no clues, and I took a cautious step forward.

The guardian's eyes flared.

I froze, but he paid me no heed. *"DEAD! They're all dead! No, no. NO! They can't be. They mustn't be."* On the heels of the guardian's wailing, a dark maelstrom of emotions roared through my mind.

A guardian has injured you, inflicting psi damage.

I staggered back. The force of the statue's grief had hit me like a physical blow. Clutching the sides of my head, I flung up walls of psi around my mind.

It did little good.

A guardian has injured you, inflicting psi damage.
A guardian has...

...

A guardian has destroyed your mind shield!

In less time than it had taken me to raise them, my mental defenses were swept aside, washed away by the storm of the guardian's despair. The worst part was I didn't even think he was trying to hurt me. Caught in the throes of his grief, the guardian appeared oblivious to my presence.

"Guardian," I called. *"Stop!"*

He failed to hear.

A guardian has injured you, inflicting psi damage.
A guardian has...

...

Warning! Your health is dangerously low at 20%.

I dropped to my knees, blood running down my nose. *"Guardian..."* I croaked, realizing I could die here.

Now, wouldn't that be funny.

After surviving everything the dungeon had thrown at me, it seemed cruel irony to die at the hands of a being who could well be one of my few allies in the Game.

A guardian has injured you, inflicting psi damage.
A guardian has...

...

Warning! Your health is dangerously low at 10%.

I coughed, expelling blood and bile. *I have to get his attention,* I thought, wiping my mouth with the back of my hand. How though? The guardian was invisible to my mindsight, and but for the gyrating light in his eyes, he was, to all intents, a statue. That didn't leave me many options.

I drew ebonheart.

If I was going to die, it wouldn't be on my knees and for lack of trying. Staggering forward, I struck at the marble figure with as much force as I could muster.

My blade clanged loudly against the statue, barely leaving a scratch.

"STOP!" I yelled. I raised ebonheart again, but before I could strike again, a fresh wave of anguish assaulted me, and I fell to the ground, overcome by a fit of coughing. *"Stop… please,"* I gasped. *"You're… killing me."*

Warning! Your health is dangerously low at 5%.

Ignoring the blood pouring down my face, I pushed myself erect. I had to bring the guardian back to his senses. Clutching ebonheart unsteadily, I readied myself. Then I realized something.

The wailing had stopped.

"Thank you," I breathed and sank back to the ground.

✳   ✳   ✳

"Wolf child, wake up."

The alien voice echoing through my mind jolted me back to awareness. *Who is that?* I wondered.

"Please. Time is short."

Moaning, I pushed back eyelids heavy with sleep and… *pain?* I'd been hurt. *"W-wha… H-how… W-was I in… get hurt?"* I mumbled incoherently.

There was a pause. *"Your injuries are my doing."*

Fragmented images trickled back. I was in the… dungeon, and the guardian… he was the one who had attacked me. My head throbbed and felt like it was about to split open—which perhaps explained why it was so hard to think straight. Stifling another groan, I rolled onto my side and drew psi. It answered reluctantly but answered nonetheless.

"You must heal yourself, or you will—"

"Shh," I rasped.

The guardian fell silent. Left to tend to myself, I painstakingly wove psi. The spell slipped through my fingers more than once, forcing me to start over repeatedly. But I persisted and finally succeeded.

Healing energy flowed into my mind, identifying and restoring the damage the guardian had inflicted.

You have restored 10% of your lost health with chi heal. Your health is now at 12%.

"Ahh," I exhaled as my memories came flooding back. I was far from hale, but I no longer teetered on the edge of oblivion.

"Wolf child? Do you still live?"

I smiled wanly. *"I do. Now, let me finish, please."* Closing my eyes again, I chain-cast chi, mending every last bit of damage the guardian had inflicted.

Your health is at 100%.

Fully restored, if still shaky, I rose to my feet and studied the guardian anew. No signs of grief marred his expression, but then, none had earlier either.

"I'm sorry," he said. *"Sorrow overcame me. I've been asleep too long and forgot how fragile fleshlings can be."*

I chuckled tiredly. *"Fragile. That's one way to put it."*

"Please forgive me—" the guardian began.

I waved away his apology. Whatever the creature before me was, he had clearly been asleep a long time and mourned the loss of the ancients as if it had occurred yesterday. *"It's alright. No lasting harm done. You stopped in time, and that's what counts."* I paused. *"I take it, you believe me now?"*

"You were right," the guardian agreed. *"Mostly."*

My eyes narrowed. *"Mostly? What was I wrong about?"*

The statue's expression did not change, but shame seeped through his mindvoice. *"My initial assessment was... hasty. Swayed by your words, I drew the wrong conclusion."* The guardian sighed. *"Not all are dead. One lives."*

I stared at him blankly for a moment before the sense of his words penetrated. *"A Prime lives?"* I asked slowly. *"Is that what you mean?"*

"Yes."

"Who?" I demanded.

"That I cannot say." The statue turned its head from left to right, seeming to taste the air. *"I sense her presence. She is hiding. Where and why, I don't know."*

My brow furrowed. What was the guardian that he could divine the presence of a Prime? And more importantly, could I believe him?

"But time grows short, and I have much to tell you."

I pursed my lips. *"You said that before. What do you mean?"*

"Your tithe," the guardian explained. *"It can only power me for a short time, and I sense nothing else about your person with the energy to keep me awake longer."*

Power him? *"What are you?"* I asked bluntly.

The statue craned his head downwards to stare at me. *"You don't know?"*

I shook my head.

"Then what prompted you to wake me?"

I shrugged. *"I saw the engraving on the plinth and thought I recognized it."* I sighed. *"I mistook it for a blood talisman."*

The guardian jerked forward, releasing another hail of stones. Startled, I jumped back. But the statue moved again, bending nearly ninety degrees to place his head inches above mine. *"You've awakened your blood?"*

I nodded.

"You're an anointed scion?"

"I am."

The guardian withdrew. *"Then perhaps there is hope."* Before I could ask what he meant, he spoke again. *"I am Kolath, a guardian construct created by the Primes millennia ago."*

I nodded, unsurprised. All signs had pointed to the statue being linked with the ancients, and Kolath's words only served to confirm that. Yet, he had named himself 'a guardian,' not *the* guardian, implying there were more of his kind. *"What is a guardian?"*

"We are the bastions of last resort," he replied.

I frowned. *"Bastions against what?"*

"The void."

I'd heard that term used before, both in reference to the aether and nether, but I was guessing Kolath wasn't talking about the aether. *"You mean the nether?"*

"Some call it that."

"What is it?"

"A rampant scourge. The antithesis of life. The death of everything if it is allowed to spread. We were charged by the Primes to hold it at bay." He fixed his gaze on me. *"The Primes of old may be gone, but new ones will arise."* He leaned forward, his mental presence thrumming with excitement. *"Tell me, how many more of you are there? Which House's scions are close to ascending to Primehood?"*

I bit my lip, realizing the source of Kolath's hope. He believed that even though the Primes were dead, the Houses still stood. For a moment, I contemplated lying to the guardian—he didn't seem to take bad news well—but I sensed doing so would be infinitely more dangerous.

"It's been centuries since the last Prime died," I said, ignoring Kolath's claim of a Prime in hiding. The more I thought about it, the more unlikely the notion seemed. *If* a Prime lived, the new Powers would not rest until she was killed. No, the entire idea was too far-fetched and was more likely wishful thinking on Kolath's part. *"The new Powers have seen to it that all traces of them have been wiped out."* I held his stony gaze. *"As far as I know, there are no other living scions."*

He stared at me. *"None?"*

I nodded somberly. *"All the Houses have fallen."*

"Are you sure?" Kolath pressed.

"Yes," I said simply.

He bowed his head. *"Then we are doomed. Without the Prime Conclave, we are lost."*

"I'm not so sure about that," I said, trying to reassure him. *"After all, the Primes have been gone a long time, and the nether has not triumphed."*

He did not respond.

"Did you hear me, Kolath? Hope remains."

Still, the guardian said nothing.

Trying a different tack, I changed the topic. *"Are the other statues in the sector guardians too?"*

More silence.

Aargh. Did despair overcome Kolath again? *"I'm not the only member of House Wolf alive, you know,"* I said, hoping that would kindle his interest. *"An envoy of Wolf lives, trapped in one of Nexus' dungeons. Do you know where I can find him?"*

Resounding silence.

I ground my teeth in frustration. Kolath himself had said time was short, yet he seemed content to let it fritter away. I needed to get him talking again. *"What can I do to help?"*

No response.

"Tell me," I insisted.

The guardian's head finally creaked upward. *"You cannot help. Only the Primes can."*

I shook my head, ignoring his despondent words. At least, Kolath was speaking now. *"Perhaps if you explained the problem, we can find a solution?"*

Silence.

As old as the guardian was, there was much he could teach me, but trying to get any information out of him was like pulling teeth. *"There must be something I can do,"* I growled.

"There isn't." Kolath shivered, releasing another puff of dust. *"There is nothing you or anyone else can—"*

He broke off.

"Yes?" I prompted and leaned forward, sure something had occurred to him.

"You cannot save us. Not as you are." Kolath paused, and I shifted restlessly. *"But perhaps you can buy us time."*

"How?"

"My brothers and sisters... they've fallen silent and are not responding," the guardian said.

"You've tried talking to them?"

Kolath nodded.

"When?" I asked.

"Just now," he said. *"I've hailed them. Even asleep, they should've heard my call. But they won't reply."*

Alarm shot through me. *"Don't do that,"* I hissed. *"Someone else might hear you."*

Kolath blinked. *"Someone else? Like who?"*

"The new Powers."

The guardian stared at me. *"You mentioned them earlier. Who are they?"*

I waved aside his question. *"Forget them. Just tell me what you need me to do."*

Kolath's gaze bore into me. *"Tell me,"* he demanded.

I sighed, regretting my earlier interjection. Taking a deep breath, I told him what he wanted to know.

Unsurprisingly, finding out how the Houses had fallen sent Kolath into a spiral of rage.

For all that the guardian claimed to be a construct, he was unlike any other I'd encountered. Granted, those didn't number very many, but I'd assumed they were all lifeless, mechanical beings with little autonomy of their own.

Whatever Kolath was, he was not that.

The guardian was sentient and possessed of an abundance of emotions—emotions which often seemed to run rampant and get the better of him. Perhaps that was a result of his great age or long slumber, but it left me doubting the soundness of his mind.

It took me longer than I liked, but eventually, I managed to diffuse the guardian's anger. Unfortunately, the reprieve was only temporary, and he started anew almost immediately.

"These new Powers, they killed the Primes?" Kolath asked me for what felt like the dozenth time.

I nodded wearily.

"How dare they?"

I said nothing.

"Do they not understand what they've done? They've placed the entire Kingdom in jeopardy!" The statue quivered, the light in his eyes pulsing ominously. *"They will learn, though,"* he vowed. *"When my brethren and I are done with them, they will regret their foolish actions."*

I opened my mouth to head off the impending outburst, then closed it with a snap. If the last hour had taught me anything, it was that nothing I did would quell the guardian.

But to my surprise, only a moment later, Kolath sagged, his rage rushing out of him like the tide. *"But it is too late,"* he lamented. *"I am not what I was, nor are my brothers and sisters."* He turned to me. *"Thank you."*

I stared at him. *"For what?"*

The guardian smiled. *"For listening to my tirade."* He sighed. *"The world has passed me by, and I'm not sure if my brethren and I serve any purpose anymore."*

I sat up, realizing Kolath was finally ready to talk. *"I doubt that. Tell me what you need doing, and we can find out."*

Kolath didn't say anything, but he closed his eyes, and a moment later, words appeared in my mind.

The guardian, Kolath, has allocated you a new task: <u>The Silent Brethren</u>. Kolath's brother and sisters are not responding to his hails. Your objective is to discover why this is the case.

I scanned the Game message avidly, not sure which surprised me more—the seemingly simplistic nature of the task or the fact that the guardian could allocate me one.

"Where can I find your brethren?" I asked after I dismissed the task message.

"I don't know," Kolath replied.

I stared at him, nonplussed.

A gravelly chuckle echoed through my mind. *"In case you've not noticed, I'm a statue. I've never visited them in person."*

"Then how did you—"

"We conversed through our minds across the breadth of the realm. My brothers and sisters could be in any sector." He paused. *"Any dungeon sector, that is. The guardians were only built in the Nethersphere. Our mission was—and still is, I suppose—to uphold the barriers and portals that hold back the nether."*

"I see," I said, not entirely sure I did, but willing to let the matter lie for now. *"And how will uncovering the reason for your brethren's silence buy more time?"*

Kolath didn't reply immediately. *"It is but the first step. I fear that if the other guardians are no longer able to communicate, they will be equally incapable of fulfilling their primary function."* He looked at me soberly. *"If the barriers fall, nothing will stop the nether from reclaiming the dungeons. And that would be bad. The Forever Kingdom cannot survive without the Endless Dungeon."*

My brows furrowed. If what Kolath was saying was true, then the guardians served a function vital not just to me but to every player and Power. *"And if I find the other guardians, what then?"*

"Help them fulfill their task however you can. Keeping the Endless Dungeon open is only a stop-gap measure, but an important one."

On the tail end of Kolath's words, another Game message unfurled.

Your task: <u>The Silent Brethren</u> has been updated. You have learned that barriers protecting each dungeon sector from the nether are upheld and maintained by the guardians. Optional objective added: Aid the guardians in fulfilling their mission.

"That sounds like a mammoth task," I breathed. *"I understand your hesitancy better now."*

There was no response.

Wondering at the reason for the guardian's latest bout of silence, I looked up to see the light in his eyes fading. *"Kolath?"*

The glow in his eyes dimmed further.

Growing alarmed, I rose to my feet. *"Are you still there?"*

"I am, but not for much longer," he whispered. *"Granting you the task has consumed the last of my energy."*

"Wait," I shouted. *"Just a little longer. Please. I have so many questions!"*

But it was too late.

The light of life animating the statue vanished, leaving only inert stone in its wake.

Your tithe has been fully consumed, and the guardian has fallen asleep.

Behind me, the crystal gate slid open again, but with my gaze locked on the lifeless statue, I barely noticed.

Damn. What now?

✳   ✳   ✳

The seconds ticked by, and I didn't move.

My gaze fixed on the statue, I scoured my mind for the least sign of Kolath but found nothing. He was truly gone.

Sighing, I swung around and left the compound, my steps heavy as I pondered my new task. In many ways, completing Kolath's quest was as crucial as fulfilling my others. Yet, it was not time-sensitive. The guardians had been asleep for hundreds of years, after all. Finding the constructs and aiding them could be delayed a few months, if not years.

And right now, I had bigger things to worry about—like what awaited me back in Nexus. I drew to a halt before the nether portal. It was time to exit the dungeon and re-enter the Game.

What will I find on the other side? I wondered.

Nearly a year had gone by. Had the city changed at all? Was the intrigue I'd been caught up in still ongoing? More importantly, did the mantises still hunt me? Were dozens of assassins awaiting my arrival on the other side of the gate?

That didn't seem likely—not after all this time—but I couldn't afford to assume I'd been entirely forgotten either. I had to prepare for the worst.

Sitting down cross-legged, I considered my player profile.

You have reached level 129. Your void armor is operational and fully charged.

Active buffs: +5% damage reduction and +2.5% resistance to air, earth, fire, water, shadow, light, and dark magic.

If the mantises *were* lurking on the other side, I didn't expect my void armor to be much help against them. Blades and poisons were the assassins' weapons of choice, and my new Class didn't increase my resistance against either.

Still, my own bladework and mind skills had improved considerably since my last encounter with the mantises, and if they expected me to be easy prey, they had an unpleasant surprise coming.

Sadly, though, my gear had taken a step backward. I still wore my bone-hide armor, and while it had grown on me over time, the cumbersome hides were no match for my previous leather armor.

I was a weapon short too. The second shortsword I'd entered the dungeon with was blunt, chipped, and about as useful as a stick. Reluctantly, I set it aside—there was no point being weighed down more than I needed to be. Ebonheart would have to suffice until I could retrieve my belongings from Kesh.

You have lost a blunt shortsword, +1.

Next, I considered the rest of my gear. The snow-cone map was the only item of real value among them, and for obvious reasons, I was reluctant to part with it. It was both a testament to my time in the tundra and a priceless navigational tool.

But I couldn't take it with me.

The risk of it falling into the wrong hands was too great, and though the chances of anyone else using it to decipher the route to the hidden sector was low, it was still possible. Sighing, I tore up the map and buried its remains in the dirt.

You have lost a snow-cone map.

I rose to my feet, leaving behind the rest of my backpack's contents. There was only one last thing to do. Closing my eyes, I drew on my stamina.

You have cast reaction buff, increasing your Dexterity by +4 ranks for 20 minutes.

You have cast lighten load, reducing your total armor penalties to 0% for 20 minutes. Net effect: +7 Dexterity and +4 Magic.

You have cast lesser imitate, assuming the visage of an elven fighter. Duration: 1 hour.

I was finally ready. *Alright, time to do this.* Drawing, ebonheart, I stepped through the dungeon's exit.

Transfer through portal commencing...

...

...

Passage completed!

Leaving sector 109. Entering the Forever Kingdom.

You have entered sector 1 of the Forever Kingdom.

I re-entered Nexus to find the city bathed in light. Behind me, the portal's glow faded, sealing the way back. Squinting in the harsh glare of the noonday sun, I studied the square.

It was as deserted as the day I'd entered the dungeon.

I shook my head ruefully. After all my precautions, finding myself in an empty square was almost... anticlimactic. But it was a welcome surprise, nonetheless. *Looks like the city hasn't changed a bit.* Sheathing ebonheart, I headed for the nearest block of buildings.

Where to? I wondered.

I was in the plague quarter's northeastern districts, and the south gate to the safe zone wasn't far away. *I'll head to the emporium first and retrieve—*

Stygian darkness flashed across the square, and mid-step, I froze.

An unknown entity has cast pulse of scouring dark.
You have failed a magical resistance check! Your lesser imitate spell has been dispelled.

I paid the Game message little heed, my attention captured by something else. The spell had not only destroyed my disguise, it had revealed the cordon of green bordering the square.

I was surrounded by mantises. Dozens of them.

They'd not forgotten me. If anything, it looked as if I was expected. Keeping my movements relaxed, I swiveled my head from left to right and counted off my foes.

There were at least forty assassins in the square.

So many. And all just for me?

Given their numbers, the mantises couldn't have been waiting here the entire time. Even for assassins as relentless as Menaq's disciples were reputed to be, standing idle outside a dungeon for over two hundred days was absurd.

There was a simpler, if less palatable, explanation.

The mantises had been forewarned. They'd *known* to await my arrival today. It meant my suspicions had been right: someone had tipped off the assassins. But instead of following me into the dungeon as I'd expected, the mantises had chosen to ambush me outside—which admittedly was the better strategy.

I'd been hoping that after my many days in the guardian tower, Menaq's disciples would've given up or, at the very least, their ardor would've cooled. Neither had happened.

I had formulated a plan for dealing with the assassins before entering the dungeon—a means of ending their hunt once and for all. But the scheme was risky, and I'd been hoping to avoid using it. Now, it seemed I had no choice.

First, though, I had to deal with the mantises in front of me. *Easier said than done.*

I turned about in a slow circle. None of the assassins had moved since showing themselves. I frowned, unsure what to make of their surprising passiveness. *What are they waiting for?*

Right on cue, two green-clad figures stepped forward, holding something large and ungainly between them.

It was a steel net.

That can't be what I think it is... can it? Holding at bay my sudden trepidation, I reached out and analyzed the item.

This is a magical net of ensnarement. It is a rank 4 item designed to entangle and hold a single subject. The net's enchantments nullify all abilities of tier 4 and lower.

For the first time, a spurt of fear shot through me.

Dying at the mantises' hands didn't concern me. In fact, I'd resigned myself to doing just that. But capture... that was an entirely different matter.

The only reason the mantises would try taking me prisoner was to remove me from the sector. If they moved me to their home territory, then they could kill me at their leisure each time I was reborn.

I can't let that happen. I unsheathed ebonheart.

At the motion, the mantises drew their own weapons. Half carried blades, while the other half held blowpipes. Given their intent to capture, I suspected the darts were dipped in something other than poison.

I grimaced. I would have to avoid both darts and net—somehow. Blade in hand, I waited.

The encircling mantises did not advance, however. With enviable patience, they waited while the pair bearing the net stalked forward.

Darting a look beyond the mantises, I began a psi casting. Unfortunately, there were no bystanders lurking nearby to bend to my use. That left only the mantises themselves to target.

My gaze flickered back to the two assassins drawing closer. The pair were raising the net—to throw at me, presumably—but my own spell was ready, and I released the casting.

You have cast mass charm.
Sixal has passed a mental resistance check!
Neewan has failed a mental resistance check!
You have charmed 1 of 2 targets for 10 seconds.

Neewan rocked to a halt, forcing Sixal to a standstill. I smiled grimly. My spell had succeeded, if only partially. But it was evidence enough that I'd come a long way since entering the dungeon, and if the mantises thought they were going to take me down easily, they were in for a rude shock.

The mantis on the left turned to stare at his bespelled companion, and I could feel the gazes of the other assassins swapping from me to the strangely behaving player.

Now, I thought, *while they are still confused.* Drawing more psi, I prepared another casting.

I wasn't sure if it was happenstance or knowledge of my limitations—my *previous* limitations—but the circle my foes had formed was outside the reach of a tier one shadow blink. Of course, since upgrading the ability, I had doubled my teleportation range—leaving some of the mantises within reach.

Rushing through the aether, I emerged behind one of the blowpipe wielders.

You have teleported 19 yards.

The maneuver caught the assassins off-guard again, and before my target could turn, I plunged ebonheart through his back.

You have cast piercing strike.
You have killed Ashyran with a fatal blow.

"Attack," I ordered, pulling free my bloodied blade from the corpse. My charmed minion reacted instantly. Dropping the net, Neewan unsheathed his swords.

Finally, realizing something was amiss, the mantises surged into motion. The swordsmen rushed in my direction while the blowpipe wielders raised their weapons. Spinning around, I threw myself forward, narrowly escaping a volley of darts.

You have evaded the attacks of 9 unknown hostiles.

Only half the projectiles had targeted me. The other ten had been aimed at my minion and thudded into him while he was still swinging into motion.

Neewan has been struck by a sleeping dart! Your minion has failed a physical resistance check and has fallen unconscious.
Neewan has been struck by a sleeping dart!
Neewan has been struck by a sleeping dart!
...
...
Neewan has suffered a critical overdose!
Your minion has died from a fatal heart attack.

My lips twisted sourly.

I'd been right about the darts. Worse yet, the mantises had caught onto my ploy quicker than I'd liked. *No matter,* I thought, rolling back to my feet. I had other tricks.

More darts hissed through the air, but having learned from Neewan's death, the mantises took pains to stagger their fire. I two-stepped over the first wave, rolled beneath the second, and cut right out of the path of the third.

I was away.

Continuing to weave an erratic path, I dashed out of the square.

The melee fighters chased after. They closed the distance rapidly, but I'd gained enough of a head start to beat them to the nearest building. Drawing close to the stone wall, I flung myself upwards, taking two quick steps on blocks of solid air to land lightly on a window ledge.

Unfortunately, the window was closed.

But it was not all bad news. The lock holding the rickety shutters closed looked flimsy and easily broken. Perched precariously, and with my left hand clinging to the top of the window's wooden frame, I bashed at the lock with the pommel of ebonheart.

It gave way immediately.

Risking a glance over my shoulder, I saw the blowpipe wielders race closer. I must've fallen out of their range, forcing them to reposition. As versatile as the small weapons were, they had their limitations too. Below me, the other mantises had sheathed their blades and had begun to climb up the building.

I sighed. I wasn't going to lose my hunters easily, it seemed.

Throwing aside the shutters, I dived into the room beyond. The chamber was empty and thick with shadows. A door lay at the far end, and my first instinct was to plunge straight through. But I hesitated, my eyes darting back to the window. *Let's see if I can't thin my pursuers' numbers.* Pressing my back against the adjacent wall, I faded into the shadows and wove psi.

A hostile entity has failed to detect you! You remain hidden.

A head popped into view in the open window, and I slipped tendrils of my will into his mind.

You have cast slaysight.
You have hidden your presence from Gieryn for 10 seconds.

Made oblivious to my presence, the mantis climbed into the room and passed me without reacting. Ignoring him, I drew more psi and flung it at the next three assassins making their way up the side of the building.

You have charmed 1 of 3 targets for 10 seconds.

Good enough, I thought, ordering my new minion to attack his former companions. Having bought myself some time, I slipped up behind Gieryn.

The mantis was scanning the room warily, searching for me, no doubt. Yanking back his head, I slit his throat without remorse.

You have killed Gieryn with a fatal blow.

Letting the corpse slump at my feet, I unfurled my mindsight. The progress of the three mantises had stalled, but others were scaling the building too. Soon, I was going to have more company than I could handle.

Time to leave.

Ducking through the open doorway, I plunged deeper into the building.

Chapter 245: Threading the Needle

The room exited into a lightless corridor.

There were a pair of doors on the right and another two on the left. Hurrying forward, I tried the first.

It was locked.

Damn, I thought and checked my mindsight. As far as I could tell, none of the rooms beyond were occupied. However, the same could not be said of the chamber behind me. It was filling quickly with assassins.

That wasn't the only bad news, though.

More mantises had stormed the building's ground floor while others had climbed past the open window—making for the second floor, I guessed. They were trying to box me in.

Hells, I cursed and padded silently down the corridor. The shadows hid me for now, but that could change in an instant.

Another closed door came into sight, one with a dull mindglow in the room beyond. Not bothering to try the door, I stepped into the aether...

You have teleported 15 yards.

... and emerged back in the real beside a sleeping dwarf—a non-player, by all appearance. Leaving him undisturbed, I sidled up to the closed door and tried the handle.

It was also locked.

Perfect. Backing away, I observed the mantises creeping through the corridor with mindsight.

They were advancing slowly but steadily. My lips twitched. My earlier ambushes had taught them caution at least, but the dozen or so approaching mantises were too many for me to handle—even with mass charm. *I wait*, I decided.

A mantis stopped before the door.

Stilling my breathing, I wove psi in readiness. The doorknob turned partway, then stopped as the lock held it back. Would he try breaking in? I wondered.

A strained second passed. Then another.

The assassin released the handle. I exhaled softly, the tension easing out of me. Too soon, it turned out. A familiar buzzing filled the corridor.

Hunter eye.

Urgh. I had no way to disguise my scent from the tracking device, nor was I about to raise a mind shield and deprive myself of the use of my psi abilities. Discovery was inevitable.

I turned my attention to the mindglows on the floors above and below. The mantises on both levels had spread out, and I identified multiple isolated targets.

Which way?

Down offered the quicker path out of the building but would also make pursuit easier.

Up then, I decided, and shadow blinked out of the room.

✳   ✳   ✳

You have teleported into Yunga's shadow.
A hostile entity has detected you! You are no longer hidden.

My target whirled, blades snaking towards me. I danced back, stealing a split-second glimpse of the room. It was little different from the chamber below and empty as well, but that would change soon.

The mantis lunged forward.

I was ready for him. Stepping to the side and out of reach of his left blade, I parried away his second sword with ebonheart and rammed my closed fist into the side of his head.

You have stunned your target for 1 second.

My foe staggered back. I followed, drawing a line of red down his torso with ebonheart. A heartbeat later, his stun wore off, and the assassin recovered his footing. Ignoring the blood pouring out of his shoulder, he sent his swords whipping back toward me.

But I was gone already.

You have teleported into Yunga's shadow.

Emerging behind my target, I sent ebonheart rushing forward. Yunga whipped around, bringing up his swords. But he was too late, and I was already inside his guard. Leaning into the blow, I buried the black blade in the mantis' chest.

You have killed Yunga.

A whistling rush of air caught my ear. Recognizing the sound, I released ebonheart and threw myself to the side.

You have evaded an unknown hostile's attack.

I rolled back to my feet to see a mantis standing in the open doorway, the blowpipe in his mouth tracking my movements. A second dart hissed out.

I sidestepped, and the projectile thudded into the wall behind me. Backing away, I drew psi.

The mantis spat out a third dart. Ducking beneath the projectile, I kept casting. A fourth missile followed in its wake, then a fifth. I dodged both.

Either running out of darts or realizing he was not about to disrupt my concentration, the assassin threw aside the blowpipe and drew his swords. But before he could take more than two steps toward me, my spell completed, and strands of psi seeped into his mind, inciting his fear centers to a fever pitch.

Biscux has failed a mental resistance check! You have terrified your target for 10 seconds.

Grinning at my success, I ignored the fear-stricken assassin and went to retrieve my sword. At my movement, Biscux's eyes widened, and jerking into motion, he bolted from the room. Chuckling, I pulled ebonheart free of the corpse.

My humor was short-lived, though. The fight had not gone unnoticed, and more assassins were converging on my location.

Sighing, I blinked out—and back into the room below.

✳   ✳   ✳

The dwarf was still sleeping, and the door, still locked.

Shaking my head ruefully—how could anyone sleep through the ruckus?—I placed my ear against the door and listened intently.

Mindsight and my senses reported the corridor beyond clear of mantises and hunter eyes. By doubling back, I'd slipped free of the assassins' net—for the time being, at least. Reaching down, I turned the key in the lock and pushed on the door.

It opened with a soft snick, but no one came running to investigate. Slipping through, I shut the door behind me and padded down the corridor, making for the same room where I'd entered the building.

I reached the chamber without incident, a little surprised to find it empty. Creeping to the window, I checked the surroundings with mindsight.

There were no hostiles in range, neither on this floor nor the one below. *Hmm...*

It beggared belief that the mantises had left this exit completely unguarded. Some of the assassins had to be hiding nearby—watching and waiting.

The question, though, was how many?

There was no way to tell, but I couldn't stay in the building. It was quickly turning into a death trap. Coming to a decision, I ducked through the window.

The drop to the ground was short, and with two-step breaking my fall, I landed softly.

You have detected a hostile entity. Zeeran is no longer hidden!
Zeeran has detected you. You are no longer hidden!

An assassin appeared where none had been before.

Somehow, despite the bright sunlight, the mantis had been hiding in plain sight beneath the window, and I had the misfortune—or was it good luck?—to land nearly atop him. Having already anticipated an ambush of sorts, I whirled about. At the same time, my foe rose from his crouch.

I raised ebonheart to strike.

He set his blowpipe to his lips.

I was a fraction faster, and before the mantis could fire his dart, I rammed ebonheart through his throat.

You have killed Zeeran with a fatal blow.

The assassin had not been alone, though.

Six more mantises materialized on the street. They'd been hiding, too, each guarding a different exit from the building, I thought. Without fuss or hesitation, three raised their blowpipes and fired.

Dropping to the floor, I rolled away.

You have evaded the attacks of 3 unknown hostiles.

The darts passed me harmlessly by to clatter against the cobblestone street. Regaining my feet, I saw the other three mantises rushing in.

The first sent his sword darting forward. Swaying back, I fended off the blow with ebonheart. The next struck at me from the left. Ducking beneath the sweeping blade, I countered with a vicious swipe at the mantis' ankles. Equal to the challenge, he jumped over the soulbound blade.

The third assassin, sneaking up from behind, struck at me with the pommel of his sword. I couldn't avoid the blow entirely but shifted far enough away that it missed its intended target—the back of my head.

Realizing how precarious my situation was and with my shoulder throbbing, I let go of ebonheart and backflipped out of reach, narrowly avoiding the probing attacks of the other two swordsmen.

I was given no chance to recover, though.

Seeing me separated from the melee fighters, the other three mantises attacked. Warned by the quiet hissing of the darts' flight, I dodged the incoming projectiles.

This isn't going so well, I thought, lurching back another step.

I was outmatched and outnumbered, and I knew, without a doubt, the only reason I was still alive was that the mantises were trying to capture— not kill.

And it was only a matter of time before they succeeded.

Breathing heavily, I turned about and fled up the street, my ears straining to pick out the telltale sound of incoming darts. But the danger, when it emerged, appeared from ahead, not behind.

I had taken barely a dozen steps before two mantises rounded the corner of the building I was making for. I didn't stop. Hurtling towards the pair, I summoned psi, and shadow blinked the moment they were in range.

An unknown entity has trigger-cast repelling field.
You have failed a magical resistance check! Your spell has been disrupted.

With an abruptness that left me reeling, I was flung out of the aether, many yards short of my target. *That's new,* I thought inanely.

Still dazed, I almost missed the inbound projectile. Jerking back at the last second, I evaded the dart and pivoted in a quick circle. Mantises were flooding into both ends of the street. I was trapped again.

And this time, I feared there would be no escaping.

Damnation. Another dart whistled through the air on course for my neck, but I stepped aside, evading it easily. A third flew in from the opposite direction, and again I ducked out of the way. Resetting my stance, I swept my gaze across my foes. More mantises were raising blowpipes to their lips, and no matter how well I dodged, I knew sooner or later, one would hit me.

There's only one option left.

Keeping a wary eye on the dart throwers, I picked out the closest group of mantises and cast mass charm.

You have charmed 1 of 4 targets for 10 seconds.

The spell barely succeeded, but one charmed foe was all I needed. Weaving through the ongoing, but staggered, waves of darts, I ran to the bespelled mantis. The other three assassins backed away, but my minion remained fixed in place, placidly watching my approach.

I was six feet from him when I gave the order to attack.

The green-clad assassin drew his blade. Realizing something was amiss, the other mantises turned upon him, swords and blowpipes raised.

They were not my minion's target, though. I was. In a rush, I closed the distance, and obedient to my will, my minion thrust out his blade.

I ran straight onto it.

The gleaming steel buried itself in my chest, piercing skin, bone, and heart with ease. Gurgling blood, I sagged listlessly. Death was only moments away. Still, a bloody grin caressed my face. I might be dying, but I'd won the encounter.

Confronted with a choice between capture and death, the decision had been easy. All that mattered was that I made it into the safe zone.

Closing my eyes, I let blackness claim me.

You have died.

Chapter 246: The Shadow Behind the Curtain

I awoke with a gasp, my eyes wide and unseeing, and my breath coming in uncontrolled bursts. I was alive. No. I was dead. I'd died. Brutally staked through the heart.

No.

I had died, yes—but by my own hand. Or at the hand of my minion rather. Death had been preferable. Now though, I was alive. Rising shakily to my feet, I studied my surroundings.

I was in the same cell I'd resurrected in before. What had Stonebeard named it? *The southeast watchtower. That's it.* But this time, the cell's doors were open, and no guard had been posted.

Fishing out ebonheart, I climbed out of the rebirth well. My quivering arms and trembling legs made that more difficult than necessary. My body was still reliving its death throes, I realized.

Drawing to a halt, I took a deep, steadying breath and, while I waited to recover, pulled up the flashing Game messages.

You have been reborn. Lives remaining: 2. Time lost during resurrection: 8 hours. Rebirth location: sector 1 safe zone. One soul bond item has been restored.

You have reached level 131!

Your dodging has increased to level 108. Your shortswords has increased to level 114. Your telekinesis has increased to level 110. Your telepathy has increased to level 106. Your null force has increased to 12.

I'd earned two levels in the encounter with the mantises, and interestingly enough, my null force skill had increased too. *Those spells I'd failed to resist,* I mused, *they must have been dark magic.*

The mantises had been prepared for the encounter—too prepared—and if not for my advancements in the dungeon, I doubted I would've been able to escape their trap. But while I found the assassins' knowledge of my abilities unsettling, I also drew comfort from it. My foes knew more about me than they should, but at the same time, their information was incomplete.

They are not infallible.

Returning to the Game messages, I considered my new attribute points. My new Class had been of little help in the confrontation, but that was because my void mage skills were yet too low to provide any meaningful resistance.

Still, increasing my Magic at this stage is not going to yield any benefits. Better to invest in something else.

Mind was my attribute of choice, yet Dexterity was the one most lacking in slots. I would need to purchase tier three abilities soon, so it made sense to invest further in it first. *That's what I'll do,* I decided.

Your Dexterity has increased to rank 36.

My player progression seen to, I dismissed the Game messages and turned my attention outwards again. Having something else to focus on had helped, and my body's shivering had eased.

Feeling ready to face the world again, I strolled through the open cell doors.

✳ ✳ ✳

The encounter with the mantises had made one thing clear: despite being absent from Nexus for nigh on a year, little has changed, at least as related to my own circumstances. If I had needed a reminder, the assassins had been it—I was still hunted.

My suspicions on *how* had crystalized, and now I was nearly certain *who* sought out my death. The *why*, though, still mystified me. But I wouldn't let not knowing stop me.

It was time to put the plan that I'd hatched what seemed like an eternity ago into play. To do that, I first needed to visit the Albion Bank.

The corridor beyond the cell was deserted, and reaching the end, I yanked open the door and stepped through. A lone figure awaited me in the room beyond.

Wilsh.

Stopping short, I studied the blackguard. The captain leaned against the opposite wall with his arms folded and a smirk on his face. He'd been expecting me.

"So," Wilsh drawled. "I see the mantises got you."

I shrugged indifferently. "It took them long enough." I let a smile stretch across my face. "And I'm fairly sure the score is still in my favor."

Wilsh's smirk faded. "That was only the beginning," he growled harshly. "The mantises have your measure now. They'll find you again—count on it—and when they do, you will die horribly." He laughed loudly. "I look forward to seeing you here again."

I cocked my head to the side, a sudden suspicion forming. The blackguard's comment implied he knew the details of my fight with the assassins. How did he know that, and for that matter, what had prompted him to wait for me here? "You know, don't you?"

Confusion marred the blackguard captain's face. "Know what?"

"Who sent the mantises after me," I said coldly. "You're working for him," I added with conviction.

Wilsh scrubbed his face clean of expression, but not quickly enough to hide the tiny start of fear my words provoked. "Of course, I know who wants you dead!" he blustered, trying to cover up his slip. "Every Dark player knows about the noob who foiled the Awakened Dead's plans. Erebus wants your blood—badly."

My lips twitched. Wilsh had just confirmed something else—he knew my true identity despite failing to analyze me during our last encounter. "But the Awakened Dead don't know I'm in the city, do they?" I was only guessing, but I didn't think I was wrong. "In fact, I'm sure if I asked around, I'd find out you didn't report my arrival to your superiors."

"And why would any Darksworn want to speak to you?" Wilsh sneered.

I smiled. "You would be surprised by who is willing to speak to me." Not waiting for his response, I resumed walking. The encounter with the blackguard captain had been fortuitous, and I'd acquired an interesting tidbit of information, but now it was time to leave.

"Oh, and Wilsh?" I began as I brushed past the captain. "If I were you, I would leave the city. Once the Dark learns you're a traitor... who knows? They may set the mantises hunting *you*."

Wilsh blanched before his face stiffened again. "You don't scare me!" he shouted.

Saying nothing, I left the watchtower.

✷　✷　✷

For the second time, I walked the streets of Nexus in a newbie shirt and shorts. This time, though, I did so proudly. With my head thrown back and ebonheart by my side, I ignored the titters and mockery of passing players as I strolled towards the Albion Bank.

Before I moved on my plan, I wanted to be certain of my suppositions. The bank would provide me with the final confirmation I needed. I'd been proved wrong about the mantises more than once already and felt the abundance of caution warranted.

And besides, I was a little anxious about what I planned. Once I set things in motion, there would be no going back, and if things didn't turn out as I hoped, the consequences could be catastrophic. Still, I couldn't keep going on like I was. I had to stop the mantises' hunt.

Reaching the building clothed in water, I skipped across the stone bridge and through the open doors. Nothing had changed since my last visit. The occupants had the same air of subdued industriousness, and the rune-inscribed watchers were exactly as I remembered.

Ignoring the startled glances of the few customers about, I made for the closest magical device, stepping boldly through its frame. As expected, my actions triggered an avalanche of Game alerts.

Watcher activated. Scanning commencing...
...
You have failed a magical resistance check.
You have failed a mental resistance check.
You have failed a physical resistance check.
...
Scans completed.
Anomalous spell(s) detected! Potential threat—
Alert aborted. An exception has been lodged on your behalf.

Once more, hidden doorways in the foyer opened, and guards spilled out despite the threat warning being rescinded. I sighed, knowing what would come next.

Sure enough, the guards tackled me with mitten gloves. They left my mouth uncovered, but I suffered their ministrations stoically and said nothing as they carried me into the adjacent interrogation room.

✳   ✳   ✳

I sat waiting for five long minutes with no one showing up. Finally losing patience, I glanced at the nearest guard. "Get Devlin," I snapped.

The guard in question gave no sign of having heard me, but I noticed one of his fellows shifting minutely. I turned to him. "You recognize me, don't you? If you do, you'll remember that Viviane herself made an exception for me. I doubt she'll be pleased to find her orders being ignored."

The guard fidgeted but remained silent. My words prompted the one opposite him to speak up, though. "That true, Shayne?"

"Yessir," Shayne replied. "The Lady gave him her token."

That seemed to decide the squad leader. "Release him." He jerked his thumb at Shayne. "And go and get Devlin."

Satisfied, I leaned back in my chair and waited.

✳   ✳   ✳

A short while later, the blue-scaled bank manager strolled into the room. He stopped short as he caught sight of me, then, with an audible sigh, seated himself in the chair opposite me. "I didn't think it was possible, but I see it's true. Welcome back."

I frowned at him. "That's an odd sort of greeting. What do you mean?"

"No matter," Devlin said, waving off my words. "I see you're determined to keep creating a stir." He threw me a pained look. "Couldn't you have chosen a less inconspicuous approach?"

I shrugged. "I needed to see you, and it couldn't wait."

Devlin's gills trilled. "See me? Why?" He grimaced, taking in my state of undress. "If this is about a loan or a request for—"

"Nothing like that," I said, cutting him off. I leaned across the table. "I have only one question for you."

Devlin frowned, but he said nothing as he waited for me to go on.

"What spells did the Watcher detect on me?" I asked.

Devlin's eyebrows shot upwards. Whatever he was expecting me to ask, it was not that. "Why do you wish to know?"

"Humor me, please."

The bank manager stared at me for a drawn-out moment, then shrugged. "Loken's tracking spell, obviously."

I nodded. "And?"

29

Devlin's eyes narrowed. "And? And nothing." He paused. "Were you expecting something else?" Before I could respond, he went on. "Michael," he said, his voice sounding strained, "please don't tell me you've just used our bank as a magical detector?"

I smiled crookedly. "I won't, then."

The bank manager dropped his head in his palms, his gills quivering, and I couldn't tell if he was laughing or crying.

I rose from my chair. "Thanks for your help, Devlin. It's time I got going."

The bank manager raised his head. "That's it?"

"That's it," I agreed.

Devlin stared at me for a moment longer and sighed. "Until next time," he said in farewell.

✳ ✳ ✳

I left the bank, my head bowed and deep in thought. Devlin and the magical Watcher had confirmed exactly what I'd suspected. There was only a single spell upon me: Loken's.

It was the final confirmation I needed. I now knew how the mantises were tracking me. And, more importantly, who had sent them.

It could only be Loken.

Originally, I'd believed Ishita was responsible. But the longer the assassins' hunt went on, the more improbable that seemed. Ishita had no means of tracking me, and whatever the spider goddess was, she was not subtle. If the Awakened Dead knew I was in Nexus, I was sure I would have encountered some of their own Darksworn before now. Yet, I hadn't.

Which brought me back to Loken.

Only the Shadow Power could track my movements. *Only* he could've told the mantises when I'd entered the scorching dunes dungeon, when I'd been in the Triumvirate citadel, and when I would exit the guardian tower.

Loken was the one who'd set the mantises on me. I was certain of it.

The next question, of course, was why. Why did the trickster want me dead? What would cause Loken to abandon his other plans for me? Only one reason came to mind. And no matter how much I tried to come up with another explanation—*any* other explanation—nothing else made sense.

Loken had to know of my bloodline.

He knew I belonged to House Wolf.

CHAPTER 247: OVERTURNING THE GAMEBOARD

Surprisingly, in the wake of my epiphany, I was not disheartened. On the contrary, my first reaction was one of relief.

Ever since meeting the trickster, I'd felt as if he toyed with me. I'd never been quite able to trust him nor take his actions at face value. Always, the Shadow Power's generosity had seemed tainted. But now, finally, I felt as if I was beginning to draw back the curtain and catch my first glimpse of the true game Loken played.

It was a game I intended to win.

But that was getting ahead of myself. There was still a lot I needed to do before I could be sure my plan would succeed. The next step was recovering my lost gear.

Shrugging off my musings, I made a beeline for the emporium. It had been months since I'd handed my items over to Cara, and I hoped Kesh hadn't seen fit to sell them. Reaching the entrance to the walled compound, I came across two familiar faces.

"Ho, ho, ho," one of the gatekeepers exclaimed. "Look who's back again!"

The second guard squinted at me. "Why, if it isn't our favorite noob," Ent chortled. "And dressed just as snazzily as the last time!"

Both giants threw back their heads and laughed uproariously. Despite myself, I grinned. The pair's atrocious sense of humor was almost homely.

"Very funny," I said, making a face. "Now open up and let me see Kesh."

Still laughing, Lake threw me a mocking bow before pushing open the gate.

✳   ✳   ✳

Kesh was in her office as she always seemed to be, leaving me to wonder if she slept in the place. As I was ushered in, the old lady looked up.

"So," she said without any inflection in her tone. "You're back."

I sighed in feigned disappointment. "You know, you could at least *pretend* you're happy to see me."

The corners of the merchant's mouth twitched, but she otherwise ignored my remark. "Sit," she ordered.

I slipped into the chair opposite her. "I take it you know why I'm here?"

Kesh looked at me quizzically. "What, no small talk? No explanation for your absence?" Her gaze sharpened. "And no excuses for using my agent as a courier or leaving me to deal with your tavernkeeper's evermore insistent inquiries?"

I smiled. "Why Kesh, you surprise me," I murmured. "I thought you were all business?"

The merchant stared at me stonily.

I chuckled, but after only a moment, my amusement faded. "What's this about, Saya?"

Despite my avoidance of her own questions, Kesh answered me readily enough. "The gnome has been writing to me regularly, asking after you. Of course, I didn't have much to tell her. All I could report was that I had no idea of your whereabouts. Needless to say, that did not satisfy the girl, and of late, her letters have grown more demanding." Kesh snorted. "She's even threatened to lodge a complaint with the Triumvirate."

Saya's threat did not seem to perturb Kesh. In fact, it was Saya's mistrust, more than anything else, that appeared to offend her.

Reaching under the table, Kesh pulled out a thick stack of letters. "But now that you've returned, you can deal with the matter and set her mind at ease."

I hesitated, then shook my head. "I can't just yet. I have something to attend to first."

The old lady's brows rose. "You should at least read her latest correspondences. I believe you might find cause for concern in there."

I was tempted but shook my head again. Whatever it was could wait one more day. Until Loken was dealt with, I couldn't afford to be distracted. "I will," I said. "*When* I get back."

Kesh's eyebrows rose higher. "Suit yourself," she said as she stowed the letters back into some unseen magical compartment.

"Do you have my stuff?" I asked, getting to the real reason I'd come here.

Kesh grunted. "I do." Reaching down again, she pulled out my bag of holding and laid it on the table before me.

Not bothering to hide my relief, I snatched up the bag and peered inside.

"It's all there," Kesh said.

"I believe you." I rose to my feet. "Thank you! I won't forget this. But now, I must go—"

"Wait!" the old lady barked. "You're leaving? Just like that? Without any explanation, after disappearing for nine whole months?"

"Sorry, I'm in a hurry."

"I can see that," Kesh muttered. "You *do* remember you've appointed me as your factor, don't you? Keep your secrets if you must, but there are important matters we must discuss—not least being the state of the tavern's finances."

I looked at her in surprise. "Is the tavern broke?"

Kesh shook her head. "On the contrary, its earnings are... considerable. You should review the books."

"I'll do that, but later," I promised. "In the interim, can you transfer a portion of its funds into my Albion account? Nothing significant," I hastened to add, "just some small change."

I'd wiped out my bank balance before entering the guardian tower, and even though I didn't intend on leaving the safe zone just yet, I realized I might need some cash on hand.

"I'll do that," Kesh said. "Just remember, the tavern books will be waiting for you whenever you're ready. Another thing: about the items you asked me to acquire—"

I waved off her words. "We can discuss that later too."

"Very well," Kesh grumbled. "I can see trying to talk to you now is useless. Go on, off with you."

I turned about, then paused as something occurred to me. "I just had a thought... can you draw up a list of all the resistance skills available in the Game? I'm particularly interested in the more powerful variants."

Kesh studied me expressionlessly for a moment. "This is for your new void Class, I take it?"

Her knowledge didn't surprise me. "Exactly," I said simply.

"I'll get on it," the factor replied.

"Thank you," I said. "Oh, and one other thing. You can't, by any chance, provide me with some directions?"

Kesh sighed. "Where to?"

"The palace of a Dark Power."

Unable to disguise her surprise, Kesh's eyes widened. "Which one?"

When I told her, her eyes grew even rounder.

✳ ✳ ✳

Hurrying out of the emporium, I headed to the Wanderer's Delight hotel. My next appointment was crucial to my plans, and I needed to be properly dressed for it. Not that I thought my gear would impress a Power, but I didn't want to risk insulting him by turning up in newbie clothes.

After purchasing a room for the day, I discovered that what Kesh considered 'small change' was considerably more than I did.

You have acquired a room key. You have lost 10 gold. Money remaining in your bank account: 990 gold.

Just how much money had the tavern made? I wondered in idle speculation. It had to be substantial if Kesh had deposited a thousand gold into my account without blinking.

"Will that be all, sir?" the hotel maître asked, breaking through my musings.

"Yes, thanks," I replied. Lifting my hand from his keystone, I headed up to my room and changed back into my old gear.

You have equipped a set of enchanted leather armor, 5 trinkets, the wayfarer's boots, and other miscellaneous gear.

The net effect of your equipped items is +2 Magic, +4 Strength, +8 Dexterity, and 26% physical damage reduction.

"Ah," I exclaimed, reveling in the tiny but significant boosts provided by my old gear. In many ways, I felt as if I'd outgrown the equipment. But if everything else went as expected, there would be enough time to see to its replacement.

Closing the room door behind me, I exited the hotel and headed to Palace Row.

＊　　＊　　＊

The street wasn't really called Palace Row, but its fringes were so heavily populated with mansions of the Game's elite that I thought the name apt.

Reaching the southern end of the street, I searched for the mansion Kesh had described. It did not take me long to find it. Just like the merchant had said, it was more fortress than palace.

Strolling casually up to the gate, I presented myself to the armed soldiers standing guard before it. Despite being in a safe zone, both were heavily armored in gleaming ebony plate mail. "Get lost," the more senior of the two barked before I could address him.

By his shoulder patch, I marked him as a sergeant. "I'm here to see Tartar," I said politely.

The second soldier snorted in disbelief. "Can you believe this moron? Who does he—"

The sergeant cut him off. "I said go away," he growled.

Reaching into my pocket, I flipped the Tartan token Talon had given me toward the legion sergeant. He caught it by reflex and glanced down. From his expression, I could tell the exact moment he caught sight of the raging bull prominently marked on its surface.

"Where did you get this?" he demanded.

"From a certain Captain Talon," I answered truthfully.

The second soldier's eyes widened. "You mean *the* Captain Talon, the captain-commander of the Ebonguard?"

I smiled. "That's the one."

The two legion soldiers glanced at each other. "Is it fake?" the second whispered.

"Don't be an idiot," the sergeant growled. "These tokens can't be counterfeited." His gaze darted to me. "Or stolen." But despite his words, the sergeant peered at me suspiciously as if suspecting I'd done just that.

Saying nothing, I waited for them to decide what to do. The conclusion seemed inevitable, anyway. Seeming to realize the same, the sergeant turned to his companion. "Fetch the commander," he ordered.

"The commander?" the soldier exclaimed. "You can't be serious. He'll skin us—"

"Go!" the sergeant barked, cutting him off.

The soldier went.

A smile toying on my lips, I folded my arms and waited.

CHAPTER 248: THE RAGING BULL

The legion commander was a tall man with graying hair and a stern demeanor. He took one look at the token before bowing respectfully and motioning me to follow him into the palace.

The commander refused to answer any of my questions, though, and after leading me into an empty anteroom, he relayed a terse set of instructions. "Stay here, and whatever you do, don't leave." His piece said, the soldier spun about and hurried away.

Turning around, I saw him disappearing through the door. "Wait!" I called, but it was too late; the commander was gone. "Damn," I muttered.

Left to my own devices, I studied the chamber. As expected, it was richly furnished with expensive-looking paintings, burnished statues, and hanging tapestries inset in the room's many alcoves. There was, however, nowhere to sit.

I eyed the two doors leading away from the room but, after only a brief hesitation, decided against chasing after the commander or exploring farther into the building. Sighing, I schooled myself to patience. *More waiting,* I groused.

Minutes passed.

Then hours, and still, I was left staring at the vacant room.

Resisting the temptation to sit on the marble floor—that would not do; this was a Power I was visiting—I began pacing. My entire plan hinged on Tartar.

If I could only speak to the Dark Power, I was sure I could sway him to my thinking, but what if the self-proclaimed god-emperor refused to grant me an audience? That I had not considered. I had been certain the envoy's token would suffice to earn me an audience. Now, I was not so sure.

Noon came and went, and still no one turned up, neither to take me to the Power nor to kick me out.

Though the temptation to leave was strong, I did not budge from the room. Was the legion commander playing a joke? Was this pointless waiting some sort of test? Or had my request to see Tartar gotten lost somewhere?

I didn't know, but I wasn't leaving until I saw the Power.

The hours ticked by, and night fell. Frustrated, short-tempered, and tired, I kept pacing. It was the only thing keeping sleep at bay. Was it time to find someone and ask them just what the hell was going on?

Maybe it is, I decided reluctantly. *How much longer can I—*

A voice echoed through the room. "You are persistent."

I spun about. The voice had emerged from one of the alcoves along the west wall, but the nook in question was empty. My eyes had passed over it enough times during my endless wait to be sure of that fact. Not even a tapestry adorned its inside.

"Who's there?" I called out.

A towering figure strode out of the alcove. Where had he come from?

The speaker dwarfed me many times over. Nothing about him spoke of subtlety, and it defied belief that he'd been hiding in the alcove all along. With each stamp of his cloven hooves, the figure set the floor shuddering. His legs, arms, and torso were covered in rippling steel plates, but they did nothing to hide the bulging muscles beneath.

The speaker's head was the most striking aspect of his appearance, though. Two ebony horns protruded from each side. Gold flecks swam in his eyes, and a drooping mustache—incongruous in his otherwise monstrous face—covered his upper lip.

A wise old minotaur?

Was this some sort of joke? But no, the minotaur striding towards me was no mundane creature. Far from it. He reeked of power—and not the ordinary kind.

This was a Power. This was the god-emperor.

"Tartar?" I guessed.

A smile touched one corner of the Dark Power's lips. "Direct, too," he murmured. Drawing to a halt before me, Tartar folded his arms across his massive chest and peered down at me. "You requested an audience?"

For a second, I said nothing—could *say* nothing.

Despite Tartar's soft-spoken words, there was nothing soft about the aura of power that surrounded him. It hit me with the force of an avalanche, and for a drawn-out moment, I was stunned speechless.

As the minotaur had drawn closer, the ethereal flames wreathing his form had surged outward to envelop me. They bore me no ill-intent—yet— but at the least hint of threat, I got the feeling they would snuff me out.

It was not only in the real that I felt Tartar's presence, though. My psi shields were up, firmly entrenched around my mind. Yet, even so, the Power loomed large in my awareness, his mind assaulting my defenses with the casual indifference of a scorching sun beating down on a dry desert.

Even the wolf in me—ever fearless—shrank back from the naked might the minotaur exuded. Unlike every other Power I'd met, Tartar's power was raw and undisguised.

Perhaps that is because I'm meeting him at the seat of his power, or maybe it is because, unlike his fellows, Tartar can't be bothered to disguise his strength.

I suspected the latter to be the case.

Recovering my equilibrium, I bowed respectfully. "I did. I received your token from—"

Tartar slashed his hand downward, leaving trails of gold in its wake. "I know where you got the token from." He paused and added coldly. "I know about your dealings with Captain Talon too. My envoy is not pleased with you."

I bowed again, lower this time. "I kept my word to him," I objected.

"That you did," Tartar said. "And in the process, you did me a service." He stared at me, eyes glowing. "It is one of the reasons you are still alive right now."

"What's the other?" I asked before I could bite back the words.

Tartar snorted. "Talon did warn me you were impertinent." The Power waved a hand, and a black obsidian throne appeared behind him. "You are a thief and a sneak," he said flatly as he seated himself. "And a deceiver too. Normally, I would not deal with one such as you."

Despite my desire to protest this less-than-flattering description, sense prevailed, and I remained silent.

Tartar steepled his hands before him. "But Talon speaks highly of your abilities, and more importantly, my envoy judges you honorable." The minotaur held my eyes, his gaze radiating a silent menace. "*Are* you honorable, thief?"

I nodded carefully, not trusting myself to speak.

The threat in the Power's gaze cooled, and he smiled. "Then, you may be of use to me in the future. That is the second reason you remain alive."

I said nothing, but my relief was palpable.

"But do not mistake forbearance for need," Tartar continued. "Waste my time or betray me, and I will see that you rue ever coming here. Understood?"

"Understood."

"Good. Now explain the reason for your intrusion."

I took a deep breath before plunging onwards. "I am here with information—and a proposition. Both, I think, will interest you." I paused, waiting to see the Power's reaction.

But Tartar only stared back at me impassively, giving nothing away.

With no other choice, I went on. "It involves Loken and a game he is running against the Dark."

Tartar's eyes flared. "The trickster," he growled and leaned forward. "What is he up to?"

"Loken has taken out a contract for my death with the mantises," I said.

"Menaq's ilk? Impossible," Tartar scoffed. "The mantises only work for the Dark."

"Or for someone they think works for the Dark," I corrected. "I know for a fact that Loken's disguises can fool even a Power," I added, thinking of how Hamish had entered Erebus' dungeon.

Despite Tartar's obvious skepticism, he didn't dismiss my words out of hand. "Do you have proof?"

"No," I admitted reluctantly. Seeing the Power's face harden, I hastily added, "But I intend to get it before sundown."

"How?" Tartar asked shortly.

I told him.

"Hmm," Tartar said, rubbing his chin with one massive hand. "A plausible plan. Tell me more..."

Inclining my head, I did just that.

✳　✳　✳

Tartar kept me for hours, questioning me well into the night. More properly, it was an interrogation, exhausting and methodical.

Throughout, I remained scrupulously honest. Still, I did not share everything, but I told Tartar enough that, by the time I was done, he acceded to my proposal.

"You best be right about this, thief," Tartar rumbled ominously after our agreement was concluded. "Otherwise, there will be consequences—for you."

I nodded, understanding full well that I played a dangerous game, but if I wanted to free myself of Loken's machinations, there was no other way.

Saying my farewells, I backed out of the antechamber. When I stepped out of the palace, I glanced up and saw dawn was not far off. Stifling my yawns, I headed to the global auction.

Despite the late hour, there was one more task I had to complete before I could call it a night. I needed a messenger to carry a missive for me, and I thought the market square was the most likely place in the safe zone to find a willing player.

Reaching the edge of the square, I scanned its depths. It was as packed as ever. *Where to begin?* My roving gaze paused on the crystalline spire in the center of the square. *Hmm... I wonder if the bards still hang out there.*

It was worth a try, I decided. Making for the spire, I cut a path through the crowds. Sure enough, I found a handful of musicians standing idle at the base of the Adjudicator. What's more, one of them was familiar.

Striding purposefully towards the half-elf, I called out. "Hello, there." Little about the bard had changed in the months since I'd last seen him. He was still dressed in the same rich cast-offs and carried a well-cared-for flute. "Shael, wasn't it?"

The bard turned around, his slanted eyes narrowing beneath his locks of flowing hair. "I remember you," he said. "The deception player with too much gold in his pocket, right?"

I smiled and stuck out my arm. "The same."

Shael shook my hand. "I'm surprised to still see you in Nexus. I'd thought a smart fellow like you would be long gone by now."

I chuckled. "It's a long story. But what are *you* still doing here? Don't tell me you haven't managed to escape the city yet?"

Shael sighed theatrically. "Keeping oneself fed and clothed in Nexus is expensive, and I've eaten through my earnings almost as fast as I've made them." He paused. "Although, to tell the truth, I've grown comfortable here, and my yearning to leave has waned."

I nodded even though I didn't comprehend the bard's attitude. If it were me, I don't think I could have hung around idle for so long, but if Shael was content with his lot, I wasn't about to question his choices.

"Speaking of coin, how do you feel about earning some?" I asked.

Shael grinned. "What do you need?"

I handed him the letter I had composed in the god-emperor's palace. "I need you to deliver this. It's for a player named Morin. You will find her in the Shadow Keep of the shadow quarter. Can you get there?"

He nodded.

"Good. Then, this is what you'll tell her..."

Chapter 249: A Foiled Jest

Less than an hour later, Shael came running back with a response. It read simply, *'I will be there.'* There was no signature, but I knew it had to be from Loken.

I smiled in relief. I'd been sure Loken was in the city and paying close attention to events. The mantises' ambush at the dungeon exit portal confirmed that, but I hadn't been quite as certain he would agree to meet.

The Shadow Power was ever fickle.

Pocketing the letter, I handed the bard the fee I'd agreed to pay him. "Thanks," I said.

"Any time," Shael replied, his face splitting into a huge grin at the shine of the gold in his hands. "And if you need me for anything else—"

"I know where to find you," I finished for him and clamped a hand down on his shoulder. "But I must run. I have a date with a Power."

The half-elf chuckled, thinking I was joking. But when my own face remained deadpan, his laughter cut off abruptly. "You're serious? Who are you—?"

Spinning around, I left him wondering as I raced towards the Wanderer's Delight hotel.

It was time to prepare for Loken's arrival.

* * *

I had no means of contacting Loken directly, hence the missive I'd sent to Morin, which I'd asked her to pass onto the Power.

I hadn't been worried about the letter not reaching the trickster. Knowing Loken, he was probably having Morin's correspondences monitored, and all I'd needed to do was get the letter delivered to the Shadow Keep.

The missive had included nothing more than a terse request to talk and the details of where and when. Loken did not have a residence in the safe zone. In fact, as far as anyone knew, he didn't have a home anywhere— which was typically mysterious of him.

But that lack was also what made my plan viable.

If Loken had insisted on meeting at a place of his choosing, my scheme would have failed then and there. He hadn't, though, and so far, everything was going as planned. But rather than setting my mind at ease, that only increased my trepidation. Events were in motion, and there was no stopping them now.

If I didn't see my plan through successfully, there would be more than one angry Power dogging my heels.

* * *

A few hours later, I was in a suite in the Wanderer's Delight, awaiting Loken's arrival. As neutral territory in the middle of a safe zone, the hotel was a popular choice for a meeting spot between factions and Powers.

When I'd explained my requirements, the hotel staff had understood what I needed and had handled everything—for a price, of course. Now, all that was required was for Loken to show up.

Sinking into the oversized stuffed chair I sat in, I closed my eyes and, through an effort of will, stopped myself from fidgeting. Loken was late. Only a few minutes, but still, it had me on edge.

What if he doesn't show? Tartar's displeasure would be the least of my worries. *He has to—*

The room door slammed open, and Loken sauntered in, a lazy grin on his face. From outside, one of the hotel's staff unobtrusively closed the door again, and I nodded to him in thanks.

My gaze flickered back to Loken. The Shadow Power was surveying the room. The suite, though large and opulently decorated, was sparsely furnished. Spotting the second of the two chairs prominently placed in the center of the room, the trickster seated himself opposite me.

"Michael," the Power greeted, lounging back. "You've finally returned!"

"Loken," I greeted neutrally.

When I said nothing more, Loken went on. "It is good to see you again. I thought you'd never escape that dungeon." He clasped a hand to his heart. "I feared for you, my boy. I really did. But nothing can keep you down, can it? You're the ultimate escape artist."

I forced myself to stay silent. I wanted to scream and rage at the Power. Nearly everything bad that had happened to me in Nexus was due to Loken and his machinations, yet here he was pretending heartfelt concern!

It was enough to set my blood boiling. *Calm, Michael. Remember the plan.*

In the face of my silence, Loken's painted black lips widened into a sly smile. "Not only did you escape, you grew admirably in the process, too, I see." Bouncing out of his chair, the Power paced a slow circle around me. "A void mage. How fascinating. It is a fairly unique Class in the Game, you know. Not one often found and even more rarely adopted. It requires, shall we say, a particular set of talents to exploit. But you, I daresay, will do well with it."

Loken drew to a halt in front of my unsmiling face. "Congratulations, dear boy. You've managed to gather a fine collection of Classes. Now, imagine what—"

"We must talk," I ground out.

I'd remained tight-lipped through Loken's near-ceaseless flow of words, but it was time to capture the Power's attention. The longer I left him at loose ends, the more likely he was to spot something amiss. "Sit. Please."

For a wonder, Loken sat and folded his hands in his lap. His back plank-straight and his eyes fixed on me, the Power gave every appearance of earnest attentiveness.

I sighed. *He's mocking me again.* Ignoring Loken's antics, I opened my mouth to speak.

The Power beat me to it. "How did you find it?"

Scowling, I closed my mouth with a snap. "Find what?" I asked after a beat.

"Don't be obtuse, Michael," Loken said in an exasperated tone. Your new Class, of course. Tell me everything!"

I eyed him for a moment, then decided this was as good an opening as anything. "Don't you know already?"

Loken cocked his head to the side in pretended ignorance.

"Your tracking spell," I growled. "Hasn't it kept you apprised of my every move?"

Loken pouted. "Now, now, don't be like that, my boy. The spell is nowhere near as precise as I'd like. Unless I am in the same sector as you, I can't divine your exact location, only the sector you're in. Nor, as you seem to think, do I spend every second of every day checking up on your whereabouts." Loken's eyes twinkled with mirth. "I *do* have other responsibilities, you know."

My eyes narrowed. Was he telling the truth? If Loken hadn't been able to track my movements through the guardian tower's sectors, he wouldn't know about the wolves or the hidden sector—both secrets I would be pleased to keep—but I couldn't count on it. Loken was lying. Almost certainly.

"What *did* happen to you in the dungeon's third level?" Loken asked, almost as if he'd been following my thoughts. You were stuck there *for months*." He waited for a moment, but when I didn't respond, he probed further. "Did you get trapped in stasis within the barrier of ice?"

I nodded shortly. "Something like that," I said and changed the topic. "It's time to talk about the future."

Loken sat up. "You're ready to attempt my task?" Not waiting for my answer, he rubbed his hands together. "Excellent. This is where I think you should—"

I shook my head. "No."

Loken looked at me strangely. "No?"

"No, I'm not ready to do your bidding," I said, annunciating each word carefully.

A flicker of emotion too quick to interpret flashed across the Power's face before he sighed theatrically. "Then why have you called me here?"

I let the silence draw out for a moment. "I know it was you."

Loken rolled his eyes. "Well, of course, it was me. Lots of things were me." He paused. "Which one, in particular, were you referring to?"

I didn't share in the Power's joke. Maintaining my grim expression, I said, "I know it was you who set the mantises hunting me."

"Ah," Loken exhaled.

That one sound was confirmation enough. But I needed to hear him say it. "Then you admit it?"

The Shadow Power shrugged, maddeningly indifferent, despite his deception being uncovered. "I can see from your expression that you're convinced. Why bother denying it? Yes, it was me."

My shoulders sagged. I'd been sure it was Loken. Still, I couldn't help a twinge of disappointment at his confirmation. It made me realize I'd been harboring a secret hope the Power would provide an alternative explanation. Now, there was no hiding from the truth: Loken had betrayed me.

"How did you figure it out?" he asked.

I gazed searchingly at the Power. There was no trace of apology or guilt on his face, nothing that suggested regret. I squashed my own sense of hurt. I understood then that Loken was not my friend nor even my ally.

He was the enemy.

"The mantises gave it away," I replied, matching Loken's matter-of-fact tone. "They were a touch too efficient in tracking my movements, and after I used the Albion Bank's watcher to confirm there were no other spells on me..." I shrugged. "There was only one plausible explanation left after that."

"Hmm," Loken murmured. "So that's why you went to the bank." He glanced at me sideways. "But that doesn't explain your visit to the safe zone's Dark district."

I looked at the Power sharply. Did he suspect?

Loken chuckled at my expression. "Come, Michael, you didn't think that would slip my notice, did you? Who did you go and see?"

Despite Loken's knowing air and relaxed countenance, I sensed a coiled tension in him. "You don't know?" I shot back.

Loken sighed. "Sadly, the Dark Powers are paranoid to a fault. A disruption haze surrounds each one of their residences, blocking all scrying attempts. I know you went there, but not who you visited." He paused. "So, who was it?"

The fact that Loken saw fit to repeat the question betrayed his interest and left me convinced he didn't know the truth. "No one," I lied. "I went looking for Menaq, but he—"

"—he doesn't reside in the city," Loken finished for me, relaxing minutely. "Ah, dear boy, you meddle in deep waters. Is that when you decided to confront me?"

I nodded mutely.

"What did you hope to gain?" Loken asked, sounding genuinely puzzled.

I held the Power's gaze. "I want to know why."

"Why?"

I sighed. "Why did you do it? Why did you betray me?"

The jester's mask that Loken wore so readily fell away, revealing, for just a moment, the consummate schemer beneath. "You know why, boy," he said coldly.

I said nothing.

"Don't tell me you haven't figured it out yet?" Loken asked, disbelief warring with amusement as his facade dropped back in place. "I expected better of you, dear boy." He paused. "Do you need me to spell it out?"

"No," I snapped. That was the last thing I wanted him to do. I breathed in deeply. Despite my resolution to remain unaffected, Loken was getting under my skin. "When did you figure it out?"

The Shadow Power studied me from beneath lidded eyes. "Oh, I suspected from the very beginning. When you first visited Hamish, in fact. You see, I'd already explored Erebus's toy dungeon myself and knew about the goblins' tannery and their prisoners." He spread his hands. "After your Class evolution, it did not take much to put it all together."

I eyed Loken skeptically. "Then why not try to kill me, then?"

"Because I thought I could use you." He threw me a mocking glare. "But when you refused my offer, I knew you had to be killed." He laughed. "Little did I know that you were going to disappear inside a hidden sector. You won't believe how happy I was when you took down Ishita's shield generator."

I frowned. "But why use the mantises? Why not your own people?"

Loken's eyes twinkled. "Habit, I suppose. Boredom, perhaps. Where's the fun in doing things the easy way? Much better," he said with a grin, "to use the Dark's own minions to see my agenda fulfilled."

I nodded slowly. That certainly fitted in with what I knew of the Shadow Power. He never seemed to do anything simply. "But *how* did you do it? How did you deceive the mantises? They only accept contracts from the Dark."

Loken studied me carefully for a moment. "Why all this interest in the how?"

It was my turn to pretend indifference. "Call it professional curiosity."

Loken laughed and peered at me shrewdly. "You want to know how to deceive the mantises, too, don't you? I gather that nothing you've tried has worked yet?"

I said nothing, but my grim expression was answer enough.

"Of course, I'll tell you! It's no great mystery: I pretended to be a Dark Power."

I affected surprise. "You can do that?"

Loken grinned. "I can."

"Which one?"

"That, I'm afraid, will be revealing too much." Loken rose to his feet. "Now, if this is all you've called me for, I'm sorely disappointed; I expected better of you. Alas, I must go."

"Wait," I ordered harshly.

Loken spun about, the amiable expression on his face gone, but before he could speak, I called out, "Heard enough?"

Loken stilled and cocked his head to the side. "Who are you talking to?"

I didn't answer, but the next moment, it became apparent as Tartar and his companion stepped out from under a tier twelve cloaking ward.

I sat back in my chair, a tight smile on my face. It was time to see how much Loken enjoyed the sting of betrayal when *he* was on the receiving end.

"We heard everything," Tartar confirmed. His gold-flecked eyes brimming with fury, the minotaur kept his gaze pinned on Loken. "Your intrigues know no end, jester."

The stick-thin figure standing in the minotaur's shadow waved his neon-green appendages in the air, signifying agreement. There was a healthy dose of rage mixed in the gesture, too, I thought. Tartar's companion was Menaq, of course. Faction head of the Mantises, and present at Tartar's behest.

I rose to my feet, hands dropping to hover near the hilt of my sheathed blades. We were in a safe zone, and conventional wisdom said I had nothing to fear, but conventional wisdom had been wrong before, and there was no telling what would happen next.

Of course, there was little I could do against any *one* of the three Powers in the room if they chose to act against me, but knowing my weapons were close made me feel safe, and I kept my hands where they were while I watched Loken to see how he'd react.

For a nearly imperceptible moment, the Shadow Power seemed frozen, his gaze jumping from Tartar to Menaq. Then, much to my consternation, a slow grin spread across his face.

Turning his back on Tartar and Menaq—in what I suspected was a deliberate insult—Loken spun towards me. "You've tricked me." He clapped his hands in glee. "How marvelous!"

I was not the only one confounded by Loken's reaction.

Tartar's brows drew down, and his mustache quivered. It was not a good sign. Menaq, who very much resembled the mantises his faction was named after, stalked forward. "How dare you use my disciples in your foul games, trickster!" He paused, seemingly overcome by rage. "You will pay for this!" he screeched.

Loken yawned. "Threats. How boring."

Damnation, I cursed, impressed despite myself by the Shadow Power's aplomb.

Menaq took another angry step, but before he could lay hands—or forelegs rather—on Loken, Tartar spoke, "Don't."

That one word was enough to keep Menaq in place and made clear where the balance of power lay between the two Dark Powers.

I sighed, disappointed by the somewhat-lackluster finale to my scheming. I'd been relishing this moment, looking forward to seeing Loken humbled and disgraced, but once again, the Shadow Power defeated my expectations. Except for that tiny split-second when his poise had faltered, Loken appeared unfazed and was already taking matters in his stride.

I should've known better, I thought. Still, the important thing was that my plan *had* succeeded, and I had to be content with that. "Do you have what you need?" I asked, addressing Tartar.

The god-emperor nodded. "Yes. You have kept your promise and have delivered the proof I requested. You have my word that the mantis' hunt will end." He said this without glancing at the other Power as if there was no doubt of Menaq's agreement.

The mantis' master shot me a glare only slightly less hate-filled than the one he'd directed at Loken. Despite this, he addressed me politely enough. "It is as Tartar has said," Menaq said. "The hunt will be called off."

"And?" Tartar prompted mildly.

"And your slaughter of my disciples will be forgiven," Menaq finished, seeming to choke on the words as he forced them out. He cast Loken a look full of loathing. "That debt will be laid at another's door."

Loken snorted derisively.

"Thank you," I said fervently to both Dark Powers, ignoring the trickster's interjection.

Menaq nodded curtly, and a moment later, the Game message I'd been awaiting arrived.

Congratulations, Michael! You have completed the task: <u>Preying Mantises!</u> As a result of your efforts, you've stopped the mantis' hunt.

The Marks on your spirit signature have changed. Using both your wiles and fists, you have accomplished what few have and survived the mantises. Not only did you put an end to their kill order, but you've also uncovered the identity of the one who marked you for death. Wolf is pleased, and your Mark has deepened.

Seeing my focus turn inwards, Tartar nodded. "That concludes our transaction, thief." Gesturing his companion forward, the minotaur headed towards the door. Pausing there, he turned to me. "When you are done here, come see me." His gaze flickered to Loken. "This is not the end of the matter," he warned.

The Shadow Power rolled his eyes but stayed silent.

"I have use for one such as you," Tartar continued, addressing me again. "And unlike some *others*, you can rest assured I will not attempt to bind you through deceit nor treat with you dishonestly. *I take care of my Sworn.*"

Despite the unsubtle taunt directed at him, Loken remained tight-lipped, his tapping foot the only sign of his impatience. With a last glare at the Shadow Power, Tartar and Menaq exited the suite.

As if he had been waiting for just this moment, the instant the door swung shut, Loken whipped around to face me.

✻ ✻ ✻

"Blowhard," Loken snorted with a contemptuous glance at the door.

I stared at the Power, surprised by his continued presence in the room. I'd expected Loken to storm out when my trickery was revealed.

My scheme, of course, had been to expose Loken to Tartar and Menaq with the expectation that once Loken's deceit was revealed, the mantises would withdraw from their hunt, and as far as that went, my ploy had succeeded.

Of course, I could have always gone to Loken himself and attempted to use my knowledge as leverage. But the trickster had gotten the upper hand on me before. It was less risky, I'd decided, to use the other Powers to trick Loken than to try and force him into a Pact on my own.

Even better, while Tartar had made no firm commitment to remove Loken's tracking spell, he had implied he would do so for the right inducement. And Dark Power or not, I felt I could expect a fairer deal from the god-emperor than I could from Loken. All in all, matters seemed to have turned out well.

Except Loken had not left.

What's he up to now?

The Power smacked his forehead with the palm of his hand. "Michael, please don't tell me," he said in a strained voice, "that you believe that bull-face's patter about honor and truth? Tartar will use you just as hard as any other Power."

My lips tightened. Once again, Loken had guessed the direction of my thoughts. "The better question," I retorted, "is what are you still doing here?"

Loken stared at me blankly.

"I just betrayed you, remember?" I snapped in exasperation. "I can't imagine we have much to talk about anymore."

The corners of Loken's mouth twitched. "Oh, that."

"Yes, that! Aren't you angry?"

The jester tilted his head to the side. "Why? Do you want me to be?"

I ground my teeth together but wisely refrained from answering.

"It was a masterful ploy," Loken admitted. "Almost worthy of me, in fact. But perhaps, not one as well thought out as you think."

I glared at the Power, not wanting to bite but eventually conceding. "And why's that?"

"An excellent question," Loken said, beaming approvingly.

"Just tell me," I growled.

Loken chuckled at my expression. "What you have failed to factor in this genius plan of yours, my boy, is the danger of Tartar's interest. You've poked the bear, or as it were, the bull. Despite that oaf's bluff exterior, he is not as simple-minded as he would want you to believe. Tartar may not be as shrewd as me, but he will be watching you now. Be careful, Michael. Be very careful."

I paid Loken's words no heed. His ploy was obvious. The trickster was trying to seed doubt where there was none. Far more confounding, though, was his lack of animosity. "You're truly not angry?" I asked, gazing searchingly at him.

"Why would I be?" Loken asked, reseating himself. "I've told you before, emotions have no part in the Game. You got the better of me, true. And well done to you for that. But in the grand scheme of things, it is only a minor blip in my plans."

I gaped at him, finding it hard to come to terms with his reaction.

Loken sighed. "You still don't understand, I see. But you will—someday. Play the Game with your head Michael, not your heart." Sitting back and steepling his fingers, Loken looked over them at me. "Now sit. We have much to talk about."

I didn't move.

Nothing was stopping me from leaving. I could walk out the door and be done with Loken. But the Power knew too much about my secrets for me to be done with him that simply.

"I'm curious," Loken said suddenly. "What made you believe I wouldn't tell Tartar and Menaq the truth about your heritage?"

I threw the Power a sharp glance, not missing the thinly veiled threat.

"I took a gamble," I said bluntly.

Loken studied me with interest. "A gamble?"

I nodded. "I judged if you wanted them to know, you would have told them already." I held the Power's gaze. "I suspect you're playing a game of your own, something that stops you from revealing my secrets."

Loken raised one eyebrow. "And you risked everything on this suspicion?"

I nodded curtly.

Loken. "*Now*, I am impressed."

When I still didn't move, Loken leaned forward. "Sit," he ordered, his face devoid of expression. "It's time we had a much longer chat."

Knowing I had no choice, and even knowing I would likely regret it, I did as Loken bade and sat.

CHAPTER 251: A MIXED DOSE OF TRUTH AND LIES

"We've nothing to talk about," I said grimly.

Loken sat back. "Come now, Michael. You know that's not true." He scanned the room in a pointed fashion. "Are there any other hidden spies?" You don't have to tell me, but I assure you, you don't want anyone hearing what I say next."

My lips thinned, realizing what subject Loken was about to broach. "There's no one about."

"I rather think you're speaking the truth," Loken said lightly. "This time."

"Tell me, then," I said, ignoring his jibe.

Loken met my gaze. "I know about your bloodline."

Despite my pounding heart, I kept my face impassive and waited for him to go on.

But Loken said nothing more.

Is that it? I wondered, my thoughts churning. *Does he not know the rest?* I examined the Power carefully, trying to penetrate his mask of affability, but Loken remained as inscrutable as ever. He was studying me just as intently as I was him, I noticed. Trying to gauge my reaction, I thought.

"I don't know what you mean," I said finally.

"Nonsense," Loken scoffed. "The knowledge is written all over your face. You are a Wolf, and what's more, you know it, too!" The Power's gaze bore into mine. "How did you learn about your bloodline? Who told you about your heritage?"

For a second, I sat still in stunned silence as I came to terms with the Power's words. *He doesn't know,* I marveled. Not the entire truth, anyway.

Loken doesn't know I'm an anointed scion!

Relief warred with disbelief and elation, but I kept my face studiedly neutral. *Don't get too excited, Michael,* I cautioned myself. *What Loken knows is dangerous enough.*

And somehow, I had to keep him from guessing the rest.

"The Game did," I said, making no further pretense at ignorance.

"The Adjudicator?" Frowning, Loken sat back. "Explain," he demanded.

"What you said earlier was true," I said carefully. "I *did* find the goblins' prisoners in Erebus' dungeon, *and* I freed them too." I glanced at the Power to see what he made of this.

His face screwed up in exaggerated concentration, Loken motioned for me to go on; he must have figured this much already.

"Freeing the dire wolves triggered the completion of a hidden quest," I said. "That's how I got my initial Shadow and Light Marks. But they weren't the only Marks I received. The Adjudicator awarded me another Mark, too— a hidden one."

"The Wolf Mark," Loken said.

I nodded. "Correct."

"And is that when the Adjudicator gave you the beast tongue trait?"

My brows rose. "You know about that?"

"You'd be surprised what a high-tier analyze can tell about a player," Loken said cryptically. He threw me a hard stare. "Now quit stalling and answer the question."

My face tightened at the Power's tone, but I didn't let anger color my response. "The trait had nothing to do with the hidden quest. At least, I don't think it did. It was a reward for soloing the sector boss."

"I see," Loken said, studying his fingernails. "Continue, then."

I shrugged. "There is not much more to tell. The Mark is what allowed my Class to evolve. Ever since then, the Game has been giving me quests to deepen the Mark, and in the process, I've been learning about Wolf too."

Loken shot me a doubtful glance but didn't question my assertion. "Tell me about these tasks," he ordered instead.

I hesitated. I couldn't refuse to answer; that would only heighten Loken's suspicions. Nor could I lie outright. The Power was too perceptive for that. "The Game tasked me to help a dire wolf pack," I said eventually.

Unexpectedly, Loken smiled. "Which is why you engineered the destruction of the Long Fangs goblin tribe." He eyed me shrewdly. "And it's because of the wolves that you are desperate to return to sector 12,560, isn't it?"

"So, you know about them," I said, making no attempt to disguise my unhappiness at the extent of his knowledge.

Loken's grin widened. "Don't mistake me for a fool, dear boy. I've uncovered all your secrets."

Not all. Just the small ones. "Now you know everything," I said in pretended disappointment. "What now?"

Loken ignored my question. "No one recruited you?"

"Recruit me?" I asked, truly puzzled. "Who would—"

"Never mind," Loken said, waving aside the question. "Just an arbitrary thought." He pursed his lips. "So. With only the Game's messages to direct you, you decided to pursue the path of the Wolf?" he asked, his voice thick with sarcasm. "Is that right?"

"Why is that so hard to believe?" I retorted. "You know I didn't want to tie myself to any Power. When the Game offered me an alternate path, I jumped at the opportunity!"

For a drawn-out moment, Loken didn't say while he studied me from beneath a hooded gaze. "What do you know about Wolf?" he asked eventually.

"Maddeningly little," I ground out. Which was true enough. "Information on him is hard to come by. I've learned that the path of the Wolf is frowned upon, and the Powers usurped him and his kind long ago. I know, too, that to uncover more of my bloodline, I need to deepen my Wolf Mark and remain unsworn."

What I'd just told Loken was, of course, not the extent of my knowledge, but I was hoping it would be enough to satisfy him that I was being truthful.

"Is that why you've stopped strengthening your Force Marks?" Loken asked.

It was an astute observation, making me doubly grateful for my secret bloodline trait. If not for it, I did not doubt Loken would've unearthed the entirety of my involvement with House Wolf. "Yes," I said reluctantly.

"And that is everything?" Loken pressed. "You don't know anything else about Wolf?"

I stared at him in feigned innocence. "What else is there to know?"

Loken didn't answer. Bowing his head, he turned his focus inwards while he considered my words.

Hiding my anxiety, I waited.

"So... Adjudicator... ... . started again," Loken mused to himself. "I wonder... ... ... this time?"

The Power's muttering was nearly inaudible, and even with my wolf-enhanced senses, I caught less than half of what he said. But it was not like Loken to speak to himself.

Did he mean for me to overhear? I wasn't sure, but I couldn't pass up the opportunity to learn more. "Did you say something?" I asked loudly.

Loken focused on me again, his eyes weighing me. Then, seeming to come to a decision, he said, "You are not the first player the Game has tried to lead astray."

Huh?

My brows drew down. "What does that mean?"

"Only that the Adjudicator has tried to revive the bloodlines before," Loken said disdainfully.

I opened my mouth to ask a question, but Loken spoke over me. "What do you know about the Houses?"

"I've heard the term," I admitted evasively. "The Adjudicator used the phrase 'House Wolf' once."

"Hmm," Loken said. "You should be thankful you don't know more. Otherwise, I would be forced to kill you."

I blinked. "Isn't that what you've been trying to do all along?"

"Oh, I don't want you dead."

"But earlier, you said—"

"I lied."

I stared at Loken. "You lied *earlier*, but *now* you're telling the truth?" I asked in a tone dripping with skepticism.

Loken grinned, openly mocking me. "That's right. I only said what I said before to encourage you."

"You're not making sense," I growled.

Loken rolled his eyes. "I thought you would've figured it out by now. The mantises were... motivation."

"For what?" I snapped irritably.

"To convince you to seek my help, of course."

I stared at him. "You're telling me you set a death squad to hunt me, all just to—"

"Not just to hunt you," Loken interjected. "To kill you too." He grinned again. "I didn't want you *dead* dead, but a little dead would have been more than alright."

I took a moment to parse that. "So, you wanted to teach me a lesson?"

Loken smacked his hands together. "Exactly!"

"For refusing to become your sworn?"

"For that too. But mostly because you refused my task."

I stared at him blankly.

Loken sighed theatrically. "The chalice, remember? Don't tell me you forgot?"

I frowned. We were back to this again? I'd thought the Paya heist was just another ploy of Loken's to get me killed. But now... I shook my head. Now, I wasn't sure of anything. When had Loken been telling the truth? Then or now? Although... it was equally conceivable he'd lied *both* times.

Gah!

Trying to sift Loken's words for truth was an exercise in futility. Setting the matter aside, I took a deep breath. "Alright," I said, fixing my attention on the Power again. "Where does that leave us? Am I free to go?"

Loken laughed with what sounded like genuine amusement. "Far from it, my boy. Now that we've got all that out of the way, we can get down to the real business—what I need you to do for me."

✳   ✳   ✳

"Why would I risk entangling myself with you further?" I asked after a beat.

Loken's face grew unwontedly serious. "You said earlier that the Powers usurped Wolf and his kind. Do you know why?"

"What does that to have to do with—"

"Hear me out," Loken interjected.

Sighing, I closed my mouth.

"Good," Loken said approvingly. "Now, do you know the reason behind our vendetta with Wolf?"

Because the new Powers hate the old, I thought but bit back the words. That was the obvious answer and couldn't be what Loken was driving at. Why the new Powers wanted the old dead, why they had revolted against the old guard, that was still a mystery to me, so I remained silent.

"You don't know, do you?" Loken said softly. He fell silent for a moment. "I was there, you know."

"There?"

Loken's gaze flicked back to me. "There when the uprising began. I was young then, an unblooded scion," he said softly. "In those days, Wolf and his fellows—Lion, Pestilence, Serpent, Dragon, and so many others—ruled the Forever Kingdom. They named themselves Primes and reigned supreme over their own little fiefdoms—Houses, they called them. Each spent their lives concerned with one thing only: strengthening their bloodlines and their

House's power." He cast me a bland look. "Do you know what the net result of all that was?"

I shook my head.

"War," Loken said softly. "War on a scale you cannot imagine. An everlasting war that slowly but surely began destroying the world."

I blinked in confusion. "How?"

"Have you ever wondered why the Forever Kingdom is the way it is, Michael?" Loken asked, answering me obliquely. "Sectors, like islands, floating in the void of the aether and nether?"

I had, but the answer, if there was one, seemed to have been lost to time. "It does seem strange," I admitted.

"It was the Primes' doing," Loken said harshly. "Their ceaseless wars spanned continents. They wielded magic the likes of which are unknown today, and in their pursuit of power, they broke the world." His face fell. "Now, the Forever Kingdom is a sad remnant of what it once was."

I said nothing for a moment. The Loken before me was very different from the one I knew—sad, contemplative, angry. Was this the true Loken or just another façade?

"Is that why the Powers destroyed the Houses?" I asked finally. I had no way to verify Loken's assertions, so I chose not to contest his words and accept them at face value.

"Yes," he responded. "It is why I rose up and took arms against my own Prime." He held my gaze. "And it is why you cannot be allowed to tread further down the path of Wolf."

"But I'm not them," I pointed out. "I am only one lowly player."

Loken laughed bitterly. "Do not sell yourself short, Michael. You are not one player. You are a spark. A spark that may ignite the flames of war and bring about the return of the Houses."

"You fear them that much?"

Loken cast me a bleak look. "Us new Powers call ourselves gods, but the sad truth is we fall short of the Primes' power. It was only through the strength of numbers that we defeated the Houses the first time around."

"So why not tell your fellow Powers about me? Why keep my existence secret?"

Loken sighed. "Balance. Those words that I spoke to you long ago in Erebus' dungeon were not lies. My duty has been, and always will be, to maintain balance in the Game."

He gazed solemnly at me. "I am not the only Power who remembers the Primes; I am not the only one who was there. Tartar remembers. Arinna too. If either learns a player is treading the path of the Primes, they will start a cleansing the likes of which this world has not seen in millennia. Sectors would be scorched, armies will be marshaled, and a crusade will be launched against every sentient beast—of any kind.

Loken held my gaze. "To purge the Primes' taint, we will lay waste to the world. We did it once and will do it again if needs be."

I stared back at him mutely, knowing on some bone-deep level that this at least was no bluff: Loken meant every word of the threat he'd just uttered.

Abruptly, the Power smiled, and the jester of old returned. "But like you said, you're only one player. I'm not yet ready to unleash such a blight on the world in the face of such a singular threat."

"Then why tell me all this?" I asked quietly.

"So that you understand the consequence of journeying further down Wolf's path," Loken replied just as softly. "Stop now while you still can. It is too late for you to assume a Force-aligned Class, but you can still become a sworn. Pledge yourself to a Power—any Power—and you will never have to worry about me again."

That I would never do, and the answer was clearly written on my face for Loken to see.

Loken's lips twitched upwards. "I thought so. Well, in that case, know that as long as you live, I will deem you a threat. Consequentially, I will be watching—always."

I expected no less. "Why not just kill me and be done with it?" I asked bluntly.

Loken chuckled. "I just might."

"But?" I pressed, sensing there had to be one.

"But," Loken allowed, "there are things you can do in your present capacity that other players can't."

Folding my arms, I sat back. "So, you need me."

"I wouldn't go *that* far."

Saying nothing, I waited. We'd finally come to the heart of the matter—what Loken wanted from me.

"I will agree to leave you alone for a time *if* you do me a favor." Loken grinned. "I *may* even remove the tracking spell."

I cast the Power a dubious look. "What favor?"

"Complete my task and steal the chalice from Paya," Loken said.

✳   ✳   ✳

I frowned to conceal my surprise.

We'd come full circle, I realized. All of Loken's lengthy explanations and threats boiled down to one thing: him wanting me to rob Paya. Just how important was this chalice?

"Why me?" I demanded.

"I told you—" Loken began.

"You fed me some vague nonsense that was more evasion than answer," I retorted. "Tell me the real reason. Why do you wish *me* to do this?"

Loken fell silent for a moment. "The explanation I gave you before was true, if not the whole truth. Paya recently came into possession of an artifact of immense value. I suspect the Awakened Dead found it in the same stretch of dungeon sectors you first emerged from."

Starting in surprise, I opened my mouth, but Loken raised his hand for patience.

"What I did *not* tell you is that the chalice is a Force artifact. It is a thing of the Dark and is powerful enough that no Lightsworn or Shadowsworn can withstand its presence for long, much less hold it." He met my gaze. "But you, unbound to any Force, will be unaffected."

Loken's knowledge of the item seemed awfully specific. "How do you know so much about it?"

"I tried stealing it," Loken said.

"And?" I prompted when he didn't go on.

"And I failed," he admitted reluctantly. "Bypassing Paya's protections was child's play. But when I reached the chalice, I couldn't pick it up. The artifact told me only one steeped in the Dark may sip from it."

"It *told* you?" I asked, sure that I'd misheard.

Loken's eyes twinkled. "Oh, did I forget to mention that? The chalice is sentient."

"A sentient item?" I asked, certain he was joking.

"There aren't many such items in the Game," Loken admitted, "but those that exist are invariably powerful."

I rubbed my lips. "What makes this one so potent?"

Loken didn't answer.

"Loken?" I prompted.

"I don't know," he said.

My brows drew down. "What? Surely you inspected it?"

"I couldn't analyze it," he admitted. "And it refused to tell me its properties."

I stared at him, at a loss for words.

"But any artifact able to injure me is surely powerful," Loken finished.

My eyes widened. The chalice was strong enough to resist Loken's analyze *and* hurt him? What was this thing? "But if it is as powerful as you say, why hasn't Paya used it?"

"She's tried, believe me, and so have others from the Awakened Dead," Loken said. "But so far, the artifact has killed or badly scarred whoever has attempted to sip from it." Loken smiled. "It seems that being Darksworn is not the only requirement."

"And now, you want me to drink from it?" I asked skeptically.

"Of course not!" Loken said primly. "I only want you to steal it. Such a powerful artifact cannot be left in the Awakened Dead's hands. Eventually, they will figure out how to use the chalice." He leaned forward in his chair. "Once you have the artifact, you may discard it in the nether for all I care. Only get it away from Paya." He looked at me from beneath hooded eyes. "Will you do it?"

My brows creased again. *Would* I do it? I asked myself. In exchange for Loken removing his tracking spell? It was what I'd been trying to do all along, after all. But... I'd had my fill of Loken's games. "No," I said.

Loken's brows rose at my blunt refusal. "Why not?"

"I don't trust you anymore," I replied. "Not to keep your word nor to twist any bargain we make to your own ends. Do what you must. Tell your fellows about my heritage if you wish. Track me. Hunt me. Whatever. But I will make no more Pacts with you."

I rose to my feet.

"Stop, Michael," Loken said.

I glanced at him, another refusal on the tip of my tongue, but Loken spoke first. "What if I remove the tracking spell on you?" he asked. "Now, and without any strings attached. Will you do what I ask then?"

Was this another trick? "Can I trust you not to put another one on me?"

Loken laughed. "If only it were that easy," he said. "I only managed to lay the tracking spell on you the first time around because of your unwitting consent. And even then, I was skirting the edges of what the Game considers permissible." He shook his head ruefully. "The Adjudicator will not allow me to reapply the spell, not when you are now so clearly opposed to being tracked."

I pursed my lips, still not convinced.

Loken watched me unblinkingly while he waited for my answer.

"I will not swear to a Pact," I said.

"And I won't ask you to," Loken said encouragingly. He studied me again, his eyes bright. "So, you will steal the chalice?"

"I will consider it," I allowed.

"Good enough," the Shadow Power said, smiling once more. A moment later, a Game message dropped into my mind.

Debuff removed. The tracking spell laid upon you by the Power, Loken, has been dispelled.

Your task: <u>Heist in the Dark</u>! has been updated. Loken has informed you that the chalice in Paya's possession is a Dark artifact inimical to Lightsworn and Shadowsworn players. Objective revised: Steal the chalice before any Dark player can use it.

"Thank you," I said, and turning about, left the room.

Chapter 252: Restart

I exited the hotel with my thoughts in turmoil.

My conversations with Loken never seemed to turn out the way I envisioned. Once again, the Shadow Power had me questioning what I knew. Was there a kernel of truth behind his words?

Had the ancients been monsters?

I wasn't sure, but ultimately, I didn't think it mattered. Whatever the Primes of old had done, I was not them. My path was my own to forge. And despite Loken implying otherwise, I was *not* doomed to repeat their mistakes.

It was clear the new Powers would not see it that way, though. They would hunt me down if my heritage came to light. Trouble undoubtedly loomed on the horizon. Still, those were problems for another day.

Today, I had cause to celebrate.

I had stopped the mantises from hunting me, *and* I'd gotten rid of the tracking spell. Both accomplishments in their own right.

Better yet, I felt I was finally beginning to unravel Loken's schemes. The Shadow Power played a deep game, no doubt, but I got the sense he'd been forced to reveal more than he wished in our conversation, laying bare some of his true motives.

The future looks brighter, I thought.

A grin slipping on my face, I let my feet lead me to the emporium. It was time for some shopping.

✳   ✳   ✳

"So," Kesh mused as I walked into her office. "You survived."

I smiled. "You don't have to sound so surprised," I said, seating myself across from her.

The old merchant scrutinized me for a moment. "From that foolish grin you're wearing, I take it your scheme succeeded?"

"It did," I agreed.

Kesh sat back in her chair. "Well, well. Don't tell me you *actually* managed to cut a deal with the mantises?"

I peered at her sideways. "What do you know about it?"

Kesh chuckled. "You told me you were going to see Tartar, and when not long after, I received word that Menaq had entered the city, it was easy to put two and two together."

I nodded slowly. "I'm impressed. Your sources are better than Loken's."

Kesh blinked owlishly. "The trickster? What does he have to do with this?"

I waved aside her question. "How did you find out about Menaq?"

Kesh eyed me speculatively but said nothing.

"If you tell me, maybe I'll tell you what happened in the meeting with Menaq and Tartar," I suggested.

"So, you *did* meet with the Dark Powers?"

I nodded.

Kesh pondered my offer for a moment before answering. "All Powers are required by city law to notify the Triumvirate when they enter the sector. It's not easy to access the list, but let's just say... I have my ways."

"Ah," I exhaled. I should've guessed. I'd known from her Pact with the Triumvirate that Kesh had a cordial relationship with the city's Powers, but I hadn't realized the extent of their dealings. "But that still doesn't explain how you tied Menaq and me together."

Kesh tilted her head to the side. "You're joking, right?"

I folded my arms and stared back at her.

"I see that you're not," she murmured, then grinned abruptly. "You're famous."

My brows furrowed. "What?"

"You didn't think the mantises' hunt went unnoticed, did you?" Kesh asked. "You were chased by Menaq's disciples on multiple occasions, and more importantly, was seen to be chased *and* escape. It's not every day that the assassins turn out in numbers on the streets to hunt a mark, you know. Of course, it got people talking!"

My frown deepened.

"For nearly a year, the entire city has been buzzing about the 'one that got away.' And the tale has only grown in the telling." Kesh snorted. "If you believe the gossip, you didn't slay a handful of assassins but scores."

"I see," I said, clenching my fists as I considered the implications of my unexpected infamy.

Kesh's lips twitched. "Oh, relax. Few know the real identity of the assassins' mark."

"That's good," I said, not bothering to hide my relief as I looked up. "How did you figure it out?"

"The reports I received from my agent in the Triumvirate citadel made it clear who the mantises were after." She eyed me for a moment. "I can't say I was surprised. You always did smell like trouble." Despite her words, a smile played at the corner of Kesh's lips.

"Trouble does seem to follow me," I allowed, grinning back.

"In case you were wondering," Kesh continued, "your latest escapade has the rumor mill churning again. Word on the street is you slew over a dozen mantises in another daring escape."

"If only," I muttered.

"We know better," Kesh agreed. She leaned across the table. "Now, tell me everything about the deal you struck with Menaq and Tartar."

Taking a deep breath, I told her.

✳　✳　✳

By the time I was done with my tale, Kesh had lost her smile again. "You swim in dangerous waters, Michael," she said, throwing me a look that made plain what she thought of my scheme.

I shrugged. "I had no choice." I'd not told Kesh everything, of course. I'd left out all mention of my bloodline and the reason for Loken's keen interest in me.

"A Force artifact," the merchant murmured, still musing over my tale. "That is no small matter."

I'd told Kesh about the heist Loken wanted me to pull off. The merchant's Pact with the Triumvirate meant she was constrained from sharing the knowledge, and given her own impressive sources of information, I thought she was more likely to discover something of value on the chalice than I was. "Will you look into it?"

Kesh hesitated. "This is not something I would normally involve myself in, but a Force artifact..." She shook her head. "That *is* worrisome. I make no promises, but I will see what I can find out. Discreetly."

"Thank you," I said gravely.

Kesh's expression cleared. "Now that that's out of the way, let's get back to business." She paused. "I take it *business* is why you're here?"

I nodded. "First, though, I want to see Saya's letters."

Wordlessly, Kesh handed over the thick pile of missives. Breaking the seal of the first, I scanned its contents.

The letter was unremarkable and contained only an account of the daily happenings in the tavern. From Saya's colorful—and sometimes quirky—tales, I got the impression that both the gnome and the tavern were thriving. Chuckling at some of the incidents she described, I set aside the letter and picked up the next.

It continued in the same vein as the previous one, as did the next dozen or so—except that with each letter, just as Kesh said, Saya's concern at my continued silence grew.

But that was not all.

In her more recent correspondents, Saya's tone grew... gloomier, less cheerful. My brows furrowed. Something was amiss. Flipping through the missives faster, I searched for any mention of what could be troubling Saya, but the gnome had studiously refrained from passing on any darker tidings. It was almost as if she didn't want to worry me.

"You sense it too, don't you?"

I looked up to find Kesh watching me, a somber look on her face.

"Something's wrong," I stated.

Kesh nodded. "I think so, but I don't know your tavernkeeper well enough to be certain if that's the case."

I grimaced in frustration. "Saya doesn't say what's troubling her, though. There's not even the least hint of what it could—"

"Check the last letter," Kesh interjected.

Doing as the merchant bade, I set aside the rest of the missives and scanned the parchment in question. One particular excerpt caught my eye.

I folded up the letter with a troubled frown. The mischief Saya had described didn't sound especially concerning, but I got the feeling she was downplaying the extent of the problem.

The Game seemed to agree, and an alert dropped into my mind.

On behalf of Wolf, the Adjudicator has allocated you a new task: <u>Tavern Trouble</u>! The missives from one of those you consider Pack suggests she needs your help. Aid Saya as soon as possible. Remember that, above all else, the wolf is the protector of the Pack. Guard your kin, scion!

Objective: Investigate the disturbances at the tavern and put a stop to them.

Just how bad are those annoyances? I wondered. If the Game itself was taking an interest, I could not afford to take them lightly. Dismissing the Adjudicator's message, I glanced at Kesh. "When did the letter arrive?"

"One month ago," she replied.

My consternation grew. Given the number of missives in the stack Kesh had handed me, I'd assumed Saya was writing more often than that. If I had to guess, I'd say she'd been penning a letter at least once a week. "But that—"

"—doesn't fit her pattern," Kesh finished for me. "I agree. I've had no contact with Saya since that last letter."

I blinked. "What? None?"

Kesh nodded grimly.

"You've tried reaching out to her, though?"

"I have," Kesh said. "But all my own letters return unopened."

My worry ratcheted up a notch. *That* could not be good.

"It's what I wanted to speak to you about earlier," Kesh added. "It's time we sent someone to sector 12,560 to investigate in person. Do I have your permission?"

"Of course," I replied absently, then paused as something occurred to me. "How *do* you correspond with Saya?" The gnome didn't have aether magic as far as I knew and couldn't directly receive remote missives.

Kesh smiled. "I have an arrangement with one of the merchants in the sector. I send him my correspondences through the aether, and he delivers them. According to *him*, nothing is amiss at the tavern." She shrugged. "But I can't vouch for him."

I pursed my lips. "So, the merchant could be part of the problem?"

Kesh nodded. "That's why we need to send someone to investigate." She paused. "One of my own agents will do, I think."

I shook my head. "No. We need to send a fighter. While protected from harm, your agents will not be able to assist Saya if necessary."

"Oh, I know that," Kesh said. "I was thinking more along the lines of stationing an agent in the sector as a permanent liaison. I don't normally open offices outside of Nexus. Still, given the artifacts the Awakened Dead have been finding in the valley's dungeon, the sector may be an ideal location for an outlet." She paused again. "Not to mention the money your tavern is raking in."

I blinked. "It's that profitable?"

"It is," Kesh replied simply.

I rubbed my chin thoughtfully, taking her word for it. If sizable amounts of money were involved, it was no wonder the tavern was drawing hostile interest. All of which made my own decision easier: this was a matter I would have to address myself. "I'll go," I said abruptly.

Kesh eyed me skeptically. "Aren't you forgetting about the Awakened Dead? You may have rid yourself of the mantises, but that will not stop Erebus and Ishita from hunting you."

"Oh, trust me, I'm not likely to forget those two." I paused. "And how do you know about them anyway?"

Kesh raised one eyebrow. "You didn't think I did my research? Seeing that I'm considering setting up an office there, I commissioned a report on sector 12,560. That's when I learned about the unusual bounty Ishita took out on you."

"Huh," I grunted. "I see."

"But in all seriousness, why go back yourself?" Kesh asked. "Wouldn't it be better to let someone handle this?"

I shook my head. "I need to set eyes on Saya myself and make sure she is alright. I feel... responsible for her." It would also be the perfect opportunity to check on the dire wolves.

I was sure Wolf's task was not just about Saya. It was also a not-so-subtle reminder—not that I needed one—that others in the valley might need my help too.

Kesh was still studying me but didn't object further.

"You mentioned earlier that the tavern had excess funds. How much do I have to play with?" I asked. If I was going to return to the valley, I wouldn't do so in haste.

This time around, I would be ready for whatever Ishita's minions could throw at me—not that I planned on letting them know I was around, but it never hurt to be prepared.

Kesh smiled. "Quite a bit, actually." Reaching beneath her desk, she retrieved a leather-bound book and placed it between us.

"What's that?"

"The Sleepy Inn's ledger," Kesh answered. "Since you appointed me the tavern's factor, I've been keeping a close tally on its profits and expenses."

Leaning forward, I peered at the pages as she opened the book. They were filled with flowing lines of numbers, rows upon rows of them, itemizing every expense and transaction.

I sat back. "Give me the highlights."

Kesh's lips twitched. "The highlights? After Saya's last deposit—which was also a month ago, I might add—the tavern has 22,350 gold available in its bank account."

My eyes widened in shock. "Did you say *twenty-two thousand*?"

Kesh nodded. "It would have been more, but Saya has re-invested a considerable sum in the tavern, upgrading the building. The renovations are complete now, though, and going forward, the monthly profits should see an increase."

"How much can I withdraw for my own use?" I asked, still trying to process the extraordinary amount.

Kesh shrugged. "All of it. The money required for the tavern's upkeep is kept in a secondary account under Saya's direct control."

"All of it..." I murmured, bowing my head to think. The Sleepy Inn had generated a shocking amount of money and, from what Kesh said, could be counted on to do so in the near future too. Having access to such wealth would make everything I planned easier—which made it all the more imperative that I lay to bed whatever troubled the tavern.

My plans took shape slowly. I knew now what I needed to do, as well as how to go about raising House Wolf *and* protect those who depended on me. But before I could finalize anything, there were a few other things I needed to find out first.

I raised my head. "Tell me what you learned about the void mage skills I requested."

Chapter 253: Windfall

Not answering me directly, Kesh set down a familiar-looking thin film of metal on the desk. It was the same emporium catalog I'd used before. Scanning the sheet, I saw it contained a list of skills.

Picking up the catalog, I read avidly.

<u>The Emporium's List of Void Skillbooks</u>

Cost: 200 gold each. Tier: Master.

<u>**Constitution skillbooks:**</u>
poison absorption (unavailable),
disease neutralization,
hardy (reduces damage from piercing attacks).

<u>**Dexterity skillbooks:**</u>
nimble (counters dexterity-based abilities),
avoid (reduces damage from area of effect spells).

<u>**Faith skillbooks:**</u>
null life,
null death,
null dark,
null light,
null shadow.

<u>**Magic skillbooks:**</u>
air absorption,
earth absorption,
fire absorption,
water absorption,
nether absorption (unavailable),
aether absorption.

<u>**Mind skillbooks:**</u>
mental fortitude (counters subversive thoughts),
kinetic rebound (reduces damage from fast-moving objects),
concentration (counters spell interruptions).

<u>**Perception skillbooks:**</u>
fade (counters all forms of detection),
conceal (counters all forms of analyze).

<u>**Strength skillbooks:**</u>
toughness (reduces damage from blunt attacks),
juggernaut (counters strength-based abilities).

"That's it?" I asked after staring at the list for a drawn-out moment. "Where are all the resistance skills?"

"Interestingly enough, void mages don't use ordinary resistance skills—those *only* increase your odds of avoiding harmful effects." Kesh shook her head in bemusement. "Your new Class does *more*. It is part of a rare set of void Classes, all of which specialize in damage reduction. Void skills not only increase a player's chance to resist an attack, but they *also* absorb a portion of the incoming damage—no matter the outcome of your resistance checks."

I nodded slowly. That tied in with the Game's description of my null force and elemental absorption skills. More surprising, though, was how much Kesh knew about my new Class. "You seem to know an awful lot about void mages," I said, leaving the question hanging.

Kesh smiled ruefully. "I researched the Class after your last visit. Voids are few and far between in the Game."

"I see." I paused. "Then there *are* other void players?"

"Certainly," Kesh said. "Though I myself have not run across one before."

Nodding thoughtfully, I bent my head to study the list of skills again—but I'd not been mistaken the first time. None of the skills on offer were comparable to the class-unique skills I'd obtained when becoming a void mage.

"Is something wrong?" Kesh asked, seeing my pensive look.

I sighed. The list contained twenty-three skills, and while many looked intriguing, none were what I sought.

"Were you hoping for something else?" Kesh prompted again when I didn't answer.

I nodded reluctantly. "I was hoping for a duplex skill."

Her brows drew down in puzzlement. "A duplex skill?"

I nodded absently. "One that counters two or more different types of damages." I paused. "Like my class-unique skills."

"Ah," Kesh breathed. "I've heard of those. But you won't find any on sale—anywhere."

I shot her a glance. "Why not?"

"Class-unique skills can only be acquired through Class stones. Only the Adjudicator has the power to create them, and when he will choose to do so—and why—is anyone's guess." Kesh looked at me oddly. "You are fortunate indeed to have earned one. Not many do. But the short of the matter is: there are *no* class-unique skillbooks."

"Oh," I said, sagging in disappointment.

I perked up only a moment later, though, as I realized just how big a boost the Class stone I'd found had given me. With it, I'd effectively gained *seven* void skills for the price of two slots. I doubted many other players had such an advantage.

It left me wondering about the nature of the Class stones, though. Did the Game configure the starting skills of each stone differently based on what a player had done to earn it?

That was what Kesh's explanation seemed to hint at. If that was so... then even if there were other voids in the Game, none of them might have *my* particular Class-unique skills.

All-in-all, I was grateful I'd listened to Ceruvax and searched out my own Class stone instead of buying one. But none of this was neither here nor there.

Shaking off my musings, I returned to my inspection of the catalog. I had a limited number of skill slots remaining which meant I could only choose three of the twenty-three skills on offer.

But which three?

My current void skills focused on negating magic and faith-based attacks. Going forward, I could also spread my skills to resist other forms of damage, but I didn't have nearly enough skill slots to cover most of them.

Disease neutralization, in particular, caught my eye. Most notably, it would make venturing into the swamp easier. Unfortunately, I could see little use for it beyond that, and I couldn't afford to choose my skills based on short-term goals.

Then there were the fade, avoid, and kinetic rebound skills. There were obvious benefits to each. But the truth was, I was more inclined to specialize.

Better to become as resistant to as many forms of mana-based casting as possible, I decided.

That would mean choosing between null life, null death, aether absorption, and nether absorption. *An easy enough decision, then.* Aether magic was not offensive in nature, as far as I knew.

"I'll take the—"

I broke off, finally noticing the additional notations next to some of the skills. "Kesh, why are two skills marked as unavailable?"

"I have not yet managed to find a seller for the poison absorption skillbook," Kesh admitted. "But if you give me another day or two, I'm sure I can source it." She paused. "As for nether absorption... that, I'm afraid, is more problematic."

I frowned. "Why?"

Kesh's lips turned down. "There is only one source of such tomes: the stygian brotherhood. They buy all nether-related spellbooks and skillbooks as soon as they hit the market and keep them for use by their own members. I could try to outbid the brotherhood for the next nether absorption skillbook that goes on auction, but that could be weeks, months, or even years from now. The only other option is to—"

"Approach the brotherhood directly," I finished. I bowed my head for a moment, thinking. "What about other nether artifacts? Does the brotherhood hoard them too?"

Kesh shook her head. "On the contrary, they sell them."

I blinked.

The merchant chuckled. "Crafting and selling stygian gear is the main source of the brotherhood's wealth. They are not the only ones to do so, but they are the best, by far." She gestured at my swords. "That stygian blade you carry was probably made by a brotherhood smith."

"Interesting. In that case, I'll take the null life and null death skillbooks."

Kesh nodded and, with a wave of her hand, caused the tomes to appear on her desk. Touching my palm to her keystone, I completed the transaction—but not without an expression of protest. "I don't see why they're so expensive," I grumbled.

Kesh smiled. "These aren't just any skillbooks. They are amongst the rarest in the Game."

I nodded, having no argument with that, and picked up the two tomes.

You have acquired a null life skillbook.
You have acquired a null death skillbook.
You have lost 400 gold.

"Do you mind?" I asked, pointing at the books.

Divining my intent, Kesh shook her head. "Go ahead."

Inclining my head in thanks, I read each tome in turn.

You have gained two master skills: <u>null life</u> and <u>null death</u>.

Null life is the art of using your void armor to ward off hostile life-based attacks or, failing that, absorb a portion of its damage. Note the benefits provided by this skill are only active so long as you have mana remaining.

Null death is akin to null life but instead attunes your void armor to necromancy, allowing you to repel—or absorb—its harmful effects.

You have 1 of 6 void mage Class skill slots remaining.

I exhaled slowly, feeling the new knowledge seep into me. My tertiary class's configuration was nearly complete, and I itched to see it done and find out how it would meld with mindslayer, but I couldn't just yet.

"What about your last void skill?" Kesh asked, seeing the tomes vanish from my hands and guessing the direction of my thoughts.

"For that, I think a visit to the stygian brotherhood is in order."

Kesh studied me curiously. "You want the nether absorption skill that badly?"

I nodded mutely. Given the hidden nether-infested sector, I suspected I would be spending a significant amount of time in the Nethersphere.

But it was for more than that that I wanted the skill.

Loken's threats had not gone unheeded. Sooner or later, the new Powers would hunt me, and when that happened, where better to hide than where few players ventured? Besides which, it was past time I acquainted myself with the brotherhood.

"Odd choice," Kesh remarked.

I glanced at her, but she said nothing further, leaving me to decide how to respond. "I have a few ventures planned in the nether," I admitted.

Kesh snorted. "Planning on becoming a rift jumper, are you? That's a dangerous hobby."

I shrugged, not refuting her assumption, and changed the topic. "I also need some new gear."

"Hmm, like what?"

"To start with, four upgrade gems," I said.

Kesh did not look surprised by the request. "That will exceed your available funds," she pointed out.

"Transfer 15,000 gold from the tavern's account," I replied offhandedly. Kesh nodded and wordlessly materialized the items I asked for.

You have acquired 4 x upgrade gems. Each item lets you improve any ability by a single tier.
You have lost 8,000 gold.

I winced. Even with the windfall from the tavern, the cost of the upgrade gems bit deep into my funds. I would have to carefully ration their use.

"What else?" Kesh asked.

I thought for a bit. Many of my skills had reached tier three, and I was eager to purchase some expert-ranked abilities, but the attribute cost was another thing that worried me. "How many attribute points do tier three abilities consume?"

"Ten," Kesh replied, confirming my suspicion.

"Ouch," I muttered. Turning my attention inwards, I checked my player profile and, specifically, my ability slot status.

<u>Unused Ability Slots</u>

Strength: 13 of 13.
Constitution: 14 of 19.
Dexterity: 9 of 36.
Perception: 3 of 25.
Mind: 47 of 71.
Magic: 21 of 21.
Faith: none.

The Strength and Magic ability slots were useless to me. I didn't have any strength-based skills, and my spell illiterate trait prevented me from acquiring Magic abilities.

Sadly, my Perception was the most constrained, and even though both my deception and insight skills were at tier three, I could not afford any Perception abilities. *I must plan my attribute distribution better in the future*, I thought.

But I *did* have sufficient spare slots to purchase expert Dexterity and Constitution abilities. And when it came to Mind, with over forty slots available, I could be more expansive.

I focused on Constitution first. The choices I needed to make there should be the simplest. "What tier three light armor abilities do you have?"

"Hmm... There are four tomes available," Kesh said. "Do you wish to see them all?"

I nodded. "That will be useful."

Kesh placed another emporium catalog before me; this one already filtered to show the four abilities in question. Leaning forward, I studied each.

Item 61,411 of the emporium's wares is the improved lighten load ability tome. This ability reduces the encumbrance from worn armor by 30%.

Governing attribute: Constitution. Tier: expert. Cost: 50 gold. Requirement: rank 10 armor skill.

Item 291,412 of the emporium's wares is the load controller ability tome. This ability is a variant of the lighten load ability, and instead of reducing your own encumbrance, it increases the weight of your foes' armor, slowing them down. Cost: 50 gold.

Item 451,478 of the emporium's wares is the lesser toughen armor ability tome. This ability temporarily increases your physical damage reduction by 10%. Governing attribute: Constitution. Tier: expert. Cost: 50 gold. Requirement: rank 10 light armor, rank 5 medium armor, or rank 1 heavy armor.

Item 931,102 of the emporium's wares is the agile fighter ability tome. This ability temporarily increases your Dexterity by +4. Governing attribute: Constitution. Tier: expert. Cost: 50 gold. Requirement: rank 10 light armor, rank 15 medium armor, or rank 20 heavy armor.

I sat back heavily. *So much for simple,* I groused. I wanted three of the four abilities, but I knew it would be foolish to select more than one.

Constitution was not one of my core attributes, and I didn't plan on investing heavily in it in the future. All of which meant upgrading one Constitution ability to tier four, then five, and so on would be challenging enough; two would be impossible.

So, which one shall it be?

Improved lighten load, I immediately dismissed from consideration. I didn't need further encumbrance reduction. My light armor skill already provided enough of that.

The physical damage reduction of toughen armor was nice, but my fighting style depended on *not* getting hit, so it was less useful than the other two abilities on offer.

Agile fighter seemed the most versatile, but it was also more expensive than load controller—an upgrade of an existing ability—and as tempting as the ability was, ten ability slots were too much to spend for it.

"I'll take load controller," I said.

Kesh summoned the item, and I wasted no time reading the tome to acquire its knowledge.

You have upgraded your lighten load ability to <u>load controller</u>. This ability increases the encumbrance of any foe within 2 yards by 20% for 10 minutes. Its activation time is very slow. Note, load controller only affects hostiles who wear armor.

It is an expert ability and requires 5 more ability slots than its advanced variant. You have 9 of 19 Constitution ability slots remaining.

You have lost 50 gold.

I smiled in pleasure. Despite some of the ability's limitations, I thought the twenty percent debuff to nearby armored melee-foes more than made up for it.

Next, I considered Dexterity. Given how many Dexterity abilities I already had, I immediately ruled out acquiring more. And besides, I had only nine free slots to play with.

I had the choice of upgrading either piercing strike, backstab, or whirlwind. All three had worked well in the past, but of the three, there was no doubt that backstab was my favorite. Its burst damage was what had made many of my one-shot kills possible. "I'll also take a tier three backstab ability tome."

Kesh laid another book on the table, and I read it too.

You have upgraded your backstab ability to <u>improved backstab</u>. This ability increases the backstab damage you inflict to 2.5x more than normal. It is an expert ability and requires 5 more ability slots than its advanced variant. You have 4 of 36 Dexterity ability slots remaining.

You have lost 50 gold.

The description of the upgraded ability was exactly what I expected, and dismissing the Game message, I turned my attention to my Mind abilities. With them, the way forward was less clear.

The upgrade gems I'd just bought would advance the abilities I'd acquired through the Wolf trials, but that still left my more 'ordinary' psi spells to consider.

The first step, I decided, would be to upgrade my existing tier two Mind spells to tier three. "Can I please get expert versions of reaction buff, mass charm, and two-step?"

Kesh waved her hands again, but unexpectedly, when she was done, four spellbooks were laid out on the table, not three.

Another variant, I thought. After peering at the spellbooks' titles, I opened and read the first two tomes.

You have upgraded your charm ability to <u>superior mass charm</u>.

This spell temporarily overrides the consciousness of 10 targets, forcing them to serve you for 20 seconds.

You have upgraded your reaction buff ability to <u>heightened reflexes</u>. This is a self-use ability that increases your Dexterity by +8 ranks for 20 minutes. You have 37 of 71 Mind ability slots remaining.

You have lost 100 gold.

The remaining two books required further consideration before opening. Both were variants of the two-step ability. Focusing on each in turn, I considered their properties.

Item 41,550 of the emporium's wares is the four-step ability tome. This ability allows you to take four steps in the air as if it were solid ground. Governing attribute: Mind. Tier: expert. Cost: 50 gold. Requirement: rank 10 telekinesis skill.

Item 231,802 of the emporium's wares is the windborne ability tome. This ability is a variant of the four-step ability that allows you to slide through the air at a faster pace but over a shorter overall distance.

The windborne ability sounded intriguing, if not wholly different from four-step, and not seeing many downsides to the implied distance limitation, I chose it without further hesitation.

You have upgraded your two-step ability to <u>windborne</u>. This ability allows you to slide along a current of wind, in any direction, up to a maximum distance of 10 yards and at 2x your normal movement speed. You have 32 of 71 Mind ability slots remaining.

You have lost 50 gold.

"Well, well," I murmured. "That will certainly come in handy."

"You're satisfied with your purchases, then?" Kesh asked.

I beamed at her. "I certainly am."

"Will that be all?"

For a moment, I was tempted to acquire more Mind abilities. But I still had the upgrade gems to use—which would require at least another seventeen more slots, leaving me with only fifteen.

There's no need to rush my choices, I cautioned myself. *Better to wait and see how these abilities perform before buying more.*

"I don't require any further abilities, thank you," I told Kesh. "But I do need a few other items."

CHAPTER 254: PLANNING FOR THE FUTURE

You have acquired 5 x rank 4 disease protection crystals.
You have lost 100 gold.

After I'd rattled off my list, Kesh laid the protection crystals I requested on the table—but nothing else.

I looked at her questioningly.

The old merchant sighed. "As much as it pains me to say this, but if you're going to visit the brotherhood, you should get your stygian equipment from them too."

I nodded slowly. I'd asked Kesh for gear tailored to rift diving. Considering the time I planned on spending in the nether, specialized equipment would be advantageous, but she was right; it made sense to get such gear from the brotherhood.

"Do you need anything else?" Kesh asked.

My gaze turned downward, inspecting my current kit. Was it time for some new equipment? I thought so, but I didn't want to spend further coin until I knew what the nether resistance skillbook and stygian gear were going to cost me. "How much do I have left?"

"Seven thousand, one hundred and eighty gold in your personal account," Kesh replied. "And another seven thousand, three hundred and fifty in the tavern's."

That's enough for a few upgrades at least, I thought happily, but before I could open my mouth, Kesh spoke up.

"You should know I've found someone willing to part with a pair of wayfarer's gloves." She paused. "Purchasing them will make a sizable dent in your funds, though."

Despite Kesh's warning, I could not contain my eagerness. "Tell me," I demanded.

"The seller is a long-time customer and, as a favor to me, has refrained from putting the item on the open market. If you want the gloves, you can get them for twelve thousand gold."

I groaned. "Twelve thousand? Really?"

"Legendary items are not cheap," Kesh pointed out. "And the gloves are amongst the least expensive in the wayfarer set. For the remaining items, you can expect to pay more. *Much* more."

I sighed.

"What should I tell him?" she asked.

I hesitated. I could afford the gloves, if barely, but acquiring them would leave me low on funds again. For a second, I considered returning the upgrade gems but then dismissed the notion. I needed better abilities more than I needed any item—even a legendary one. "Can you ask him to hold them for one more week? I will have an answer for you by then."

Kesh eyed me for a moment. "A week," she agreed eventually. "But no longer."

I nodded.

"Now, if that concludes all your purchases, can we discuss the matter of sector 12,560?"

I nodded again.

"When do you plan on leaving Nexus?"

I rubbed the side of my face, thinking. The day was late, and I felt drained; the conversations with Loken and Tartar had been taxing in more ways than one. *Better to start the venture in the valley fresh,* I thought.

"Tomorrow morning," I answered.

"Perfect," Kesh said. "Then I'll have one of my agents ready to accompany you at first light tomorrow. Will that be acceptable?"

"Of course." I paused. "Out of interest, where do you plan on setting up your outlet in the sector?"

Kesh snorted. "That's a good question. It will have to be in the safe zone—everywhere else in the valley is too dangerous—but thus far, I've had no luck finding a premise. Given the sector's growing popularity, no one is willing to sell property there. It's hard to negotiate remotely, though, and my agent should have better luck once she reaches the sector."

I stroked my chin. "Hmm. What about using the tavern?"

Kesh grimaced. "I'd prefer my own premises. The emporium prides itself on providing a premium service, after all. But if no other opportunities present themselves, I may just take you up on your offer."

"You would be welcome." I smile slyly. "But, of course, renting space in the tavern will cost you a percentage of the profits."

"Of course," Kesh murmured. "How does ten percent sound?"

"I was thinking more like twenty."

"Fifteen," Kesh countered.

I thought about it for a moment, then nodded. "Deal."

The merchant snorted. "You are not very good at this, are you? Most players would've driven a harder bargain."

I shrugged. It better served my interests to keep Kesh happy than to squeeze her for every percent of profit.

Something else occurred to me. "You should send Cara."

Kesh blinked. "Who?"

I slapped my forehead. I had forgotten Cara was not the agent's real name, just what I called her.

"Your agent in the plague quarter," I clarified. "I'm used to dealing with her already."

Kesh stared at me owlishly. "Careful, Michael. There is a good reason my agents' identities are cloaked behind veils of secrecy. Don't get too close to the girl, or you will jeopardize her—and me."

I inclined my head, accepting the rebuke. "Understood."

"Anyway, I don't think it's wise to send *that* agent," Kesh continued. "The girl is nearing the end of her term and already has a well-established relationship with the knights."

I was curious about what Kesh meant by 'term,' but I didn't think she would take kindly to me probing further into the nature of her agents. "But I trust Ca—" I began.

Spotting Kesh's incipient frown, I corrected myself—"the agent. Sending her will serve both our interests, especially since we don't know the state of things in the valley."

Kesh's frown deepened, but she didn't object further. "Very well, but make sure you heed my warning."

I nodded.

"But if you wish the citadel agent—" Kesh glanced at me— "or as you would have it, *Cara*, to accompany you, then I will need a day more to transfer her out of her current posting." She looked at me. "Are you prepared to wait?"

I hesitated. I was reluctant to delay my return to the valley, but Saya had waited a month and the wolves even longer to hear from me; another day would not matter much. "Alright."

"Good, that's settled then," Kesh said. "I'll see you the day after tomorrow."

Rising to my feet, I bid farewell to Kesh and left the compound.

✻   ✻   ✻

A little later, I was back in my room in the Wanderer's Delight. Night had fallen, and my body craved rest, but I had a few more tasks to complete before I could sleep.

Sitting cross-legged on the bed, I glanced down at the four upgrade gems spread out before me. They were for what I'd come to think of as my scion abilities: astral blade, chi heal, mind shield, and shadow blink.

Shadow blink was at tier two and the others at tier one, and while all four scion abilities could be upgraded to expert rank, I only had enough upgrade gems to get two there. I *could* still buy more gems, but the cost was exorbitant, and for now, I had to choose which of the abilities to upgrade.

Shadow blink first, I think.

It was one of my most-used abilities, and upgrading it to its full potential was essential. Touching a hand to the gem, I willed my choice to the Game.

Ability gem activated.
Creating ability tome...

...

Tome creation halted. There are 2 expert variants available for the shadow blink ability.

Variant 1: <u>long shadow blink</u>. This variant increases the range of shadow blink to 50 yards.

Variant 2: <u>shadow bounce</u>. This variant modifies the base ability, allowing you to perform 2 consecutive short shadow blinks in a single cast, stunning each target for 2 seconds in passing.

Choose your tier 3 shadow blink ability tome now.

"More variants," I murmured. I'd anticipated an upgrade along the lines of long shadow blink, but the shadow bounce variant was unexpected.

It was interesting...

...but ultimately less enticing than long shadow blink.

While a mini stun and double jump were great, they didn't improve the ability in a manner I liked. I mostly used shadow blink to catch my enemies off-guard, and even if long shadow blink limited me to a single target, striking—instantly and suddenly—from *much* farther away was a lot more appealing.

My decision made, I willed my choice to the Adjudicator.

You have acquired a long shadow blink ability tome.

The ability gem vanished, leaving a small leatherbound book in its stead. Picking up the book, I absorbed its knowledge.

You have upgraded your shadow blink ability to <u>long shadow blink</u>. This mind spell allows you to teleport to any living entity within 50 yards, taking your shadows with you.

Perfect, I thought.

My gaze slid to the remaining three gems. My next decision was harder. Mind shield, chi heal, and astral blade were all at tier one, and while I had an inkling of how they would advance, I couldn't be certain. On top of that, I needed six gems to upgrade all three fully.

Let's prioritize by use, I decided and activated the next two gems.

You have acquired a lesser chi heal ability tome.
You have acquired a lesser astral blades ability tome.

Upgrading mind shield would have to wait—I didn't use it much, anyway. Picking up the spellbooks that had appeared, I read them one after the other.

You have upgraded your chi heal ability to <u>lesser chi heal</u>. This spell allows you to restore 20% of your lost health with psi.
You have upgraded your astral blade ability to <u>twin astral blades</u>. This spell manifests two psi daggers in your hands. Note, both your hands must be empty.

Hmm.

The chi heal upgrade was expected, the astral blade one... less so. I'd been hoping for a longer-lasting spell or a bigger blade. Still, the ability would be useful when attacking from range.

My gaze skipped to the last gem.

Which of the two abilities did I take to tier three? If their upgrade paths followed the same pattern as shadow blink, then I was likely to be given an option between two variants. There was no way to anticipate what they would be, though.

So, I went with the ability I considered more crucial: chi heal.

Ability gem activated.
Creating ability tome...
...

Tome creation halted. There are 2 expert variants available for the chi heal ability.

Variant 1: <u>moderate chi heal</u>. This variant increases the restorative effects provided by chi heal to 30%.

Variant 2: <u>quick mend</u>. This variant modifies the base ability, allowing you to trigger-cast a lesser chi heal.

Choose your tier 3 chi heal ability tome now.

"Well, well," I exclaimed, rubbing my hands in glee. "This is more like it." The second variant suited me perfectly, and despite its lower healing benefit, I had no hesitation in acquiring the ability.

You have acquired a quick mend ability tome.

You have upgraded your chi heal ability to <u>quick mend</u>, transforming it into a trigger-cast spell.

Trigger-cast abilities are pre-cast and automatically invoked under specific conditions. They are an essential part of any caster's arsenal and, most notably, are used by mages to activate their shields and other defenses. Beware, though, that trigger-cast spells are not infallible. If you incur high burst damage or take a critical hit, the ability may fail to trigger before death claims you.

Quick mend allows you to automatically invoke a lesser chi heal when your health falls below a predefined percentage. It may also be used normally and without trigger-casting. Note, this ability's weaves will dissipate after 1 hour if unused.

You have 14 of 71 Mind ability slots remaining.

My tasks completed, I laid down flat on the bed and stared up at the ceiling. My head felt too full, with the knowledge of my new abilities swimming in it. Once more, my combat effectiveness had undergone a step change, and I was eager to test out the new spells.

But that would have to wait for tomorrow. I stifled a yawn. For now, sleep beckoned. Folding my hands behind my head, I let my thoughts drift.

There was one aspect of my player profile I'd not seen to: upgrading slaysight. That was not an oversight, though, but a deliberate choice. I'd decided to forgo advancing the ability until *after* my Classes melded. There was a chance—if only a minimal one—that I would lose the ability in a future meld. And if that happened, there was no reason to waste a Class point unnecessarily. *Better if I—*

I broke off, interrupted by another yawn.

That's enough thinking, I thought tiredly and closed my eyes. Before I knew it, I was fast asleep.

I awoke early the next morning and, without delay, exited the room. I had an entire 'free' day before I left for the valley, and I intended to put the time to good use. Making my way through the hotel, I deliberated on what to do.

My goals had multiplied rapidly.

In addition to visiting the valley, there was the hidden sector to explore, Ceruvax to find, and Kolath's mystery to uncover, as well as deciding what to do about Loken's quest and Tartar's interest.

The nether-infested sector in the guardian tower was central to my plans for House Wolf, and returning to it was a priority. However, exploring the sector was a mammoth task and not an undertaking to try completing in a day.

Finding the last Wolf envoy was just as important. Based on Cyren's information, I suspected he was in the saltmarsh dungeon. But locating the dungeon's entrance was going to be a problem. Making contact with Ceruvax would also have to wait.

Then there was Kolath's task. I knew little about what it would entail or where it would lead. And while I was determined to pursue the matter, I did not foresee making headway soon. I set it aside, too.

Finally, there was Loken's quest.

I was ambivalent about the mission. On the one hand, given the trickster's machinations, I felt little inclined to do what he wanted, and the task itself would undoubtedly be dangerous. But on the other hand, Loken was not a Power I could ignore. For better or worse, I'd attracted his attention, and he knew about my bloodline.

There were also more intangible benefits to the task. I sensed the chalice was important to Loken, making the mission a unique opportunity to learn more about the Shadow Power's motivations—which would be reward enough. *Loken's mission bears thinking upon,* I decided, *but it's not a job I can tackle just yet.*

Slipping out of the hotel foyer, I paused on the threshold. It was time to decide which way to go. Sighing, I glanced down the street in both directions.

I had more than enough to do, but none of my main tasks were achievable in a day. That left only my secondary objectives to consider, namely completing my Class and... collecting a few bounties.

To complete my Class, I needed to visit the stygian brotherhood. Their chapterhouse lay deep in the plague quarter, though, and going there was better left for later in the day. *In the meantime, let's see what bounties are available.*

Swinging left, I strolled towards the market square.

✳ ✳ ✳

I'd come a long way since first attempting to become a bounty hunter, and while money was no longer a motivator, there were also other reasons to join the guild.

First and foremost, I suspected full guild members had access to the other Nexus quarters—something I thought would become more important the longer I stayed in the city. Then, too, there was the matter of gaining allies.

I could not raise House Wolf on my own. I would need, if not allies, then friends. And as a factionless, Force-unaligned group, the bounty hunters guild was the ideal organization to reach out to. Of course, I still knew little about the guild, but the easiest way to learn more of them was to rise up through their ranks.

And for that, I need to complete bounties.

Coming to a stop in the safe zone's central square, I scanned the area. The global auction was as busy as ever, and I could see no sign of the noticeboard. But I had asked for directions on the way over and knew it was on the west end of the square. Wading through the crowds, I searched for the board.

Five minutes later, I drew to a halt, staring at the wooden monstrosity planted in the ground in front of me. I'd been slightly concerned about finding the noticeboard in the sea of people, but I needn't have worried. The bounty board was unmissable.

It was both many times larger and sturdier than the one in the wolves' valley. And instead of being full of tacked-on pieces of paper, the noticeboard held only four steel posters, each firmly fastened to the board's broad wooden face.

I glanced at the players beside me. Most rushed by, not paying the noticeboard any heed. But the few that stopped, stood back and stared intently at the steel posters.

As I watched, a robed human caster pulled out a piece of paper and scratched furiously on it, all while shooting glances at the board. Following his gaze, I saw a string of words marching down the surface of each metal poster.

They're like Kesh's catalogs, I thought. Fascinated, I stepped forward and inspected one of the metal sheets more closely.

The number 'One' had been carved into the wood above the poster, and not unexpectedly, all the bounties scrolling through it were tier one.

To my right, I noticed a disfigured elven woman with a broadsword peeking over her shoulder, sauntering up to another poster. She touched the metal sheet—briefly—before walking away with a satisfied look on her face.

Hmm, now what was that about?

Curious, I walked over to the poster and touched it myself, prompting a Game message to appear.

Welcome, probie! You have 1 of 5 active jobs logged in your BHG ID. Do you wish to add bounty 10,380 to your log?

Replying in the negative, I looked to my right—in the direction the fighter had headed. The elf was gone. *She must be a bounty hunter*, I thought, regretting the missed chance to speak to a fellow guild member. Shrugging off my disappointment, I pulled out my BHG ID.

The Game message I'd just received implied I had an active bounty—which was news to me.

When I'd entered the guardian tower, I'd had three bounties. I'd failed the first after the allotted time had run out, and while I'd received no similar messages on the other two bounties, I had assumed they'd lapsed too. Bounties were not exclusive, after all, *and* nearly a year had gone by.

Surely in the interim, someone else had completed the other open jobs?

Apparently not, I thought, staring down at my BHG ID.

One job was still listed on the rear of the card. Running a finger along the finely etched letters, I called up the job description.

Job number: 428. Job name: Hunt for a Criminal. Tier: 4. Bounty: 150 gold. Payment is guaranteed by the guild, and the job is available to both guild members and non-members. Job description: Knight-captain Orlon requires assistance in apprehending a convicted thief named, Anriq. The thief escaped custody and is thought to be in the saltmarsh district. The mark is a player and a known werewolf. Knight-captain Orlon can be found in the Triumvirate citadel.

I pursed my lips thoughtfully. So, the werewolf was still at large. What did that say about this Anriq? Was he too difficult to capture? Or was it the terrain that daunted my fellow bounty hunters?

A shout broke through my musings. "Hey, buddy! Get out of the way. You're blocking the board."

Returning my BHG ID to my pocket, I waved in apology to the heckler. *Well, it looks like I'm heading to the saltmarsh district today, after all.*

✳ ✳ ✳

Before leaving the square, I scanned the noticeboard for other bounties. If I was going to head into the saltmarsh, it made sense to tackle any other jobs I could find in the region.

To my delight, I found two other bounties listed.

Job number: 1015. Job name: District purge. Tier: 4. Bounty: 300 gold. Payment is guaranteed by the guild, and the job is available to both guild members and non-members. Job description: A group of sea hags has once more taken up residence in the saltmarsh. Find and kill them lest their nest attracts more of their kind. To claim the reward, deliver the nest mother's scalp to knight-captain Orlon in the Triumvirate citadel.

Job number: 271. Job name: Tongues and feet. Tier: 4. Bounty: 200 gold. Payment is guaranteed by the guild, and the job is available to both guild members and non-members. Job description: A herbalist from the Shadow quarter requires a batch of reagents harvested from yellow-spotted frogs. The creatures are indigenous to the saltmarsh and can only be found within its depths. To collect your reward, deliver 5 yellow-spotted tongues and 10 yellow-spotted feet to any guild office.

Even not knowing what a sea hag or yellow-spotted frog was, I accepted both bounties without hesitation, reasoning that if the jobs were too hard, I could simply forgo completing them.

You have been granted authorization for bounties 1015 and 217.
Your BHG ID has been updated. Active bounties: 3 of 5.

Before leaving the safe zone, I had one more stop to make. Dashing into the emporium, I made a few quick purchases.

You have acquired 2 x crystals of rank 6 disease protection.
You have lost 1,000 gold.
You have acquired a hunter's alchemy stone. It is a rank 4 item capable of extracting and storing rank 4 alchemical ingredients from slain creatures. This item only works on animal lifeforms and cannot be used to obtain materials from plant life.
The enchantment can be replenished with mana. Currently stored ingredients: 0 / 500.
You have lost a small alchemy stone and 350 gold.

I still had the two cure disease potions I'd purchased from Trexton, but with money less constrained now, I saw no reason not to employ better protection against the saltmarsh's virulent infections.

The cost of the enchantment crystals went some way to explaining why the saltmarsh bounties seemed unpopular. They were amongst the oldest bounties on the board.

I also upgraded my alchemy stone, realizing I would need the additional storage, as well as a mechanism for collecting rarer reagents. I would've preferred a rank five harvesting tool, but like most other rank five items, it was too expensive to consider buying yet.

Reaching the safe zone's south gate, I crushed one of the protection crystals in my hand.

You have activated a single-use enchantment, casting a ward of disease protection around yourself. For the next 4 hours, you will be shielded from tier 6 and lower infections.

Taking a deep breath, I stepped into the plague quarter. I was finally ready for a day's outing in the saltmarsh, and it was time to see what horrors it held.

I stopped when the street I was following south through the plague quarter came to an abrupt end. I'd reached the saltmarsh district.

Before me was the marsh itself, it stretched out as far as the eye could see, miles of brackish water filled to the bursting with bulrushes and other vegetation. What I had not expected, though, were the derelict buildings. There were entire blocks of them—dilapidated, abandoned, and sinking.

Some buildings were missing, no doubt already completely submerged. Others looked like they were well on their way there. *So,* I mused, *at some point, all this was part of the city proper.*

What had happened?

The sea had plainly rushed in to flood the district, but why had that been allowed? And why had the region not been reclaimed? The Powers could certainly have achieved either. Shaking my head at the mystery, I turned my attention to the marsh itself.

Here and there, ripples marred the otherwise still-surface of the water. Insects flitted about, but there were no birds. Nor players. In fact, it was eerily quiet.

I glanced behind me.

The plague quarter's grim buildings stared back.

Reassured that I hadn't somehow been mysteriously teleported elsewhere, I swung back to face the saltmarsh. The district's borders were clearly delineated, the marsh having swallowed the roads leading into it to form a perfect rim.

I grimaced unhappily. The nearest building was too far away to flit over the marsh with windborne. If I were going to enter the district, I would have to wade through the water. It looked shallow enough, but who knew what manner of creatures and pestilence hid beneath the murky surface?

Dropping to my haunches, I inhaled deeply.

And immediately regretted it.

The marsh's scents left much to be desired. Mixed in with the saltiness of the sea was the stench of decay and things best left unmentioned. I did *not* want to spend any longer in it than necessary. Rising to my feet, I unfurled my mindsight.

Every lifeform within twenty yards impinged on my awareness. Predictably, they were all innocuous enough—small fish and mud crawlers. No yellow-spotted frogs, though. I snorted. As if I would be that lucky.

Still, I had a plethora of targets to choose from. Fixing my awareness on the most distant lifeform I could see, I cast shadow blink.

You have failed to teleport behind a mud crab. This entity is too small to provide a stable exit point.

That's... dastardly.

I sighed. There was no getting around it. I would have to wade through the marsh. Reconciling myself to the idea, I bent my thoughts to my objectives.

So, how do I go about this?

I had three bounties to complete, and no further guidance other than my targets were somewhere in the saltmarsh. Originally, I thought that sufficient, but I'd not anticipated the marsh being this big. From the looks of it, I could spend many long hours within its depths, and that was only considering what I could see.

Nothing for it but to begin.

Closing my eyes, I cast my buffs.

You have cast heightened reflexes, increasing your Dexterity by +8 ranks for 20 minutes.

You have cast load controller, granting you a 10-minute encumbrance aura that slows any armor-wearing foe within 2 yards by 20%.

You have trigger-cast quick mend. When your overall health falls below 30%, it will instantly heal you for 20%.

Ready to venture into the swamp, I took a step forward.

My foot plonked through the water with an audible splash and found solid—if muddy ground—beneath. I took another step to stand knee-deep in the water.

Brown sludge seeped into my leggings.

Urgh.

My mouth twisting distastefully, I kept going. The height of the water rose until I was submerged waist-deep in filth. Thankfully, though, it leveled off about ten yards in. I did *not* want to contemplate swimming in the marsh. Picking one of the derelict buildings, I waded towards it.

My target was a half-rotted timber structure that looked ready to tip over, but for all that, it was three stories tall and loomed over the nearby buildings. It would make for an excellent vantage point.

Something stung me.

Tier 5 disease resisted! You have failed to contract Typhili!

Drawing to a halt, I stared at the Game message. I'd been in the swamp for less than a minute, and already I'd been exposed to infection.

It's a good thing I bought those protection crystals. My cure disease potions would hardly have sufficed. *Now, let's hope I don't encounter anything worse.*

Slapping a hand to my neck to kill the offending insect, I moved on. Ten yards from the wooden building, I stopped again. It was time to test-run one of my new abilities.

Reaching into my mind, I wove strands of psi into solid air. The weaves expanded into a ramp that reached up to a second-story window, and with no little trepidation, I stepped onto it.

You have cast windborne.

Spell-manifested wind formed at my back, and in the next instant, I was gliding up the ramp of air—visible only to my eyes—at breathtaking speed.

"Wow," I gasped, forgetting my distaste for the marsh as I was propelled off the windslide and onto the windowsill. Though the timbers were rotted, they bore my weight easily, and I clung to the outside of the window while I caught my breath and let the excess water and sludge drip free from my armor.

Windborne was... different.

Its speed buff was a huge bonus, as was the fact that I could create the windslide in *any* shape I desired. I grinned. I could run circles around my foes—and all through the cast of a single spell. Used correctly, the ability would be devastating in combat.

My excitement fading, I turned my attention back to the building and peered through the gaping hole that served as a window. The inside was nothing more than the shattered remnants of a room, one with holed-through floors, broken walls, and rotted furnishings.

But it looked safe enough.

Nevertheless, I inspected the chamber a second time over with mindsight. The ability confirmed what I saw. The building was empty. Well, empty, if you discounted the thousands of little mindglows that I knew to be insects.

Not delaying further, I slipped through the window and gingerly lowered myself onto a beam that seemed more solid than the rest. The log creaked but held.

To my right was a half-rotted staircase leading up to the top floor, and beneath it was a hive. Most of the mindglows in the building originated from there. Each tiny creature—no larger than my fingernail—was uniformly crimson. Their eyes and carapaces glinted in the shadowy darkness, giving them an ominous cast. Reaching out with my will, I analyzed one of the insects.

The target is a level 6 blood fly.

Blood flies are indigenous to the saltmarsh and carry all manner of diseases and infections. They derive their name both from their blood-red color and their uncanny ability to sense warm-blooded creatures.

There were thousands of flies nesting on the support beams beneath the staircase. I glanced up. Unfortunately, none of the holes in the floor above were big enough for me to fit through.

To reach the next floor, I would have to pass within a few feet of the tiny monstrosities. Humming quietly to themselves, they seemed dormant, though, and with my ward of disease protection, I didn't think I had anything to fear from them.

Balancing my weight carefully, I tiptoed towards the stairs.

Multiple hostile entities have detected you! You are no longer hidden.

Hmm, that was quick. The noise emanating from the nest increased, and a few flies lifted off the beam to buzz angrily around me. Pausing, I eyed the tiny insects warily. One zipped through the air, straight for my face.

Making no move to stop it, I waited.

A level 5 blood fly has stung you! Tier 4 disease resisted. You have failed to contract Mong Fever!

Another dozen flies dived down in the wake of the first.

Twelve blood flies have stung you!
Tier 6 disease resisted...
Tier 5 disease resisted...
...
Your health has decreased to 99.999%.

"Ouch, that hurt," I murmured, smirking at the flies that continued to flit impotently around me. Certain now that the insects were no threat, I continued onwards.

More flies lifted off their perches to whiz threateningly about me. I ignored them. The sooner I got up to the next floor, the sooner the insects would realize I was no danger—to them or their hive. Accompanied by a growing swarm of flies, I placed a foot on the first stair.

That proved a mistake.

The wood groaned loudly beneath me. It did not give way, though. Unfortunately, that was the least of my problems. Spurred on by the noise, the entire hive roused itself to deal with the threat—me.

A blood fly swarm has attacked you. Multiple diseases resisted. Your health has decreased to 99%.

"Damnation," I growled, flapping feebly at the flies as I climbed the next step. The tiny buggers swarmed over me, crawling into my mouth, ears, and nostrils. A few even managed to penetrate my leather gear to buzz beneath. Revolted, I slapped uselessly at my armor.

A blood fly swarm has attacked you.
A blood fly swarm has attacked you.
Your health has decreased to 97%.

I'd underestimated the little blighters, I realized. Each fly's attack was no more than a pinprick but, taken all together, their damage was not so negligible.

If this keeps up, I can be in real trouble.

There was no need to panic, though. All I needed to do was lose the swarm.

Dashing up the stairs, I set about doing that.

Chapter 257: Hidden Amongst the Reeds

Wood creaked and broke, causing my foot to plunge through the stairs more than once. I didn't let it slow me down. Each time, I caught myself before I could stumble and raced onwards.

I reached the third floor still encased in blood flies.

Your health has decreased to 91%.

Second by second, the volume of the swarm's buzzing increased. I assumed it was the blood flies' manner of voicing their anger, but I had little attention to spare the phenomenon.

I had to find a way onto the roof.

There, I thought, spotting a hole in the ceiling big enough to fit through. Summoning psi, I formed a ramp of air.

You have cast windborne.

I accelerated up the windslide, leaving most of the swarm behind in the process. A moment later, I was flung onto the roof. Somersaulting off the windslide, I landed on bended knee.

My gaze flitted left and right, taking stock of my surroundings. I was on the roof, and it was empty. More than half of the support beams were gone, making crossing the rooftop treacherous. For the average player, anyway. Given my own agility, I foresaw no problems.

The next building is close enough, I thought. I could reach it easily with windborne, and from there, the structure beyond. If I strung together enough windslides, I could outrun the swarm. I was sure of it.

The swarm buzzed through the hole.

The windslide had let me temporarily escape their clutches, but they were back now. Though, instead of immediately resuming their assault as I expected, the blood flies rose higher in the air. I frowned. Did they mean to dive down in attack?

That wasn't it.

The swarm's buzzing increased to a fever pitch. I winced, rubbing the sides of my head as the sharp sound hurt my eardrums. *Is this a new sort of—*?

I broke off.

Cloudy trails of red were streaming up from the adjacent buildings. And they, too, were buzzing.

More blood fly swarms.

Fleeing over the rooftops was out of the question.

My gaze swung back to my original foe. The swarm still hovered in the air, and was it my imagination, or did the little blighters seem smug?

I scowled in response. "Don't worry," I growled. "I will still have the last laugh." Ducking back into the hole from whence I'd come, I dropped into the building again.

✳   ✳   ✳

None of my abilities or weapons would be effective against the swarms. I could spend all day hacking into the blood flies and still not make a dent in their numbers, and none of my spells—not even mass charm—was remotely useful.

That did not mean I was helpless.

I had other options.

Returning to the room where I'd encountered the first blood swarm, I ducked under the staircase and got to work. It was a tight fit, but that was perfect for what I planned. Rubbing my thumb across the blue rune on the trapper's wristband, I activated the item.

You have passed a thieving skill check!
You have removed 2 trap-making crystals from your trapper's wristband.

As the enchanted crystals fell into my waiting hands, I cast set trap. To deal with the flies, I needed an area-of-effect ability. I didn't have any of those myself, but my traps made up for the lack. My eyes and fingers humming with spelled-energy, I began preparing a killing ground.

A swarm funneled down the hole in the ceiling.

I ignored the insects. I doubted the creatures had the intelligence to understand what I was about, but if they did and fled, that was all the better.

Seeing me crouched beside their nesting ground, the blood flies did not hesitate and buzzed angrily in attack.

Your health has decreased to 90%.
Your health has decreased to 89%.

I kept working, not bothering to brush aside the insects covering my hands or eyes. Releasing the enchantment on the first crystal, I extracted a trigger and set it on the floor next to me.

You have placed a pressure plate but have failed to conceal the trigger due to the presence of nearby hostiles.

Two more swarms dove down from the ceiling and streamed through the intervening space to engulf me.

Your health has decreased to 75%.
Your health has decreased to 72%.

I was weakening rapidly, and my visibility had been cut to zero. Unfazed, I continued assembling the trap, working by touch and feel alone. Carefully lowering the second crystal, I placed it next to the pressure plate and set the magical weave between them.

You have connected a fire enchantment to a pressure plate.
A firebomb trap has been successfully configured!
Your health has decreased to 65%.

My work was almost done.

There was only one more thing to do: trigger the trap. But first, I had to ensure my targets were all in place. Turning my attention outwards, I focused on the surrounding swarms.

The space around me was so thick with flies, their mindglows formed a solid wall in my mindsight. How many swarms does that make?

Seven, at least, I thought. I'd lost count at some point.

Your health has decreased to 60%.

Is that all of them? I wondered. I wasn't sure, but I couldn't afford to wait any longer. Lowering my hand, I slapped it down onto the pressure plate.

You have triggered a trap!

Raging hot flames blossomed into life.

At the epicenter of the inferno, I squeezed my eyes shut and hugged myself tight as the fire washed over me. There was nothing to do but to bear the pain, my only consolation knowing that as much as I was suffering, the blood flies were hurting worse.

You have failed a magical resistance check!
Your health has decreased to 23%. Quick mend triggered, restoring 20% of your lost health!
A blood fly swarm has been killed.
A blood fly swarm has been killed.
A blood fly...

As quickly as the magical flames appeared, they vanished.

Relieved, I collapsed against the floor, my body still riddled with pain. I was charred and singed but no worse for wear. *Nothing a few heals won't rectify.*

Around me, it was blessedly quiet—absent the buzzing of even a single blood fly. My cracked and burned lips spread into a smile.

The trap had worked.

✳   ✳   ✳

A little later, I was whole again.

Dropping into a crossed-legged, I considered the waiting Game messages.

Your thieving has increased to level 79. Your telekinesis has increased to level 111. Your elemental absorption has increased to level 12. Your chi has increased to level 105.

I snorted. The battle against the swarms had not been worth the effort. My gains were negligible, and I'd nearly died in the process.

Speaking of the flies... Turning my attention outwards, I studied the area.

Nothing remained of my foes but ash.

They'd died easily enough once I employed the right tactic against them. But the encounter gave me pause and made me question if I was as prepared as I thought for a trip through the saltmarsh. Still, I was committed now, and there was nothing for it but to go on.

And besides, it was not like I was in a dungeon; I could always turn back if necessary.

Rising to my feet, I returned to the building's roof. My head constantly swiveling left and right, I kept a wary eye out for blood flies, or anything else for that matter. I would not make the mistake of underestimating the saltmarsh's insect-life again.

Just as I'd hoped, I had a clear vantage of the district from the top of the building. To the east and west, the train of dilapidated wooden buildings continued without end. No doubt, many of them housed more colonies of blood flies. Feeling no desire to tangle further with the swarms, I turned my attention south.

At the farthest edge of my sight was a mass of heaving, turbulent gray, topped with ephemeral streaks of white.

The sea.

Something shifted in my mind, and a sense of longing overcame me. I was convinced that some part of me—the 'me' from before the Game or one of the fallen scions—had some deep, unfathomable connection to the ocean.

But as quickly as the sea piqued my interest, it lost it, too. Something else had attracted my gaze. Along the shoreline was a mighty fortress.

It was the sole structure in the district that was entirely free of the marsh. Built atop a rocky outcropping and battered by the ocean on one side and bordered by the marsh on the other, the mammoth stone construction was replete with towers and defiant spires that reached up to the sky.

Now, what is that? I wondered, feeling an almost irresistible urge to explore the ancient structure.

I quelled the thought immediately.

I'm not going there, I thought, refusing even to consider the possibility. I would have to cross nearly the entirety of the saltmarsh to reach the distant fortress, and I only had eight hours of disease protection to work with. *Some other time, maybe.*

Turning away, I studied the rest of the saltmarsh. Deeper into the district, the number of ruins dropped notably—perhaps, having been exposed to the marsh for longer, they had succumbed more fully to its clutches—and the marsh's surface was an almost unblemished field of bulrushes and other reeds.

But only nearly so.

Here and there, the occasional ruins still fought off the saltmarsh's attempts to swallow it.

One particular set of marble pillars caught my eye. They were in the same state of disrepair as the rest of the structures in the district, but interestingly enough, they were situated in a stand of trees.

A forest grove.

The trees were formed from thick, tall boughs, certainly not the kind one would expect to find in a marsh, and looked old enough to have been in the district before the saltmarsh invaded.

It was not the pillars nor the grove that had attracted my attention, though: it was the figures I could see walking between the trees. Narrowing my gaze, I focused on one of the distant specks.

The target is a level 117 coral hag.

Every sea hag began life as an ordinary witch. But at some point in their lives, lusting after the dormant power in the oceans, they gave themselves, body and mind, to primal sea spirits. Reborn thereafter as true denizens of the oceans, the hags have a singular purpose: spreading their master's watery domain. All landbound creatures are anathema to the hags, and they will do their utmost to purge the lands of life.

I smiled, not at all put off by the Game's daunting description. I finally had a lead on one of my bounties, and it was time to hunt.

CHAPTER 258: CONTACT

It took me two hours to reach the forest grove.

Although the swamp teemed with life—mostly insects and creatures too small to pose a threat—there *were* a few larger occupants, but with mindsight to guide me, I was able to detour around them without trouble.

Still, the trip was far from pleasant.

Lacking any form of higher ground to ease my journey, I was forced to wade through the marsh the entire distance. Needless to say, that left me soaked and miserable. The sludge penetrated every layer of my armor, and I could feel *things* crawling over me.

Repressing yet another shudder, I pushed aside the bulrushes in front of me and took a soggy step forward. I had cause to both thank and curse the marsh reeds. On the one hand, they did a good job of disguising my presence, but on the other, they slowed me down and made judging my position difficult.

Still, I was sure I neared my destination. *It can't be much—*

I broke off as I spied a line of green foliage peeking over the top of the reeds. The grove had finally come into sight again. Drawing to a halt, I studied my target.

Just as I'd noted from a distance, the trees forming the grove were giants of their kind, with their upper branches topping even the city's many high walls. The lower barks of each wooden behemoth were flaked and rotted— courtesy of the saltmarsh, no doubt. But the decay did not seem to have penetrated far. The trees' trunks remained unbent, and their upper reaches bore the unmistakable green sheen of health.

That's where I go, I thought, craning my neck upward.

Moving silently—no mean feat in the marsh—I waded closer and reached the treeline without incident. Dappled shadows filled the grove's interior, the overarching trees filtering out the bright sunlight. Placing my back against the broad trunk of the closest tree, I peered around the edge.

None of the hags were around, but that was to be expected; I'd chosen my entry point carefully. No other creatures were visible either, and mindsight reported the waters ahead to be starkly empty, absent even the occasional small life present elsewhere in the marsh.

Oddly, though, the trees themselves teemed with life.

According to my mindsight, each was coated in a layer of tiny unseen creatures. I frowned. *More insects?* Reaching out with mindsight, I analyzed one.

The target is a level 1 seaworm.

Seaworms are small sea organisms and, though innocuous-looking, can be deadly in numbers. They are usually found accompanying a sea hag who oftentimes use the worms' unquenchable appetites to scrub a region free of life.

Hastily, I stepped back from the trunk sheltering me.

Dropping into a crouch and ignoring the water that lapped at my face, I studied the tree with new eyes. After the incident with the blood flies, I knew better than to underestimate any foe, no matter how small, and the information analyze had yielded made clear what the worms were about.

They were eating the tree.

Running my gaze up and down the massive tree trunk, I tried to spot the elusive seaworms, but they defeated even my impressive sight. *Maybe, they're beneath the bark.*

I hesitated, debating my next move. I'd planned on using the trees to strike at the hags from above, but I couldn't do that until I understood the full extent of the threat the worms posed. Realizing I had no choice, I reached out to the tree and yanked free a rotted piece of bark.

Worms spilled out.

My lips turned down as I watched the dozens of tiny forms wriggling in the water. They were as numerous as the blood flies and appeared just as intent on their 'prey.' Twisting their hairless pink bodies around, the worms swam back from whence they'd come. Cupping my palm, I scooped up one before it could get away and drew it closer for a better look.

But the worm wasn't interested in complying. Quicksilver fast, the creature wriggled through a seam in my glove and vanished beneath.

A seaworm has bitten you for zero damage!

A seaworm has infected you with maritoxin, a paralytic that slows your movements by 0.01% for 10 seconds. Maritoxin is a stacking toxin; further doses will increase its debilitating effects.

"Bloody hell," I muttered. Pulling off my glove, I shook the worm free before it could do more damage. Plopping into the water, the wretched creature turned back towards the tree.

Such single-mindedness could not be normal. *They have to be under the sea hags' command,* I decided. My gaze drifted back to the trees. That made the wooded giants too dangerous to traverse. I sighed. It seemed that if I wanted to proceed, I would have to fight the hags at ground level—and while hip-deep in water.

Not good. Not good at all.

But I wasn't about to give up just yet. Pulling the shadows around me, I cast my buffs and waded into the grove.

Your Dexterity has increased by +8 ranks for 20 minutes.
You have gained an encumbrance aura for 10 minutes.
You have trigger-cast quick mend.

✳   ✳   ✳

Whoosh... swish.

My ears pricked. What was that sound?

Drawing to a halt, I listened intently. My advance into the grove had barely begun, and I was less than a few yards beyond the treeline. But what few sounds there were in the lifeless grove carried unnaturally far, and I'd been forced to move even slower than I'd had in the marsh.

A noise came again. *Plop!*

My brows creased. It sounded as if something had hit the water, and close by too. Was it a falling branch? It couldn't be anything else. Mindsight reported the area ahead to be clear of life.

I wasn't about to take any chances, though.

Bending my knees, I lowered myself deeper into the water until only my eyes were visible above the surface. Then, moving glacially slow, I slipped into a patch of reeds—there was no escaping the marsh reeds; they were everywhere—and carefully separated a couple of brown stalks to peek through.

A hostile entity has failed to detect you! You are hidden.

A solitary sea hag was up ahead.

Inching my head left and right, I checked for more foes but spotted none. The hag was, by all appearance, alone. More worrying, though, was the fact that she didn't appear in my mindsight.

Her mind's shielded.

It was the only explanation. That made things more difficult but not impossible. Letting my gaze rest on the hag, I studied my foe.

At first glance, the sea-witch appeared human. Her long dirty-brown hair was tangled and matted, and she was dressed in a sealskin robe that hugged her hunched-over frame. A closer look at her seamed face and yellowing teeth shattered the illusion, though.

The hag's teeth were razor-sharp, and she had far more of them than any ordinary human. The seams on her face told a different tale, too. They were not a result of age but formed from the gills that lined her cheekbones.

Then there were her clawed hands and scaled skin. The hag was covered in scales similar to Devlin's, the Albion Bank's manager. But where his scales were a brilliant blue, the hag's were muddy brown and emerald green.

Attempted camouflage? I wondered. The sea-witch was standing stock-still, her gaze roaming attentively over the surroundings. A sentry, I decided. Reaching out with my will, I analyzed her.

The target is a level 121 tidal hag.

Hmm. My target was of lower level than me, and rightfully, I should have no trouble eliminating her, but I knew well that some abilities could make levels count for little, and I had no idea what powers the hags possessed.

It was a safe bet that the hag had water magic, though, and as a witch, I didn't expect her to be physically adept. The sea hag didn't carry any weapons that I could see either but judging by the length of the claws tipping her fingers, I didn't think she needed any.

I strike hard and fast, I thought, slipping ebonheart and my stygian shortsword free from their sheaths. Keeping both blades beneath the water, I summoned psi.

You have teleported into a tidal hag's shadow.

I stepped out of the aether with my target still oblivious to my presence. Rising tall, I raised both swords and stabbed down.

A tidal hag's spell: <u>impervious ice</u> has triggered, blocking all incoming damage for the next 2 seconds.
Backstab failed!
Backstab failed!
A hostile entity has detected you! You are no longer hidden.

Both my blades bounced back, repelled by the wall of ice that materialized between them and my target. "Goddamnit!" I growled between clenched teeth.

The sea hag spun around, hands outstretched and palms flat. Staggering back, I fled the gleaming claws searching for my throat.

You have evaded a tidal hag's attack.

My foe wasn't done yet. Her eyes flashed white, and realizing a second attack was incoming, I stepped to the side.

You have evaded a tidal hag's attack.

A bar of frost shot by, missing my nose by scant inches. I raised my blades, knowing I had to go on the offensive again, but the water and the muddy ground were slowing my movements, and my foe was already launching her next assault—*she* didn't appear to have any trouble maneuvering.

Darting forward, the witch raised upturned palms in my direction. I threw myself to the left, but I couldn't avoid the attack this time and twin lines of searing cold struck my chest.

You have failed a magical resistance check!
A frost ray has injured you!
A frost ray has injured you!
Your void armor has reduced the elemental damage incurred by 5%.

The force of the magical projectiles flung me backward, plunging me into the marsh. More frost rays followed and, seeming to have no trouble penetrating the murky water, struck me dead center again.

A frost ray has injured you!
A frost ray has injured you!
…
Quick mend triggered!

My back hit the marsh floor, and more ice attacks drove into me, keeping me pinned underwater. I spared the Game messages no attention, though. The frost rays were doing more than injure me—they were also freezing the water.

She is going to encase me in ice, I realized with grim certainty.

Ignoring the ongoing assault and my rising fear, I opened my eyes wide and searched for the hag. The muddy water made it difficult to see, but I thought I could see the hazy outline of a shape looming over me.

That has to be the hag.
Fixing on the blurred form, I shadow blinked.

You have teleported into a tidal hag's shadow.

It worked, and I emerged from the aether upright and behind my target. The hag spun around, her expression of surprise almost comical as she reorientated her frost-rimmed hands on me.

I was already in motion, though. My movements short and jerky, I thrust ebonheart into the hag's chest, followed by the stygian blade a moment later.

You have critically injured your target. You have killed a tidal hag!

The light faded from the sea-witch's gaze as she sank into the water. Chest heaving, I stared down at the corpse. *Damn,* I thought, *that was a tougher fight than I bargained on. I hope—*
At a betraying slip of noise—barely heard over the sound of my own painful breaths—my head whipped upward. Other seal-clad shapes, hands rising, were slipping toward me. Not questioning my instinctive response, I dove into the marsh reeds a split-second before a flurry of frost beams could decapitate me.

You have evaded the assault of 3 unknown hostiles.

Reinforcements had arrived.
And this time, they had numbers on their side.

Chapter 259: A Game of Cat and Mouse

In the wake of the near miss, my heart pounded furiously. *That was too close,* I thought. Staying under, I waited for my pulse to slow and reflexively cloaked myself.

You are hidden.

The shadows wrapped comfortingly around me like a warm blanket, and I felt calm descend. I was far from safe, but as much as water was the hags' ally, darkness was my friend, and in its embrace, I felt my worries fade.

My foes would not easily find me—no matter their numbers.

Still submerged, I relocated position, slipping carefully between the reeds. While I did, I took stock of the situation.

Before diving beneath the water, I'd spied three sea hags approaching, and more were surely on the way. It had been my plan to quietly stalk the witches and pick them off one by one. But them coming to me... that could work to my advantage too.

They deserve a proper welcome, I thought savagely.

First, though, I had to make certain I was ready to face the newcomers. Turning my focus inwards, I pulled up the flashing Game messages and checked on my status.

Warning! Your health is at 30%.

Your dodging has increased to level 109. Your sneaking has increased to level 104. Your two weapon fighting has increased to level 105.

Your chi has increased to level 107. Your telekinesis has increased to level 112. Your insight has increased to level 125.

Your elemental absorption has increased to 17.

Void armor inoperative. Current charge: 0%. Replenish your mana to reactivate!

Damnation! I cursed. My void armor had been exhausted, and my health was low. I was in no condition to continue the fight just yet.

Recuperate and replenish first, I decided.

Directing my thoughts to the potion bracelet still snug on my arm, I willed it to inject a potion into my bloodstream. It cost me a valuable consumable, but chi healing would take too long.

You have restored yourself with a full healing potion. Your health is at 100%.

I only had one mana potion on my belt—a full one—and while I was loath to use it, finding a quiet spot to channel mana was also out of the question. Yanking the flask free, I set it to my lips and swallowed its contents while still underwater.

Your mana is now at 100%. Void armor restored.

That done, I stole into a dense clump of reeds. It was past time to come up for air. Unbending carefully, I pushed upward until my nose rose above the surface.

Multiple hostile entities have failed to detect you! You are hidden.

A sea hag was skimming across the marsh a few yards to my right. A pair passed by on my left, submerging their heads every few seconds to search the water's depth. A few feet in front of me was another hag. She, remarkably, was standing *on* the water.

All of them were absent from my mindsight.

Not daring to move—or even breathe deeply—I kept my gaze fixed on the water-walking hag. Her eyes narrowed to slits, the witch was pivoting about in a slow circle.

How many foes surrounded me? I couldn't tell, but I was sure there were more hags to my rear as well. *How did they converge on me so quickly?* I wondered.

Another sea witch glided across the marsh and stopped before the one in front.

"Have you found him yet?" the water-walking hag hissed.

The second hag bowed deeply. "No, mother."

My ears perked up. *Mother?* Was this the leader of sea hags, the one whose scalp I needed to collect? It seemed likely. Judging the risk acceptable, I reached out with my will and analyzed the hag.

The target is a level 140 hag mother. Hag mothers are notoriously vicious. They tolerate no contenders and demand unquestioning loyalty from their followers. Consequently, finding more than one mother in any coven is rare.

The Game's response provided the confirmation I needed. Dismissing the message, I returned my attention to the pair's conversation.

"... is he, Malina?" the mother demanded.

"We're not... sure," Malina replied, ducking her head to avoid her leader's penetrating gaze.

The hag mother took a step forward, flexing her claws. "Don't tell me you let him escape?"

Malina jerked back. "No! He must still be in the grove. The outer wards were activated when he was spotted, and they have not been tripped."

The hag mother tilted her head to the side in consideration. "Is he sheltering in the trees?"

Malina shook her head. "We've thought of that. Caulis has communed with the worms. They sense no one nearby."

"Are you sure?" the mother pressed. "The grubs' thoughts are not easy to interpret."

"Caulis is sure," Malina said, stressing the other hag's name in an apparent bid to disavow responsibility. "*She* is the worm keeper."

A frown flickered across the mother's face, but she didn't refute the other hag's assertion. "Find him," she ordered in what was a clear dismissal.

The second hag inclined her head but didn't move.

"Is there something else?" the mother asked, studying her subordinate in surprise.

Malina hesitated. "Caulis can't be certain, but she thinks... she thinks..."

"Spit it out," the mother snapped.

"Our intruder might be a wolf."

The hag mother blurred across the intervening space and, in a prodigious display of strength, picked up the other hag by the neck. "What?" she hissed.

"O-one of-of the... worm-s-s tasted him-m," Malina gasped as she struggled to breathe in the mother's chokehold.

The mother squeezed, digging her claws deeper into her captive. "One worm?" she scoffed. "That's hardly a reliable indicator."

Malina bobbed her head. "I ag-g-ree, mother, b-but Caulis insisted I tell you."

For a drawn-out moment, the hag leader said nothing. Then in a sudden burst, she opened her hand and spun around to consider the vacant marsh. "Is he here for the other one?"

Malina picked herself up and massaged her bloodied neck. "He must be."

"Excellent," the mother pronounced. "That raises the stakes. Find him and bring him to me—alive."

"Yes, mother," Malina replied. Bowing deeply, she began to slip away.

"Oh, and Malina," the mother said without turning around.

Her subordinate paused.

"If he escapes, I will hold *you* responsible."

Malina stiffened, and her face twisted in a snarl, but she said nothing as she retreated. A moment later, the hag mother left, heading in the other direction.

I watched them both go, a thoughtful look on my face. The trip into the marsh was turning out to be a lot more interesting than I'd anticipated.

✳   ✳   ✳

My first instinct was to follow the hag mother, but I squashed the urge. As tempting as the idea of cutting off the head of the snake was, I could not bank on scoring a quick kill against the hags' leader, and the fight was sure to draw the rest of the sea witches.

My second thought was to go in search of the other 'wolf.' Whether it was a *real* wolf, a werewolf, or another Wolf Marked player, I had no idea, but all three possibilities were equally intriguing. Still, I didn't act on that urge either.

The mysterious wolf would have to wait. First, I had to deal with the hags. Remaining where I was, I laid my first trap.

You have connected a trap element to a sound glass trigger.
A poison cloud trap has been successfully configured!

Unfortunately, neither the trip wires nor the pressure plates were suitable for the marsh's environment, and given the unpredictability of the water's movements, I didn't think it was wise to use the motion pins either—which left only the sound glasses to employ as triggers.

My choice of trap elements was similarly restricted. Still, I felt the poison clouds and fire enchantments would do well enough. Swimming underwater, I came up for air in another clump of reeds. It was only a few yards away from the first trap.

Cautiously, I scanned the area. The hags were still looking for me, probing both the waters beneath and the trees above, but their search cordon had spread out to cover more ground, leaving me more freedom to maneuver.

Turning a slow circle, I tallied up my foes. There were twelve hags, but Malina and the hag mother were not among them, so I could not count on the ones I could see being the entirety of the coven's strength.

Were fourteen hags too many? I didn't think so.

Bending down, I placed the next two enchanted crystals, affixing each to a reed stalk.

A firebomb trap has been successfully configured!

Lifting my head, I searched for another viable location. *There*, I thought, spotting another promising mass of bulrushes.

Slipping deeper into the water, I moved on to set the next trap.

✳   ✳   ✳

Remaining trap-making crystals: 0 of 40.
Your thieving has increased to level 89.

Ten minutes later, all my traps were set.

I'd employed every trap-making crystal at my disposal and seeded a large area, transforming it into a killing ground. Fortunately, the crystals in the trapper's wristband were not pre-configured but created on demand, allowing me to use the wristband's full complement of crystals for the two types of traps I desired.

Rising higher out of the water, I surveyed the innocuous-looking reed patches. Unlike on previous occasions, I'd not concentrated the traps together. I'd spread them out deliberately, leaving a safe path—if a crazily contoured one—through the trapped ground.

Ducking back down, I opened my backpack and, retrieving more mana potions, slotted them in my potion belt. I would have no time to meditate or channel mana in the coming clash.

I was almost ready. Casting my buffs, I focused on the closest hags—a pair about forty yards to my left.

Time to get this show started, I thought and summoned psi.

Twin psionic daggers materialized, one appearing in my right hand, the other in the left. In one smooth, unhurried motion, I let both blades fly.

The ethereal violet daggers flew true and struck both my targets dead center.

A tidal hag's spell: <u>impervious ice</u> has triggered. Backstab failed! Your target's spell has blocked your attack.

A coral hag's spell: <u>water shield</u> has triggered. Backstab failed! Your target's shield has blocked your attack, absorbing its damage.

Multiple hostile entities have detected you! You are no longer hidden.

Both hags spun around and, seeing me, screamed in warning. The cry was quickly taken up by the other witches in the grove, and I could almost feel the spells being directed my way.

I remained where I was.

Taking my deception further, I grinned and waved insouciantly at the pair I'd attacked. Despite the surprising nature of the second hag's spell, the astral blades had done precisely what I hoped: they had triggered my quarries' defenses.

The two hags raised ice-rimmed hands.

Now, I thought and stepped into the aether.

Blinding white ice lanced out of the witches' upraised palms. But I was no longer where they aimed.

You have teleported 41 yards.
You have evaded a tidal hag's attack.
You have evaded a coral hag's attack.

I emerged behind the first hag and, before either witch could so much as register my presence, lunged forward with ebonheart. This time, my blade encountered no resistance.

You have killed a level 124 tidal hag with a fatal blow.

The coral hag spun around. I didn't bother facing her, though. Burning through her shield would take too long, and I was acutely aware of the other witches racing toward our position.

Diving into the marsh, I wrapped myself in shadow.

You are hidden.

It was time to lead the hunters on a merry chase.

Chapter 260: The Maze of Traps

I didn't stay under long. When I judged myself a safe distance from the coral hag, I resurfaced.

"There he is!"

Three sea witches were directly ahead of me, only one of whom was protected by an ice shield. Not troubling to analyze my targets, I let fly with my astral daggers.

Your attack has failed! Your target's spell has blocked your attack.
Your attack has failed! Your target's spell has repelled your attack.

Not unexpectedly, both ethereal blades failed to score a hit. More surprisingly, one of my daggers was heading straight back at me. Diving left, I threw myself out of the way.

Unfortunately, that put me squarely in the path of another projectile, one fired by an unseen hag to my rear.

You have been hit by an ice dart.
Your void armor has reduced the elemental damage incurred by 5%.
You have failed a magical resistance check! You are <u>frozen</u>. Duration: 3 seconds.

"Got him!" a hag crowed.

In an eyeblink, ice encased me, freezing my limbs and robbing me of forward momentum. Like a stone, I dropped back into the marsh. But while I was immobilized, I was not stunned, and the dark water provided plenty of cover. Drawing on the shadows, I concealed myself.

You are hidden.

A block of ice on the marsh floor, I waited. The hags were surely rushing in to finish me. Would they find me?

It did not take long to find out.

You have been hit by 4 frost rays.
You have evaded the assault of 6 unknown hostiles.

Lines of ice crisscrossed the water as the hags fired blindly into the marsh. I was struck thrice, but the spells that hit me didn't renew the frozen debuff, and a moment later, I was free. Immediately, I released the psi I'd been holding ready.

You have cast windborne.

I shot out of the water, propelled upward by a near-vertical ramp of air. The converging hags, astonished by my sudden appearance, shrank back.

I ignored them. It was time to enter my maze of traps. Focusing on a more distant foe, I blinked.

You have teleported into the shadow of a coral hag.

The sea witch behind whom I'd appeared spun around, but she was too late. I'd already submerged myself in the marsh again.

You are hidden.

Magical projectiles pounded furiously at the water. I paid them no heed. It was less than ten yards to the first trap trigger. Swimming underwater, I slipped past the sound glass and resurfaced.

Peeking out of the water, I checked my rear. A second witch had joined the coral hag, and both were scanning the marsh for me. My lips turned down. I had been hoping to snare more of my foes.

But two would do.

Releasing the shadows wrapped around me, I waited for the hags to spot me. They did so almost immediately and gave chase without a second thought.

Still, I waited.

A heartbeat later, the pair fell into the invisible circle marking the trapped area. This time, I'd made sure to separate trap and trigger by a large distance, ensuring I would be unaffected.

"Come and get me!" I roared.

You have activated a trap!
A tidal hag's spell: <u>impervious ice</u> **has triggered.**
A coral hag's spell: <u>water shield</u> **has triggered.**

Plumes of green gas billowed out, swallowing my pursuers, but they came on, undeterred by the toxins eating at their defenses. Spinning around, I recloaked myself and continued my flight.

An ice dart flew over my shoulder.

I didn't turn around. My stealth was intact, and the hags were firing blindly. The pair were catching up, though.

But I didn't mind that.

Scanning the area, I identified the next closest group of hags. They were forty yards to my right. *Not near enough to pose any threat*, I decided. Glancing over my shoulder, I locked gazes with my chosen target and, in one motion, blinked and struck.

You have teleported into the shadow of a tidal hag.
You have backstabbed your target for 2.5x more damage!
You have killed a tidal hag with a fatal blow.

One down.

Yanking ebonheart free from the corpse, I drew stamina and psi again and wove a second flurry of spells.

You have cast whirlwind, piercing strike, and windborne.

The second hag was slow to realize the danger and was still half-turned away. Materializing the windslide in a tightly wound arc about her, I launched an all-out offensive and struck at the witch from multiple directions—all seemingly at once.

Your target's shield has blocked your attacks.

Your target's shield has blocked your attacks.
Your target's shield has...
...

Halfway through my spiral, the hag's defenses crumbled, and I buried ebonheart hilt-deep in her chest.

You have killed a tidal hag with a fatal blow.

A frost dagger whizzed past.

Flinging my head up, I glanced in the direction it had come from. The other hags were converging fast. *Time to reposition.*

Diving into the marsh, I headed towards my next trap.

✳ ✳ ✳

A minute later, I was hunkered down in the reeds beside the third sound glass, uncloaked and waiting.

Spells and angry cries from the hags filled the air, but so far, they'd failed to find me, but not from a lack of trying. The murky water made hiding easy, and I took full advantage, popping in and out of the marsh at every opportunity to launch stinging attacks whose purpose was to irritate rather than hurt.

Now, a pair of green clouds hung low over the marsh—from the dispersing toxins of the first two traps. The twenty hags on my tail plunged heedlessly through. They weren't afraid of the poison; their spelled defenses saw to it that the damage was minimized or nullified entirely.

Multiple hostile entities have detected you! You are no longer hidden.

"Found him!" Malina crowed from the front of the pack. Exhorting those behind her to greater speed, she raised her hands and prepared a casting. The sea witch had joined the hunt a while back, but of the hag mother, there was no sign yet.

Pity, I thought. The next bit promised to be... interesting.

The volume of spells coloring the air increased. I paid them no heed, though, as I watched my pursuers through narrowed eyes. Crossing over an invisible line etched in my mind, the hags entered the killing ground.

That's far enough, I decided, crushing the sound glass in my hand.

The trigger activated.

And a pulse raced down the magical weave connecting the trigger to the trap element ten yards away. The fire enchantment ignited, and flames gushed out. The fire was not large. Small and contained, it barely singed the hags, but that was not the flames' purpose.

A tongue of fire touched the poison cloud.

My vision flashed orange.

A split-second later, an avalanche of sound and air rolled over me—the toxic gases had ignited.

Hags were tossed asunder. Here and there, a spelled shield winked out, and I carefully marked each position. A moment later, thick black plumes swallowed the sea witches, and silence descended upon the marsh. Rising to my feet, I slipped into the smoke.

It was time to kill.

✳ ✳ ✳

Even blinded by smoke and dazed by the explosion, the hags did not make for easy prey. I could not see them nor track them with mindsight, but my sharp hearing did not let me down, and I soon located my first target.

It was Malina.

"Caulis, get rid of this wretched smoke! The rest of you, call on your—"

Drawing up behind the sea witch, I wrapped my left hand around her mouth and slashed open her throat.

You have killed Malina with a fatal blow!

Letting the corpse sink, I ducked back into the water.

"Malina?" someone hollered. "What's wrong?"

There was no answer, of course, and more cries followed, some perplexed, a few scared, but most angry. The hags were scattered and confused but regrouping fast. I judged I had just enough time for two more kills.

"Answer me, sister! Where are you?"

I waded silently toward the speaker. If memory served, it was a hag whose shield had failed.

A drop touched my face. Then another. I looked up.

It was raining.

I frowned. *Rain from a cloudless sky?* It was no natural weather phenomenon. *This is the hags' doing.* The black smoke was already dispersing, pushed aside by cooling streams of water and air.

I was not going to reach my target in time, I realized.

A half dozen mindglows appeared in my mindsight. It couldn't be the hags, though. Their minds were shielded. My frown deepened. *Now what?* Reaching out with my will, I analyzed one of the invisible shapes.

The target is a level 109 water elemental.

I grinned, worry forgotten.

The hags had summoned additional support, but their ploy had backfired. The creatures' minds were unshielded, providing me with convenient beacons with which to locate their mistresses. Drawing in psi, I shadow blinked to one of the newcomers.

You have teleported into an ice elemental's shadow.

I emerged from the aether still cloaked and less than two yards from my intended victim. Ignoring the elemental, I crept up behind its hag mistress and readied ebonheart.

Perhaps, I will score more kills after all.

✳   ✳   ✳

You have killed a coral hag with a fatal blow!
You have killed a tidal hag with a fatal blow!
You have killed a tempest hag with a fatal blow!

I slew three more of my pursuers before the smoke dispersed entirely. By this time, the hags had drawn together for mutual protection, looks of grim determination replacing their cries of outrage.

I may have hurt my foes, but they were far from done.

Hidden amongst the reeds around the next trap trigger, I observed the hags from fifty yards away. Would they be so foolish as to keep pursuing me? I wondered.

"Malina, where are you, you misbegotten toad? When I get my hands on you, I swear I will wring your bloody neck!"

At the screeched command, I turned in the direction of the speaker. It was the hag mother accompanied by another pair of sea witches.

The coven's leader had finally made an appearance.

"She is dead, mother," one of the hags from the huddled group said.

The hag mother snorted. "Good riddance. She's botched things enough already. Report, Caulis."

"Eight dead in total. Twelve remaining." Caulis' gaze slid to the hag mother and her companions. "Now fifteen."

The hag mother scowled. "Then what are you fools doing cowering over there? Spread out and find him!"

Caulis' mouth worked soundlessly, but she didn't protest the order. "As you wish, mother."

Smiling, I readied myself. The game was still on.

✳   ✳   ✳

Five minutes later, all my traps were triggered, transforming a large section of the grove into a smog field.

The hags called down more rainstorms, but given the increased smoke and patches of reeds that had caught fire, they were less successful in clearing the air.

Not everything went my way, however. My previous ambush had made my foes wary. Changing tactics, they hung on the fringes of the smoke patches while they tried clearing them with jets of water and ice. But complying with their leader's orders, the sea witches *had* spread out—giving me a few choice targets.

I was done hunting lesser prey, though. It was time to land the big fish: the hag mother herself.

The coven's leader was still on the battlefield. Accompanied by her two bodyguards, she stood unconcerned in the center of the smog field—water walking again—and studied her followers with a jaundiced gaze. All three witches were wrapped in ice shields. Ordinarily, that would suffice as protection against a sneak attack.

But I had a plan.

Hidden in a nearby clump of reeds, I began my assault. *First, a distraction.* Drawing on my stores of energy, I wove a spell of deception.

You have cast ventro.

"Need a little help?" I whispered mockingly. "Your followers seem to have trouble finding me."

The trio's gazes whipped in the direction my voice had emanated from—conveniently turning their backs on my true position.

I rose out of the water. *Second, the rush.* Not waiting to see what further action the coven leader took, I released my next spell.

You have cast windborne.

Spell winds formed at my back, propelling me upwards. I was too far to reach the hag mother directly by windslide, but I didn't need to. Rocketing off the currents of air, I arced silently through the smoke-filled sky.

I'd plotted my trajectory perfectly.

Through slitted eyes, I watched the top of the hag mother's shield rushing up. She remained oblivious to my descending form.

Third, the strike. Raising my blades, I empowered them with stamina.

You have cast whirlwind, increasing your attack speed by 100% for 3 seconds.

You have cast piercing strike, doubling the damage dealt on the next attack.

I drew level with the hag mother—passing just inches behind the rear of her shield—and struck, moving in a blur.

You have backstabbed a hag mother for 5x more damage!
Your target's shield has blocked your attacks.

Ebonheart clanged off the hag's shield. Undaunted, I struck again with my second sword.

You have backstabbed a hag mother for 2.5x more damage!
Your target's shield has blocked your attacks.
A hostile entity has detected you! You are no longer hidden.

An instant later, my feet hit the marsh's surface. Whipping past my target, I plunged through the water and, striking the mud floor, pulled the shadows tight about me.

You are hidden. Multiple hostile entities have failed to detect you!

Fourth, rinse and repeat.

Pushing off the marsh floor, I surged upward through the water to strike at the hag mother from below.

You have backstabbed a hag mother for 2.5x more damage!

Your target's shield has blocked your attacks.
You have backstabbed a hag mother for 2.5x more damage!
Your target's shield has been destroyed! You are no longer hidden.

My lips twitched upward in a satisfied smirk. I'd done it. I'd broken through the hag mother's defenses. Now for the final step. *Finish her.* With a contemptuous glance at the downturned palms of the three hags—and the attacks they were likely directing my way—I shadow blinked.

You have teleported into the shadow of a hag mother.

Frost and ice splashed harmlessly into the water at my abandoned position. At the same time, I brought ebonheart and the stygian sword curving inwards.

Both blades met at the hag mother's neck.

Cold steel cut through skin, bone, and flesh effortlessly, and a moment later, the sea witch's headless corpse dropped at my feet.

You have killed a hag mother with a fatal blow.

Now, that's how you—

Twin jets of water and ice struck me from either side, cutting short my celebrations. Spinning around, I turned to face the closer of the bodyguards.

The battle was far from over.

Hefting my blades, I threw myself at the hag.

CHAPTER 261: THE OFFERING OF A HAG

"Stop!"

The command rang across the grove, harsh and demanding, and in response, the hag I was charging lowered her hands.

For a split-second, I contemplated following through with my attack anyway. But then curiosity and common sense caught up. Pulling back my swords, I altered my trajectory to dive past the hag and back into the marsh.

Surging up from the water again, I whipped around. Both bodyguards were watching me impassively. I eyed them suspiciously, but even under my stare, neither made any move to attack.

I inched my head to the side, not willing to let either bodyguard go unobserved for any length of time, and studied the other hags out of the corner of my eye. There were fourteen in total, approaching from all sides and with their hands conspicuously lowered.

Was this a trap?

If I didn't move soon, I would be surrounded. Instinct was urging me to flee, but I sensed nothing false in the sea witches' sudden passiveness. They truly seemed to have given up the fight.

I can't take the chance, I decided. Hefting my blades, I prepared to dive back into the marsh.

"Wait, wolf," a hag called out. "We wish to parley."

I turned in the direction of the speaker, this time recognizing the voice. It was the witch the hag mother had addressed as Caulis.

"Get back then!" I snarled and pointedly raised my bloodied blades. "Or I will resume my slaughter."

Rage suffused many of the hags' faces, but Caulis herself appeared unperturbed by the threat. "As you wish." Raising her right hand, she called out, "Pull back, sisters."

Obediently, the sea witches retreated.

Pivoting in a slow circle, I observed them through narrowed eyes but again sensed no deception in their movements.

"We only want to talk," Caulis repeated.

My gaze jerked back to the hag. "You said that, but I don't believe you. Why would you after I killed your leader?"

For the first time, emotion flickered across Caulis' face. "That misbegotten fool?" she spat. "She deserved to die. You've done our coven a service by ridding us of her."

The former bodyguards' hands twitched at this, but Caulis threw them a hard stare, and the pair subsided. After giving them a warning glance of my own, I turned back to the hags' spokeswoman. "And so, you are what? The coven's new hag mother?"

"I am," Caulis confirmed.

No one gainsaid her.

"What about the others I killed?" I asked, moving the conversation on. "Do their deaths mean nothing to you too?"

For a moment, the coven's new leader remained silent. "Ever since we came to this blighted city, we've all been marked for death. That my sisters died hurts, but that fourteen of us remain alive? That gives me cause for hope."

I frowned. "I'm not sure I understand."

"We are not the first coven to enter Nexus," Caulis said. "But none who came before ever returned to the sea, and I and my sisters fully expected to die on this bedeviled shore. Gretna was arrogant to think she could establish a foothold here, in the very heart of the players' domain."

Gretna must've been the former hag mother. "So, what do you want from me?"

"A cessation of hostilities, nothing more," Caulis answered.

"I thought your kind hated all landbound life?" I scoffed.

"We do," Caulis replied equably. "But living matters more."

I grunted, finding no cause to object to that. "What do I get in return?"

"Your life."

I snorted derisively. "That's not yours to give."

"The life of another then."

I blinked. "Who?"

"The wolf we hold prisoner."

I raised a questioning eyebrow. "What makes you think I can't take him from you if I wanted to?"

"You may have slain some of us, but the outcome is by no means assured if we resume battle."

"I've been doing well enough so far," I said mildly.

Caulis shook her head in frustration and tried another angle. "The worms have your companion. You will not free him of their jaws without our aid."

The new hag mother seemed to be under the mistaken impression that I knew her prisoner, but I didn't enlighten her. And besides, Caulis was right about the battle's outcome being uncertain, if not for the reasons she thought.

I'd used all my traps and much of my stash of mana potions to replenish my void armor between fights. More importantly, though, I was running out of time and couldn't afford another protracted engagement. The first disease protection crystal was nearly spent, which meant I had less than four hours to finish matters in the grove *and* leave the saltmarsh.

"How can I trust you?" I asked at last.

"You players can see the true nature of objects, yes?"

I nodded.

Caulis drew something out of her robe and threw it to me. I made no move to catch the item, and it plopped into the marsh to float on the surface. "That is all you need to free your friend."

Glancing down, I analyzed the small object.

The target is a basic commune rod. This item has been crafted from the same coral that gave birth to seaworm colony 12,402. The hags have imprinted it with the mental commands necessary to control the colony.

Available orders: eat, withdraw, sleep. This item has no prerequisites to use.

"Do you see?" Caulis asked.

I nodded. "Where is the prisoner?"

"In a hollow carved out of the largest tree in the grove." She studied me. "Do we have a deal?"

I chewed over Caulis' words a second longer. "We do. Go."

Silently, the new hag mother turned around and headed south. The other sea witches followed, gliding across the marsh in her wake.

✳ ✳ ✳

After verifying that the sea witches had indeed departed, I pocketed the commune rod, then returned to the spot of the hag mother's demise and dived to the marsh floor.

A moment later, I resurfaced with my prizes.

Holding the corpse in one hand and the head in the other, I pursed my lips as I considered the grove. I needed somewhere secure to search the body. I couldn't do that in the water, which left only the trees.

Dropping the head momentarily, I pulled out the commune rod. *Let's see if this works.*

Closing my eyes, I focused on the seaworms industriously eating away at the nearest tree. *"Sleep,"* I breathed, projecting my thoughts through the crystal.

For a wonder, the worms' responded. In a matter of moments, their mindglows dulled, and their frantic movements slowed to a crawl.

"Huh," I grunted. "What do you know? It works."

I'd half expected the commune rod to be defective, some trick of Caulis' to push through her deal. But it seemed the sea hags had wanted to leave the city as much as I'd wanted them gone, and she'd negotiated in good faith.

Picking up the hag's head, I dragged it and the corpse into the tree's lower branches. The worms remained quiescent throughout, and I turned my attention to the waiting Game messages.

Once again, many of my skills had advanced. Ignoring the usual skill level up messages, I focused only on the skills that had ranked up.

You have reached level 133!

Your dodging has increased to level 111 and reached rank 11.

Your elemental absorption has increased to level 23 and reached rank 2, increasing your chance of resisting harmful elemental effects by 5% and decreasing the damage you suffer from them by 10%.

I smiled, pleased by my player progress. Without having to think about it, I invested my new attribute points.

Your Dexterity has increased to rank 38. Other modifiers: +8 from items.

Next, I considered the hag mother's body. She wore no jewelry and only had two items of note: a pair of soft-scaled boots and a sealskin robe.

Yanking off the boots, I inspected them first.

You have acquired the rank 3 item: boots of the flying fish. This item allows the wearer to walk over water as if it were solid ground and requires a minimum Magic of 12 to equip.

The boots were interesting but not worthy of replacing my wayfarer's boots. Storing them in my backpack, I considered the sealskin robe. I had to peel it off the corpse and, to my surprise, found the inside bone dry.

Thoughtfully, I analyzed the garment.

You have acquired a rank 2 sealskin robe. This item has been enchanted to keep the wearer dry and warm in even the coldest seas. Additionally, it increases your water magic by +10. This item requires a minimum Magic of 8 to equip.

"Too bad I didn't find this earlier," I muttered, glancing down at my water-logged clothes. It would've saved me a soaking.

Inspecting the inside of the robe more closely, I found it was lined with pockets. All the pockets, but one was empty. Rifling through it, I pulled out a fistful of items.

You have acquired 3 x coral flowers, 1 x toad tongue, 4 x yellow-spotted frog feet, 20 x marsh weed, and 1 x yellow-spotted frog tongue.

"Well, that's handy," I remarked, studying the cache of reagents in surprise, especially the frog feet and tongue. They were the exact items I required to complete bounty job two hundred and seventy-one.

Turning about, I stared out into the grove. There were at least eight other hag corpses resting at the bottom of the marsh somewhere, and I needed to loot them too.

But first, time to recuperate.

✳   ✳   ✳

You have replenished 100% of your psi and mana through meditation and channeling.

You have activated a rank 6 disease protection crystal.

You have acquired 8 x sealskin robes, 27 x coral flowers, 4 x toad tongues, 8 x yellow-spotted frog feet, 80 x marsh weed, and 6 x yellow-spotted frog tongues.

You have acquired a hag mother's scalp.

Job 1015 update: Task complete. Visit knight-captain Orlon to collect your reward.

Job 271 update: Task complete. Visit the guild office to collect your reward.

A little later, I was finally done with my chores and ready to move on. Rising to my feet, I equipped my cat claws and scaled up the tree's broad trunk, not stopping until I reached the topmost branches. From there, I surveyed the grove.

Most of the trees were the same height as the one I was perched on, but one tree, in particular, loomed over the others.

That must be the one Caulis spoke of.

Taking up the commune rod in my hand again, I ordered all the seaworms infesting the grove to slumber. I had no idea if the worms would ever wake on their own again but judged putting the nasty little creatures to sleep safer than commanding them to retreat—that would leave the worms in the marsh, and *that* I did not want.

When mindsight confirmed the coast was clear, I leaped off the branch and glided along a windslide to the neighboring tree, and from there, to the next.

Reaching my destination—the grove's tallest tree—I dropped back into the marsh. Immediately, I saw that Caulis had not led me false. A large dulled mindglow was concealed inside the tree.

That has to be the mysterious wolf.

And if I was reading his mindglow correctly, the wolf was stirring.

Chapter 262: A Wolf in Chains

Like the tree itself, the prisoner was riddled with seaworms—*thousands* of them. But they were all dormant, which explained why the wolf was only awakening now.

How is he still alive? I wondered. The hags had not mentioned how long they'd been holding their captive prisoner, but I'd gotten the impression it had been for some time.

Metal clanged. Wood creaked. And bits of dead bark fell.

The wolf was coming out.

I backed away from the tree to give the newcomer space. The creature was probably half-crazed and in no mood to be friendly. Letting my hands hover near my blades, I waited.

A figure stumbled out.

I was not sure what I was expecting, but a naked human was not it. Stumped for words, I stared at the tall young man. He was filthy. Mud caked his hair, brown streaks dripped down his arms, manacles were fastened around his feet, and slumbering worms covered nearly every inch of his body. But for all that, the 'wolf' was clearly human.

He's a player, too, I realized a second later as I read the spirit signature clouding his form.

The target is Anriq. He bears a Mark of Greater Dark, a Mark of Lesser Shadow, and a Mark of Wolf pack-brother.

The werewolf criminal.

I shook my head, amazed at my luck. For once, fortune seemed to be favoring me. I had come to the grove to complete one bounty, but here I was, on the brink of completing *three*.

Anriq, meanwhile, was grunting and staggering about in a circle—he'd been chained to the tree—and was frantically swiping at the clinging worms. He wasn't doing a very good job, though.

"Need a hand?" I offered.

The wolf-man flung up his head and pinned me with an ugly stare. The whites of his eyes showing, the youth bared his teeth and growled menacingly.

Hmm, it looks like I wasn't far off the mark. He seems half-feral.

"Easy there," I said soothingly. "I'm not going to—

Claws extended from his fingers, and in a sudden frenzy of motion, he slashed at the steel chains imprisoning him, shearing them clean through in a single strike.

My eyes widened, impressed by the ease with which the captive had slipped his chains. Still, I couldn't help but wish he'd stayed imprisoned a little longer. He seemed to be focusing on *me* as the target of his animosity. Backing farther away, I showed him my empty palms.

The gesture did not appease Anriq.

Surging forward, he charged me. Bracing myself, I prepared to meet him, but I made no move to draw my weapons—I was not about to kill the only other Wolf Marked player I'd met before we even had a chance to speak.

Only a second later, though, the youth gave me cause to question the wisdom of my tactics. Even as his feet flew over the water—senseless worms flying free—Anriq was changing.

Coarse brown fur spurted from pink flesh; claws extended from toes; ears elongated, canines revealed themselves, and a snarling snout appeared where none had been before.

Worse yet, the youth got bigger.

Bloody hell, I thought, watching the onrushing figure—more beast than man now. Having closed the gap to less than three feet, Anriq was already as big as a dire wolf and still growing.

Perhaps, this wasn't the—

You have been hit by a werewolf's charge.

Trying to stop my opponent was impossible.

I might as well have been trying to hold back the tide. Against Anriq, the half-dead prisoner, I'd fancied my chances. Against Anriq, the werewolf, I stood no chance.

The youth plowed into me, and I flew backward, helpless to fend him off or even slow his charge. And for the second time in my short sojourn in the grove, I was struck helpless.

You have failed a physical resistance check! You are <u>battered</u> (limbs immovable, abilities restricted). Duration: 3 seconds.

Cursing my luck and flat on my back, I sank to the marsh floor with the werewolf's weight bearing me down. Anriq's assault had only just begun, though. Sharp canines ripped into my shoulder, and clawed feet raked my abdomen.

Anriq has critically injured you!
Anriq has critically injured you!
Quick mend triggered!
Warning! Your health is dangerously low at 40%.

He wasn't going to give me a chance to explain anything, I realized, and grappling underwater with the stronger werewolf was the last thing I wanted.

I need to buy time, and then I need to put some distance between us.

Directing my thoughts to the potion bracelet, I injected a restorative concoction into my bloodstream.

You have restored yourself with a full healing potion. Your potion bracelet has 1 of 3 charges remaining.

Soothing trails of liquid spread through my body, closing my wounds and healing my injuries, but I was still battered and unable to move or use my abilities. My foe, meanwhile, did not let up on his frenzied assault.

Anriq has injured you!

Anriq has injured you!
...
Warning! Your health is dangerously low at 25%.

In a breathlessly short space of time, my health flashed red again. Trapped underwater and helpless to do anything else, I injected myself once more.

You have restored yourself with a full healing potion. Your potion bracelet has 0 of 3 charges remaining.
Warning: you have imbibed 8 alchemical mixes in the last 24 hours! Consuming further brews in the next 24 hours may trigger unwanted and irrevocable side effects.

The Adjudicator's warning was alarming but less so than the huge swathes of damage the werewolf was wreaking on my body. And besides, my potion bracelet was empty, so it mattered little in my present circumstances.

For now, I had no choice but to watch and wait.

Anriq has injured you!
Anriq has ...

...

You are no longer <u>battered</u>.

The lethargy infecting my limbs and the fog around my mind vanished, and I wasted no time in weaving psi in a bid at escape.

You have cast windborne.
Anriq has injured you!
Warning! Your health is dangerously low at 18%.

More than three-quarters dead and bleeding from multiple bites and gashes, I rocketed out of the water on the windslide that manifested beneath me.

My ploy did not, however, get rid of my werewolf hanger-on.

Refusing to let go, Anriq hung on tenaciously and was borne up with me. Still, our abrupt upward velocity startled the youth, and his frantic pawing stopped for a moment. Taking advantage of his distraction, I wove another spell.

You have cast slaysight.
Anriq has failed a mental resistance check! You have terrified your target for 10 seconds.

The spell completed just as the windslide came to an end, and my foe and I tumbled off, still attached. In freefall, I glanced down at my captor.

But he was no longer that.

My spell had transformed our roles, and magic-induced fear suffused Anriq's face. Meeting my eyes, the werewolf blanched and loosened his grip. Grimly, I shoved him away, and we hit the water, separated by a distance of a few feet. Resurfacing quickly, I spun around in search of him.

But I needn't have bothered.

The werewolf was cutting through the water as fast as he could in panicked flight. My shoulders sagging in relief, I wrapped myself in shadow and set about healing myself.

✳   ✳   ✳

Whatever had caused Anriq to attack me drove him still, and barely seconds after his terrified debuff lapsed, the werewolf returned. But strong as he was, his senses were not finely honed, and he passed within inches of my hiding spot without finding me.

Concealed amongst the reeds, I studied the player. Anriq's earlier transformation was complete. He was at least twice my height in his full wolf form and looked a formidable foe. But now that I had more time to observe the youth, I saw that his beast form bore as many signs of his recent captivity as his human form had.

Anriq's wolf skin hung loose on his frame, and tufts of his fur stuck out oddly. White scars riddled his torso, but they were slowly closing over even as I watched.

The werewolves' famed regeneration, I thought, remembering Barac's offhand comment from months ago. It must've been the same regeneration that had allowed Anriq to survive the worm's jaws for as long as he had.

The youth was stalking through the grove, sniffing and snarling. *He's still half-feral,* I decided. Not leaving the shadow's safety, I reached out with my will and ensorcelled him again.

You have terrified Anriq for 10 seconds.

Once more, the werewolf took off, fleeing, but only seconds later, he returned, gnashing his teeth in anger. *Stubborn,* I thought. But so was I. Pitilessly, I terrified him again.

And again.

And again.

Each time Anriq returned, his frustration palpable. I paid his anger scant heed, though, and bewitched him, in turn, every time.

We kept at it for nearly an hour.

Finally, something gave, and on his umpteenth return, the wolf shrank down, transforming into a haggard and very naked human. "Show yourself, coward!" he yelled in a hoarse voice.

"Why should I?" I asked, projecting the words with ventro.

In a flash, Anriq descended on the spot from where my voice had emerged. Crowing in victory, he slashed at the reeds with claw-tipped hands.

I chuckled, watching his near-berserker fury. "You won't find me that easily."

Chest heaving, the youth swung around to the new reed patch I spoke out of. Realizing I was toying with him, he didn't charge, though. "Where are you?" he demanded.

"Somewhere close," I replied vaguely. "Now, are you ready to talk, or do you want to decapitate a few more bushes?"

Anriq's face devolved into rage, but he quickly suppressed it. Hugging himself tight—to rein in his fury, I suspected—the werewolf player stared out over the grove.

He still hopes to find me, I thought.

"You can tell Dathe I'm not returning," Anriq half-growled.

My brows creased. "Who?"

"Don't take me for a fool," he spat. "I *saw* your Wolf Mark."

I scratched my head. "Perhaps that makes sense in your mind, but I'm afraid I'm not following you."

"You're one of his!" Anriq accused.

"Whose? If it's this Dathe you mean, then certainly not."

"Don't lie to me!" Anriq roared.

"Why would I bother?" I countered. "Believe me, if I wanted you captured or dead, you wouldn't still be walking free."

"You want it!"

"It?" I asked, shaking my head in bemusement. "There you go again, assuming I know what you're talking about. Why don't you do me the courtesy of pretending I don't and explain what you're going on about?"

Anriq didn't say anything. Fuming in silence, he scanned the marsh.

Patiently, I waited him out. I held all the cards at this point, and the werewolf player had to know it.

"Dathe is the pack leader," he said finally.

"Ah, I see." I paused. "And of which pack would that be?"

Anriq's brows drew down sharply. "What are you playing at?" he snarled. "There is only one werewolf pack, and Dathe is their leader."

I nodded slowly, finally realizing where this was going. "This pack... they are hunting you?"

"Yes!"

"And you think I'm part of it?"

Anriq's only response was a menacing growl.

Deciding to take that as assent, I concluded, "Which is why you attacked me when you saw my Wolf Mark."

"Congratulations, you've solved the mystery," Anriq spat scornfully. "Now, if we are done with this charade, will you show yourself? Or will you continue to cower in the dark like a dog?"

"There's just one problem," I said, overlooking the insult. "You see, I don't know this Dathe, nor am I part of his pack." Anriq opened his mouth to retort, but I spoke over him. "*Which* you would know if you read my Marks correctly."

The youth closed his mouth with a snap. "What's that supposed to mean?"

"Precisely what I said." Rising to my feet, I let the shadows around me dissipate.

Anriq whirled around to face me, hands clenching and muscles tensing as he prepared to charge.

"Read my spirit signature again," I ordered, ignoring his threatening stance.

He did not comply at once, and I resigned myself to a second tussle. Then I felt a tingle wash over me.

Anriq has recognized your Wolf Mark!

Anriq's eyes widened. "Y-y-ou're an alpha!" he gasped.
Folding my arms across my chest, I grinned. "Exactly."

"You can't be one of Dathe's!"

I nodded. "That's what I've been trying to tell you."

Spinning on his heel, Anriq paced across the grove, the waist-deep water barely checking his stride at all. I watched him, slightly envious. *Having all that Strength must be nice,* I mused.

"No pack can have two alphas," the youth said aloud.

I said nothing, knowing he was working through the implications of my Mark.

"That means..." Anriq spun around to face me, something akin to joy touching his face. "Dathe is dead! You killed him! You must have if you are the new—"

I shook my head, interrupting him before he could become too excited. "I'm afraid not. I didn't lie to you before. I've never met this Dathe."

The werewolf's face fell. "Then... how?"

"I'm the alpha of another pack," I said, stating the obvious.

"*Another* werewolf pack?" Anriq asked eagerly.

Once more, I was forced to disappoint him. "I'm not a werewolf, nor have I met any before today."

"What then?" A glimmer of something unrecognizable—*disgust?*—flickered across Anriq's face. "Don't tell me you've forced yourself onto a pack of *ordinary* wolves? Why would they accept you? And for Powers' sake, how did doing that gain you a Wolf Mark!"

I grimaced. "That's not it either." I held up my hand before he could speak again. "I will not share any of the details behind my Wolf Mark. Sorry, but you haven't earned that right."

The werewolf took my refusal in his stride and fell silent for a moment. "What Class are you?" he asked eventually.

The question, an apparent non-sequitur, caught me off-guard, and for a second, I hesitated. But then, seeing no reason not to tell him—plenty in the city already knew part of what I was—I answered. "I'm a mindstalker."

"That's not a Force Class," Anriq rasped, eyes narrowing. "Is it?"

"It's not," I agreed.

"Then to which Power are you sworn?"

"I'm not."

"Not?" Anriq asked, perplexed.

"Not sworn to any Power or Force," I elaborated.

Anriq's face paled as he went white as a sheet.

"Are you alright?" I asked, taking a step closer to him.

Anriq shook his head—in denial of what, I wasn't quite certain. "That-s-s not-t... possible," he said. "You must be sworn. You must!"

"Why?" I asked. My answers seemed to have triggered some deep-seated fear in the youth, and he was on the verge of panic. I took another step forward, but Anriq's gaze jerked toward me, and I froze.

Is he going to bolt?

But no, he remained stock still, staring at me with wild eyes. "No werewolf had been allowed to forgo swearing himself to a Force," he said finally. "For that to happen—" Anriq licked his lips. "For you to be..." He gulped. "It's just not possible," he finished lamely.

"But I'm not a werewolf," I repeated. "Whatever rules govern your pack doesn't apply to me."

The reminder calmed the youth, but only for a moment. "Another impossibility," he whispered.

"Why?" I asked curiously.

"Only werewolves can achieve a Mark as steeped in Wolf as yours," Anriq replied.

That was not quite true, but I let his statement pass uncontested.

"Well, others can," the werewolf amended a moment later, "but not without becoming..." Once more, he ran aground. Taking a deep breath, he continued, "The only other possibility is that—"

He knows, I thought in dread. *He must.*

"—you are a scion," he finished.

My thoughts churned. Just like that, my secret was out in the open. This time, though, I wasn't sure if I could stop it from spreading.

The dire wolves' elders had told me my blood would awaken of its own accord as my Mark deepened. Unexpectedly, Anriq seemed to know that too, which must be how he figured out the truth.

There is going to be no lying my way out of this, I realized. Unable to explain away Anriq's reasoning, I said nothing.

But that was enough for the youth. "It's true then," Anriq breathed. "You *are* a scion of House Wolf."

Keeping my face impassive, I stared back at him.

Despite my own shock, my mind had not stopped working. There were other implications—besides the obvious ones—to Anriq's conclusion. Foremost among them was that the werewolves had to know about the ancient bloodlines. How else would Anriq conclude what he had? And that, in turn, meant...

Will I find other scions among them?

The thought prompted a complex mix of emotions—relief that I was not alone, delight at finding potential pack brothers, suspicion at how they survived in Nexus, and finally, resentment that there could be others like me.

Then, the wolf in me stirred as another more disturbing question rose in my mind: would my candidacy for Prime be contested?

My lip curled up in an involuntary snarl. I would brook no competitors. None.

This is not the time for such musings, I told myself firmly. Clamping down on my errant thoughts, I refocused on Anriq.

He was still staring at me, his expression a mix of awe and reverence. His attitude had shifted markedly in the interim, I noted. Was that because of my alpha Mark or the fact that I was a scion?

Perhaps, it's due to both.

"You've awoken your blood, truly?" he asked.

I nodded wordlessly. Denials wouldn't work now, but perhaps the truth could serve me just as well.

"How did you do it?"

I waved aside the question. "That's a long and dreary tale. And someday, perhaps, I will share it, but not today." I held his gaze. "Now, tell me, how do you know about the bloodlines? The Powers jealously guard all knowledge of the ancients."

Anriq was silent for a moment. "That, too, is a long tale. But I will tell you if you wish."

"I do."

Anriq sighed. "My pack—former pack—has in its possession an item called the Wolf Torc. It is an artifact of the ancients, and when analyzed, it talks of the scions and the blood."

"An artifact," I murmured, my interest piqued. "Who has it?"

"The pack leader, Dathe."

"Of course." I should've realized as much myself. Something else occurred to me. "Is this item the 'it' you were referring to earlier?"

Anriq shook his head. "No."

"Oh," I said and turned back to the matter at hand. "So, what does the Torc do?"

Anriq looked at me in surprise. "You don't know?"

"No."

"So, it's not for the Torc you've come?" he persisted.

"I said so already," I said irritably. "Now, tell me what it does."

Anriq inclined his head. "The Torc connects the lycan guard to its commander."

The youth's answer made even less sense than I expected. "What does *that* mean?" I asked with a frown.

"You truly don't know, do you?" he marveled, but before I could vent my impatience again, he went on, "The Torc is a blood-binding device. It forges an unbreakable tie between the lycan commander and the guard. With it, the commander can compel his soldiers to fulfill his orders."

"The artifact sounds... fascinating." *And powerful.* "I assume the werewolves *are* the lycan guard?"

"Correct," Anriq replied. "And Dathe is the commander."

I rubbed my chin. "How did you escape his clutches then?"

"The Torc doesn't directly enforce obedience." Anriq's lips twisted. "It can be used to inflict pain, though. I've seen weres who refused Dathe's commands burn from the inside out." He shuddered. "But to answer your question, I fled *before* Dathe could bind me."

"I see," I said. "But none of that explains why the Powers let your pack be. Surely, they know of the artifact."

"They do," Anriq confirmed. "It was the Triumvirate themselves who bequeathed the Torc to the pack."

"What?" I asked, startled. "They *gave* it to the werewolves? Just like that?"

Anriq's lips twitched in an almost-smile. "No, not 'just like that.' The Triumvirate had conditions, namely that every werewolf assumes a Force

Class. The pack didn't know why initially, but we figured it out over time. It was to stop our blood from awakening."

"Ah," I said, understanding dawning at last. Sulan had said something similar all those months ago, which made me realize something else: there could be no scions amongst the werewolves. Not if they couldn't awaken their blood. Mollified by the insight, the wolf in me subsided.

"And if you don't adhere to the Triumvirate's conditions?" I asked, returning to the conversation.

"They have promised to wipe out the pack, down to the last player."

My lips turned down. "That sounds like the Powers, alright," I muttered. "But threat aside, the Triumvirate must want something. What do they gain from giving Dathe the Torc?"

"Soldiers," Anriq answered promptly. "We patrol the saltmarsh on their behalf and keep the marshmen at bay." His spine straightened a touch in an unconscious gesture of pride. "No one is more aptly suited to this task than us werewolves. No one else can *live* here and do what we do except us."

"Marshmen?" I asked, focusing on the most critical aspect of what he'd said. "Who are they?"

For the first time, Anriq appeared uncomfortable with my questions. "Primitives," he said, not meeting my gaze. "They, too, live in the marsh and consider it theirs by right."

"I haven't seen any," I said slowly.

"You won't," the youth replied dismissively. "They are even better at hiding than you."

"But—"

"I've answered all your questions," Anriq broke in. "Now, will you answer some of mine?"

I hesitated, but what he asked was only fair. "Go ahead."

"What *are* you?" Anriq asked.

"Just a player," I replied.

The werewolf snorted.

"No, really," I said. "I'm an ordinary player, if one a little different from most. Early on in the Game, I had the good fortune to be Marked by Wolf, and since then, I've walked a different path."

I could see from Anriq's expression that he wasn't convinced, but he didn't pursue the matter further. "What's it like?" he whispered.

"What's what like?" I asked, confused.

"Having your blood awakened."

"Oh," I said, never having given the matter much thought. "It's different. Scary. But natural as breathing too."

Anriq nodded as if he understood. "Why are you here? No one just wanders into the saltmarsh."

I pulled out the hag mother's scalp and held it up. "I came for her." I paused. "And you."

Anriq made the connection quickly. "You're a bounty hunter?" he asked disbelievingly.

I grinned wryly. "Of sorts."

"And now that you've found me? Will you claim my head too?"

My smile died, and I eyed him speculatively for a moment. "That's still to be determined," I replied, being deliberately vague. "We need to have a much longer conversation first." I scanned the soggy grove. "But not here," I decided. Reaching into my backpack again, I pulled out another item and threw it at the werewolf.

You have lost a sealskin robe.

Catching the garment easily, Anriq bent his head down in inspection.
"Put that on and follow me," I ordered. Not waiting for his response, I turned on my heel and headed north out of the grove.
For a moment, the only sounds breaking the marsh's silence were my own. But then, a second sound intruded as the youth waded through the water in my wake.
I smiled. Anriq had accepted my invitation.

CHAPTER 264: A PERVERTED TRIAL

The casual invite to Anriq had been a test, of course.

I couldn't deceive him with lies nor bind him by magic, which left only one option: winning his trust with the truth. Determining how far *I* could trust *him* had been the true purpose of my act of disinterest. So far, the werewolf was proving to be exactly what he appeared—an earnest young man who had run afoul of his pack.

Still, there were a lot of unanswered questions surrounding Anriq.

Namely, how deeply were the werewolves under the Triumvirate's spell? Why had Anriq run away? What had the hags wanted from him? And most importantly, how did he feel about the ancients?

Would he betray me at the first opportunity?

Or was he a potential ally?

All these thoughts and more ran through my mind as we waded north through the saltmarsh. I couldn't afford to tarry in the grove any longer. There were just over three hours left on my last disease protection crystal— not that I cared to share that information with Anriq—and so despite the manifold mysteries remaining to be solved in the marsh, I reluctantly headed out.

During the two-hour journey, I plied Anriq with questions, some subtle, others less so. He answered everything more forthrightly than I expected, but on some subjects, he was surprisingly cagey.

* * *

"So, what *are* werewolves?" I asked, deciding to begin my 'interrogation' with an innocuous-seeming question about which, admittedly, I was more than a little curious. Who better to ask than a werewolf himself? "You appear human—most of the time, at least."

Anriq chuckled from beside me. "You won't believe how many times I get asked that."

I cast my new companion a sidelong glance. He seemed more at ease in the open marsh than he'd been in the grove and kept pace easily with me. If anything, I was the one slowing him down. Before we'd set out, I'd given him some rations. The youth had gulped them down in short order, accelerating his regeneration, and now all signs of the wounds he'd suffered while in hags' clutches had vanished.

"Quite simply, we are players who carry the were-trait," Anriq continued. "Some begin the Game bearing the trait; others earn it later." He shrugged. "Sometimes all it takes is a bite from another were-player. Other times, the requirements can be more onerous. Only the Adjudicator understands why."

"Then, werewolves are not the only weres. There are other types too?"

"Oh yes."

"Hmm," I mused, considering the possibilities. "And becoming a werewolf has nothing to do with your Class?"

"Not at all," Anriq said. "Although, there are some Classes that are were-specific—such as my own."

I glanced at him again. His comment reminded me I'd not yet inspected him fully. "Can I analyze you?"

"Go ahead," Anriq replied, but despite the werewolf's easy acquiescence, his gaze grew wary.

Reaching out with my mind, I sent probing tendrils of will toward the werewolf.

The target is Anriq, a level 102 were-rampager and human. He bears a Mark of Greater Dark, a Mark of Lesser Shadow, and a Mark of Wolf pack-brother.

Warning: this player has been branded a criminal by the sector's ruling faction, the Triumvirate. Aiding him in any manner may result in charges being brought against you.

My eyebrows rose, surprised both by the youth's comparatively low level and the Adjudicator's warning. I suspected it was the criminal brand that had Anriq worried, but I chose to ignore it entirely. The Triumvirate were not my enemies, but nor was I inclined to further their agendas.

"You're Darksworn?" I guessed, considering the strength of his Dark Mark.

Anriq nodded, his tension easing at my lack of reaction to the analyze. "The were-rampager is a melee-based Class and quite popular amongst werewolves. It enhances our already powerful beast forms even further, making weapons and armor superfluous."

My eyes narrowed thoughtfully. "Most of your pack is Darksworn, too, then?"

"Yes, but that doesn't mean we—they—are a Dark faction. The werewolves serve the Triumvirate. No one else."

"Is that so?" I said, glancing at him sharply. "Are you sworn to one of the Triumvirate then?" Analyze had not revealed Anriq to be marked by any Power, but I didn't place as much faith in the ability as I once had. His Mark could be hidden.

"I'm not," Anriq denied. "The Triumvirate considers every werewolf to be a follower." His lips twisted. "But they have not chosen to 'honor' any besides Dathe with the bond of a Sworn. It's through Dathe that they enforce their control over the pack."

I held Anriq's gaze, weighing him carefully. I sensed no untruth in the youth's words, but he could simply be a better liar than I credited. If he served a Power, any Power, there was no way I could trust him. But if he didn't...

"Which of the Triumvirate is Dathe sworn to?" I asked finally.

"Rampel."

I nodded, unsurprised. "What else can you tell me about Dathe?"

"He is cruel," Anriq answered promptly. "Sadistic. Evil."

"Strong words," I murmured.

He reared back in affront. "You don't know him! You would feel the same if you've seen even a tenth of what Dathe's done."

"Alright, I'll take your word for it," I said, not wanting to rile him further. "How long has Dathe had the Torc?"

"Decades, or so says pack gossip. He won it from the previous pack leader over a century ago."

I pursed my lips. "So Dathe is not the first werewolf leader to possess it?" Just how long had the Triumvirate kept the werewolves on a leash?

Anriq shook his head. "No. The pack has been around for centuries, and ever since anyone can remember, the Torc has always been held by the pack leader. Any werewolf may challenge the alpha for the right to possess it. Dathe himself has killed dozens of contenders during his reign." His face turned glum. "But there haven't been any new challengers in years. No one can defeat Dathe."

"What's the challenge?" I asked idly.

"Some sort of ritualized combat," Anriq replied. "I've heard some of the elders refer to it as the Combat Trial."

I drew breath sharply. "Are you sure?" I whispered.

He glanced at me oddly, noting my intense gaze. "That's what the elders call it anyway."

That name can't be a coincidence, I thought, coming to a full halt. *It has to be another of Atiras' Wolf Trials.* "This Trial... where does it take place?"

"Within the pack's lair—the ruined keep of the lycan guard. There is a room in the keep's basement; the only time it's used is during the challenge." He paused. "There are strong enchantments about the chamber. Amongst other things, it keeps the room in pristine condition."

"Where is this keep?"

"On the southern edge of the mash. You can't miss it."

The fortress along the shoreline, I thought, realizing of which building he spoke. "And the victor's prize is the Torc?"

Anriq nodded mutely.

"The loser just hands it over willingly?" I asked skeptically.

Anriq snorted. "No, the trials are to the death—*final* death. I'm not sure how the Trial's enchantments work, but they stop any defeated contenders from ever arising again."

The penalty for failure in the Mind Trials had been final death, too. Now, I was sure of it. The Combat Trials were another of Atiras' Trials.

I have to find this chamber.

On the tail end of the thought, a Game message dropped into my mind.

On behalf of Wolf, the Adjudicator has allocated you a new task: A Perverted Trial. You have gained information on the location of another of Atiras' Trials. If your source is correct, the Triumvirate have manipulated the Wolf Trials to serve their own ends. Wolf is incensed by this perversion of the ancient ways and requires you to end their vile practices.

Objective 1: Explore the sea fortress and confirm the Combat Trial's location. Objective 2: Wrench control of the werewolf pack from the Triumvirate. Objective 3: Punish any pack leaders complicit in the pack's subjugation.

I dismissed the Game message. Even without its prompting, I had ample reason to find the Trial.

"Can only werewolves enter the Combat Trial?" I asked as I resumed wading through the marsh.

"Of course—" Anriq began, then broke off. "You know, now that you mention it, I'm not sure." He peered at me. "It may be that the elders consider anyone marked by Wolf to be a suitable candidate."

I nodded, hoping that was the case.

"Don't get your heart set on wearing the Torc, though," he warned.

I glanced at him. "Why not?"

"For one, the Torc is soulbound. Dealing final death to Dathe is the only way you'll get it, and no one has come close to succeeding at that. For another, not even Dathe can wear the bloody thing."

I frowned. The Torc's soulbound properties came as no surprise. For such a powerful artifact, it was not unexpected. But that the pack alpha couldn't employ it caught me by surprise. "Why can't he use it?"

"Oh, Dathe can use it alright. It's just unwearable." Anriq shifted uneasily. "No pack leader has *ever* worn the Torc. It's commonly believed among the pack that the Triumvirate tinkered with the relic to keep the alpha from running off with it. The damn thing works, but it can't be worn—or moved."

My frown deepened. "So, where does Dathe keep it?"

"In a magical chest crafted by the Triumvirate." He pulled out a slim key. Where he'd been hiding it, I had no idea. "The chest itself is immovable and can only be opened by this."

My eyes widened. "Is that the mysterious 'it'?"

Grinning, the werewolf nodded.

"You stole the key from Dathe?" I guessed.

Anriq's grin widened.

I chuckled, then guffawed. "Anriq, I think I'm beginning to like you. Come, tell me everything, and leave nothing out."

*　*　*

Three hours later, Anriq and I stood at the edge of the saltmarsh district. I had delayed my departure from the region to complete my questioning. Given Anriq's status as a criminal, that seemed safer than venturing with him into the plague quarter's more populous areas.

I had learned most of what I'd wanted to know from the werewolf, except when it came to the marshmen. On that subject, Anriq had been surprisingly closed mouth, repeatedly stating their secrets were not his to share. Eventually, I abandoned the topic entirely and questioned him on other things.

Anriq, it turned out, had been the hags' prisoner for months. The sea witches had been experimenting on him in an attempt to divine the secrets of his regeneration. He had fallen foul of them while wandering the marsh.

On the run from Dathe and his cronies, the young werewolf had been alone, without help, and easy prey for the hags.

Surprisingly, Anriq had not stinted on sharing information on the werewolf pack itself. Given the specific details he had shared, I no longer harbored any doubts about his loyalties.

Anriq hated Dathe's and his masters. He'd fled the pack to escape the alpha's harsh rule, but Dathe, no fool, had convinced the triumvirate knights to declare Anriq a criminal, effectively trapping the youth in the saltmarsh—the one place in the city that other players rarely ventured.

But life alone on the saltmarsh was not easy, and though he did not ask it, I could tell from the werewolf's imploring looks that he desperately wanted out—which left me with a difficult decision to make. My disease protection enchantment had nearly run its course, and it was time to go.

The question was: did I leave alone?

"What now?" Anriq asked, unconsciously echoing my own sentiments.

Turning about, I faced him squarely. "I have one last question for you."

"Yes?" he asked eagerly.

I hesitated, not sure if I wanted to know. "You've accepted my lead awfully quickly. You've not questioned me once since we left the grove; you've followed me unhesitatingly; and you've answered all my queries more fully than I'd any right to expect." I paused. "Why?"

Anriq shrugged. "You're an alpha."

I stared at him, waiting for him to go on, but when he didn't, I exclaimed, "That can't be all there is to it! You must have more reasons than that."

Anriq remained silent for so long I didn't think he would answer. "You're an alpha," he finally repeated. "But I get the impression you've not been one for long. Correct?"

I frowned, unsure what he was getting at but willing to hear him out. "That's true."

"That explains your confusion. You don't yet comprehend what it means to be pack," Anriq said.

I wanted to be offended, but there was no judgment in his tone, only dry statement of fact.

"To be part of a pack..." Anriq's gaze grew distant. "... is to be complete. There is strength in a pack. Comfort. Order, too. Its call is fierce—nearly irresistibly so at times. There have been many nights when I've lain awake, regretting my decision to leave my pack mates. Even hating Dathe as I do, and even knowing the punishment awaiting me on my return, I've nearly gone back—simply to belong again."

He met my gaze. "No wolf can walk alone forever. Not you. Not me. You're an alpha, and in that, there is hope for me to find a pack again—one untainted by Dathe. Do you understand now?"

I nodded slowly. What Anriq described, I'd felt myself. Not to the same extent the youth had, but enough so to understand the allure he described.

Taking a deep breath, I turned around. "Come on then. It's time we got going."

Anriq didn't move.

I glanced over my shoulder. Hope, desperation, and fear vied on the werewolf's face. "I— I... can't leave," he said. "Nexus is too dangerous for me. If the knights find me, they will—"

"I know," I said. "But I intend on getting you out of the city, and I think I know someone who can help. Will you trust me?"

For a drawn-out moment, Anriq said nothing. Then, he climbed up the bank bordering the saltmarsh. "Yes," he whispered.

Chapter 265: Wolves at Bay

The day was still young—just past noon—when Anriq and I exited the saltmarsh district.

It was also the busiest time of day in the plague quarter, and more than a few people were about. Still, I didn't think that would be a problem.

Anriq and I were just two more players walking the streets, and so long as we didn't draw any attention to ourselves, there was no reason the passersby should pay us any heed. Admittedly, Anriq in the hag mother's robes and boots—he couldn't use the boots' enchantments but stood out less in them than he would've barefoot—cut a strange figure but no more than many other players.

At first, things went exactly as I expected, and no one cast us a second glance. We slipped northeast through the quarter, avoiding the more crowded streets around the public dungeons and cutting a wide arc around the knights' citadel—we *definitely* didn't want to go near there.

I planned to stash Anriq in one of the abandoned houses in the quarter, then visit Kesh and Cyren. Because of the shield generator around Nexus, I couldn't simply buy a portal scroll and teleport Anriq out of the city. But if anyone knew how to sneak someone out of the sector, it would be Kesh or Cyren. They would tell me—for a price, of course.

Unfortunately, things didn't turn out as I hoped.

Halfway through the quarter, Anriq gripped my arm. "What?" I whispered, turning towards him. The plan was for the werewolf to remain silent and follow my lead—which he was obviously *not* doing.

Anriq, though, was gazing fixedly down the street and did not notice my ire. "I've been spotted," he hissed.

My head whipped around. Eight players were standing idle on a street corner about a hundred yards ahead. One of them was pointing in our direction—at Anriq, more precisely—and another was whispering excitedly to his companions while shooting us sidelong glances.

You have passed a mental resistance check! Multiple neutral entities have failed to analyze you.

The group was definitely onto us. "How in hells did they spot you?" I muttered.

"I was analyzed," he replied.

"But why would they pick you to analyze in the first place?" I wondered. "There are lots of other players about."

"One of them must be a spotter," Anriq answered. Sweeping his gaze from left to right, he scanned the nearby streets. "Do we fight or flee?"

"What are spotters?" I asked slowly, ignoring his own question.

"Players carrying detection wards," Anriq replied absently. "The wards alert the spotters when a criminal is close by. The knights use them all over the city."

For a moment, I was struck speechless. "It would've been nice if you told me about them *before* we encountered one," I managed eventually.

"I'm sorry, it slipped my mind," Anriq said, ducking his head. "I've been in the marsh too long."

I opened my mouth, another retort ready, but a flash of movement on my left drew my attention. I glanced down the street. The group who'd spotted us was in motion, sprinting closer with weapons drawn.

"We'll talk about this later," I said. Yanking on Anriq's arm, I pulled him down a side street. "For now, we flee."

✳ ✳ ✳

Running flat out, Anriq and I fled east through the quarter. The werewolf had no stealth or deception skills, which left us only two options: fight or flight.

Fighting, I judged, was the worse choice. A pitched battle would only draw further attention, and once more players realized they had a criminal in their midst—one with a bounty on his head no less—a true hunt would begin.

Unfortunately, fleeing didn't work either.

No sooner had we disappeared down the side street than a horn trilled out, playing a series of honks in a distinct, if peculiar, pattern.

"The alarm has been raised," Anriq said before I could ask what it meant. "That sound will let everyone know that a criminal is on the loose in the quarter," He looked at me bleakly. "It will bring the knights down upon us. And others looking to earn their favor as well."

Sure enough, a group of players further down the street turned around at the horn's call and, seeing us running, pointed our way.

This just keeps getting better, I thought sourly.

"There he is! That's the criminal!"

"Get him!"

Cursing foully, I turned north.

Anriq pulled up next to me. "Shouldn't we be heading south? Back to the saltmarsh?"

"No," I said in a clipped tone. I had a second, closer destination in mind. Besides, returning to the saltmarsh meant abandoning the werewolf, and I wasn't ready to do that yet.

"So, where are we going?" Anriq panted.

I was onto plan B. It was an escape option I'd been hoping not to exercise, but it didn't look like there was much choice now. "The guardian tower," I said.

Anriq wrinkled his nose. "What's that?"

"A public dungeon where we can lose those on our tail," I said. "Now save your breath and run!"

Swerving left down one street, I raced to its end, then turned right up the next, navigating by memory alone. We couldn't be more than five minutes from the dungeon. *We'll make it,* I thought grimly.

More cries and shouts echoed in our wake, and the horn continued to warble, the sequence it played out growing more complex. I suspected it was communicating our location, but I could do little about that.

Turning down another street, I drew up short.

A dozen players were waiting. Holding their weapons at the ready, they blocked our way. "Charge!" the ogre at the fore roared.

"Back," I yelled. Spinning on my heel, I dashed into the closest alley.

Anriq followed without question, and behind him, I heard the other players give chase. Reaching the end of the alley, I skidded to a halt.

"This is a dead end," Anriq began worriedly. "How are—"

"Shh," I ordered. Throwing back my head, I gauged the height of the adjacent buildings.

Damnation. They were all too tall to scale in the time we had left, even with windborne to aid us. Pulling out my last invisibility potion, I tossed it to Anriq. "Drink that."

The werewolf glanced at the flask in his hands, and his eyes widened as he realized what it was. "What about you?"

"Don't worry about me. I'll be fine. Now down that quickly and hide."

The werewolf did as I bade. "What if we're found?" he asked as he faded from sight.

"Then we fight," I whispered.

Pulling the shadows around me, I concealed myself too.

✳   ✳   ✳

A few seconds later, a handful of players dashed into the alley.

Five hostile entities have failed to detect you! You are hidden.

"They're not here!" one shouted.

"They must be. I saw them come here myself," a second replied.

Cloaked in darkness and with my back braced against the alley wall, I focused on the second speaker. He was a dark elf and was examining the alley minutely—as if he could see more in the shadows than his fellows. *If this comes to a fight,* I thought, *he will have to die first.*

Realizing I needed to know what we were up against, I examined each member of the enemy party in turn.

The target is Augur, a level 141 wild druid and dark elf.
The target is Dreyn, a level 120 crusader and human.
The target is Taufil, a level 118 wizard and gnome.
The target is Usmatrik, a level 131 ranger and lizardman.
The target is Mesina, a level 150 summoner and human.

More bad luck, I groused. Each of the hostile players was of high enough rank to pose a credible threat, but I'd faced worse odds before, and this time I had help. I glanced at where I knew Anriq to be.

The werewolf, shining bright in my mindsight, sat still and unmoving. Even though he was of lower level than the hostile players—and without arms or armor—I knew from personal experience Anriq would be able to hold his own in a fight.

Let's hope it doesn't come to that.

I wasn't prepared to bank on luck, though. Keeping my movements slow and controlled, I equipped my cat claws and set to climbing.

Five hostile entities have failed to detect you! You are hidden.

Ten seconds later, the enemy party was still in the alley.

"You're sure they're here?" Dreyn asked.

"I am," Augur replied.

"Because if you're wrong," Usmatrik began, "we're going to lose out on a massive payday. The others won't—"

"I'm not wrong," Augur insisted. "Now quite yakking and spread out."

Splayed against the wall, I sighed. The party wasn't going anywhere. About forty seconds remained on Anriq's invisibility, and when that time ran out, a fight was inevitable.

I have to be ready before then. Anchoring a clawed hand in another crack, I kept climbing.

✳   ✳   ✳

I reached the top of the building with ten seconds to spare. Along the way, I'd cast my buffs.

Your Dexterity has increased by +8 ranks for 20 minutes.
You have gained an encumbrance aura for 10 minutes.
You have trigger-cast quick mend.

Perched on the rooftop, I extracted my climbing rope and affixed it to a roof eave. Then I drew my blades and waited.

The five players had split up and were searching the alley in pairs while the last one—Mesina—and her pet wraith kept watch at the alley mouth. Other players rushed by the entrance without stopping or were warned off by the summoner.

The party seemed intent on ensuring no one else could claim the criminal's scalp.

Which suited me just fine.

Through mindsight, I saw Anriq unbend from the crouch he had fallen into earlier. He had to have realized the potion was about to wear off, too. I wished I had a means of coordinating my attack with the werewolf, but that was impossible, and I could only hope he didn't do anything foolish.

Drawing in psi, I prepared a casting. A second later, Anriq blinked back into sight.

"There he is!" Taufil exclaimed. The wizard, wrapped in a magic shield, was pointing his staff in the rampager's direction.

Anriq was already in motion. Surging forward, he leaped towards his closest foe—the crusader, Dreyn. Mid-air, the werewolf shifted, his robe and clothes falling away as he transformed from man to beast.

The wizard's warning proved timely, though. Pivoting about calmly, the crusader raised his shield and set his stance. At the same time, the rest of the party readied their attacks.

It was the moment I'd been waiting for.

With the enemy focused on Anriq, my own assault would pass unnoticed until too late. Letting the rope uncoil to the alley floor—it was our escape route—I released the casting I'd held ready.

You have cast mass charm.
Mesina has failed a mental resistance check!
A level 150 wraith has failed a mental resistance check!
You have charmed 2 of 2 targets for 20 seconds.

My lips twitched upward. My charm spell had done better than I'd expected, and *both* the summoner and her pet fell under my control. "*Attack!*" I ordered, yanking on the leashes I'd wrapped around their minds.

Without hesitation, the ethereal wraith and human summoner rushed to the closest of their former comrades—Usmatrik.

The ranger, meanwhile, had just released the arrow he had nocked. It struck Anriq squarely as he crashed into the crusader but had no discernable impact. Ignoring the barbed shaft in his side, the werewolf battered at his target with tooth and claw.

But just as the ranger's attack failed, so did Anriq's.

The crusader employed his shield to push aside his foe's slavering jaws while his thick steel armor sufficed on its own to rebuff the werewolf's claws.

The remaining two party members weren't slow to act either. Lightning streaked across the alley and into Anriq's rear. It slowed the werewolf's assault a touch, but he kept attacking.

A second arrow whizzed through the air; this one was fired from the druid. It also struck its target, but instead of punching a new hole in Anriq's side, the projectile unleashed a mass of thorny vines that wrapped themselves around the werewolf.

The druid would be my next target. Stepping through the aether, I emerged unnoticed behind him.

You have backstabbed Augur for 4x more damage!
You have killed your target with a fatal blow.

At a hiss of sound, I threw myself sideways.

You have evaded Usmatrik's attack.

Rolling to my feet, I risked a glance over my shoulder. The ranger was raising his bow to fire at me again, but before he could release the projectile, the undead wraith was on him, wrapping oversized hands around the lizardman's neck.

The startled ranger turned around—only to be struck by a flaming bolt launched by Mesina. Smiling grimly, I left Usmatrik to his fate and turned my attention to the wizard. He had not noticed the carnage behind him yet.

Drawing psi, I formed a slide of air between me and Taufil and dashed along it, blades raised. Catapulting off the end of the windslide, I leaped down on my unsuspecting target.

You have cast whirlwind and piercing strike.
You have backstabbed Taufil for 5x more damage!
Your target's shield has blocked your attacks.

Ebonheart bounced off the wizard's shield, but I'd only just begun my assault. Empowered by whirlwind, I launched a furious sequence of attacks.

Your target's shield has blocked your attacks.
Your target's shield has blocked your attacks.
...
Your target's shield has been destroyed! You have killed Taufil with a fatal blow.

Slipping free my blades from the corpse, I glanced up to see Anriq wrench off the crusader's head.

Anriq has killed Dreyn.

Where tooth and claw had failed, raw strength had succeeded. The werewolf had literally torn apart his smaller foe. Looking up from the dismembered corpse, Anriq gazed at me, waiting for instruction. I motioned for him to follow. We still had two more targets to kill.

Your minions have killed Usmatrik.

At the message, I turned around in time to see the ranger's burned and bloodied body hit the ground between the summoner and her pet. It couldn't have been more than twenty seconds since the battle had begun, and already it was nearly done.

Only one more to deal with.

"Let's end this," I called to Anriq over my shoulder. Not waiting for his response, I dashed toward the summoner.

Halfway to my target, my charm spell fizzled out.

I didn't let that daunt me, though. The party's sole survivor—still dazed and reeling from the aftereffects of her bewitching—was easy prey. Ignoring the wraith that moved to intercept me, I blinked through the aether.

You have teleported into Mesina's shadow.
You have killed your target with a fatal blow.

The wraith wailed and, a moment later, vanished unsummoned in the wake of its master's death.

I glanced at Anriq again. "Good work there," I said wearily. "Now, let's get—"

You have been struck by a tranquilizer dart.
You have failed a physical resistance check! Lethargy has begun spreading through your body. Time remaining until you are completely asleep: 3 seconds.

You have been struck by a poison arrow.

You have failed a physical resistance check! You have been poisoned with an unknown toxin. Your health is degenerating by 1% per minute.

I staggered forward, eyes widening. To my rear, new signatures blossomed in my mindsight. Another enemy party was entering the alley, I realized.

Hells, can't we catch a break?

Across the alley, Anriq met my eyes.

"The rope!" I croaked, fighting back the spreading coils of sleep. "Get to the—"

But I got no further.

Finally overcome by the tranquilizer, I slipped into darkness.

I awoke slowly.

My gaze was cloudy, and everything was hazy. Blinking rapidly, I waited until my eyes cleared before studying my surroundings.

Murky water, rotting wood, and the dank overpowering smell of decay filled my senses. *I'm in the saltmarsh*, I realized. More precisely, I was in one of the dilapidated buildings infested with blood flies. Despite the unappealing surroundings, I was pleasantly surprised to find I was not dead.

How did I survive?

Turning my head to the side, I noticed a robed and barefoot figure.

Anriq.

The werewolf sat with his head bowed and his arms wrapped tightly around his knees. *He must have brought me here,* I thought gratefully. Pushing my hands against the floor, I tried to sit up, but it felt as if red hot pokers were being thrust through my body, and with a gasp, I fell back.

At the sound, the werewolf raised his head and stared at me through eyes red and bleary. "You're alive!"

I chuckled. "I'm tougher than I look," I croaked. Even talking hurt. My throat was parched, and my lips were cracked. "What happened?" I asked, forcing myself to speak.

"A second party ambushed us," my companion replied. "You were hit first, but I managed to get you out using the rope."

"You climbed the rope *while* carrying me?" I asked, startled.

Anriq's lips twitched. "Werewolves are nothing if not strong," he said. "Besides, you don't weigh much."

"But weren't you struck?"

He shrugged. "I was, but what they hit you with didn't affect me nearly as badly. My Constitution is nearly as high as my Strength, and I was able to shrug off the attacks."

"Impressive," I murmured, thinking that whatever Anriq said, it couldn't have been as easy as he made out. "Then what happened?"

The werewolf sighed. "A long and dreary chase that lasted hours. Those players were persistent."

Hours? Frowning, I turned my head and stared out of the room's only window. My senses had not deceived me. It was still bright outside. "How long have I been out for?"

"The better part of a day." Anriq paused. "The tranquilizer was potent. It was meant for someone my size, I think."

My eyes widened in alarm. "Almost a whole day? But the sun's still up."

Anriq glanced out the window and grunted. "Huh, that's true. Looks like dawn's arrived."

Dammit. That meant it was time to meet Kesh already. Heaving myself upward, I tried to rise again, this time with more urgency, but once more, my body failed to heed me. "Anriq, help me up," I pleaded.

Uncoiling, the werewolf did as I asked. Fresh waves of pain coursed through me, but I clamped my jaws shut, holding in the screams that demanded to be let out.

Anriq studied me worriedly. "You shouldn't move."

"I must," I replied through gritted teeth.

The werewolf fell silent. "Have you checked your Game messages?" he asked finally.

I shook my head. "Why?"

"You should," Anriq prompted. "I couldn't identify the second toxin in your body, but it took a toll on you. I tried healing the damage, but nothing I gave you worked."

"You tried—?" I asked, growing more alarmed. "What did you give me?"

Mutely, Anriq held up a handful of spent potion flasks. "Sorry, I didn't have any of my own," he said, mistaking the reason for my concern. "I took these from your backpack." Frowning, he pointed to the empty vials. "The healing potions helped some, but not for long. What poison did they hit you with?"

"I don't know," I replied absently, less worried about the toxin—it must've washed out of my body by now—and more concerned with the potions' effect. Turning my attention inwards, I studied the waiting Game messages.

You have reached level 135!
Your chi has increased to level 111 and reached rank 11.
Your sneaking has increased to level 110 and reached rank 11.

You have imbibed 17 alchemical mixes in the last 24 hours and have developed an adverse reaction! You have gained the trait: <u>potion resistance</u>. Due to your overuse of potions, your body has grown less responsive to their restorative effects. This trait reduces the beneficial impact of all brews consumed by 1 rank.

It was worse than I thought.

I'd been hoping the penalty would be something like a curse—a curse I could remove—but a trait… that was permanent.

Right, this ain't good. It was a further complication I didn't need. My gaze flitted to Anriq, who was inspecting me worriedly.

It's not his fault; he didn't know.

But the Adjudicator was not done delivering bad news. More Game messages vied for my attention. Dreading what else awaited me, I opened them.

Your health is dangerously low at 20%.
You have contracted Typhili, a level 5 disease! Warning, the contagion in your body is approaching critical mass and will soon morph into a deadlier version.

"Dammit," I swore, beginning to regret not dying instead.

"What's wrong?" Anriq asked.

"Help me," I rasped. "I've got to get out of here."

"But shouldn't you heal first?" Anriq protested. "Your health, it's not good. What if—"

"No!" I growled. "I have to leave the saltmarsh immediately!" Quickened by anger, my pulse raced, and my breathing grew faint.

Calm, Michael. Or you might get your wish and die here, after all.

I took a steadying breath. "Please. Get me out as fast as you can."

Saying nothing further, Anriq reached down and slung me over his back. "As you wish."

✳ ✳ ✳

A few minutes later, Anriq and I were crouched atop the bank leading down into the saltmarsh. Thankfully, the district's edge was nearly as unpopular as the marsh itself, and no other players were about. Reaching into my backpack with a shaking hand, I extracted the disease cure potion Trexton had mixed for me so long ago.

"Are you sure you should be taking that?" Anriq asked in trepidation.

"I have no choice but to," I said, staring morosely at the flask. "It will take too long to find a mage willing to cure me."

While Anriq had carried me out of the marsh, I'd filled him in on the reason for my distress. Needless to say, the werewolf had been distraught—despite me absolving him of any blame for my newly acquired trait. To take his mind off matters—and my own, too—I had made him recite the tale of our escape.

It turned out that Anriq had had an eventful day and night. He'd spent nearly the entire time chased by multiple groups of players and had only lost them when he'd ventured deep into the marsh. Now, he was almost as spent as I was.

Despite his misstep with the health potions, Anriq had done far more to help me than I'd anticipated. I'd fully expected the werewolf to flee the alley alone, leaving me behind to die. If he had done so, I would have borne him no ill will.

That he hadn't... that he had carried me out at great personal risk to himself, it spoke of the youth's integrity. But my survival had come at a cost, and now I had a difficult decision before me. I refocused on the flask in my hand.

If I didn't drink it, death was assured.

But if I *did* consume it, then I risked more debilitating effects.

It was either lose big or lose small. I didn't have lives to spare, though, so in the end, the choice was simple. *Here goes.* Uncapping the flask, I downed its contents in a single gulp.

You have cured yourself of Typhili with a rank 6 cure disease potion.

You have imbibed 18 alchemical mixes in the last 24 hours! Your potion resistance trait has advanced to <u>potion resistance II</u>. The second tier of this trait reduces the restorative effects of all brews consumed by 2 ranks.

"Ah," I exhaled, feeling the potion magically purge the contagion from my body.

"Did it work?" Anriq asked anxiously.

I nodded, saying nothing of the additional unwanted effect. "Let me see to my healing now." Glancing down, I inspected myself in a cursory fashion but then paused as I noticed fresh bite marks on my arm.

"Oh, about that," Anriq said, following my gaze. "I bit you."

"You *bit* me?"

Anriq nodded sheepishly. "When the potions failed to work, I tried giving you the werewolf traits. I was hoping it would take this time." He paused. "I guess it didn't."

"Oh," I said. Not knowing what else to say, I closed my eyes and healed myself. Then, for good measure, I invested my new attribute points and restored my reserves of psi and mana through meditation and channeling.

Your Dexterity has increased to rank 40. Other modifiers: +8 from items.

Feeling whole again, I rose to my feet and surveyed the area. The sky had brightened considerably. *Kesh and Cara must be getting impatient by now.* "Come on," I said. "Let's get moving."

The werewolf did not budge.

I shot him a questioning glance. "What are you waiting for?"

"I'm not coming," Anriq said.

My brows drew down. "Why not?"

"You will be safer without me," he replied, ducking his head despondently.

I stared at him in silence for a moment. "Don't be afraid. We will—"

Anriq's head jerked up. "I'm not scared!"

I inclined my head. "Poor choice of words on my part," I apologized. "But I think we can do better the second time around. If we're careful and avoid any crowds, I'm certain I can get you safely through the plague quarter."

Anriq shook his head stubbornly.

"We didn't go through all that for nothing!" I said in exasperation. "I promised to get you out of the city, and I will."

"But you don't even know how you will manage it yet," Anriq pointed out.

"That may be, but I have contacts who will help."

"I'll wait here until then," Anriq said. "It will be safer—for both of us."

I stared at him searchingly. "Are you sure?"

He nodded.

"Alright," I conceded reluctantly. It wasn't distrust that made me hesitate. Anriq had proven his loyalty beyond question, and I didn't fear him betraying my secrets anymore. He was Pack, and that was that. No, what worried me was leaving him alone again.

But the werewolf's suggestion *did* make sense. He had survived a long time in the saltmarsh on his own, and there was no reason he couldn't manage for a few more days. "I *will* be back. Count on it."

Saying nothing, Anriq just nodded.

I bit my lip. Somehow, I always seemed to be leaving behind those who I considered pack. But it couldn't be helped this time. I had to go. There were others also depending on me. "Where will I find you when I return?" I asked finally.

"Leave a message in the trunk of the tree where you found me," he said and, turning away, headed for the marsh.

Stepping forward, I stopped him. "Thanks for getting me to safety."

Anriq shrugged uncomfortably, not looking at me. "It was no more than my duty."

I smiled. "Nonetheless, I'm grateful."

He nodded mutely again and waded into the marsh. Silently, I watched him go. Then, turning about, I headed north.

Chapter 267: Criminal Behavior

My appointed meeting time with Kesh had come and gone, and so, despite wanting to visit the stygian brotherhood, I hurried north towards the safe zone's south gate.

I had only one detour to make—a visit to the bounty hunters guild.

As I made my way through plague quarter, I kept a wary eye on the passing players, but despite yesterday's events, no one looked at me suspiciously, and I reached the guild without incident.

Bounding up the stairs to the fortified building, I banged on the studded metal door with a closed fist. It opened a smidge, and two familiar storm-gray orbs peeked through. "Well, well, look who's come to visit."

"Hello, Eyes," I said.

"If it isn't the infamous bounty hunter himself," the doorkeeper said. "The talk of the city and celebrated slayer of mantises. Tell me, boy, how many assassins did you kill today?"

"Cut it out and let me in."

Bobbing up and down in the air in a parody of a bow, Eyes floated backward and let the door yawn open. "Not enjoying the fame?" he asked, dropping the mocking tone.

"Not in the least," I muttered, unsurprised that the guild was in the know about recent events.

"So, what brings you to us today?"

"I have a couple of bounties to hand in," I replied, then grinned. "Soon, I'll be a full guild member like you."

Eyes snorted. "Not like *me*." He paused. "You've completed the probationary tasks?"

I nodded.

"Let me fetch Han then," he said and disappeared through the inner door.

✳ ✳ ✳

"Welcome back, Michael," the guild's client liaison officer said as she stepped into the foyer.

I turned around from the painting I'd been studying to face her. In a striking black and gold suit, she was as immaculately attired as the first time I'd met her. "Hello, Hannah."

"Sit, please," she added, seating herself.

While I made myself comfortable, the guild officer studied me with undisguised curiosity. I bore her scrutiny impassively.

"You've created quite the stir," the dark-haired woman said eventually.

I grimaced. "It couldn't be helped."

"That's not what I heard tell," she said, a smile tugging at her lips. "But all that is done now. You've settled matters with Menaq, haven't you?"

I threw her a sharp look. "What do you know about it?"

"Oh," she replied vaguely. "We hear things."

"Huh," I grunted, realizing she wasn't about to share her sources.

"But you haven't come all this way for idle chatter," she said briskly. "Eyes tells me you've completed some bounties?"

I nodded.

"Card, please," the brown-haired woman said, all business now.

I handed over my BHG ID.

Hannah closed her eyes as she inspected the object. "You have the scalp and reagents?" she asked after reading the card's contents.

"I do." Removing the items in question from my backpack, I gave them to her.

You have lost a hag mother's scalp, 5 x yellow-spotted tongues, and 10 x yellow-spotted feet.

"Thank you," Hannah replied. "I will see these get to the clients." She touched my BHG ID again. "And here is your reward."

Jobs 1015 and 271 have been completed. You have gained 500 gold. Money remaining in your bank account: 6,330 gold.

"What about the third bounty listed here?" Hannah asked when she was done. "Have you managed to find the werewolf?"

Keeping my face impassive, I shook my head. "Not yet, but I will," I said with pretended determination.

"Too bad," Hannah said lightly, "but the two bounties you've completed will suffice." Pocketing the ID card, she pulled out another and handed it over.

Wordlessly, I took the item.

You have acquired a BHG ID. This is a writ of authorization, marking you as a junior member of the Bounty Hunters Guild. As a junior member, you can actively pursue 10 bounties at any one time.

Your BHG ID has been updated. Active bounties: 1 of 10.

Congratulations, Michael! You have achieved full membership status in the bounty hunters guild and completed the task: <u>Probie!</u> This task has no impact on the Marks on your spirit signature, and they remain unchanged.

My eyes narrowed as I read the Game messages. "Junior... member?" I asked, leaving the question hanging.

"Not what you were expecting?" Hannah asked, arching one eyebrow. "As a junior member, you will qualify for higher-tiered bounties." She leaned forward. "But it also means you must complete your annual job quota. No more going a year without fulfilling any bounties. Understood?"

"Completely," I said. "What's the quota?"

"Five jobs per year."

That didn't sound too bad. "Does this mean I can also attempt bounties in the other city quarters?" I asked, trying not to appear too eager.

"Not quite," Hannah murmured. "Those sorts of jobs are reserved for senior members only."

There always has to be something else, I thought, holding back a sigh. "And how many jobs do I need to complete to qualify for that?"

The liaison officer cast me an amused look. "From here on out, promotions in the guild are a matter of quality, not quantity. Complete whichever bounties you desire. Based on your on-job performance, the guildmasters will determine when you are ready to advance."

Well, that's... vague. But all I said was, "I see." Rising to my feet, I nodded to the still-seated woman. "Then I guess we're done here. Goodbye, Hannah."

"One second, Michael," the liaison officer said, stopping me before I could leave.

Turning around, I looked at her questioningly.

"What are your plans now?"

I tilted my head to the side. "Why do you ask?"

Hannah hesitated. "There may be a job we need you to do for us in the near future."

"What sort of job?"

Hannah seemed reluctant to continue despite having broached the subject in the first place. "You'll get all the necessary details in due course *if* we decide to proceed. For now, make sure to stay in touch."

"Of course. I am always at the guild's service," I said with no trace of mockery.

Turning about, I headed for the exit, feeling Hannah's gaze on me the entire way.

✳   ✳   ✳

Setting aside my disappointment, I left the guild headquarters at a fast walk. Money aside, I'd been hoping my guild membership would earn me the right to enter the other city quarters. That had turned out not to be the case, but I had no time to dwell on the matter.

It was time to leave the sector.

I slipped through the safe zone's south gate without stopping. The triumvirate knights on duty threw me hard stares but made no move to bar my way. *Odd,* I thought, thinking the guards were more focused than usual.

From the gate, it was a short walk to the emporium, and I was ushered inside. Striding briskly through the compound, I entered the old merchant's office.

Kesh was not alone.

A red-robed figure stood silently beside her chair. *Cara.* Smiling, I nodded at the agent. She returned my greeting with a careful nod of her own.

"You're late," Kesh said laconically.

I glanced at the merchant. "Sorry, I had a few errands to finish first."

"They didn't by any chance involve a werewolf?" she asked wryly.

With difficulty, I kept my surprise from showing. "No. But that's a strange question. Why do you ask?"

"Oh, no reason, *except* that the knights' offices are awash with reports of a criminal sighting," Kesh replied, casting me a disapproving look. "The criminal in question—a werewolf, in case you were wondering—was spotted several times in the plague quarter yesterday." She leaned back in her chair. "Interestingly enough, he was not alone and on multiple occasions was seen with a player bearing a remarkable resemblance to yourself."

Despite my growing alarm, I kept my expression deadpan. This had to be the reason for the gate guards' hard looks and Hannah's question about the werewolf bounty.

"But," Kesh continued, ignoring my strained silence, "despite multiple attempts, no one was able to analyze the second player." The old woman's gaze darted back to mine. "Which is fortunate because if the mysterious player *had* been identified, he, too, would be branded a criminal."

Kesh's warning was as clear as day, and I inclined my head in acknowledgment. The merchant either knew of or strongly suspected my involvement in yesterday's events but, for whatever reason, was turning a blind eye.

And intriguingly enough, she'd chosen to deliver her message in front of Cara.

"Out of interest," I asked casually, "how *would* a criminal flee the city?"

Kesh snorted, not appearing the least surprised by the question. "He won't do it using the teleportation points in the safe zone if that's what you're thinking. The wards around the safe zone are impossible for even most Powers to confound."

I nodded, having known as much already. "Are there other teleportation points in the city?"

It was Cara who answered. "No. The Triumvirate maintain tight control on all players and Powers entering and exiting Nexus. The only way to leave the city unsanctioned is by employing a nether portal in a connected dungeon."

Kesh cast the agent a sidelong glance but did not admonish her for speaking out—another interesting fact that I squirreled away for later consideration.

"But you should be careful, Michael," Cara continued, making no pretense at speaking obliquely. "The Triumvirate closely monitors any dungeon with an exit that leads out of the city."

I nodded to her in thanks. It confirmed my fears; I wasn't going to get Anriq out any other way except through the guardian tower. The real challenge, though, was getting him from the nether-infested sector to somewhere safer.

And where would that even be?

"That's enough talk of criminals for now," Kesh interjected. "Back to business." She looked at me. "You're ready to leave?"

"Almost," I promised. "I need to replenish some of my supplies first."

"What do you need?"

I told her, prompting another shake of disapproval from Kesh—it was a long list. "You're too hard on your gear, Michael." But in spite of the admonishment, the merchant materialized the requested items.

Your potion bracelet has been refilled with 3 full healing doses.

Your trapper's wristband has been replenished with 20 traps.

You have acquired 2 x full healing potions, 2 x full mana potions, 3 x major mana potions, and 2 x rank 4 cure poison potions.

You have acquired 4 x crystals of rank 6 disease protection and 2 x crystals of rank 5 poison protection.

You have lost 3,500 gold.

Despite my new potion resistance trait, I restocked on potions. I would endeavor not to use them, of course, but in an emergency, they could make all the difference.

Acquiring more enchantment crystals was also essential—notwithstanding the cost—and I purchased ones that offered protection against disease and poison.

Poison had nearly proved my undoing on multiple occasions. Despite this, I wasn't tempted to acquire the poison absorption skill or the disease neutralization one, for that matter. I had to play the long game, which meant filling my last skill slot with the nether absorption skill. And while it was not ideal, I would combat any toxins and contagions I contracted with consumables.

My traps were something else that needed attention. They were due for an upgrade, but before I purchased tier two traps, I had to advance my set trap ability first. I wasn't ready to expend the Dexterity points necessary to do so, though. Better traps would have to wait.

My gear attended to, I offloaded the unwanted loot I'd collected from the hags onto the merchant's table. "I need to get rid of this stuff too."

Kesh eyed the items silently before waving her hand and making them disappear.

You have sold a lot of miscellaneous equipment for 300 gold.

"That's it?" Kesh asked.

I shook my head. "I need a few ability tomes, too."

"Which ones?"

I took a moment to gather my thoughts. Since my last visit to Kesh, I had pondered my attributes and player growth more deeply. My Perception abilities were the only ones I'd not upgraded recently—but not by choice. The unhappy truth was that I didn't have sufficient ability slots for the attribute.

Worse yet, in the foreseeable future, I would be investing my new attribute points in Dexterity, Mind, *and* Magic. Dexterity and Mind contained my core abilities, and while I had no Magic abilities, raising the attribute was necessary to improve my void armor.

All of which meant my Perception abilities would fall further behind.

At the moment, I had *six* Perception abilities—far too many to consider upgrading. *I will have to forgo advancing at least three of them,* I decided.

But which ones?

Turning my attention inwards, I called up the necessary player data.

<u>**Michael's Perception Abilities (22 of 25 slots used)**</u>
improved analyze: tier 2, slots used: 5.
improved trap detect: tier 2, slots used: 5.
conceal small weapon: tier 1, slots used: 1.
facial disguise: tier 1, slots used: 1.
superior ventro: tier 2, slots used: 5.
lesser imitate: tier 2, slots used: 5.

Analyze was essential. The ability had, in the past, provided critical information on my foes and would only become more valuable as I upgraded it further. The same applied to trap detect. It allowed me to venture alone—something most players wouldn't dare do—into dungeons and... other places. Both abilities were keepers.

That makes two.

Conceal weapon had proved less than useful, and I disregarded it from consideration without hesitation. Ventro, on the other hand, had been a lifesaver many a time. Still, I didn't see value in upgrading the ability further. Projecting my voice up to a distance of twenty yards was sufficient for most purposes.

That left facial disguise and imitate to consider.

Given my increasing notoriety amongst Powers and players, having a disguise of some sort was essential. Both abilities had weaknesses, though.

Facial disguise covered only my face but allowed me to maintain an illusion in combat. Imitate, while wrapping my entire body, took up more Perception slots and fell apart the moment I took damage.

Deciding between the two was no easy matter.

My gaze flickered back to Kesh. The merchant was tapping her fingers impatiently, but I needed more information before making a choice. "Can you show me the available ability tomes for facial disguise and imitate?"

Kesh sniffed. "If it will help you make up your mind quicker, then yes." Tapping a rapid sequence on one of the emporium's catalogs, she set it down on the table before me.

Leaning over, I studied the slate's contents.

Item 10,301: <u>improved facial disguise</u> ability tome. This tier 2 ability enhances the illusion wrapped around the caster's face, masking not only his features but also his voice. Additionally, tier 1 analyze data is falsified.

Item 10,302: <u>superior facial disguise</u> ability tome. This tier 3 ability enhances the illusion's robustness, allowing it to function within a safe zone. Additionally, tier 2 analyze data is falsified.

Item 10,303: <u>master facial disguise</u> ability tome. This tier 4 ability further enhances the illusion's sturdiness allowing it to falsify all the caster's analyze data.

Item 10,304: <u>mimic</u> ability tome. This tier 5 ability physically transforms the caster's face, making his disguise impenetrable to nearly all forms of detection. Additionally, your spirit signatures may be falsified.

Item 4,121: <u>improved imitate</u> ability tome. This tier 3 ability expands the spell's versatility, allowing the caster to disguise not only his voice, apparel, and appearance but also his size and scent. Additionally, tier 1 analyze data is falsified.

Item 4,122: <u>superior imitate</u> ability tome. This tier 4 ability improves the spell's durability, allowing the caster to maintain the illusion around himself for an entire day and even during combat. Additionally, tier 2 analyze data is falsified.

Item 4,123: <u>master imitate</u> ability tome. This tier 5 ability enhances the spell's robustness allowing it to function in a safe zone and falsify all the caster's analyze data.

Item 4,124: <u>doppelganger</u> ability tome. This tier 6 ability physically transforms the caster, making his disguise impenetrable to nearly all forms of detection. Additionally, your spirit signatures may be falsified.

"Wow," I whispered, studying the upgrade path of the two abilities in fascination. Both imitate and facial disguise eventually became extraordinarily powerful, and while there was no doubt imitate was the better of the pair, it also demanded more ability slots.

I looked up from the catalog. "Out of interest, how many slots does a tier five ability occupy?"

"I told you before, I trade in goods, not information," Kesh said, sounding exasperated. "Now, I've been more than generous in what I've shared so far, but if you want to—"

"The attribute cost increases by five from tier two to four," Cara interjected. "And doubles from tier four to five."

Kesh threw her subordinate a frosty glare, which Cara ignored but, caught up in what the agent had said, I barely noticed. "That would mean a tier five ability requires... *thirty ability slots!*" I exclaimed, aghast.

"Correct," Cara confirmed.

"Well, damn," I muttered. I'd heard on multiple occasions before that the jump between tier four and five was insurmountable for most players, but the implications of that had never really sunk in.

Until now.

Thirty attribute points were more than I'd planned for, not just for a Perception ability but for *any* of them. Given the exorbitant attribute cost, it was unlikely I would be able to acquire more than a handful of tier five abilities.

This elevates the importance of my Class abilities and my blood memories, I realized. Neither of the two required ability slots. *A fact that I'm going to have to exploit.*

I would have to think more about the matter later, but for now, it was clear that cheaper was better. "I'll take the tier two facial disguise ability tome." I paused. "You might as well also include a tier three analyze, tier three trap detect, and tier three facial disguise."

"Good," Kesh said, some of her ire disappearing. She materialized the books, and we completed the transaction.

You have acquired a <u>superior analyze</u> ability tome. Governing attribute: Perception. Tier: expert. Cost: 50 gold. Requirement: rank 10 insight skill.

You have acquired a <u>greater trap detect</u> ability tome. Governing attribute: Perception. Tier: expert. Cost: 50 gold. Requirement: rank 10 thieving skill.

You have acquired an <u>improved facial disguise</u> ability tome. Governing attribute: Perception. Tier: advanced. Cost: 25 gold. Requirement: rank 5 deception skill.

You have acquired a <u>superior facial disguise</u> ability tome. Governing attribute: Perception. Tier: expert. Cost: 50 gold. Requirement: rank 10 deception skill.

I didn't have the necessary slots to use any of the tomes yet, nor had I decided which one took priority, but I would keep all four close until then.

"What else?" Kesh asked.

"Nothing," I said. I'd been intending on upgrading another Dexterity ability but decided to hold off for the time being.

Kesh grunted. "Have you made up your mind about the wayfarer's gloves?"

I shook my head. "Not yet, but I should have an answer for you when I return from sector 12,560." I paused. "But there is something else you can do for me in the interim."

Kesh waited for me to go on.

"I didn't get a chance to visit the stygian brotherhood yesterday. Can you approach them on my behalf? You know what I need already."

Kesh pursed her lips. "How much should I tell them?"

I frowned. "What do you mean?"

"The brotherhood are an inquisitive lot. They will want to know who wants the gear and why." She looked down her nose at me. "The skillbook, especially, will attract a lot of questions. Unless I satisfy their curiosity, they will not sell the book, and even then, they still might not."

"Tell them what you deem necessary," I said, trusting her judgment.

Kesh nodded. "Then I guess it's time you two got going." She glanced at Cara. "You clear on your tasks?"

"I am," the agent replied. Gesturing to me to follow, she glided towards the door.

Cara and I did not exchange any words until we exited the emporium. Once through the gate, I turned to her. "I'm sorry. I've just realized I didn't consult you before my request to Kesh. I hope you don't mind the trip?"

Cara chuckled. "Not at all. It'll make for a welcome change, actually. My time in the citadel was... well, boring. Not much interesting ever happened there." Her hooded face turned in my direction. "Except for you, of course."

I nodded, glad she was not angry. "What has Kesh told you?"

"About where we are going? She's given me the basic rundown on the sector. I know the valley is in turmoil, contested by all three Forces, and is ripe for expansion." Cara tilted her head to the side to study me curiously. "Kesh has also told me you've done quite well for yourself over there." She paused. "Odd. I would never have pegged you for a merchant."

I shrugged. "That's less my doing than Saya's."

"Saya? This is the player you've been corresponding with by letter?"

I nodded. "She's been running the tavern for... almost two years." *Has it really been that long?* "And mostly, things seemed to have gone well, but of late, Saya's had some difficulties, and now, we've lost contact with her."

"You're worried?" Cara asked, her tone grave.

"I am," I admitted. "There have been no missives from the tavern in over a month, and while Saya is capable enough, she is no fighter."

"Whatever trouble is plaguing the tavern, it can't be too bad," Cara said reassuringly. "It's located in the safe zone, after all."

I sighed. "I hope so." I banished my gloomy thoughts. "But enough of the sector; we'll find out how matters stand there soon enough. What happened in the citadel after I escaped?"

Cara shrugged. "There's not a lot to tell. The mantises vanished almost immediately. It was as if they knew you'd left."

Which they probably had once Loken had told them.

"After that, the plague quarter pretty much returned to normal," Cara added. "Until yesterday." She laughed. "You really do have a talent for creating a stir."

I sighed again. "Speaking of yesterday... do you know if there is a way to remove a trait?"

Despite her concealing hood, I could feel Cara's surprise as she stared at me. "Why would you want to?"

"I seem to have acquired one not to my liking," I replied reluctantly.

"One not to your—" Cara began. "Oh. You mean a negative trait. Which one is it?"

"Potion resistance."

"Ah... that's too bad."

Suspecting the worst from her words, I nevertheless asked, "How do I rid myself of it?"

Cara shook her head. "You don't. Traits are forever. The only possibility is acquiring a *second* trait to offset the effects of the first."

I lifted my head, hope blossoming. Another trait? *Now, there's a thought...*

Cara, though, was quick to dispel my excitement. "But the likelihood of finding the *right* trait is vanishingly small unless you have the necessary Class. In this case, that means an alchemical one—which you don't have."

"Damn," I muttered, deflating again. "I'm stuck with it, then?"

Cara nodded. "I'm afraid so," she said sympathetically.

I felt silent for a moment, pondering what this meant for me. "Is potion resistance common?" I asked finally.

"Not ordinarily," Cara replied. "You usually only hear tell of the trait after prolonged player battles, and even then, it does not affect everyone equally. Some are more susceptible than others. The important thing, though, is not to let the trait advance once you've contracted it." She paused. "I'm sure you've realized this already, Michael, but I'll say it anyway: avoid imbibing any potions in future. You *don't* want to become addicted."

I shuddered. "Now, there's a cheerful thought." Deciding against probing further, I turned my attention to the surroundings.

The streets had grown busier in the interim, and I realized we were nearing the global auction. Turning right down another road, I detoured around the market square to avoid its perpetual crowds. "Just how are we getting to the valley, anyway?" I asked suddenly. "Kesh didn't tell me."

Cara did not remark on the change of topic. "Kesh has given me the sector's coordinates. I will open a portal to its safe zone."

My eyebrows rose in surprise. Cara was getting us there? Somehow, I'd assumed that Kesh had arranged for transport with the Triumvirate knights. "I didn't know you had aether magic."

"There is a lot about me you don't know," Cara said, sounding amused.

"That's true enough," I agreed with a smile of my own. "Hmm... how many can you transport?"

"There is no limit as such. As long as I have mana, I can hold the portal open." Cara glanced at me. "Why do you ask?"

My eyes narrowing in thought, I let my gaze rove over the auction's crowds. "I have an idea." Gesturing for Cara to follow me, I swung left and into the busy square.

✳ ✳ ✳

The conversation died again when we entered the square. The crowd's constant din made talking impossible, as did the steady stream of players flowing past. Leading the way, I forged a path for Cara and me, but the going was slow.

Feeling guilty for leading the agent into this mess, I glanced back. To my surprise, Cara was faring better than I was. The surrounding players were giving her a wide berth, seemingly more afraid of brushing up against her red cloak than they were of bumping shoulders with me.

More at ease, I pushed on into the center of the square. Reaching the statue of the Adjudicator, we broke out of the crowds. "Sorry," I apologized to Cara. "I'd forgotten what the auction is like."

"Oh, it's no bother," she replied. "I know the square well."

I quirked an eyebrow, marking the fondness in her tone. "You spent a lot of time here, then?"

"I did in my younger days when I was—" She shook her head. "But that's all ancient history, and I'm sure of no interest to you."

On the contrary, I was intrigued, but before I could say so, Cara went on.

"I'm more interested to find out why we are here," she finished, looking at me expectantly.

I didn't answer immediately. I hadn't explained to Cara the reason for this detour. To some extent, that was because I wasn't certain how she'd react, but mostly it was because I didn't know if the one I was looking for would be here.

Turning around, I scanned the base of the Adjudicator's statue.

"It's not anything to do with the Adjudicator?" Cara asked, a note of trepidation entering her voice.

"Definitely not," I replied emphatically. "I'm looking for—" I broke off as I spotted a familiar figure. "Wait, I see him. Shael!" I called out, waving to attract his attention.

The half-elf looked up, and recognition lit his face.

"Michael," Shael greeted warmly as he walked over. "I'm surprised to see you back so soon." He made a show of looking me up and down. "And in one piece too. I guess you survived that date, then?"

I could feel Cara's quizzical gaze, but I only laughed. "That I did, and more. You're still here, I see."

"As always. Do you have another job for me?" He flashed a quicksilver grin. "I hope you don't mind me saying, but I hope it pays as well as the other. That was easy money and all for the work of five minutes!"

"I'm afraid I have something a bit more long-term in mind this time," I murmured.

Shael's brows creased. "What do you—" The bard broke off as he finally noticed Cara standing silently beside me. "And who's this? A lady and one of Kesh's famed agents as well, if I'm not mistaken." He bowed in an elaborate flourish. "Greetings, noble lady."

Cara shook in obvious amusement but did not respond to the bard. "Who's your friend, Michael?" she asked, and although it went unvoiced, I heard the real question beneath: is he why we are here?

I inclined my head. "Shael is one of my first acquaintances in Nexus, courtesy of a chance-met encounter. He's been stuck in the city for a long time. Too long, in fact. Anyway, he guided me truly, and I have a mind to repay the debt." I threw her a questioning look. "If I can."

Cara caught my drift immediately and nodded in assent.

Shael, meanwhile, was darting puzzled glances between us. "There is no debt, my friend," he said. "You paid me for the questions I answered, remember?"

"Perhaps," I allowed. "Still, your information led me true, and the least I can do in return is offer you an opportunity."

"What opportunity?" Shael asked, looking less enthused now.

"A chance to leave Nexus," I replied quietly.

Shael's face went blank. "I'd rather you pay me in coin."

I shook my head. "That's not possible, I'm afraid. The job in question is in another sector entirely. We are on our way there right now."

"I told you I've grown comfortable here," the half-elf replied, an edge to his voice.

That was when you couldn't leave, I thought. "You did," I agreed and held his gaze. "But I still offer you the choice. Will you stay? Or come with us?"

For a drawn-out moment, Shael didn't say anything, then his eyes narrowed. "And what do you get in return?"

"Backup," I replied succinctly.

The bard frowned.

"The sector we're going to is contested," I explained. "Multiple factions are there and in numbers. In truth, I'm not sure exactly what sort of mess we'll be walking into, and I will be more comfortable with someone to guard my back."

"The conflict itself should prove to your advantage," Cara interjected. "You may even find a patron."

I cast her a sidelong glance. What did she know about the bard that I didn't? But now was not the time to ponder the matter. I refocused on Shael. The cheerful demeanor he wore like a mask had disappeared as he considered our words.

Everything I'd said to Shael was true, if perhaps not the whole truth. I didn't expect to find myself in any pitched battles, nor did I expect Shael to provide direct combat support.

I was thinking farther ahead—*much* farther ahead—past whatever troubles were afflicting the tavern today. In the long run, Saya would need a combat player to support her with any other problems that might crop up. And Shael had already proved himself trustworthy.

Besides, what tavern doesn't need a bard?

Shael's gaze flitted to Cara. "Why isn't Kesh providing you with a guard escort?"

I shook my head. "Too conspicuous. I hope to go unnoticed if I can." I glanced at Shael meaningfully. He was a deception player, just like me. "And you, I know, can blend in better than most."

Shael shifted uncomfortably. "Will it be dangerous?"

"Undoubtedly."

"Will I be paid?"

My lips twitched, knowing I had convinced him already. "Handsomely."

The bard thought about it for a moment longer. The conclusion was forgone, though. "I'm in," he said heavily. "But I have a feeling I'm going to regret this."

I grinned, not in the least daunted by his misgivings. "Excellent. Let's get going then." Spinning about to face the demarcated teleportation area, I led the way back into the crowd.

*　＊　＊　＊*

The area was as busy as I remembered.

When we reached the platform's base, Cara placed her hand on my arm. "You two wait here," she said softly and ascended the stairs to speak to one of the knights on duty.

While the pair spoke, I let my gaze rove over the teleportation dais. A never-ending stream of portals opened and closed, spilling out more players or swallowing just as many. But not everyone was using portals, I noticed. Some vanished or appeared without the requisite shimmering curtain of white.

A scarred elven woman, in particular, attracted my interest. Standing alone on the dais, she was not intoning the words of a spell under her breath; instead, she was fidgeting with the bracelet wrapped around her left arm.

Almost as if she felt my gaze, the player looked up and stared right at me. *She's the bounty hunter I saw in the square the other day,* I realized. The elf nodded at me—in recognition of a fellow guild member, I thought—and I waved back. Then, before I could even think of stepping over and speaking to her, the elf pressed a stud on her bracelet and disappeared.

Now, how did she do that?

"Well, you seem to have landed on your feet," Shael said, speaking up before I could pursue the matter further.

I turned to him. "What do you mean?"

The bard grinned and idly twirled the flute in his hands. During our walk over to the platform, he seemed to have regained his equilibrium. "Oh, only that when you arrived in Nexus, you were a wet-behind-the-ears noob. Now, look at you," he said, gesturing at me. "Rubbing shoulders with Powers, bearing fancy swords, *and* with an emporium agent as a companion." He smiled. "Not only that, but you're also rich enough to sponsor a beggar bard out of this damnable city."

"Oh, I'm not paying the Triumvirate for the portal," I replied. "Cara will be opening it herself."

Shael chuckled. "No, my friend, on that score, you are sorely mistaken. One way or the other, you *are* paying for this trip."

Before I could ask him what he meant, Cara waved us over, and we stepped onto the platform.

"We've been granted permission to leave," she said. "You two ready?"

I nodded and glanced at Shael.

"Past ready," he said, with none of his earlier qualms.

"Then let's not delay any longer," Cara said. Raising her arms, the agent materialized a portal. The promptness of the shimmering curtain's appearance caught me by surprise, and I took an involuntary step back.

By the time I recovered, Shael and Cara had already vanished. *Damn, they're eager.*

My own emotions were a mixed jumble of elation, excitement, and trepidation. At long last, I was returning to sector 12,560. And even though I'd been looking forward to this moment for months, I couldn't help but wonder what the valley had in store for me.

Time to find out, I thought and stepped into the portal.

Transfer through portal commencing...

...
...
Passage completed!
Leaving sector 1. Entering sector 12,560 of the Forever Kingdom.

CHAPTER 270: OLD STOMPING GROUNDS

You have entered sector 12,560 of the Kingdoms.
This area is part of the Forever Kingdom's wild borderlands. It is currently neutral territory, unclaimed by any faction or Force. No additional restrictions apply to this region.
You have entered a safe zone.

I stepped out into a square that was, at one time, both familiar and unrecognizable. Turning a slow circle, I took in my surroundings. The village was the same size and shape it had always been, its configuration of streets and buildings unchanged.

But everything else about it was *different*.

The dirt roads had vanished, replaced by neatly paved blocks of stone. Then there were the buildings. Every structure looked like it had been rebuilt from the ground up, and not from simple logs either, but with brick and mortar.

The buildings had grown too. Where before, most of the village had consisted of simple log cabins, now I was surrounded by multi-storied structures. But none of that was what startled me the most.

It was the fortifications that did. Or the lack thereof.

The double ring of walls that had hemmed in the safe zone was gone, vanished like they'd never been. Loken had told me Mariga—Amgira, I corrected—had destroyed the goblin fort before leaving the sector, but I'd never contemplated what that meant for the village.

"It's beautiful," Cara murmured.

She was right, I thought, turning my gaze upon the mountainside laid bare all around us.

Shael chuckled. "It's prosperous, that's what. This place practically screams money." The bard scratched his chin. "How does a borderland sector get this rich *and* remain neutral territory? Every nearby faction should be scrambling to claim this place!"

"Who says they aren't?" I asked.

The bard looked at me sharply.

"Look there," I said, pointing to the forest at the base of the mountain slope on which the safe zone was perched. Caught up by the changes to the village, I'd not noticed before, but the valley's wooded interior was not as pristine as it had once been.

Huge swathes of trees had disappeared, ravaged by fire and magic, and gray ash clouds still hung over multiple locations. *A battle is raging down there.*

Shielding his eyes from the sun overhead, Shael narrowed his eyes and peered where I pointed. "Is that... smoke?"

I nodded.

"You weren't kidding," the bard said. "It looks like a war zone down there."

"And this is the combatants' staging area," Cara added quietly.

Turning away from the forest, Shael and I followed her gaze. The agent was examining the passing players.

There were many more of them than I remembered—and they were all armed to the teeth. *Faction soldiers,* I thought. Hurrying back and forth in differing directions, the groups of players glared at one another with undisguised hate, and if not for the fact that we were in a safe zone, I suspected many would've gladly drawn blood.

Shael sucked in air between his teeth. "I count at least eight different factions present."

The bard, I noticed, was studying the soldiers' colors and badges.

"From Dark, Shadow, *and* Light," he finished in a half-strangled voice. "Damn, Michael, what is this place?"

"I told you the sector was contested," I pointed out.

"But not by *all* three Forces!" Shael half-shouted.

I glanced at the bard curiously; this was the most upset I'd seen him.

Heads turned our way, and Shael lowered his voice. "A faction war is one thing, but a Force war? That's likely to bring out the major Powers, and trust me, my friend, when they clash, you don't want to be around." The bard ran a troubled hand through his hair. "Hells, I won't be surprised if there are envoys in this sector already."

I winced.

The bard noticed. "There are, aren't there? Tell me," he demanded. "Whose envoys are present?"

"Tartar's most likely," I said.

Shael's eyes grew round.

"One of Loken's, too, probably." I rubbed my chin in thought. "And I won't rule out the possibility of Amgira—Arinna's envoy— also being present."

The bard went pale as a sheet. "That's... that's..." Seemingly at a loss to finish, he dropped his head in his hands. "Powers, Michael," he groaned. "Why have you brought us here?"

Unexpectedly, Cara laughed and placed a hand on the bard's shoulder. "There, there. It's not all bad. I've been informed—reliably so—that Michael here is on speaking terms with both Tartar and Loken." She glanced my way. "And I imagine, if he must, he'll find a way to ingratiate himself with Arinna, too."

Shael groaned louder. Not unsurprisingly, Cara's words provided scant comfort.

✳   ✳   ✳

Sadly, that was not the end of the matter. Shael had more questions, but I pleaded off answering. "I'll explain later *after* we get to the tavern."

"But—" Shael began.

"I agree," Cara interrupted. "Let's get going. We're attracting far too much attention as it is."

I threw her an indecipherable look. From her earlier words, I gathered that Kesh had informed the agent about my meeting with Loken and Tartar, but I couldn't decide whether that was a good thing or not.

"Lead on, then," Shael conceded grudgingly.

Nodding sharply, I turned left. "This way," I said and headed in the direction of the tavern. Cara strode after me, and a moment later, Shael did so too.

While the three of us wove through the streets, I studied the passing buildings more closely. More than half were festooned with faction banners and flags.

They've been turned into barracks, I realized, watching a squad of wounded soldiers being escorted up the steps of one such building. It made sense. Nowhere else in the sector would be safer for injured players to recover.

The remaining buildings had been transformed into shops. On my left, I spotted an apothecary, on my right, a smithy, and on the next street over, a bank. All the homes were gone. *The original owners must've made a fortune*, I mused, eyeing the many merchants on display.

Our group was attracting its own fair share of attention, too, I noticed. Or rather, Cara was. Every merchant who spotted her kept their attention fixed on the agent's red-robed form until she disappeared from sight.

"Wow, Cara," I murmured, studying the emotions playing across the watching merchants' faces. "Looks like you're even more infamous than I am. What has Kesh done for her agents to warrant such... attention?"

"Oh, only what every merchant dreams of doing," she replied lightly. "Undercut the competition and secure a hold on the market."

Shael snorted. "That's an understatement. The old lady has quite the reputation in Nexus. She's known to own the biggest clients and rarest items." He scanned the watching faces. "That's why they're afraid. They're scared the emporium has come to steal their business."

Cara laughed but didn't refute the bard's words.

"In fact," Shael continued, "I wouldn't be surprised if we don't see a sudden flurry of sales in the sector." He grinned. "This would be a good time to..."

I stopped paying attention as we turned a corner, and the Sleepy Inn came into sight. I knew it was the tavern because it stood in the same place, but nothing else about it was recognizable.

That's the Sleepy Inn? I marveled.

The building was six stories tall—twice as tall as it had been when I'd left. Like the rest of the town, it had undergone a transformation into a brick-and-mortar building, but the changes were more extensive than that. Colored glass panes covered the windows, stone statues decorated the roof, the walls were brightly painted, and flowerpots hung everywhere.

Renovations, eh? I thought, eyeing the cheerful-looking building. It looked like a bit more than that. Keeping my gaze fixed on the tavern, I hurried my steps. Now that my destination was in sight, I was eager to get inside.

Which was how I missed the crowd of approaching players.

"Whoa there, fellow," one of the group said before I could barge into him.

Paying the speaker no mind, I sidestepped him and attempted to slip past his companions. The tavern entrance was only a few dozen yards farther up the street, and I could spot its doors thrown back in welcome.

The crowd closed ranks.

Rebuffed, I drew up short, and behind me, I felt Shael and Cara do the same. *What the hell?* I cursed, finally turning my gaze upon the group. The players' faces were set in hard lines, and their gazes were cold.

They're barring my way—deliberately, I realized, belatedly recognizing the group's intent.

A hand patted my shoulder. The group's speaker. "Relax, fellow. Where are you going in such a hurry?"

Shrugging off the offending arm, I glared at my questioner.

He threw up his hands, displaying empty palms. "We mean you no harm. We just want to chat before you head on off."

Remaining tight-lipped, I stepped back and let my gaze flit over the group. Did they recognize me? Was that why they'd stopped us?

But none of the two dozen players arrayed before me looked like Awakened Dead. Sure, their expressions were unfriendly, but the naked hatred Ishita's followers felt for me was absent. I wasn't about to take any chances, though.

Reaching out with my will, I analyzed the party's leader.

The target is Pitor, a level 141 human warrior. He bears a Mark of Minor Dark, a Mark of Lesser Shadow, and a Mark of Kalin.

I did not recognize the name Kalin, but he had to be a Power, which meant the player before me was his follower. *And perhaps, even Sworn too.* I grimaced. I'd tangled with enough Powers already, and I didn't need more enemies.

"What do you want?" I asked, making an effort to keep my tone neutral. I didn't quite succeed.

"No need to get riled up," Pitor said soothingly. "We only want to talk."

I folded my arms across my chest. "Then talk."

"You're going to the tavern, aren't you?" Pitor asked.

My gaze sharpened. "What of it?"

Pitor smiled. "I thought so. But before you head on, there are a few things you should know."

He had my full attention now. "Go on."

"It's simple, really," Pitor said, his tone friendly. "Staying there—" he jerked his thumb to point at the tavern—"is dangerous."

My arms tightened about themselves. "Dangerous," I whispered. "How?"

"Well, that's the thing," Pitor replied, still smiling. "Guests have been disappearing all month—dying, I'm told—their throats slit the moment they leave the safe zone."

I knew where this was going now. Saya's notes hadn't said anything about disappearing guests, but they *had* made mention of intimidation attempts, and that, I was sure, was why Pitor and his gang had waylaid us.

My blood boiled, and anger thrummed in my veins, but I forced it down. "Is that so?" I asked casually. "And who is killing these guests?"

Pitor shrugged innocently. "No idea. Of course, we've offered our assistance, but the gnome in charge is too proud to accept help from the likes of us." He grinned toothily. "So you see, if you stay there, you're taking your life in your hands." Striding forward, he placed a hand on my arm. "Personally, I wouldn't risk it."

I went still, dangerously still. Pitor sensed nothing amiss, but Cara must've because she stepped forward, her robe brushing against me.

Pitor's gaze flickered to her before returning to rest on me. "You look like you can take care of yourself, but who knows what might happen to your companions?"

My hackles rose. And all I wanted to do was bare my teeth and rip out Pitor's throat. But this was a safe zone. *Relax, Michael. Don't show him the big bad wolf—not yet. You're just another player. Harmless.*

And besides, it will be all the sweeter if he doesn't see it coming.

"We will take our chances," Cara said, breaking the tension.

Pitor frowned. "You're going to let the merchant do the talking for you?" he asked, keeping his gaze fixed on me.

I shrugged; the gang leader clearly didn't realize the entirety of what Cara was. "She's the one paying the bills." Brushing past him, I stepped towards the wall of players at his back.

The group did not budge.

I glanced over my shoulder at Pitor. "Are you going to tell your people to move? Or are we going to find out what the Adjudicator thinks of this?"

Pitor's eyes narrowed. "You're a fool not to heed our warning, friend."

Saying nothing, I took another step forward.

Pitor waved his hands, and the players dispersed. With Shael and Cara following in my wake, I stepped through their ranks. I was certain now of the source of the tavern's troubles and eager to put an end to it.

But first, it was time for a long-delayed reunion with Saya.

The street beyond Pitor and his men was deserted. That was no accident, I knew. The blockade we'd just passed was responsible. My gaze slid to the opposite end of the street and picked out a second cordon.

I grimaced. Pitor's operation was no two-bit scheme. He was going to great pains to keep people away from the tavern. Why, though? Was it simple extortion?

"I'm guessing you know the owner," Shael said in a low voice as he hurried to my side.

Looking over my shoulder at the players behind us, I didn't answer immediately. They were still watching us with narrowed eyes and hands resting on weapons. Still, the stop at the blockade had not felt targeted, and Pitor hadn't seemed to realize I was the tavern's owner.

In fact, unless Saya had told someone, I doubted anyone but Kesh, Cara, and the gnome knew who actually owned the tavern. Well, Loken did, but he didn't really count, and whatever game Pitor was running, it was too crude to be the Shadow Power's doing.

Shael doesn't need to know the whole truth, not yet. Best to keep the knowledge contained.

I turned back to the bard. "In a manner of speaking," I replied obliquely.

"I thought so," he said. "That's why we're here, then? You got a job to protect the tavern?"

"Exactly, right." I hesitated. "But it's more than that. The tavernkeeper is a friend."

Shael glanced at me. "This is the gnome that fool was referring to?"

I nodded.

"Well, I'm eager to meet her then."

I studied the bard curiously. "Are you sure you want to entangle yourself in this? Your earlier, uhm... concerns about the sector were warranted. It was shortsighted of me not to explain how things stood in the valley before bringing you here. And now this." I stared at him soberly. "If you want to walk away, I understand."

"Nah, I don't." Shael chuckled. "And you don't have to tiptoe around my feelings, you know. What I experienced earlier was panic—plain and simple. In my defense, going from the safety of Nexus to an active warzone was a real shock to the system, that's all." He shook himself. "But I'm good now and will do whatever I can to help."

I glanced at Cara. She had remained silent throughout our exchange.

Feeling my gaze upon her, she said, "There is little those thugs can do to harm me; my protections are greater than they can hope to overcome." She paused. "And besides, part of my directive is to help you resolve matters here however I can."

"Thank you," I said, nodding gratefully to both of them. I had no plan yet for dealing with Pitor's gang, but I was sure with the pair's help, things would be that much easier.

We reached the tavern's entrance, and without pause, I hurried up the steps and into its depths.

✳ ✳ ✳

Stepping through the doors, Shael, Cara, and I entered a nearly deserted room. Just as I feared, the tavern was as empty as the streets outside had suggested it would be.

There were still a few patrons, but they numbered less than a double handful. The players, intent on not drawing attention to themselves, nursed their drinks and did not look up at our appearance. *They're scared*, I thought.

Our entrance did not go entirely unnoticed, though. Two waiters swung in our direction, a comical look of relief on their faces.

"Welcome to the Sleepy Inn," the first greeted, a tall blonde-haired girl who looked no older than twenty. Her face was all sharp angles, but her gray eyes were full of warmth.

The second waiter, a thin and gangly boy, strode silently beside the girl as she hurried towards us. His features bore a striking resemblance to the girl, and I suspected they were siblings.

Incongruously, both players were armed. Beneath the aprons wrapped around their bodies and the dirty rags draped over their shoulders, the youths wore chainmail armor and had weapons strapped at the hip.

Strange sorts of waiters, I thought, and promptly analyzed both.

The target is Teresa, a level 25 human blade devotee. She bears a Mark of Minor Light.

The target is Terence, a level 22 human swordsman. He bears a Mark of Minor Light.

My brows rose. "You two are *not* civilians?"

Teresa smiled. "We're not, but we get that question a lot. We're just helping out. The owner is our friend."

"Speaking of whom..." Terence glanced over his shoulder. "Saya!" he hollered. "We have guests."

"Coming!" a familiar voice called from somewhere above.

"Please, sit," Teresa said, ushering us towards one of the nearby empty tables. "Saya will be with you now."

Obligingly, Cara and Shael trailed after the girl. I followed more slowly, scanning the room.

The tavern's common area had grown, expanding into the kitchen at its rear and the smaller side rooms until it took up what I assumed to be the entirety of the ground floor. The inside was as gaily decorated as the outside, too. Flowerpots, magelights, and colorful baubles hung everywhere.

But despite the cheerful décor, there were plenty of signs that the tavern had fallen on hard times. Some of the flowers were withered, cracked pots were left unrepaired, and most of the magelights stayed unlit—not to mention the sea of empty tables.

My hands closed into fists. The trouble plaguing the tavern had to have been going on for a lot longer than a few weeks. *Just how long has Saya been forced to deal with Pitor and his ilk on her own?*

At the sound of soft footfalls coming down the stairs, my gaze jerked upward. A moment later, a short figure appeared.

It was Saya.

The gnome had aged. Lines creased her face, her hair was frayed, and bags rimmed her eyes. *She's changed,* I thought, wondering where the adventurous young soul who I'd rescued from the wyvern had vanished to.

The tavernkeeper's eyes drifted unseeing past me to alight on Shael and Cara, and some of the worry clouding her gaze lifted.

I winced, pained to see the hungry hope in her eyes at the appearance of new guests. *I should have come sooner,* I thought guiltily, never mind the impossibility of such. I took a step forward, and the gnome's gaze jerked back to me.

For a moment, Saya stared blankly, not recognizing me, then realization hit, and she gasped. Meeting her gaze, I smiled. "Hi, Saya. I've finally—"

Hurtling forward, she flung herself at me. "Michael!" she squealed, drawing the attention of everyone in the room.

I staggered backward, nearly bowled over. Indifferent to the spectacle we made, Saya hugged my legs tightly and buried her face in me.

"I knew you'd come," she cried, her voice muffled so that no one else could hear. Not that I thought Saya cared just then. She was trembling, and sobs of relief—at least I hoped it was relief— wracked her body.

I patted her back awkwardly. "I'm sorry it took me so long," I replied quietly. "I would've come sooner if possible."

Wordlessly, Saya squeezed me tighter.

Staying silent, I held her until she regained her composure. Finally, Saya stepped back and looked at me through reddened eyes. "How did you know we needed you?"

"I received your letters yesterday."

Saya's brows creased. "But I sent nothing yesterday."

I nodded. "It was a batch of old letters. The latest one mentioned the trouble you were having with—"

"Let me see it," Saya interrupted.

Silently, I handed her the missive in question.

Saya's frown deepened as she read the letter. "But I sent this weeks ago! Where did you get it?"

"Kesh gave it to me," I replied.

"But... But what about the other letters I sent since then? Did she not have them?"

I shook my head. "This was the last correspondence Kesh received. Your silence worried her enough to bring the matter to my attention." I hung my head. "Sadly, I myself have been out of contact with Kesh for the last few months. It was only two days ago that I saw her again."

Saya squeezed my arm. "What matters is that you're here now." Her face tightened. "But that merchant... I will have to do something about him," she whispered.

My eyes narrowed as I stared at the grim-faced tavernkeeper. The look
on Saya's face was not one I recognized, and it almost seemed as if she was
contemplating murder. What had happened to her in the intervening time to
make her so... bloodthirsty?

"Saya," I said softly.

Lost in her thoughts, the gnome did not look up.

"Saya," I repeated louder.

Finally, she met my gaze.

"Tell me what's happened," I said gently.

Saya stared at me wordlessly for a moment, then deflated, the bleakness
fading from her expression. "It's a long tale, Michael." She pulled me
towards the table where the others sat. "Come, you'll want to sit for this."

*　　*　　*

Saya insisted on serving us herself.

Shooing away her young waiters, she brought the food and drink and
refused to answer any questions until we'd eaten our fill. Gradually, the
attention of the other patrons drifted away, leaving us free to talk.

After the dishes were cleared away, Saya re-emerged from the first floor,
where I understood the kitchens and tavern offices had been relocated.
Seating herself at the table, she introduced herself.

"And who are your friends, Michael?" she asked.

I turned to the half-elf. "Shael here is a red minstrel from Nexus. He did
me a favor two years ago, and today I returned it by getting him out of the
city."

Saya bobbed her head in greeting, but I didn't miss the shrewd glint in
her eyes as she assessed the bard and, more particularly, his flute.

Shael bowed in his chair. "Nice to meet you, good lady. I admit when
Michael told me he had a job for me, this was not what I was expecting, but
you have a lovely place here, one that should be filled to the bursting every
night! I assure you we will see that happens. Mostly, though, I hope we will
become friends."

Ignoring the bard's expansive promise, I turned to Cara. "And this is
Cara, Kesh's agent. She's here to set up an emporium outlet and help as
necessary."

Cara inclined her head. "It's a pleasure, Saya."

"Likewise," the gnome replied. "I may never have met your mistress, but
I feel like I know her already. I learned a lot through our correspondences, so
much so that I've come to depend on her advice." She sighed. "Which is why
I found her silence this past month so difficult."

"Kesh is the wisest of merchants," Cara agreed. "And I believe she's
taken a liking to you, too." Amusement threaded her voice as she added,
"I've been given strict instructions to see you safe." She paused. "But more
to the point, now that I'm here, your communication can resume. I will act
as an intermediary for your messages."

Saya sat up, her face shining. "Thank you," she said fervently.

Before Cara could respond, I leaned forward across the table. "Right, now that the introductions are out of the way, tell me what's happened."

Saya's face darkened, and I could almost see the worry settle on her shoulders again.

I bit my lip, wishing I could take back my words. Why couldn't I have found a more tactful way of broaching the subject?

Saya's gaze drifted towards the open door. "You must've run into our persecutors on your way here ...?"

I nodded grimly. "Some player named Pitor stopped us for a *chat*."

"I know him well," Saya said thinly. "He is one of Yzark's underlings."

I frowned. "Yzark?"

Saya nodded. "He is the Marauder boss in charge of their operations in the sector." Her jaw tightened. "*He* is the one who has decided to target the tavern."

I leaned back in my chair. Saya's words implied that the efforts against the tavern were more extensive than I'd initially thought. *There is more going on here than I realized. My original assumptions may be wrong too.* "These... marauders, they are extorting you for money?"

Saya snorted. "I wish. They don't want money; they want the tavern."

"What?" I asked sharply.

Saya gestured to the street outside. "The whole point of all their harassment is to force me to sell."

The gnome stressed the word 'me' ever so slightly. I didn't think the others had noticed, but I took her point: the marauders believed Saya to be the tavern owner.

I nodded minutely in acknowledgment of her message, and Saya went on, "The Marauders want the tavern, but not for the reasons you'd assume." She paused. "They're not interested in the money it makes; they're after the building itself. The tavern is the largest structure in the safe zone, centrally located, and would make for an ideal base."

My eyes narrowed. "Base for what?"

"Controlling the sector."

I went still. "The Marauders are a *faction*?"

Saya nodded mutely.

I squeezed my eyes shut for a moment as the implications sunk in. "One large enough to challenge Tartar?"

I hadn't seen any evidence of the legions in the sector yet. Still, I couldn't believe Tartar or Captain Talon had abandoned the valley, not after all the trouble they'd already gone through to wrest control of it from the Awakened Dead.

To my surprise, Saya shook her head. "Far from it. Everything I've managed to learn about them suggests they're one of the smaller factions in the Game."

My face scrunched up in confusion. "Then, what makes them believe they can—"

"I think I know what's going on here," Shael interjected.

I turned to the bard. I'd almost forgotten about my two companions, so caught up had I become in Saya's explanation. "You do?"

He nodded. "I've heard of the Marauders. They're a Shadow faction led by the Power Kalin. It's true they are a minor faction, but they have a reputation for punching above their weight." He met my gaze. "They're power brokers."

I stared at him blankly.

"What the bard means," Cara said, "is that factions like the Marauders—and they're not the only ones—seek out war-torn sectors where the bigger factions have failed to score a decisive victory and insert themselves as middlemen."

Shael nodded. "It's when a resource—be it a mine, dungeon, or even a sector—is too important for one of the big guys to let another control that the Marauders come into play. They swoop in, take ownership, then *sell* access to whoever wants it." His lips twisted in disgust. "They don't care who they grant access to—so long as they pay."

I digested his words. *Power brokers, indeed.* "And the other factions allow this?"

Shael shrugged. "What choice do they have? The Marauders may be vultures, but they still serve a valuable function. It's either allow someone unimportant like the Marauders to control this sector or—"

"—go to all-out war," I finished for him grimly.

"Exactly," Shael replied. "If the major factions bring their full might to play in this sector, it would quickly be turned into a wasteland."

"Thereby destroying the very thing they sought to possess," I murmured. "That implies..." I glanced at Saya. "Has the war in this sector come to a standstill?"

Her lips turned down. "That may be overstating the situation. Skirmishes occur between the factions daily." She paused. "But I suppose there haven't been any big battles of late, and none of the factions appear close to gaining control of the sector. Since the Howlers' defenses were destroyed, no one has managed to refortify the village."

I nodded absently, recalling that controlling access to the safe zone was one of the key requirements for taking ownership of the sector.

"Just which factions are we talking about?" Shael asked curiously. "I heard Tartar mentioned, but not who the other players are."

"Three Powers have armies in the sector," Saya replied. Raising her hand, she ticked them off on her fingers. "Tartar. Loken. Muriel."

I frowned. That Tartar was still here did not surprise me. But that Loken had brought a warband into the valley caught me by surprise. It was unlike the trickster to act so directly. "Loken has an army here? And who is Muriel?"

"He does," Saya said. "His forces are led by an envoy. I've never seen her personally, but the rumors of her are too prevalent to ignore. As for Muriel, she is a major Power of Light and the one responsible for prosecuting the war on their behalf."

"Muriel?" I mused. "Not Arinna?"

Saya stared at me blankly. "Arinna? Why would she have an interest in this sector?"

I wave aside a question. "Not important. What happened to Ishita and Erebus? Have they abandoned the valley?"

"Not entirely," Saya replied. "The Awakened Dead have retreated to the dungeon. For the moment, they only seem interested in holding its entrance secure."

Well, that was a bit of good news, at least and meant I wouldn't have to worry about tripping over Ishita's followers. "I noticed you didn't list Kalin as one of the contesting Powers," I said after a moment.

"Because he isn't," Saya said. "While the Marauders do have a force present in the sector, they don't have the numbers the big three do. Kalin has avoided conflict with the others, and they are just as content to ignore him." She grimaced. "Despite my pleading, neither Loken, Tartar, nor Muriel's people are willing to step in to protect the tavern."

"I see," I said and bowed my head to think. In some ways, the situation in the valley mirrored the one of two years ago. Then, it had been the goblin tribes fighting for control of the sector; now, it was the Powers themselves. Somehow, though, I didn't think my previous tactics would work.

Still, there must be some way to see Saya and the tavern through this. Not to mention the dire wolves. I'd steadfastly not been thinking about them. Surviving in the war-torn valley, one rife with players, could not be easy for the pack.

I raised my head. "You've painted a bleak picture, Saya, but I'm sure there must be a way to extricate the tavern from this mess. First, though, I need you to recall every last detail about all *five* forces in the valley." I held her gaze to make sure she understood. "Tell me everything and leave nothing out."

The gnome took a deep breath. "Alright. Then, to begin with, you'll want to know about..."

CHAPTER 272: VALLEY IN DISTRESS

Saya spoke for hours, detailing everything she knew about the armies in the valley.

It turned out Captain Talon was still present in the region. He and his legion were entrenched in the valley's center, allowing the tartans to respond to threats to the village in the south *and* strike at the dungeon to the north.

For now, the Awakened Dead retained enough strength to bar any of the other forces in the valley from entering the nether portal, although rumor had it that Tartar had also launched a secondary attack against Erebus from the Nethersphere itself. The news made me smile. The Awakened Dead seemed to be in all sorts of trouble, and I dearly hoped they failed to survive.

The Dark's main opposition in the sector was Muriel. Cara and Shael described her as a major player in the Game. For reasons I didn't understand, the Unity Council—Light's governing body—had assigned her responsibility for capturing sector 12,560.

Despite being the newest entrant in the valley, Muriel had brought the largest force to bear. Her army grew daily and already outnumbered the combined might of Tartar and Loken. She, too, had encamped her people in the valley's center and, other than for the occasional foray north or south, seemed content to wait until she was strong enough to overwhelm her foes with numbers alone.

Loken's army was the smallest of the trio and, as far as anyone could tell, was made up entirely of archers and light infantry. Shadow frequently raided the armies of Dark and Light, but the attacks amounted to little more than probes and feints. For now, at least, Loken seemed unwilling to commit to a pitched battle.

Perhaps unsurprisingly, given the size of Loken's army, his envoy had eschewed the valley's center for the western mountain slopes. In fact, my first thought upon hearing of it was that they were using the dead wyvern mother's cave network as their hideout.

The most interesting bit of information Saya shared, though, concerned Loken's envoy. Unlike her Light and Dark counterparts, the trickster's commander did not walk openly, and no one knew her true identity. Misdirection, guile, and illusions seemed to be her modus operandi.

The envoy did not appear averse to taking the field herself. She often struck without forewarning and disappeared before reinforcements could arrive. And while her attacks were little more than pinpricks, she was a definite thorn in the side of Light and Dark. Intrigued, I made a mental note to learn more about the mysterious envoy if I could.

It might have seemed passing strange that none of the three armies had chosen to entrench themselves around the village—it was the key to owning the sector, after all—but until the sector was claimed, the village was as much a threat to an occupying force as it was a safe haven.

Anyone could portal into the safe zone and in whatever numbers they wished, which meant an army encamped near the village would be exposed to attacks from the rear—the safe zone—*and* from the other forces already in the valley. It made claiming the sector a strategic nightmare.

Eventually, of course, someone would move in to control the village, but that would likely only occur *after* they'd dealt with the other threats in the valley.

The three armies—four if you counted the Awakened Dead in the dungeon—complicated matters in the valley enough on their own, but unfortunately, there were other forces to contend with, too.

Rumors of the purported wealth of the sector and its dungeons had spread far, attracting the Game's worst elements, and a host of smaller factions—the Marauders included—had entered the valley, seeking to eke out what advantage they could.

As Saya relayed her tale, my worry grew exponentially. As ugly a picture as the gnome painted, she was shielded from much of the chaos in the safe zone. It was the wolves who'd bear the brunt of the danger.

Damnation, I must check on them—and soon.

I was sure Duggar would've taken the pack into hiding again, but the risk of discovery was high with so many players in the valley. *One problem at a time.*

"What of the goblin tribes?" I asked as Saya finally ran down.

"The Red Rats have retreated into the dungeon with Erebus' people. The Howlers remain with Talon, supplementing his legion. The last I heard, they've increased their numbers in the valley, bringing in more troops from their home sector."

I wondered if Hyek was still alive and what he'd make of me now, but it was only a bit of idle speculation; I had no intention of tangling with the goblins or Talon's legions again.

"You said the Marauders' camp is nearby," I said, turning to the next matter. According to Saya's sources, the Marauders showed no interest in the dungeon to the north and didn't stray far from the village. "Why are the other factions letting them remain so close?"

"I don't think they see the Marauders as a threat," Saya said. "Mostly, I believe that's because the Marauders don't have the numbers to retain control of the safe zone."

"How many players did the Marauders bring into the sector?" Cara asked, voicing a rare question.

Saya shrugged. "I'm not sure. But at a guess, five hundred."

Cara glanced at me. "That will not be enough. To claim a sector requires a controlling force of at least one thousand."

I nodded. Captain Talon had told me much the same on my previous visit to the sector. "Then confirming the Marauders' numbers will be one of our priorities." Before anyone could ask how I proposed doing that, I moved the conversation along. "In your last letter to Kesh," I said, looking at Saya, "you mentioned 'taking steps' to protect the tavern. What did you do?"

"I hired mercenaries to escort customers into and out of the safe zone." She grimaced. "That did not pan out so well."

"What happened?" I asked.

"The Marauders bribed them," she said. "And those that couldn't be bribed, they killed."

"I see," I muttered. "And that merchant you mentioned earlier, am I correct in assuming he is the one Kesh appointed to relay your messages?"

After a sideways glance at Cara, Saya nodded.

"When last did you speak to him?" I asked.

"Three days ago," Saya replied in a clipped tone. "He *assured* me Kesh was receiving my missives and *claimed* to have no idea why she wasn't responding." She growled unhappily. "Obviously, he lied on both accounts. I plan on paying him a visit tonight."

I didn't think that would be a good idea and turned to Cara, believing her to be the better choice, but Shael spoke before I could.

"Let me talk to him," he said.

Saya and I shot the bard curious glances.

Seeing our expressions, Shael grinned. "You want to know why the merchant betrayed Kesh, who paid him, and how much, right?"

I rubbed my lips. "Hmm... yes."

"Then leave it to me to find out," he replied. "No offense to the ladies, but gathering information is part of what I do best." His grin widened. "And besides, I have a few tricks up my sleeve for winning over a mark's confidence."

He was talking about his deception abilities, I realized. Had he ever used them on me?

"Alright," I said before I could ponder the question too deeply—I *didn't* want to know. "The merchant is all yours."

Saya opened her mouth, but I waved aside her impending objection. "You have enough to worry about here. Let Shael handle the merchant."

Closing her mouth, she nodded reluctantly. "You have a plan?"

"Maybe," I said. "Getting the tavern's customers back is another priority." I bowed my head to think for a moment. "I want you to hire more mercenaries."

Saya stared at me. "Why? Because it worked so well last time?"

I shook my head, ignoring her sarcasm. "No, this time, keep them in the safe zone. The Marauders are using the blockades as a show of force. Nothing is stopping us from doing the same. Have the mercenaries wear badges bearing the Sleepy Inn's insignia and instruct them to gather everywhere in the village that the Marauders do. At the very least, it will show Yzark's people we aren't intimidated. And if we are lucky, the mercenaries' presence will comfort the tavern's patrons enough that they will overlook the Marauders' threats."

"That makes sense," Saya conceded. "But what about the ambushes outside the village?"

"*I'll* put a stop to that," I replied grimly.

Wisely, she didn't ask how.

"Another thing," I said after reflecting on the matter further, "make sure to source the mercenaries from the bounty hunters guild."

"The guild?" Saya asked dubiously. "I don't think they have many members in the sector. It might be better to use one of the smaller factions."

"No, it has to be the guild," I said, growing more enamored of the idea the longer I considered it. This would be an ideal test of their trustworthiness. "Reach out to the guild's headquarters in Nexus if you have to. Kesh can help with that." I glanced at Cara, and she nodded in confirmation. "Liaise directly with a player named Hannah. She is the guild's customer liaison and will help with the necessary arrangements."

"I'll do so," Saya said, "but, on its own, a display of strength will not be enough to bring back the customers." She stared directly at Shael. "We will need something more."

The bard took the hint. "I'm at your service, good lady," he said, flourishing his flute. "Fortunately, music is the *other* part of what I do best."

"Thank you, Shael," Saya said warmly.

"Perfect," I said. That took care of one of my companions. I turned to Cara, but she seemed to divine my thoughts before I could speak.

"I can delay securing a premise for the emporium for a few days," she said. "That is assuming I can even find one." She glanced at Saya. "In the meantime, do I have your permission to begin trading from the tavern?"

Saya brightened considerably as she realized what Cara was suggesting. "Of course! And I'll make sure everyone knows that the Sleepy Inn not only has a bard again, but it's also playing host to Nexus' most famous merchant." She grinned. "If those two things don't bring the tavern's patrons back, nothing will!"

✳ ✳ ✳

With Cara and Shael's immediate plans decided upon, Saya waved Terence and Teresa over to show the pair to their rooms. After the four left, Saya and I sat alone at the table in companionable silence.

"Thank you," the gnome said softly.

I looked up at her in surprise. "What for?"

"This," she said, spreading her hands to encompass me, the tavern, and the departing Shael and Cara. "I was at a loss about what to do. I had no one to turn to. Oh, Teresa and Terence helped as much as they could, but the pair are young and in desperate need of help themselves. On top of that, Kesh wasn't answering my letters, the mercenaries I recruited betrayed me, and customers were dying." She sighed. "It felt as if it was all spinning out of control." She looked at me through bright eyes. "But now, I feel as if there is hope for the tavern again."

"It's not your fault, you know," I said quietly, responding to the underlying emotion behind her words. "You were alone and without resources."

"I should have done better," Saya replied, hanging her head.

I shrugged. "So should have I."

She raised her head to stare at me mutely.

"I left you here alone." *And the wolves too.* "I should've planned better, anticipated, if not this, then something like it." I shook my head. "The war was inevitable. I should have foreseen the consequences."

"It's not—" Saya began.

"—my fault," I finished for her. I held her gaze. "Nor is it yours."

Saya smiled tremulously, getting what I was driving at, and we lapsed into silence again, each lost in our thoughts.

"You know you haven't said what your own plans are," she said eventually.

I looked up at her. "I plan on paying the Marauders a visit," I said, not elaborating further.

"I thought as much," Saya said before glancing out the open door. The day was still young. "You will wait for nightfall?"

I nodded.

"Be careful, Michael. The Marauders may be brutes, but they are not stupid. Their camp will be well-guarded."

"I won't underestimate them," I promised. Motion at the stairs drew my eye; the young waiters were returning. Seeking an opportunity to change the topic, I jerked my head towards the pair. "What's their story?"

Saya followed my gaze. "Teresa and Terence are twins. They arrived in the valley as part of a larger group. Treasure hunters, no less. Somehow, the pair convinced the company leader to take them on as apprentices. Sadly, the entire group was killed." She smiled grimly. "Not once, but multiple times. To no one's surprise, the company disbanded after that, and those that could fled the sector. The twins were not amongst them."

I winced. "They couldn't leave?"

"They had no money and nowhere to go." Saya sighed. "Their story, so like mine, spoke to me, so I gave them a place to stay. They've been grateful for the work—and coin—and even though they're not civilians, they've done their best to help."

"You trust them?" I asked.

"Completely," she replied.

"That's good," I said, studying the twins thoughtfully as they moved about the tables, checking on the other patrons. The pair's gear was basic, and they had no levels to speak of. But that was not necessarily a bad thing.

They likely haven't acquired their third or even second Class yet.

It was food for thought, but I had more important things on my mind right now.

I rose to my feet. "You had best show me to my room, Saya. I have a long night ahead of me, and I should get what rest I can before then."

I awoke a few hours later.

Rising from my bed, I walked over to the shuttered window and peered outside. Just as I thought, night had fallen, and I spent a moment studying the village below. At my request, Saya had given me a room on the top floor of the tavern, leaving me with an unobstructed view of the village.

Everywhere I looked, there were buildings bathed in light and scores of players hurrying about. It was a reminder — if I needed one — that the wolves' valley was no longer the backwater it had been during my last sojourn.

Picking up my backpack and weapons, I made my way to the tavern's ground floor. It promised to be a long night, and a hearty meal would not go amiss.

The sounds of gentle music floated up as I entered the common room. *Shael*, I thought. A quick count of the patrons revealed that they had doubled from earlier in the day. The tavern was still a far cry from full, but already things were improving.

Glancing at the small stage at the back of the room, I waved to the bard. Seated on a stool and playing his flute with a contented expression, he nodded back without interrupting the flow of music. I smiled. I'd made the right decision in bringing him along.

Turning around, I surveyed the room. The twins were stationed behind the bar, but of Saya and Cara, there was no sign. The patrons, themselves, were captivated by the music and gave Shael their full attention.

Or nearly all did.

Four men sitting at a corner table were ignoring the music entirely. My smile faded. That was not the only thing that marked them as different from the other patrons either. All four bristled with weapons. Nor were they doing anything to avoid attention. In fact, they stared straight at me.

More trouble? I wondered, stilling.

The oldest of the four, a grizzled dwarf with scars running down his arms and gray in his plaited beard, rose to face me. "You Michael?" he yelled over the music.

Scowling, some of the patrons turned to shush him but, on seeing the dwarf's expression, quickly looked away. They were not the only ones to react. On my left, I sensed the twins leave the bar. Like me, they suspected trouble, but unlike me, they were drawing their weapons.

Idiots! What are they thinking?

I shook my head sharply at the pair. This was a safe zone. Threatening another player was a surefire way to get yourself killed, and besides, the four at the table looked like they would eat the two alive.

Reluctantly the siblings re-sheathed their weapons but refused to take their gazes off the newcomers.

The exchange did not go unnoticed by the dwarf. "Get lost, kids," he growled, again with no regard for who heard. "This is a conversation for adults." Drawing out an empty chair, he plunked it back down and scowled at me. "You need an engraved invite or what?"

On the stage, the music missed a bit, and turning towards it, I saw Shael look at me questioningly. "Keep playing," I mouthed in response. Whatever this was, it was better I handled it alone.

Ignoring the patrons' shooting glances and casting a second warning glance at the twins, I strode across the room and, with a nonchalance that was not entirely feigned, sat in the chair the dwarf had pulled out.

All four newcomers stared at me. Avoiding their hard gazes, I studied them in turn. *Newcomers*, I mused, *is an apt term for them.* Something about their demeanor led me to believe they'd just arrived in the sector.

So, how do they know who I am already?

The dwarf to my right was dressed in scaled leather armor that left his bulging biceps uncovered. Two long-handled warhammers were strapped across his back, and judging from the size of his arms, the dwarf wielded each one-handed.

To my left was a figure wrapped in cloth from head to foot, leaving only his eyes showing. If not for his garments being jet-black instead of bright green, I would've mistaken him for a mantis.

Two armor-clad figures sat across me. One was an orc, the other, a human, but that was the only difference between the pair. Their gear was identical. Their armor was the same shade of gray, they carried the same assortment of weapons, and even the inscriptions engraved on the handles of their broadswords were indistinguishable from one another.

Huh. Strange party.

"You don't talk much, do you?" the dwarf drawled.

I let my gaze drift to him. "I'm still waiting for you to introduce yourselves."

One corner of the dwarf's mouth twitched. Was that a smile?

"I'm Beorin." He pointed a fat finger to my left. "That's Snake." He waved at the other two across the table. "And those two clowns are Moarg and Mauser." He slapped both hands down on the table hard enough to cause it to jump. "There. Now we're all caught up. That make you feel better?"

Ignoring his tone, I asked, "Who sent you?" It was clear to me someone had. What I wasn't sure yet, was for what purpose.

Beorin pulled out a slim rectangular shape and laid it on the table. He nodded to the others, and they did the same. Glancing down, I instantly recognized the four cards.

They were BHG IDs.

"I'm a senior member of the guild," Beorin added, "and these laggards are part of my squad."

Snake snorted but didn't dispute the dwarf's words.

"I see," I said, feeling some of my tension ease. The four were not assassins as I'd first assumed. I knew the IDs could not be faked, but it didn't pay to be careless. Reaching out with my will, I analyzed them.

The target is Beorin, a level 181 hammer monk and dwarf.
The target is Snake, a level 172 fiend slayer and dark elf.
The target is Moarg, a level 155 armsmaster and orc.

The target is Mauser, a level 155 armsmaster and human.

"Satisfied?" Beorin asked, clearly having felt my inspection.

I nodded. "You appear to be what you say. Why are you here?"

He guffawed. "You don't know? Hannah sent us, of course."

I blinked in surprise. It couldn't have been more than a few hours since she'd received my request. "That was fast."

"The lass was always quick on the draw," the dwarf replied, taking a sip from his tankard. "More to the point, she told me the guild may require your services shortly." He belched loudly. "Until then, I'm to do what I can to keep you alive."

I raised an eyebrow. "You're bodyguards?"

"Nothing of the sort!" Beorin retorted. "We'll do the job your factor—" he meant Kesh—"paid us for, but nothing stops us from helping out a fellow guild member in our free time, eh?"

I eyed the four skeptically, not buying it. Saying nothing, the other three stared back at me impassively. I couldn't get a read on them, but they seemed to have scant interest in the conversation and appeared content to let their squad leader do the talking.

Beorin took another long draw from his tankard. "Speaking of the job— it true that all you want us to do is stand around town, looking tough?"

"In a nutshell, yes."

Beorin stared at me for a moment, then shrugged. "It's your coin." He sipped his drink again. "Though for the amount you're paying, if that's all you want, you're a rich fool indeed," he muttered under his breath.

I was sure the dwarf hadn't intended on me hearing him, but he had not accounted for my wolf-like hearing. "Are there only four of you?"

Beorin shook his head. "We're just the advanced party. The rest of your bodies will get here tomorrow."

"How many?"

"Two, maybe three score hunters."

I whistled softly, amazed anew by Hannah's efficiency. Sixty mercenaries were more than I expected the guild to supply on short notice. "Excellent. You've met Saya?"

"The little gnome? Yeah."

"You will report directly to her and follow her orders. To the letter," I said, stressing the last bit.

"No problemo," Beorin replied casually. "Any other instructions?"

"Yes," I murmured, thinking of the dwarf's earlier words. "Rich, I may be, but perhaps not as foolish as you believe. There *is* something else you can do for me."

Mid-drink, Beorin paused. Setting down his tankard, he looked at me with more cunning than his otherwise bluff exterior had suggested. "Go on," he said slowly.

I smiled. The dwarf was not quite as simple as he was trying to make out. "It concerns the Marauders. I may need your squad to detain a few of them tonight."

He eyed me askance. "Detain how?"

"Stop them from leaving the safe zone."

Beorin snorted. "Lad, I'm not sure if you noticed, but there are only four of us, and from what I've heard, there are a damn sight more Marauders than that around. How do you expect—"

I cut him off. "They will be in newbie clothes. Unarmed and unarmored."

"That so?" The dwarf's eyes narrowed, and I could almost feel him reassessing me. "You're planning on doing some killing tonight?"

I shrugged. "I might."

Beorin grinned. "You're going to the Marauder's camp, aren't you?"

He's a shrewd one. Dangerous too. "Perhaps," I replied casually.

"Want some company?" Beorin asked. "The four of us have done a bit of night raiding a time or two ourselves. We could—"

"No, thank you," I said, politely—but firmly—declining his offer. Beorin's squad might look handy to have around in a fight, but I didn't know them.

Beorin laughed, not offended by my refusal. "Alright, suit yourself."

"Good, that's settled then," I said and made to rise.

"They told me about you, you know," he said abruptly. "Said you killed a whole bunch of mantises."

I sat back down. "Who did? Hannah?"

Beorin sniffed. "Not Han; she won't tattle on clients. Eyes was the one. You know what else he said?"

I waited.

"That you're damnably stubborn, arrogant, and reckless."

I rolled my eyes. "Look, if you don't want to do what I ask, that's fine, but I can do without the—"

"Eyes *also* said you're bloody dangerous and crafty to boot. That true?"

I sighed, tiring of the conversation. "Who the hell knows?"

Beorin grinned. "Can't argue with a response like that. Fine, we'll do it."

I blinked. "What?"

"You go out and have fun, laddie. And don't worry about any of your slaughtered sheep returning to their camp. We'll keep them nice and tender and waiting for you."

"Uh... thanks," I said and beat a hasty retreat before the dwarf could restart the conversation.

∗　∗　∗

Unfortunately, the bounty hunters weren't the only ones to accost me. No sooner had I sat down at a nearby table, hoping for a quiet meal, than I was interrupted again.

This time by the twins.

"What did they want?" Teresa whispered as the pair slipped uninvited into the chairs across from me.

Folding my arms, I glared at her. "*I* want supper."

Teresa waved a hand airily. "It's on the way." She glanced over her shoulder at the bounty hunters' table. Nursing their drinks, the four did not look over.

"Saya said they're bounty hunters," Teresa said. "That true?"

Before I could respond, Terence chipped in. "You think they'll apprentice us?"

"No," I replied succinctly.

The pair exchanged puzzled glances, no doubt confused by who I was answering. I almost smiled but managed to keep my scowl in place. I did *not* want to encourage them to linger.

Unfortunately, the pair were not so easily daunted. "Saya has told us a lot about you," Teresa said, changing tack without skipping a beat.

I said nothing.

"We want to come with you," Terence added.

That drew my attention. Did everyone know where I was going? "I'm not going anywhere," I said mildly.

"Your backpack suggests otherwise," he replied promptly. "You wouldn't have it with you unless you planned to venture out. We don't care wherever it is you're going; we just want to tag along."

I snorted. "You two don't have enough levels under your belt. It's too—"

"From what Saya tells us," Teresa cut in, "you were much the same level when you first entered this sector."

I glanced at her. "The valley was a very different place then. Now it's a war zone. You will be in—"

"We know all about how dangerous the valley is," Terence said, rolling his eyes. "We've died out there twice already."

I stared at him. "Twice? How many lives do you have remaining?"

"Idiot," Teresa hissed at her twin. "Why'd you have to tell him that?"

That answered my question. "You two are on your last lives," I accused, "*and* you still want to leave the village—at night?"

How reckless could they be?

Teresa scowled. "Look, we're both more than grateful for all Saya's help, but sitting here, we're not gaining any levels. It will always be too dangerous for us to venture out. Day or night." She bit her lip. "But if *you* help us—just for a few levels, mind you—we'll take it from there."

I shook my head. "I won't be responsible for you two dying. What I attempt is too—"

"Just once," Terence said, staring at me beseechingly. "We won't bother you again. Promise."

I was drearily tired of being interrupted, but I let the interruption go unremarked.

"Take us," Teresa pleaded.

"No."

The girl clenched her hands into fists. "Why?"

I held back a sigh. The twins didn't seem like they were going to give up, and once more, I recalled how much I needed allies to rebuild House Wolf. But tonight's work was too grim for the pair. They deserved a chance, though, and my help, too, if only to repay the debt I owed them for aiding Saya.

"What if we—" Terence began.

I held up my hand. "You two can't accompany me, not tonight. But I *will* take you out hunting tomorrow."

The twins' eyes lit up. "We've your word on it?" Teresa asked.

"You do," I said, wondering what I'd gotten myself into. "Now scat and let me eat in peace," I added, seeing my food approach.

Chapter 274: Wolf on the Prowl

After a satisfying, if rushed, meal, I headed back to my room. There was a reason I'd asked for a room on the top floor. It gave me easy access to the roof in case I needed to make a quick exit.

Putting out the chamber's only magelight, I opened the shutters and peeked out. My room overlooked the tavern's main entrance. My original plan had been to leave through the front door, but I'd already attracted too much notice.

Best to avoid further attention.

Peering left and right, I studied the street and spotted Pitor. The same two groups of thugs kept watch on the tavern, but I was sure they would leave soon. From what Saya told me, I knew the Marauders manning the blockade changed shifts twice daily.

Once they left, I would follow.

Equipping my cat claws, I ducked out the window and climbed to the roof, no more than another blotch of darkness in the night. The tavern's ground-floor exits were being watched, but I was sure no one would think to surveil the roof itself.

Pulling myself onto the roof, I ran silently across its tiled surface and peered at the adjacent building. It was a smaller structure, only three stories high, and was separated from the tavern by a road, but the gap was easy enough to ford with windborne. Calculating my trajectory, I materialized a solid ramp of air and slid down to the neighboring building.

I touched down lightly with nary a sound.

Staying crouched, I extended my senses and waited to see if anyone had noticed. No alarms were raised. Smiling tightly, I made my way to the opposite end of the building and, using my clawed gloves, descended to the street below.

✴ ✴ ✴

Slipping out of the safe zone was a trivial matter.

The walls around the village had been destroyed, and no one bothered keeping watch on the players streaming in and out any longer. Reaching the treeline, I cloaked myself in shadow and cast facial disguise, taking the guise of an unremarkable human fighter.

Even at this hour, players still moved through the forest. Most belonged to companies of soldiers, returning to the safe zone to take shelter for the night. Despite the changes in the valley, players remained afraid of the darkness, although this time around, the monsters they feared were other players.

Scaling a tall tree on the village's northwest perimeter, I turned about to keep watch on players exiting the safe zone. Saya hadn't been able to get the exact location of the Marauder's encampment. If I had to search for it myself,

I knew it would take me the greater part of the night to find. Much easier, I decided, to follow my marks to my destination.

An hour later, as the stream of incoming players slowed to a trickle, my quarries appeared—two dozen of them, to be precise. Shaking myself alert, I carefully examined the faces of the approaching Marauders. Sadly, Pitor was not among them.

It's the group from the other blockade, I thought.

Pitor's team could not be far behind, but while I'd been relishing the opportunity to silence the human warrior, one group of Marauders was as good as another.

Rising into a half-crouch, I tiptoed across the tree bough, stalking my prey from above.

✳　✳　✳

The Marauder team headed dead west, traveling parallel to the mountain slopes. Tracking them from high above in the trees, I went unnoticed.

For thirty minutes, I did nothing but watch and analyze my foes. The group consisted of a mix of spellcasters, fighters, and rangers—a *substantial* number of rangers, which was perhaps unsurprising given the environment the Marauders were operating in. Best of all, though, every player's level was below my own—a welcome change from my usual encounters.

The main body of fifteen traveled in a tight-knit group under a half-dozen magelights while the nine rangers formed a large screen around them. But surprisingly, none of the party's scouts took to the trees. *That will make this easier.*

Unfurling my mindsight, I scanned the surroundings again. This time around, I detected no other players nearby except the Marauders. Satisfied we'd ventured far enough from the village not to run into anyone else, I cast my buffs.

Your Dexterity has increased by +8 ranks for 20 minutes.
You have gained an encumbrance aura for 10 minutes.
You have trigger-cast quick mend.
You have cast facial disguise. Duration: 1 hour.

I peered down through the branches one last time. The column of warriors and spellcasters, laughing and joking amongst themselves, were still oblivious to my presence. *Time to act,* I decided and dropped back to wait for the rearmost scouts.

The rangers were traveling in pairs, two on each flank, except at the front, where there were three. With my mindsight opened, I sensed the mindglows of the scouts guarding the party's backtrail before I saw them. *Their stealth is quite good,* I thought grudgingly as I waited for the pair to draw closer.

You have detected 2 hostile entities.
Sunchild is no longer hidden! Krato is no longer hidden!
Two hostile entities have failed to detect you!

The scouts were almost directly beneath me now, and the main body had marched out of sight. Spinning psi, I slipped tendrils of will into the minds of both players.

You have cast slaysight. You have hidden your presence from 2 of 2 targets for 10 seconds.

Perfect, I thought as the spell went off without a hitch. Lowering myself off the tree branch, I dropped to the forest floor and landed with a soft thud.

The first scout froze. "You hear that?" Sunchild whispered.

Krato broke off from scanning the surroundings to frown at his partner. "Hear what?"

I was directly in front of the pair—less than two yards away, in fact—but blinded by slaysight, they didn't see me. Drawing my blades silently, I rose to my feet.

"I swear I heard a—" Sunchild began.

Darting forward, I rammed ebonheart through his throat, stopping him short.

You have killed Sunchild with a fatal blow.

Krato gaped at the sudden appearance of the bloody hole in his companion. His shock lasted only a heartbeat, though. Recovering, the ranger whipped his head back and forth and grabbed for the weapon at his waist.

He didn't stand a chance.

Flowing deftly around the scout, I plunged both my blades through his back, ending his life as abruptly as I had his partner's.

You have killed Krato with a fatal blow.

Letting the corpse drop at my feet, I listened intently. The main column of Marauders had not broken off their advance, nor did I hear any other scouts approaching.

My kills had gone unnoticed.

Sheathing my blades, I looted the bodies, then took off in a curving run south.

It was time to take out the other scouts.

✳   ✳   ✳

You have killed Heron.
You have killed Lilith.
You have …

You have acquired 7 caches of miscellaneous items.
You have reached level 136.
Your shortswords has increased to level 121 and reached rank 12.
Your two weapon fighting has increased to level 112 and reached rank 11.
Your telepathy has increased to level 111 and reached rank 11.

Taking out the other rangers was almost child's play. Using a combination of charm, slaysight, and shadow blink, I'd cut a deadly arc around the party, eliminating their scouts one by one.

Now, it was finally time to deal with the rest of the Marauder team. Perched on a tree and directly in their line of march, I waited for the main column to appear in the clearing below.

"... think I stand a chance?"

"Don't be daft! Geta will eat you alive."

"Yeah, man, listen to Mel. That wench likes a man with a little more meat on his bones."

"Ask Turton. He *knows* exactly what I'm..."

My lips twitched upward. The spellcasters and fighters appeared none the wiser of their companions' fate. *Dumb and happy.* And coming to me like lambs to the slaughter.

Just the way I planned.

Drawing upon my psi, I sent tendrils of my will rushing into the center of the enemy column, simultaneously breaching the mental defenses of eight players.

You have cast mass charm. You have charmed 8 of 10 targets for 20 seconds. Two players have passed a mental resistance check.

Hosen has detected your mental intrusion!

Ah well, I thought as two Marauders resisted my attempted bewitching. I supposed another perfect result was too much to hope for, but eight minions could manage the job as well as ten.

Even if one of the Marauders had been alerted.

Hosen's head swung back and forth. He hadn't spotted me, but he clearly sensed something amiss. "Ambush!" the priest yelled. "Draw your weapons!"

The orc at the front of the column swung about and frowned. "What are you on about now, Hosen? There's no one—"

I was still choosing individual targets for each of my charmed minions to assault, but in the wake of the priest's warning, I realized I couldn't afford to be picky.

"*Attack,*" I whispered.

Eight players drew their weapons and threw themselves at their former companions, slashing with blades, chopping with axes, or unleashing their magic with staffs and wands.

It was glorious mayhem.

Blood spurted. Limbs were hacked off. Entrails were spilled. Fireballs roared to life. Ice expanded underfoot. Roots thrust up from the ground.

And through it all, players died.

Your minions have killed Turton.

Your minions have injured Melancholy.

Your minions have injured...

...

"What are you fools doing!" the orc roared. He still hadn't realized what was happening. "Stop this at once!"

"I told you, we are under attack," Hosen shouted from inside a dull bubble of ash. "There's a psionic lurking nearby."

My eyes narrowed, having no trouble overhearing the two above the clash of blades and spells. The priest was more perceptive than I anticipated. *I've got to do something about him.*

That was easier said than done, though. Hosen was already shielded and surrounded by five other unaffected and angry players—one had died already. But there was no reason for me to risk myself in melee combat. Shrouded in the trees, I had the upper hand.

I'll do this from afar, I decided and formed two astral daggers in my hands.

"Well, find him then!" the orc bellowed.

"On it already," Hosen snapped back. A moment later, a white star exploded in the clearing. Ducking my head, I shielded my eyes from the harsh light.

Unfortunately, the priest's casting was more than a simple light spell.

Hosen has cast seeking star of shadow.

You have failed a magical resistance check! You are <u>**shadow touched**</u>**. Duration: 60 seconds. For the length of the debuff, you cannot hide from any player bearing a Mark of Shadow.**

You are no longer hidden.

Raising his hand, Hosen pointed unerringly at me. "There he is!"

"Damn," I muttered, letting the half-summoned astral blades fade away. This was *not* part of the plan. I had not intended on letting the Marauders catch sight of me, not when I could use mass charm to whittle them down from the shadows. A faceless demon in the woods was much scarier than a foe to whom you could put a face.

But now, I had a choice: run or fight.

"Well done," the orc crowed, spinning around to glare at me. "Now dispel his casting, and let's kill the pest!"

I fight, I decided my face hardening.

My overarching plan for dealing with the Marauders required them to fear me, and that would not happen if I fled with my tail between my legs at the first sign of trouble.

Drawing psi, I stepped through the aether and into the chaos raging in the clearing.

CHAPTER 275: A TEAM LEAD ASTRAY

My first target, of course, was Hosen.

Disregarding the battling players about me, I materialized behind the priest' cloudy gray shield.

You have teleported 25 yards.

My blades a blur, I struck at him supernaturally fast.

You have cast whirlwind and piercing strike.
Your target's shield has blocked your attacks.

I failed to get through with my initial assault, but the priest's shield would give away—eventually. I struck again, bringing ebonheart down in a blow that would've cleaved Hosen in two had it connected.

Your target's shield has blocked your attack.

The priest spun around, hands spread and palms out, but there was no fear in his eyes, only... anger. Cloying tendrils of shadow seeped out of Hosen's fingers, through the gray shield, and towards me.

My eyes narrowed to slits. Whatever spell the priest had cast, I did not want to feel its touch. The safest course was to retreat out of range, but I was not about to break off my attack. Not yet.

Maintaining the tempo of my assault, I watched the sinewy strands of shadow draw closer. The first reached striking distance.

Evading its touch, I hit the priest's shield from the left. Another tendril neared.

Bobbing beneath it, I double-tapped the gray bubble protecting Hosen with both my blades. The third sinew inched closer.

Contorting my body out of the way, I swept ebonheart across the face of the priest's shield again. Then, the fourth tendril was on me.

Still off-balance from my last maneuver, I could not escape. Spelled-shadow bit into my hand, and I jerked back my arm, hissing in pain.

You have failed a magical resistance check!
You are <u>death touched</u> for 10 seconds. Hosen has begun leeching your life at a rate of 1% per second.

More tendrils crowded me—far too many to evade *and* attack. *Time to regroup,* I decided. Jumping back, I glowered at the priest while considering my next move.

From the safety of his shield—which looked in no danger of collapsing yet—Hosen smiled in mocking invite.

I wasn't baited.

Another frontal attack was not going to work. But a rapid-moving assault might. Quick as thought, I mapped a tight corkscrew around the priest. Spinning psi, I began materializing the windslide. *Let's see how he likes it when—*

A blur of motion out of the corner of my eye was my only warning. Without questioning the instinct that prompted it, I dropped to all fours.

A half-giant bulldozed past.

In her wake, she left upturned soil, broken foliage, and scattered leaves. My reflexes had saved me, but not entirely, and her foot brushed me in passing.

Lorita's charge has grazed you. You have failed a physical resistance check!

Your spellcasting has been interrupted!

You are <u>dazed</u> (reaction time slowed). Duration: 3 seconds.

As fleeting as the impact was, it still sent me flying across the clearing, limbs flailing. But Lorita's charge *also* took me out of her and Hosen's immediate reach.

I hit the ground with a resounding thud, and the air whooshed out of me. Groaning, I sat up. *Gotta keep moving.*

A shadow fell across me.

Damn, not again. Knowing that attempting to dodge was a bad idea right now, I did the only other thing I could think of: I reached into the mind of the foe looming over me and wrenched.

You have terrified Hurin for 10 seconds.

Slaysight did not let me down; in a heartbeat, mind-numbing fear overtook my foe's limbs. Scrambling back, I found myself staring at the orc I'd spied at the head of the Marauder column. His face pale and trembling, Hurin was locked motionless with his hammer hanging uselessly above his head.

At my movement, the orc glanced down, and he paled even further. Dropping his hammer, he turned about and fled—

—directly onto the blade of one of the charmed fighters.

Your minion has killed Hurin with a fatal blow.

Well... that was fortuitous.

Hurin's death was a reminder that I could just as easily die in the clearing from misfortune as from anything else. *Which is why I shouldn't be here.*

But it was too late to back out now, and there was still a fight to be won. Lumbering to my feet, I took stock of the battle.

About ten other players remained standing in the clearing, half of whom were bespelled and doing their best to keep the unbewitched Marauders at bay. Lorita and two other warriors had gotten away from my minions, though, and were fast approaching from my right. But they hadn't closed the distance yet, so I searched for Hosen.

The priest was lowering his staff in my direction.

Time for round two, I thought and dove through the aether just as Lorita cut down Hurin's killer.

You have teleported into Hosen's shadow.

I emerged poised to strike and slashed first with ebonheart, then my stygian blade. Both scored direct hits on the priest's shield.

Hosen whirled around, a spell on his lips.

I didn't hang around to see what foulness he conjured up this time. Reworking my failed casting from earlier, I laid down a ramp of air and jumped on.

The priest's face contorted in confusion as I floated around him. Zipping along the windslide, I struck at his shield, first from the right, then from the rear, and finally from the left.

Hosen's expression changed again, concern displacing befuddlement. Corkscrewing about my foe, I continued my assault.

He tried to track me, of course, but I was moving too fast for him to target, and inevitably, on my third circuit, Hosen's shield cracked. Not giving the priest time to register that happy fact, I buried ebonheart deep into his torso.

You have killed Hosen with a fatal blow.

I guess round two goes to me.

Somersaulting off the windslide, I landed beside the corpse. Lorita and her two cohorts—human knights—were waiting for me. But I was ready for them, too.

As the trio converged, I slipped under the half-giant's opening blow, parried away the first knight's sword, and slashed at the second, forcing him to break off his attack.

Tevin has evaded your attack.

Despite the first exchange ending in a stalemate, the three fighters backed away and exchanged concerned glances. Perhaps, they were stunned by the speed of my counters, or maybe they were reevaluating their strategy.

I didn't really care.

Not letting the opportunity go abegging, I swept my gaze across the clearing. As far as I could tell, only one other uncharmed Marauder was alive, and he was being mobbed by my remaining five minions. They wouldn't stay *my* minions much longer, though.

Maybe, I should—

With a sudden bellow, Lorita dashed forward, and my attention snapped back to her. Realizing she was repeating her earlier charge, I flung myself out of the way.

This time, I managed to sidestep the attack entirely, but the two humans had anticipated me and moved in for the kill.

The first knight chopped down with his broadsword. There was no time to dodge. Crossing my shortswords before me, I blocked the strike— barely—but the force of the blow sent me staggering back.

That's when the second knight acted.

In a nearly perfectly executed maneuver, he lunged forward, the tip of his glittering sword pointed at my heart. Knowing I couldn't avoid the onrushing blade, I stepped *into* the attack.

My unexpected tactic foiled the knight's aim, and instead of running me through as he intended, his blade bit through my shoulder.

Luri has injured you.

The wound hurt like hell, but I ignored the pain. Dropping my stygian blade, I gripped the hilt of the knight's broadsword and yanked, driving it deeper into my shoulder.

Luri has critically injured you!

My actions savaged my shoulder further, but more importantly, they brought my foe within arm's reach.

Luri's eyes widened as he realized too late what I intended. Smiling a bloody grin, I thrust ebonheart—held low all this time—up and under the knight's breastplate.

You have killed Luri with a fatal blow.

Footsteps pounded across the ground behind me. Still pinned by the knight's sword, I couldn't dodge. But I didn't need to. Squeezing my eyes, I searched for the nearest mindglow and blinked away.

You have teleported into Tevin's shadow.

The second knight sensed my presence at his rear and threw himself to the side before I could strike at him. *Damnit*, I cursed, lamenting the missed opportunity.

I stalked after.

A sun ray has injured you!
Your void armor has reduced the light damage incurred by 5%.
A magic rock has injured you!
Your void armor has reduced the elemental damage incurred by 10%.
Quick mend triggered! Your health is at 45%.

Magic exploded into my shoulder blades, nearly throwing me to the ground. Catching myself in time, I chose a direction at random and ducked into a roll in anticipation of further attacks.

A fireball roared past.

Climbing back to my feet, I spun about in search of my latest attackers. But even as I did, I realized what had happened. My charm spell had lapsed, releasing the spellcasters under my mental control. Sure enough, I spotted all five of my former minions facing me, their faces a rictus of anger and hate.

My foes in the clearing had just gone from two to seven.

Fight or flee? I wondered, feeling a sense of déjà vu as I asked myself the same question again.

One of the five spellcasters had already wrapped himself in a magic shield, and another—incanting words rapidly—appeared about to do the same.

However, in the case of the other three mages, rage seemed to have overcome common sense.

The three had gone straight on the attack without taking the time to see to their defenses. It was the trio who had launched the first salvo of magical projectiles, and even now, they pointed their wands my way, preparing a second assault.

I can't forgo this opportunity, I thought, convinced by the three to stay in the fight.

If I gave the mages enough time, they would eventually raise their defenses. Five shielded spellcasters would not be easy to defeat. Three *unshielded* mages, on the other hand...

Drawing psi, I mapped out a convoluted path to my targets—no point making myself an easy target—and cast windborne.

The mages released their second wave of attacks a half-second before I finished my own spell. Jumping onto the windslide, I shot upward and *over* the incoming projectiles.

You have evaded 3 magical projectiles.

The mages' heads jerked upward, the same bewildered expression mirrored on all three faces. An amused chuckle escaped me. The abysmal failure of their assault had left my foes confounded—as did my aerial approach.

From the left flank, Lorita and Tevin rushed in to intercept me, but I was moving too fast for them to catch. And besides, the windslide kept me out of the reach of ground-bound foes—temporarily, at least.

Drawing closer to my first target, I readied ebonheart. The mage raised his wands in a warding gesture. It made no difference. As I rushed past, I slashed out with the black blade, slicing clean through the Marauder's wands *and* neck.

You have decapitated Xerces.

The windslide curved left, carrying me to my second target. Belatedly, the mage realized he should run, but he, too, failed to escape as I rammed ebonheart hilt-deep in his back.

You have killed Hoffman with a fatal blow.
You are no longer <u>shadow touched</u>.

Sadly, my windslide had come to an end, and I dove off. The third mage had been too far to reach with it. Meanwhile, I spied the two shielded mages lowering their staffs. They were finally shifting from defense to attack.

But I wasn't planning on hanging around where I was. Weaving psi, I blinked out. And back again. Appearing behind the last unprotected mage, I wrenched back her head and slit her throat.

You have killed Soraya with a fatal blow.

The remaining four Marauders spun around to face me, their faces carved rock and seething hate. But there was an element of fear in their expressions too. I'd slain more than ten of them in less than sixty seconds.

Time to disappear. Waving insolently, I somersaulted backward and wrapped myself in darkness.

You are hidden.

"Where'd he go?" Tevin whispered.

You have healed yourself. Your health is at 65%.

"He's hiding," the first mage replied. "Be careful. He's still close."
"What *is* he?" the knight asked, nervously eyeing the darkness.
The mage shrugged. "An assassin, probably."
"Who would send assassins after us?" Tevin wondered.
"Who cares?" Lorita screeched. "Just find him!" Hefting her axe, she rushed toward the spot where I'd disappeared.
The second mage broke off his chanting. "Don't be a fool, Lorita," he ground out harshly. "If you go out there, you're dead. He is waiting for us to panic. *Don't* give him what he wants."

You have healed yourself. Your health is at 85%.

The half-giant hesitated for a moment, then retreated to the mage's side.
"Good," the mage pronounced. "Now, let's stick together. If we do that, he can't get at us. All you two need to do—" he pointed to Lorita and Tevin— "is protect us. Leave finding him to Inga and me." Not waiting for their responses, the mage resumed chanting.

You have healed yourself. Your health is at 100%.

Crouched down a mere ten yards away, I opened my eyes. I'd used the temporary respite from action to heal myself while listening to the Marauders with half an ear. As the full sense of the mage's words penetrated, I smiled indulgently.
It was a good plan, but not good enough.
The mage was correct: I *did* want to separate them. But if they didn't comply on their own, I had other ways of meeting my objectives. Opening my backpack, I retrieved a stone bottle. Holding it ready, I reached into the minds of the fighters.

You have cast slaysight. You have terrified 2 of 2 targets for 10 seconds.

Surging upward, I flung the bottle at the four Marauders huddled together.

You have ignited a smoke bomb, creating a smoke cloud.

The reaction was instantaneous. Tevin and Lorita took off running, feet pounding against the ground as they burst out of the gray clouds and into the forest.
"Fools!" the overbearing mage yelled after them. "Come back here. At once!"
Naturally, the two fighters didn't respond, and for the time being, I forgot them; I would find them again soon enough. Narrowing my focus instead on the mage's mindglow, I stepped through the aether.

You have teleported into Greaves' shadow. You remain hidden.

Wrapped in shadow and smoke, I was invisible to my targets. Taking ebonheart in a two-handed grip, I struck at Greaves' shield.

You have backstabbed Greaves for 5x more damage!
Your target's shield has blocked your attacks.

The mage spun around, his swishing robes betraying his movements. "He's here!" Greaves cried. "Help me, Inga!"
I sensed the other mage turning towards me, but I didn't stop my attack. The two spellcasters could no more see me in the billowing smoke than I could them. Empowering my arms, I pounded on Greaves' shield twice more, dealing huge swathes of backstab damage each time.
It was enough.

Your target's shield has been destroyed!

"Inga, do something!" Greaves yelled. "My shield is—"
Ebonheart flew forward to where I knew the mage to be and slid easily through cloth and skin to bury itself in my foe's torso.

You have critically injured Greaves.

"Aiyee! It hurts!"
I'd failed to land a killing blow, but that didn't matter. Retracting the black blade, I adjusted my aim and struck again.

You have killed Greaves.

One down. Swinging around, I stalked through the smoke toward my second target. I didn't get far, though.

Inga has cast self-immolation.

Flames roared outward from the mage, consuming him, me, and the lingering smoke cloud.

You have failed a magical resistance check! You are <u>burning</u>. Duration: infinite. The debuff will remain in effect as long as the source spell is being channeled.
Your void armor has reduced the elemental damage incurred by 10%.

Magical fire wreathed me from head to foot. Squeezing my eyes shut, I screamed. I couldn't help it; the pain was stupendous. Superheated skin charred, and flakes fell off. Simply thinking was difficult.
But one thought kept me upright: Inga had to be hurting as much as I was, or nearly so.
The spell he'd cast was a gamble, damaging him as it did me. In the split-second I'd had before the fire had overtaken me, I'd seen the mage's shield flicker out, consumed by his own flames.
I... just... need... to... get... to... him.

I took a shaky step forward. More of my skin sloughed off. Shadow blinking was out of the question. Wrapped in pain as I was, using any of my abilities was beyond me.

I took another step.

The health potion on my bracelet cried out to be used, but I ignored the temptation of quick relief. I had to learn to fend without it. *It's only pain,* I told myself.

I took another step.

Vaguely, the sound of another scream penetrated, a twin to my own. It was Inga. I forced blistered eyes open. A blurred shape swayed in front of me. *Almost... there.*

Pulling ebonheart back, I thrust. The blow was a feeble imitation of my previous ones, and the point wavered noticeably as it sunk into my target.

Nonetheless, the blow sufficed.

You have killed Inga.
Flames extinguished. You are no longer <u>burning</u>.

With a relieved gasp, I collapsed to the still-smoking ground. *Not... out... of... danger... yet.*

I marshaled the dying strands of my will, and before unconsciousness could claim me entirely, I blanketed myself in darkness.

You are hidden.

✳ ✳ ✳

Two hostile entities have failed to detect you!

I groaned softly, jerked into some semblance of consciousness by the Game message.

"... they're dead," a voice said bleakly.

I recognized the speaker. It was Tevin. I quietened my breathing, in no condition to fight yet.

"And the assassin?" another asked. *Lorita.*

"I don't see his body. He must've fled."

"Keep looking," the half-giant ordered.

"We shouldn't be here," Tevin argued. "Let's head back to camp. Yzark must be informed."

"Shut your gob," Lorita growled. "And do as you're told."

The knight didn't object further, but his steps were heavy as he stomped deeper into the clearing.

A hostile entity has failed to detect you!

I didn't dare move. Pain still clouded my mind, leaving my senses impaired and unable to pinpoint the two fighters, but I knew they were close.

Turning my attention inwards, I drew psi. Before I could do anything else, I had to attend to my wounds. Chain-casting quick mend, I began nursing myself back to health.

Less than a minute later, Tevin threw up his hands again. "I can't find him. I told you: he's not here!"

"He must be," the half-giant insisted, although she didn't sound so certain anymore. "I didn't see any footprints leading away."

"Footprints?" the knight echoed incredulously. "Did you not notice the assassin flying?" he asked, his tone scathing.

Lorita snorted. "He can't fly."

"Then what do you call…"

Another Game message dropped in my mind, and I stopped paying attention to the pair's bickering.

Your health is at 100%.

Silently, I rose to my haunches. *Time to end this.*

✳   ✳   ✳

Ten minutes later, I was still in the clearing. And was I not alone. Instead of killing Tevin and Lorita, I'd taken them prisoners.

Disarming and capturing the two Marauders had gone off without a hitch, and now the pair were trussed up securely and watching me with burning intensity.

Leaving them to stew a little longer while their fears ran wild, I looted their companions' corpses. The dead Marauders were chockful of items, too many to sift through just yet, so, without hesitation, I dumped everything into my bag of holding.

You have acquired 15 caches of miscellaneous items.

After my scavenging was done, I reviewed the battle results.

You have reached level 138.
Your light armor has increased to level 113 and reached rank 11.
Your telekinesis has increased to level 120 and reached rank 12.
Your null death has increased to level 11 and reached rank 1.

Not bad, I thought. I'd gained two more levels and advanced a bunch of skills, three of which had ranked up, too. I strode towards my prisoners. Now, though, it was time to decide what to do with them.

I had two choices: kill both or kill one and let the other go.

I pursed my lips. Going with the first option would mean abandoning my plan for the Marauders—something I would've scoffed at earlier but, after the difficult battle, deserved weightier consideration—whereas the second was necessary to discover their camp's location. I paced a circuit about the prisoners, thinking hard.

"Who are you?" a glaring Lorita demanded suddenly.

"More to the point, *what* are you?" a more subdued Tevin inquired.

I ignored both questions. *The human knight is the one I need,* I decided. Lorita was too temperamental. If I let her go, odds were she would turn back and hunt me—no matter how futile that was.

I stopped short, realizing I'd made my decision already.

The battle with the Marauder team had been touch-and-go more times than I cared to count. But I *had* prevailed in the end, and that's what mattered.

That's it, then. I go ahead with the plan. Taking a moment, I reflected on just what that was.

Ambushing the Marauder team had not been a whim. I'd done it precisely so that I could let some go—after suitably terrorizing them, of course. Not only would the freed prisoners lead me to their camp, they would *also* raise the alarm.

Both actions served my purposes.

Taking out five hundred Marauders in a fortified camp was too risky. *Even I knew that.* I snorted. No matter what Eyes had told Beorin, I wasn't that foolish or reckless.

But... five hundred Marauders spread out and searching for a lone assassin? Against such, in the forest, *and* in the dark, I fancied my chances.

Of course, I couldn't expect all the Marauders to leave their camp and go searching for me, but every one that I managed to kill in the forest would be one less to deal with when I *eventually* penetrated their camp.

Which brought me back to my prisoners.

Rounding on the pair, I buried ebonheart in the half-giant's throat without preamble.

You have killed Lorita with a fatal blow.

Tevin stared at me, aghast. "What did you do that for?"

"So you understand who you are dealing with," I replied mildly. Crouching before the knight, I held his gaze. "I want you to deliver a message for me."

"A message?" he sputtered. "Why would I— Wait. You're letting me go?"

"This time," I said with an evil smile. "You will tell Yzark what happened here and make sure he knows I'm coming for him. You understand?

Not about to question his good fortune, Tevin nodded vigorously. He squinted at me for a moment longer than strictly necessary, and I felt a failed analyze attempt ripple over me.

"Stop that," I ordered sharply.

"Sorry," Tevin gulped as he realized he'd been found out. "But what name should I give him?"

"You will tell him," I went on, ignoring his question, "that by the time I'm done, every Marauder in the valley will be dead. I will slay each ten times over if necessary. If he wants to avoid that fate, he will pack up and leave now."

"He won't listen," Tevin objected.

"Make him." Rising to my feet, I cut the knight loose. "Get going."

Making no move to leave, the near-naked human—I'd relieved him of his armor and weapons—stared at me.

"Go!" I snapped.

Scrambling to his feet, Tevin fled.

Smiling to myself, I gave him a minute's head start, then followed in his wake.

The Marauder did not go far.

Thirty minutes later, Tevin stumbled to a halt in front of a tall palisade. Twenty yards behind him and perched on a stout tree branch, I paused, too, taking in the scene below.

The trees on the other side of the wooden wall were just as dense as on this side. I frowned. That either meant we'd not reached the Marauder's camp or... the Marauders were using the trees for cover.

Glancing left and right, I spotted the palisade curving inwards in both directions. *This has to be their camp,* I thought. *No one builds a wooden wall in the middle of nowhere.*

Reaching up to another branch, I pulled myself higher up the tree to get a better look. But I didn't venture closer to the camp just yet—who knew what wards the Marauders had set.

In a matter of moments, I reached the tree's uppermost branches and peered down between the foliage. Almost immediately, I spotted five dull glows within the encircling walls.

Those are campfires—shrouded campfires.

Despite it not being in a clearing, I was certain I'd found the Marauders' camp. But it was smaller than I expected. *That base can't hold five hundred. Half of that, maybe.*

I glanced down at Tevin. The knight was standing in front of the palisade and windmilling his hands frantically—*trying to get the attention of someone inside?*

A gate slid open.

If I hadn't witnessed its opening myself, I wouldn't have spotted the gate's seams in the wall, even with my keen eyesight. Two players hurried out, approaching the near-naked knight.

Schooling myself to stillness, I trained my ears upon them.

"... Tevin, is that you?"

"By the Powers, Kenneth, of course, it's me. Thank Kalin, I made it!"

"What happened to you?" Kenneth asked.

The second guard chuckled. "Did a serline kill you?"

Tevin scowled. "That's not funny, Jorge."

"Ah, c'mon. Admit it, it was a little—

"Where's the rest of your team?" Kenneth interrupted.

"Dead," Tevin replied, bowing his head in shame.

For a moment, the gate guards said nothing, staring at the knight in shock. Finally recovering, Kenneth laid a hand on Tevin's shoulder and shook him. "*All* of them?"

Tevin nodded mutely.

"What, serlines get them too?" Jorge asked half-jokingly.

Both Tevin and Kenneth ignored him.

"An assassin got us," the knight explained haltingly. He looked around with a belated sense of caution. "Let's get inside. I'll tell you all about it after I report to Yzark."

The three hurried away, and with a thoughtful frown, I watched them go.

✳   ✳   ✳

After Tevin and the guards disappeared, I turned my attention to the camp itself.

The Marauder base was only a few miles west of the village but was well hidden, and I doubted I would have found it without searching for hours.

Mentally marking the location of the gate, I paced a slow circuit around the camp along my treetop highway. The palisade was a uniform twenty feet in height all around. There were no other gates—not that I could spot, anyway—nor walkways, nor towers. In fact, except for the wooden walls, the camp had no physical defenses.

There were guards, I knew that.

But I only knew about them because I'd spotted the pair greet Tevin. When I inched closer and inspected the camp with mindsight, I came up with...

... nothing.

I rubbed my chin thoughtfully. I was in an ancient oak ten yards from the concealed gate, and from where I sat, I could see directly into the camp.

But I saw no players.

Either the camp was empty... or its interior was hidden from both physical and mental sight. *The base must be warded, but to what extent?*

Reaching into my backpack, I extracted a pair of black goggles and put them on.

You have equipped the spectacles of ward seeing.

With new eyes, I looked on the camp again—and whistled in silent appreciation.

Dappled strands of magic danced in my sight. What the Marauders' base lacked in physical protections, it more than made up for in magical defenses. A network of wards crisscrossed the palisade, the ground below, and even the air above the camp.

Getting through that mess will not be easy.

But it *was* possible.

My thoughts flashed back to the last time I'd been confronted by a warded wall. That encounter had not ended well. *Alright,* I conceded, *it's only possible if there are no unseen wards.* Bowing my head, I considered the likelihood of the camp being protected by tier five spells.

All the Marauders I'd encountered had been tier three players. That was not to say there couldn't be rank twenty players in the base, but the notion seemed far-fetched.

This wasn't Nexus, after all.

I have to trust that what I see with the spectacles is the full picture, I decided. Doing so was a risk, but a small one. Raising my head again, I analyzed the lines of magic riddling the base and searched for a way through.

✳   ✳   ✳

Fifteen minutes later, I had a route through the Marauders' defenses mapped out, but I made no move to follow it yet. It had been thirty minutes since Tevin had disappeared into the camp.

What's taking so long?

If the Marauder boss was going to take the bait and dispatch his men in search of me, it would happen soon, but the night was passing by, and I couldn't sit waiting forever.

I'll give it another thirty minutes, I decided. Making myself comfortable on my treetop perch, I pulled up my player profile. It had been a while since I'd reviewed it in detail.

<u>Player Profile (Partial): Michael</u>

Level: 138. **Rank:** 13. **Current Health:** 100%.
Stamina: 70%. **Mana:** 100%. **Psi:** 100%.
Lives Remaining: 2.

<u>Attributes</u>

Available: 3 points.
Strength: 17 (13)*. **Constitution:** 19. **Dexterity:** 48 (40)*. **Perception:** 25.
Mind: 71. **Magic:** 23 (21)*. **Faith:** 0.
* *denotes attributes affected by items.*

<u>Active Buffs</u>

Damage reduction: Life: 0%. Death: 5%. Air: 10%. Earth: 10%. Fire: 10%. Water: 10%. Shadow: 5%. Light: 5%. Dark: 5%. Physical: 26%*.

Additional resistance (excluding inherent resistance provided attributes): Life: 0%. Death: 2.5%. Air: 5%. Earth: 5%. Fire: 5%. Water: 5%. Shadow: 2.5%. Light: 2.5%. Dark: 2.5%. Physical: 0%.

Immunities: Entanglement: tier 2 spells*. Mind spells: tier 2 spells*.
* *denotes buffs affected by items.*

<u>Skills</u>

Dodging: 114. **Sneaking:** 115. **Shortswords:** 124. **Two weapon fighting:** 115. **Light armor:** 113. **Thieving:** 89.
Chi: 113. **Meditation:** 137. **Telekinesis:** 120. **Telepathy:** 113.
Insight: 133. **Deception:** 109.
Channeling: 25. **Elemental absorption:** 25. **Null force:** 15. **Null life:** 4. **Null death:** 11.

I smiled in satisfaction. My skills continued to improve; a few were even closing down on tier four.

My void skills, though, had a long way to go. While the battle with the hags and the Marauder team had raised them some, I realized I would have to make a concerted effort to bring them in line with my other skills.

If only there weren't so much to do.

Perhaps, tomorrow, after I found the dire wolves, I would train my void skills. I'd run across plenty of low-level creatures in the valley during my previous visit, and if I went looking, I was sure to find suitable monsters this time around. The engagements would have to be 'real' fights, though. Otherwise, the Game would not award me with skill increases.

I turned back to the Marauder camp. Of course, all that was assuming everything went off as planned tonight —which was far from certain at this point.

In the meantime, I think it's time to spend those three attribute points.

I could dump them in Dexterity again... or I could invest them in Perception. Doing so would allow me to utilize one of the ability tomes currently weighing down my backpack.

Perception, it is, I decided and willed my desire to the Adjudicator.

Your Perception has increased to rank 28.

"Excellent," I murmured. I now had six Perception ability slots available. That would suffice to upgrade one of my existing abilities.

Which one should it be? Analyze, facial disguise, or trap detect? Upgrading analyze would be of the most immediate benefit, but I preferred a longer-termed strategy.

Working towards a more comprehensive facial disguise fit that bill. Being able to mask my face even while in a safe zone would increase the effectiveness of my disguises—something I greatly desired.

Extracting the ability tome in question from my backpack, I began reading.

You have upgraded your facial disguise ability to <u>improved facial disguise</u>. This tier 2 ability enhances the illusion wrapped around you, masking not only your features but your voice too. Additionally, players who attempt a tier 1 analyze on you will see a falsified name, level, and species.

You have 2 of 28 Perception ability slots remaining.

Closing my eyes, I let the new knowledge settle in my mind. The improvement provided by facial disguise's tier two variant was negligible and perhaps not worth four whole ability slots, but it was the tier three variant I sought.

It would make the investment worthwhile in the end.

At a soft creak from below, my eyes snapped open. Glancing down, I saw the gate to the Marauders' camp opening.

Finally, I thought and rose to my haunches.

✳   ✳   ✳

A double column of players streamed out. Their expressions were uniformly grim, and they all held their weapons at the ready. Narrowing my gaze, I counted off their numbers. When the gate finally slammed shut, I'd reached fifty.

I whistled soundlessly in silent appreciation.

By any normal measure, fifty players were overkill for hunting a lone assassin. More impressive yet, every Marauder in the company was buffed and ready for war. I could tell that just by looking because of the glowing bubbles surrounding each mage.

Whatever else the Marauder boss was, he was a careful and astute commander. *Fifty players. All in one big party. And with their defenses up already.*

Ambushing them will be a tad more difficult than I anticipated, I acknowledged in wry understatement.

So, what did I do?

My gaze dropped to the front of the column passing beneath me. Tevin was there—in new gear—as well as another player who I didn't recognize. Both were in animated conversation. Lending my ear, I listened in.

"...telling you, Myka," Tevin was saying. "Whoever this guy is, he's impossible to spot!"

Myka—a lanky elf with a multi-hued headdress—snorted. "And I'm telling you, stop worrying. Our Hound is a specialist. Once she picks up his spoor at the ambush point, she will be able to track him wherever he goes—no matter how high you think his stealth is." He glanced at the player marching directly behind him. "Isn't that right, Hound?"

"Don't call me that," the woman so-addressed growled. "I have a name. Use it."

Myka sniggered. "Ah, but I much prefer Hound. It has such a nice ring to it. Don't you think Tevin?"

The knight, wisely, refrained from commenting. "What if he kills her?" he asked with an apologetic glance at the short woman.

Myka rolled his eyes. "That's what her protective shield is for. Or did it somehow escape your notice?"

"Much good a shield did Greaves," Tevin muttered.

"Well, I'm not Greaves," Myka bit out irritably. "I swear, to hear you speak, you'd think this assassin was a bogeyman."

"But you didn't see him charm the others. It was—"

"Enough, Tevin," Myka said wearily. "We have psionics of our own to protect us." He held the knight's gaze. "He's just a player, you know. We'll find and kill him soon enough."

"Even if he is an Elite?" Tevin persisted.

"He's not an Elite," Myka snapped, his patience seeming to wear thin. "Our spies in the village have been keeping close track of everyone who has entered the sector. We know where they all are. This player, whatever he is, is not that."

"I hope you're right," Tevin muttered under his breath before falling silent.

I let the pair slip out of range as the rest of the column marched past. Their conversation had been revealing—to say the least—and gave me food for thought.

The so-called Hound was particularly disconcerting.

The short woman was nothing to look at and, except for the magic shield surrounding her, didn't warrant any especial attention.

I hesitated to analyze her, though.

If she *was* a tracker, it stood to reason her Perception was high, increasing the chances that she would resist or even detect my analyze attempt—and I was not about to risk that.

I wondered how she tracked her quarries. By sight, sound, scent, or mindglow? Or through some other means I didn't know about?

But the Hound hadn't spotted me hiding in the tree high above. So either her Perception wasn't high enough to penetrate my stealth, or she'd simply not looked my way.

The same reasoning also applied to mental tracking. The moment I'd heard Myka mention psionics, I'd woven a mind shield about my consciousness, but that wouldn't have helped me if the Marauders had already been searching for my mindglow.

I have to know just how strong their psionics are, I decided. Lowering my mind shield, I opened my mindsight.

It was disturbingly empty.

Not a single mindglow appeared despite the fifty players marching beneath me. *Aargh*, I cursed and restored my mind shield. If the Marauders' psionics were powerful enough to shield the entire company, chances were, they would quickly nullify my psi abilities.

Had it been a mistake to let Tevin go?

Perhaps. But it was too late to change that now. I glanced down at my chameleon belt and the enchantment crystals secured there. The good news was that I had the means necessary to hide from the Hound and, if it came to it, from the psionics, too.

I can't take on this enemy column, though.

They were too well-prepared for my tricks. My gaze drifted back to the Marauder camp. But maybe *they* weren't.

I didn't immediately head into the Marauder camp.

If the Hound could track me from the ambush spot to here—and at this point, I had to assume she could—then first, I had to lead her astray.

Which meant laying a false trail.

Not attempting to conceal my scent or mind, I headed due south until I reached the valley's southern border. *This is good enough*, I thought, looking around. *Let the Hound track me this far and no farther.*

Extracting a pair of enchantment crystals, I crushed both.

You have activated a scent concealment crystal, masking your scent for 4 hours.

You have activated a mental concealment crystal, hiding your consciousness for 8 hours.

With my protections in place—and hopefully now invisible to the Hound's senses—I retraced my steps north, traveling swiftly until I reached the trees bordering the Marauder base. Pausing there, I studied the crisscrossing weaves of magic encasing the camp.

The spellcasters who had set the wards had layered them in the shape of a dome—one that did not extend above the treetops. Naturally, the strands forming the dome were thickest at ground level and around the palisade, but up top, along the upper reaches of the trees, there were... gaps.

Not large ones, but big enough for an agile person who knew just the right angle to contort his body to slip through.

First, though, I had to get *above* the wards.

Setting my hands on the trunk of the ancient oak sheltering me, I got climbing. I didn't stop until I reached the topmost branches. Stepping onto a slender bough, I bounced lightly. It bore my weight without protest.

Perfect.

Running across the branch, I launched myself into the night sky, forded the expanse of open air between, and touched down on a tree *inside* the camp. Crouching down on the quivering tree limb, I glanced down.

The camp's wards were below me. This close to the wall, they were a densely packed mess, but I didn't intend on dropping into the base from here. Slipping through the tree, I made my way to its far end.

Then leaped again.

As I landed, the next branch creaked alarmingly but did not give way. Heaving a sigh of relief, I inched towards the tree's central trunk before looking down again. The wards had thinned.

But not enough.

Fixing my gaze on the next tree, I repeated my maneuver, then thrice more, each time flitting silently from tree to tree, until I was perched in the bosom of a redwood near the center of the camp.

Once more, I looked below.

Here, at last, there was a hole in the dome large enough to slip through. Moving slowly, I lowered myself down the tree until I landed on a branch a mere foot above the gap in the wards. I'd reached my chosen insertion point.

Peering into the lattice of magic, I studied the path I needed to take. There were five layers of spells to bypass, but they were stacked tightly enough that a single windslide would carry me through.

I paused, tense with anticipation. The moment of truth had arrived. Either I would sail through the Marauders' defenses or... I would be caught like a fly trapped in a web.

Exhaling a slow breath, I mapped the windslide's path with more care than was my wont. Then, tucking in my limbs, I stepped onto the ramp of air.

I was on my way.

✳ ✳ ✳

I zipped through the wards in a giddy rush and touched down on a stout branch before I realized it.

Multiple hostile entities have failed to detect you! You are hidden.

A plethora of sights, sounds, and noise assailed me. The transition was so sudden that for a moment, I was dazed and left wondering if I'd not tripped the wards after all. Then sense prevailed, and I realized the wards did more than protect the camp.

They *also* hid it from external observation.

Safely nestled in the redwood, I craned my head from left to right and let information seep in.

Magelights were wrapped around the lower trunks of the trees and affixed to the inside of the palisade, brightly illuminating the Marauder base. The gate through which Tevin had passed was also clearly visible from my vantage point, and I noted it was the camp's only entrance.

Everywhere I looked, players strolled, laughed, or caroused. Most were gathered around raging campfires that, for some reason or the other, the wards had not hidden entirely. Seen from inside the camp, though, they were more like bonfires.

There were ten campfires in all, but only half had been lit. Each campfire was set outside a large, rectangular-like tent, and through the open flaps of some, I spied rows of bunk beds.

Saya's estimates were wrong.

The thought popped into my head unbidden. Examining it, I realized why. There were about ten dozen Marauders visible in the camp, and assuming none were already sleeping in the khaki tents, the enemy's numbers were far short of five hundred.

One hundred and twenty Marauders in camp. Twenty-three dead. Fifty searching for me in the woods. And another fifty in the village, blockading the tavern.

That put the Marauders' full complement in the sector at nearly two-hundred and fifty.

Still a lot, I thought wryly as I considered the ten rectangular tents. They were barracks, and I judged each large enough to house about two dozen players—which matched my tally of the Marauders' numbers.

But there was also an eleventh tent. Dirty-brown, circular-shaped, and significantly smaller than the others, it sat directly beneath me.

A command tent? For the Marauder boss?

It seemed likely. The interior of the tent was not visible from where I perched, but I had other means of seeing. Unfurling my mindsight, I scanned inside.

A single mindglow shone within.

Hmm... I let my gaze drift away from the tent. None of the players in the camp were shielded, and other than the two guards at the gate—the same two who'd greeted Tevin—there were no sentries. No one looked up either or appeared concerned about a lurking assassin.

This was not a camp on high alert.

I can probably get away with analyzing the players, I decided. Even if I was detected, they might not think anything of it. Refocusing on the mindglow in the round tent, I cast analyze.

The target is Yzark, a level 148 orc blood-drinker. He bears a Mark of Lesser Dark, a Mark of Greater Shadow, and a Mark of Kalin.

I smiled beatifically. *Got you.*

✳   ✳   ✳

I spent another twenty minutes carefully observing the Marauders, analyzing each in turn. I'd been right, none of them, not even Yzark, was tier four. Level-wise, it put me and my foes on equal footing. Factoring in my scion traits, unusual Classes, and rare traits... well, then, the advantage was squarely with me.

One-on-one, at least.

My biggest challenge was the Marauders' numbers, but I'd known that coming in and had a few ideas of how to better the odds.

My observations revealed something else, too. The number and size of the tented-barracks were not a coincidence. Each tent housed a single team of Marauders—twenty-four by my best guess—and their commander.

By and large, each team remained a tight-knit unit, eating and making merry at their own campfire. Occasionally individual Marauders would drift to another group, but they would always return to their fellows.

The commanders were invariably the highest leveled player in each team and notable by the deference the other Marauders paid them. I counted five commanders in the camp, including Pitor. He and his team must've returned from the village while I'd been dealing with Hurin's party.

Oddly, Pitor and Yzark were the only two Marauders who bore Kalin's Mark. Pitor was also the second highest-level player in the camp. Did that make him Yzark's second-in-command?

Probably, I decided and turned my thoughts on how to deal with the Marauders.

My initial idea was to poison their food. I still had the three vials of viper's venom I'd looted from Wengulax, and using poison was a strategy that had worked well for me against the Fangtooths in the Erebus' dungeon.

But the Marauders had five pots cooking at the moment, one at each campfire. The other five campfires were unlit—courtesy of the teams out in the field. Still, five pots were four too many.

Unlike the goblins, the Marauders were players and would be alerted the *instant* they were poisoned. Which meant I either poisoned all of them at once—an impossibility in the current circumstances—or none at all. I couldn't risk losing the advantage of surprise while some of my foes were still unincapacitated.

The same reasoning applied to the use of my traps. Never mind that I didn't have enough to deploy against ten dozen players.

Which left only...

... slaying the Marauders in their sleep.

It was a strategy not without problems of its own. I would have to remain hidden until the camp settled down for the night—and then hope no one awoke at an inopportune moment.

Not to mention, I ran the risk of the Hound returning before I was done. Yes, my scent was masked, and yes, my mind concealed, but I had no certainty those measures would suffice against the tracker.

But on the plus side, the longer I waited, the more intoxicated my foes would become. None of the Marauders looked like they were rationing their drinks.

Killing my foes in their sleep is the best strategy open to me.

Bracing my back against the stout trunk of the redwood, I closed my eyes and settled down for a long wait.

Two hours later, I opened my eyes.

The Marauders' raucous laughter and loud singing had died down, leaving only the sound of clinking glasses and soft murmurs, but nearly half the camp was still awake. It was not the lack of noise that had shaken me from my trance, though.

It was the sound of the gate opening that did.

Rolling into a crouch, I peered intently at the palisade. The two Marauder teams accompanying Myka and the Hound had returned.

Damnation, I cursed and rechecked my protections. Everything was as it should be. Glancing up through the branches at the wards beyond, I wondered if I should retreat.

But no, once past the wards, I would be blind to what was happening inside the camp, and the Hound was *already* here. There was no point in leaving just yet.

Better to remain still and trust in my protections.

Staying where I was, I watched the incoming Marauders. The two teams broke off, each heading to a different unlit fireplace. But not Myka and the Hound.

Both made their way straight to the command tent—and me.

A hostile entity has failed to detect you! You are hidden.

Clenching my blades, I spun psi in readiness. If the Hound showed the least sign of suspicion, I would flee the camp with windborne. Then the night would devolve into a running battle through the forest—perhaps not be a bad thing. It was how I'd originally anticipated taking on the Marauders.

A hostile entity has failed to detect you!

The Hound and Myka drew closer, Tevin not with them. Neither looked up. Not daring to breathe, I waited. The pair paused at the closed tent flap.

A hostile entity has failed to detect you!

"Come," a harsh voice called.

Myka ducked within, then the Hound.

I exhaled slowly. I'd gone unfound. Either the tracker was not as good as Myka thought she was, or my protections were better.

"What do you have to report?" Yzark growled from inside the tent.

Banishing my musings, I listened in. Despite the orc's voice being muffled by the tent, his words carried clearly to me.

"Nothing," Myka replied airily.

"Nothing?" Yzark asked, the ire in his voice undisguised.

Before the elf could reply with another flippant comment, the Hound interjected. "I picked up our quarry's trail in the clearing Tevin showed us, then lost it at the southern mountain slopes."

There was a pregnant pause.

"You lost it," the Marauder boss repeated. "I expected better from you, Misha."

So, that's the Hound's name.

"I was lucky to track him even that far," she said.

"Why?" Yzark asked sharply. "Is he that good?"

"Hardly," Misha snorted, then laughed humorlessly. "But it's hard to spot tracks left on tree bark."

More silence.

"Back up," Yzark commanded. "Are you saying the assassin is traveling *by treetop?*"

"Yes," was the clipped response.

"What is he? A bloody elf?" Yzark muttered.

"Hey, I resent that," Myka interjected. "Not all elves are tree-huggers, you know. Why, my own—"

"Shut up, Myka," the orc roared.

The elf complied immediately.

"Better," Yzark said in a milder tone. "Go on, Misha. You were saying?"

"There is not much to add," she said. "If I hadn't picked up our quarry's scent in the glade... I wouldn't have been able to follow him at all."

Well, well, I thought. *That tells me all I need to know about the Hound's abilities.*

"Where did the assassin go after ambushing Hurin's team?" Yzark asked.

"He came here," the short woman replied.

"Here?" Yzark sounded startled. "And you didn't think to mention this earlier?"

I could almost sense Misha's shrug. "He didn't do anything except perhaps study the camp and mark its location before heading south."

"Where you lost him?" the orc prompted.

"Correct," she replied, not sounding happy about the fact.

Yzark began pacing, his footfalls echoing loudly. "This is an interesting foe we face," he mused. "He appears out of nowhere, kills an entire team, issues meaningless threats, finds our camp, then disappears again. Does this make sense to either of you?"

Neither Myka nor Misha replied that I could hear, but I imagined they were shaking their heads.

"Did you learn anything else about him?" Yzark asked.

"Nothing that Tevin didn't tell us already," Misha said. "He's short. Fast. Wields two blades, one of them an ebonblade, the other a—"

"Stop!" Yzark snapped. "Did you say an ebonblade?"

"That's right," Myka said, answering before Misha could. "When Tevin described the weapon, I immediately recognized it as an ebony shortsword." He paused. "But it can't be a *real* ebonblade, can it? If Captain Talon wanted us gone, he wouldn't have sent a lone assassin."

"You're sure it was an ebonblade?" Yzark pressed, ignoring his subordinate's question.

"That, or a very good fake," the elf replied.

A chair creaked as the orc sat down. "Get Tevin in here. And Pitor, too," he hissed. "At once!"

* * *

Silence descended in the tent again as Misha and Myka ran out to do Yzark's bidding. While they were gone, I tried to puzzle out why the orc had fixated on the detail regarding the ebonblade.

What did he know or suspect?

I was no closer to uncovering the answer, though, before Myka and Misha returned with Tevin and Pitor in tow.

"Pitor, describe the player you observed arriving in the sector this morning," Yzark ordered without preamble.

A pause. "Which one?" the human fighter inquired.

"The bodyguard of Kesh's agent whom you foolishly allowed to enter the tavern!" Yzark roared back.

"Oh. Him." Pitor shifted. "I take it you don't mean the bard?"

"Of course not, you imbecile!" Yzark scoffed.

"Right. Got it," Pitor replied weakly. Even from outside the tent, I could tell he was nervous, but there was nothing wrong with the Marauder's memory. Taking a deep breath, he described me in exacting detail.

Yzark swung to Tevin. "Is that the assassin who attacked your team?"

"It sounds like him," the knight replied cautiously. "But his face was... different."

"Faces can be more easily disguised than gear," Yzark retorted. "It's him. I'm certain."

No one said anything for a moment.

"But why is that important?" Myka finally dared to ask.

"Because he was with Kesh's agent. That makes him one of *her* lackeys." Yzark began pacing again. "Civilian though she may be, Kesh is a player of means. She is not to be trifled with, nor are the Powers she has aligned herself with. Either the Triumvirate have an interest in this sector." He stopped short. "Or Kesh does."

Yzark snapped his fingers. "Pitor, that merchant we bribed, the one who was relaying the tavernkeeper's messages, did he tell us to whom they were addressed?

"No, boss."

"Could it have been Kesh?" Yzark muttered. "Has the gnome been trying to elicit the emporium's help all along?"

Silence.

"That must be it," Yzark said, answering himself before anyone else could. "And now, Kesh has decided to take a direct hand in events. Hence the agent and the assassin." He sat down. "This is bad. Kalin must be informed."

Pitor made a move towards the tent flap. "On it. I'll dispatch a messenger imm—"

Yzark cut him off. "No. I will not go empty-handed before our lord. We will send word to Kalin *after* we capture and question the assassin."

"How will we do that?" Tevin asked brightly.

Yzark ignored him. "Misha, Myka, take your teams back out and scour the spot where you lost his trail."

"But we've already been—" the Hound began.

"Go!" Yzark barked. "You will depart immediately." The orc lowered his voice threateningly. "And don't return without something to report."

Wordlessly, the two fled the tent to do the Marauder boss' bidding.

"Why are you still here, Tevin?" Yzark inquired mildly.

Mutely, the knight dashed out after the others.

"Sheesh, Yzark," Pitor chuckled nervously when the pair were alone. "You're in a mood tonight. What's—"

"You will accompany Misha and Myka."

"What!" Pitor exclaimed. "Why should *I* go?" he whined.

"That's an interesting question," Yzark said softly. "Maybe to redeem yourself? If you hadn't waited all day to report on the arrival of Kesh's agent, we wouldn't be in this mess."

"How was I to know—"

"Or maybe," Yzark said, his voice rising, "you should go because you're my second-in-command? Kalin will want someone to blame in case this all goes wrong, and that *won't* be me."

"Powers, Yzark. Are you really going to—"

"Or maybe," Yzark roared, "you should go simply because I *ordered* you to?"

Prudently, Pitor swallowed further protest. "As you wish," he said stiffly and stomped out of the tent.

✳   ✳   ✳

The conversation in the tent left me grinning stupidly.

Myka and Misha were leaving—again. Unwittingly, Yzark had removed the biggest threats to my plan—the Hound, the psionics, and the most alert Marauders. Having caroused most of the night, the rest of the players were too far gone in their cups to pose much danger.

This just might work, after all.

Sitting back down against the trunk of the redwood, I watched the two teams leave. The gates slammed shut behind them, and calm descended on the camp.

The minutes ticked by, and little by little, more Marauders retired to their tents. Beneath me, I heard a heavy sigh and the creak of a bed. Yzark, too, was going to sleep.

I resumed my vigil, and time slipped by. With every passing hour, the silence deepened, until, an hour past midnight, I judged the entirety of the camp—except the two gate guards—asleep.

I rose to my feet. The camp was a mess, with discarded dishes and cups strewn everywhere. The shadows were thicker, too, the magelights having dimmed as their charges waned.

Casting my buffs, I dropped to the ground, gaze fixed on the gate. I'd hours to prepare and knew in exactly what sequence I would execute my plan.

The two sentries would be the first to die.

Bent in a half-crouch, I padded closer. Neither guard spotted me, too focused on stealing sips from the bottle they passed between themselves.

Two hostile entities have failed to detect you.

I closed the distance to five yards. Three. One. And still, neither Marauder spotted me. I shook my head. *Some guards these are.*

Rearing up to my full height, I yanked back the head of the closer one and plunged ebonheart through his back. A soft moan escaped my victim as the bottle he clenched fell from suddenly-lifeless fingers.

You have killed Justin with a fatal blow.

The second guard's gaze jerked down, following the broken bottle. "Ju-sh-tin, yoush alrigsh? Thatsh good shit you're spilling. Givsh it here!"

Sighing in disgust, I stepped over the corpse and towards his near-senseless partner. *No need to waste psi blinking behind this one.*

The guard peered owlishly at me. "Hey, whosh are—"

With more force than strictly necessary, I rammed my stygian sword through his throat.

You have killed Hakien with a fatal blow.

Letting the body drop, I swung back to face the camp.

Not a single mindglow flared—all retaining the subdued hue of dormant minds.

I shook my head again. I had the sneaking suspicion that tonight's work was going to be both bloodier and easier than I'd anticipated.

Chapter 280: A Grim Night's Work

I was right.

Not a single soul stirred as I padded from bunk to bunk, murdering the Marauders in their sleep. After the first dozen victims, I got the killings down to an artform.

Clamping my left hand over my target's mouth, I placed ebonheart under the ear and behind the jaw, then thrust inward—not rushing—and severed the brain stem in one single motion. Only a bare handful awoke to realize their fate, and they were stunned and dispatched before they could call out.

I kept my mindsight open the entire time, spotting the errant few from the other tents who awoke in search of more drink or to relieve themselves. A short teleport, a quick thrust, and they, too, were laid to rest.

In nearly no time at all, my grim work was done.

Every Marauder in all five tents was dead. One hundred and twenty souls killed in what seemed an eyeblink.

Standing outside the command tent, I shivered involuntarily. Even having planned the murders and hoping for such an outcome, the blood on my hands made me sick to the stomach.

But I was not done yet.

One other person in the camp was still alive—Yzark. I'd been saving him for last.

Concealing my identity with facial disguise, I drew aside the flap to the orc's tent and skulked inside. He was still asleep, his mouth half open and his nostrils flaring in time to his snores.

I edged closer until I was beside the bed and only bare inches from the Marauder boss' exposed throat. The Adjudicator had listed his Class as a blood-drinker. I didn't know what that was, but it didn't sound pleasant.

Moving slowly, I sheathed ebonheart. Unlike his fellows, Yzark would not die an easy death.

The Marauder was fully dressed. He wore an ornate white robe and had a brace of curved daggers, a half-dozen potions, and a few enchantment crystals on his belt. His arms were riddled with tiny scars that looked self-inflicted, and even asleep, his face was etched in angry lines.

Moving with painstaking care, I freed the orc of his weapons.

You have acquired 3 x rank 4 sacrificial daggers. The properties of these items have been shielded from direct inspection.

Interesting, I thought absently as I set aside the daggers. Normally, I would only loot my targets *after* they were dead, but I intended on chatting with the Marauder boss and didn't want to leave him his weapons—in case he somehow managed to overcome me.

Knives taken care of, I relieved the orc of his potions, too.

You have acquired 6 x minor health regeneration potions. Each potion will gradually restore a player's health at a rate of 0.2% per second over 2 minutes.

The potions were also intriguing and, if I had to guess, had been specially crafted for Yzark.

Next, I unwound a length of rope. Pushing one end under the bed, I pulled it gently over Yzark's arms and torso before wrapping it beneath the bed again.

The orc's hands twitched.

Pausing in my work, I glanced at the Marauder's face, but he showed no other signs of restlessness. Resuming my toil, I wrapped the orc in a few more layers of rope.

Finally, I returned to the head of the bed.

Yzark's snores had not abated. Extracting the three vials of viper's venom from my backpack, I unstoppered each and held them ready.

Here goes.

In a burst of motion, I upended the vials into the orc's open mouth, shoved his jaw shut, forced him to swallow, and then yanked the rope tight around his body.

You have lost 3 x vials of viper's venom.
You have poisoned Yzark!

The Marauder boss' eyes snapped open, his mouth working in wordless shock. Instinctively, he tried to rise. But with his arms pinned to his sides and his torso tied to the bed, he was going nowhere.

Realizing he was trapped, but not knowing how or why, Yzark's struggles grew more frenzied. Unsheathing ebonheart, I rested the tip on his throat. "Stop," I ordered.

The orc froze.

In an instant, Yzark's face cleared, scrubbed free of emotion. Then, with deliberate care, his head turned in my direction. "Who are you?"

I stared at the orc in silent admiration. If I'd not witnessed his frantic struggles of a second ago, I would almost believe him to be at ease. "Who I am is of less concern than why I'm here," I replied mildly.

You have passed a mental resistance check! An analyze attempt by a hostile entity has failed.
Yzark has failed to pierce your disguise.

"What have you done to me?" Yzark asked, his voice still calm and betraying no sign of his failed attempt to inspect me.

I cocked my head to the side. "What? Haven't you checked your Game messages yet? That's sloppy."

The Marauder's eyes narrowed a touch before turning blank again—he'd not appreciated the admonishment. A second later, his eyes grew even more deadpan. *I guess he's finally realized he's poisoned,* I thought wryly.

The orc's tongue flickered out to touch his lips. "That taste. I know it. It's—"

"—viper's blood," I finished. "I imagine you will be dead within the minute."

Yzark displayed no reaction to the news of his impending demise. "Viper's blood," he repeated. "Mantises use that."

I smiled, neither refuting nor confirming his conjecture.

The Marauder's eyes drifted towards the tent flap. Realizing what he was doing, he jerked his gaze back to me.

"No one's coming," I said lightly.

Yzark said nothing, but his face tightened fractionally.

My smile deepened. The orc's mask was growing brittle. "Your people are dead. All one hundred and twenty of them; slain in their sleep. Tomorrow, I expect, they will be cursing the impulse that caused them to drink themselves senseless." I wagged my finger at him. "That was not wise of you, allowing them such excess."

Yzark's lips thinned. "I don't believe you."

I shrugged. "That matters not. You will discover the truth for yourself soon enough."

Yzark gaze sharpened—*trying to pick the truth from my lies? Probably*—but I gave nothing away, and his eyes dropped from my face to study my gear.

A moment later, the orc's nostrils flared. He was staring at the bared blade at his throat, I noticed.

"You're no mantis," he stated.

"Are you sure?" I asked coolly.

"Nor do you work for Tartar," Yzark went on, ignoring my interjection, "despite the ebonblade you carry."

"Hmm..." I screwed up my face in pretended confusion. "Was that who I got this sword from?"

Anger burned in the orc's eyes. "Don't toy with me, human. Tell me who you are?"

I rolled my eyes. "We're back to this again, are we? I won't tell you, no matter how many times you ask."

"Why are you here then?" he barked.

I smiled indulgently. "A *much* better question. Two reasons, actually." Raising one eyebrow, I waited expectantly.

But, ignoring my prompting, Yzark said nothing.

I sighed. "Oh, very well, be like that." Leaning down, I whispered in his ear, "For one, I'm here to tell you, you were wrong." I paused again.

This time Yzark couldn't resist. "Wrong about what?" he ground out.

I leaned back. "Wrong about me working for Kesh. It's the other way around."

Yzark's eyes narrowed, and I could almost see the alarm in them growing as he worked through the implications.

"Yes," I said. "I was here. The entire time. And I heard *everything*. Now, you know how poorly your wards serve you. I can reach you whenever I wish."

Yzark was struggling to control his expression now, but he retained enough of his composure not to respond to the implied threat. "And the second thing?" he growled.

I smiled approvingly. "I'm here to deliver a message. This sector is ours. Tell Kalin that if he persists in trying to claim it, it will not go well for him—" I stared hard at the orc—"nor you, for that matter."

The Marauder's lips quivered. "You said 'ours.' What did you mean?"

"Did I say that? You must be mistaken." He wasn't, of course. The misdirection had been deliberate on my part.

Beads of sweat broke out across the orc's brow, but I didn't kid myself that it was my words that had prompted it.

It was the poison.

I was surprised, though, that the viper's blood had taken this long to show itself. Did Yzark have some sort of internal resistance to poison? Would he survive its effects?

Just in case, I pressed the point of ebonheart deeper against the orc's bare skin. *I might have to do this the usual way, after all.*

"You're *his*, aren't you?"

I blinked, refocusing on Yzark. "Come again?"

"You're his. You must be," he spat. "These *games* you play, they smack of him. You even talk like him."

Somehow, I kept my eyes from widening. *He thinks I work for Loken. How... ironic.* But now that Yzark had made the accusation, I realized that I *had*, albeit unconsciously, been channeling Loken.

The entire reason for my conversation with Yzark was to intimidate him. I was not so naïve to believe slaying the Marauders would be enough to make the Power behind them back down.

Kalin would only send more of his people next time. Sadly, I lacked any real strength to threaten him directly. Certainly, no Power—even a minor one—would fear a tier three player.

Hence, I'd resorted to using lies and innuendo and was attempting to deceive Yzark—no fool himself—that a shadowy force lay at my back.

It seemed, though, I'd fooled myself in the process, too.

In crafting my mysterious persona, I'd unknowingly modeled myself after Loken. A disturbing realization at first. But the more I thought about it, the more I realized how apt a subject he was.

Who better to imitate than the trickster himself?

If Yzark did end up believing I worked for Loken, well then, that was just dandy. The trickster *was* one of the more notorious Powers in the Game. The very suspicion that I acted at his behest should set Kalin quaking.

And if, in the process, I managed to create some trouble for Loken, why, that wouldn't go amiss either.

Yzark's mind, meanwhile, was turning frantic circles as he drew connections that didn't exist. "Did his envoy send you? She did, didn't she? That wench has been unhappy since the day we arrived. We will not bow to her threats! Nor will the Shadow Coalition! They *approved* this venture. When Kalin complains, there will be repercussions. Not even Loken will be able to—"

"You're beginning to bore me, Yzark," I said mildly. Leaning my weight into ebonheart's hilt, I slid the black blade through the orc's throat.

You have killed Yzark with a fatal blow.

You have slain a soldier of Kalin, earning his ire!

Sighing, I stepped back. The orc's ramblings had just begun to get interesting, but they'd also made me realize I had to cut short our conversation.

As intriguing as Yzark's mention of Loken's envoy and the Shadow Coalition were, I knew little about either. I'd already succeeded in my objective: seeding doubt, and perhaps a measure of fear, in the Marauder's mind. But if I'd let the conversation run on, I was afraid the orc would catch on to my ignorance, making it less likely that my deception would hold up.

The wiser course had been to quit while I was ahead.

I only hoped I'd done enough.

Ducking out of the tent, I surveyed the camp. My work this night was far from done. There was still a mountain of loot to collect—and sort—and more Marauders to slay. I'd not forgotten about the Hound and Myka's teams nor the other two blockading the tavern.

I kill them, too, then return to the village.

Striding forward, I got to work. I still had a lot to do to prepare for the arrival of the other Marauders.

Chapter 281: A Mountain of Loot

Before searching the camp, checking my Game messages, or attending to the dead, I secured the gate.

I didn't expect the Marauder teams to arrive until dawn, if then, but if any returned early, I could not afford to be caught unprepared. The wards about the camp would prevent the players from sensing anything amiss on their approach, but once they passed through the gate, it wouldn't take them long to figure out something was wrong.

Which is why I trapped the gate—or rather, the mustering ground just inside.

You have successfully configured 20 traps.

After laying my traps and hopefully leaving a nasty surprise waiting for whoever next entered the camp, I dragged the bodies of the gate guards into the closest tent.

Hands on hips, I eyed the two corpses. Both reeked of alcohol, vomit, and... other things. Still, I needed the garments of at least one of them. *Justin's will do.* Holding my nose, I stripped off the dead Marauder's outer garments—cloak, hat, shirt, and pants—and equipped them over my armor.

Of the four Marauder teams at large, Myka and Misha's groups worried me the most. They had gone out together, and I expected them to return as a unit too. Worse yet, they knew enough to guard against some of my tricks—which is why I intended on using *different* ones this time around.

The two teams from the village were less of a concern. They *might* return early—warned by the reviving dead—or they might not return at all if they waited for their replacements. Either way, after my gains tonight, I was sure I could handle a single Marauder team on its own.

Speaking of gains...

Turning my focus inwards, I finally opened the Game messages that had been insistently flashing for attention.

You have reached level 150!
Congratulations, Michael! You are now a tier 4 player. Your experience gains have decreased further. For achieving rank 15, you have been awarded 1 additional attribute point.

Your sneaking has increased to level 124 and reached rank 12.
Your insight has increased to level 143 and reached rank 14.
Your thieving has increased to level 102 and reached rank 10, allowing you to learn tier 3 abilities.

The night's deeds had earned me comparatively few advances in skills, but murdering over a hundred players had not been without benefit—in this case, it had amounted to twelve player levels, fourteen attribute points, and one Class point.

A significant jump in strength by any measure.

Sadly, though, while I'd finally joined the ranks of tier four players—achieving level-parity with most players in the Game—none of my skills had made it that far yet.

But they will, I vowed.

That, though, was a task for another day. Right now, I had attribute points to spend. *First, I need to bump up my Perception.*

My plan for dealing with the remaining Marauder teams involved a touch of deception, and if I were going to deceive the Hound's senses, a bit more Perception would not go amiss.

Your Perception has increased to rank 31.
You have 11 attribute points remaining.

I spent three attribute points on Perception, advancing it just enough to upgrade facial disguise. Opening the requisite ability tome, I began to read.

You have upgraded your facial disguise ability to <u>superior facial disguise</u>. This tier 3 ability enhances the robustness of the illusion wrapped around you, allowing it to function within a safe zone and for extended periods of time. Additionally, players who attempt a tier 2 analyze on you will see a falsified name, level, species, Class, and health status.
You have 0 of 31 Perception ability slots remaining.

A tier three illusion and over thirty ranks in Perception should be enough to defeat the Hound's senses, I told myself, not sure if I was convinced.

I shrugged. If it didn't work, it didn't. I couldn't afford to overinvest in Perception. However, I had more attribute points to spend, and turning my focus inwards again, I added everything to Dexterity.

Your Dexterity has increased to rank 51. Other modifiers: +8 from items.

I smiled, pleased by the changes to myself.

The additional eleven attribute points had made a perceptible difference, and I was noticeably faster. Now, no matter how many Marauders came at me, they would have a hard time pinning me down. Not to mention, I'd also gained enough ability slots to purchase more Dexterity abilities once I returned to the village.

My grin widened. Already, the tasks before me didn't seem as daunting anymore. Swinging around, I faced the silent tents.

There was only one more thing left to do: loot the dead.

✳   ✳   ✳

I'd not overestimated the amount of equipment there was to plunder.

A hundred and twenty dead Marauders equated to a veritable mountain of gear—far more than I could hope to carry, even with my bag of holding. Then, too, there were the consumables lying about the camp—drinks, rations, animal skins, alchemy ingredients, and so on. Some of them were valuable in their own right.

Just stripping the bodies and sorting the items took hours.

Making sure to keep everything out of sight of anyone who stumbled through the gate, I collected all the equipment in an empty tent and created three piles: items not worth enough to carry away, gear for selling, and equipment to keep for myself.

Naturally, the last pile was the smallest.

Sitting on an upturned crate, I leaned forward to inspect my booty more closely. *There are some interesting pieces here.*

A dull pounding interrupted me.

Sitting back, I frowned. Where was that sound coming from? I was certain there was no one else in the camp.

The sound came again, louder this time.

It's the gate! I realized. Whoever had arrived was early; dawn was at least an hour away. Dashing out of the tent, I raced towards the palisade, weaving psi as I did.

You have cast facial disguise, assuming the visage of Justin. Duration: 3 hours.

Panting hard, I skidded to a stop before the gate.

The pounding continued. "Open up, you fools! We're tired, hungry, and sore!"

I recognized the voice: it was Pitor.

"Goddamnit, if you two are sleeping, I'll—"

I slid open the gate a touch. "I'm awake," I slurred in Justin's voice. The facial disguise spell saw to it that I mimicked the dead guard's tone exactly. "Now, stop that damnable racket. You're giving me a headache."

You have passed a mental resistance check! Pitor has failed to pierce your disguise.

Shoving open the gate wider, Pitor brushed past me. Behind the disgruntled Marauder, I saw Myka and Misha's teams looking just as exhausted and haggard as he'd had reported.

"What took you so long?" Pitor demanded querulously.

"Boss did," I replied succinctly.

"Yzark's still awake?" Pitor asked in surprise while I slid the gate back all the way and let the fatigued players in.

They shuffled past me, heads down and clothes saturated with dust. Had they actually scaled the mountain in search of me? It looked that way.

More importantly, the mindglows of all fifty Marauders were visible, and none of the mages had their shields active—*and why would they? They are returning to their home base, after all.*

All in all, the returning Marauders painted a sorry enough picture that I almost felt bad about what was going to happen to them.

But only almost.

Pitor waved his arms. "Hey Justin, you listening to me? I asked you a question."

"Ye, ye, I heard you," I groused. "The boss is awake and in a mood. He wants to see y'all."

Pitor sighed. "Alright, I'll head to his tent now."

"Not just you," I said, stopping him.

He swung back, scowling.

Opening my arms, I took in the entire company. "He wants to see *everyone*. You're all to wait here," I said.

Pitor opened his mouth to protest.

"Boss' orders," I finished.

The Marauder threw me a sharp look but didn't protest. "Myka, Misha," he snapped. "Form up your teams. The boss is coming, and he'll not be pleased to see the state you lot are in."

Pitor, I noticed, didn't have a speck of dust on his clothes. *He* obviously hadn't bothered climbing the mountain.

Myka and Misha were both put out by the order but nevertheless complied. As she shoved her people in line, the Hound's weary gaze swept over me in passing.

You have passed a mental resistance check! Misha has failed to pierce your disguise.

A triumphant smile slipped fleetingly across my face, but I hid it before anyone noticed.

"Where's Hakien?" Pitor asked, belatedly realizing the other guard was missing.

The last of the Marauder company entered the base, and I slid the gate closed behind them. "Gone to fetch the boss," I replied reasonably.

"But—"

"Pitor," Misha called out suddenly, her voice sounding odd, "when did we start placing traps around the gate?"

"What?" he asked, marching up to her. "What have you found?"

Remaining slouched and doing my best not to appear as if I was hurrying, I advanced towards the pressure plates I'd set in an out-of-the-way spot.

Misha pointed to something buried in the ground less than two yards away. "There's one there." Swiveling a little, she gestured to a second spot. "And another there."

"That can't be right," Pitor said, looking puzzled. "We don't have any in stock." He glanced over his shoulder at me. "Justin, what the hell is going on?"

I met his gaze across the stretch of open ground separating us. "The boss will explain everything," I assured him and stepped onto the twenty triggers I'd stacked atop one another.

You have triggered a trap!
You have triggered a trap!
You have...

...

In one glorious instant, the twenty traps activated—half poison clouds, and the other half, firebombs.

The resulting explosion was cataclysmic.

Flames mushroomed upwards, clearing the treetops and reaching skyward. My vision flashed white, and even at what I'd deemed a safe distance, I was blasted off my feet.

I hit the palisade hard, breaking my nose and cracking a few ribs in the process. I didn't care, though. Damage messages were scrolling through my vision.

Pitor has died. You have slain a soldier of Kalin, earning his ire!
Inzamin has died.
Misha has died.
Myka has died.
...

The list went on and on. Compared to what happened to the players in the epicenter of the explosion, the injuries I'd sustained were nothing.

Yikes. Rising to my feet, I dusted myself off. All fifty Marauders had perished, and not a single mindglow remained. It defied my wildest expectations.

Craning my head back, I stared skywards. Already the flames were vanishing. "That must've been visible in the village," I muttered, wondering if that would send the other two Marauder teams racing home.

Wafting away the lingering smoke, I strode towards the closest body part. I didn't have much time left, and I still had my looting to complete.

You have reached level 152!
Your deception has increased to level 111 and reached rank 11.

I sighed as I closed the Game messages.

Despite killing fifty players, I'd gained only two levels—not unexpected given the new disparity in rank and tiers between the Marauders and me—but it was disheartening, nonetheless.

Even more disappointing, deception was the only skill to go up during the encounter. My reaction to the Game alerts, however, was nothing compared to my response to the teams' loot—or the near lack thereof.

A depressing side-effect of the cataclysmic explosion was that it destroyed all but the hardiest of equipment. As a result, picking through the remains did not yield as many choice items as I had hoped.

Still, I reminded myself, *it isn't as if you haven't gathered an impressive haul already.*

Restoring the mustering ground to its original state as best I could—I still had two more teams to greet—I hurried into the tent where my loot awaited.

Right, time to examine my new gear. Picking up each piece, I inspected it minutely.

You have acquired 73 gold coins.

You have acquired a <u>large bag of holding</u>. This item contains an enchantment to store any object you can lift with two hands. Courtesy of the enchantment, the bag, and its contents are weightless. Only inanimate materials may be kept in the bag. Currently stored items: 0 / 200.

You have acquired a goliath's ring, +8 Strength.
You have acquired an acrobat's ring, +8 Dexterity.
You have acquired an adept's ring, +6 Magic.
You have acquired the sharpshooter's band, +4 Perception.
You have acquired the hale stone, +8 Constitution.
You have acquired a savant's ring, +4 Mind.

You have acquired the rank 4 shortsword: the <u>faithful blade</u>. This item increases the damage you deal by 40% and bears the enchantment: recall. Recall is an activated ability that causes the sword to return to the caster's hand if he is within 10 yards. This item requires a minimum Dexterity of 16 to wield.

You have acquired the rank 4 set of light armor: <u>ranger's kit</u>.
This item decreases the damage you sustain by 40% and has been enchanted to increase the wearer's stealth skill by +4 ranks. This item requires a minimum Constitution of 16 to equip.

You have acquired 2 x rank 4 strength enhancement crystals, 2 x rank 4 dexterity enhancement crystals, and 3 x rank 4 magic enhancement crystals.

You have acquired 20 x acid bombs, 15 x smoke bombs, 15 x ice bombs, and 20 x fire bombs.

You have acquired the bomber's belt. This item can hold up to 20 bombs and has been enchanted to prevent the accidental detonation of your stored devices.

You have acquired the Magister's Cloak. This item is indestructible and part of a legendary set. Find more pieces in the set to increase the benefits received. The Magister's Cloak increases your Magic by +4 ranks and repels physical attacks in the same manner as armor, providing +8% physical damage reduction.

You have acquired an aetherstone bracelet. This is a rank 5 artifact that allows you to traverse the aether and teleport from one sector to another using the coordinates stored in one of its five aetherstones. Before the bracelet can be employed, the relevant coordinates must first be etched. This item requires a minimum Magic or Faith of 20 to use.

Aetherstones are rare gems that can forge transitory connections to the Forever Kingdom's ley line network through the expenditure of mana. The aetherstone bracelet is limited in how it can interface with the network and will only allow teleportation from inside a Kingdom safe zone. The destination, however, can be any known Kingdom key point. The bracelet cannot be employed in a dungeon, nor will it bypass magical barriers like sector shield generators.

Currently stored locations: 3 / 5. Available locations: sector 24,401 safe zone, sector 12,560 safe zone, and sector 1 safe zone.

I sighed happily; the new gear was an upgrade over my old equipment in nearly every aspect. Pleased anew by my haul, I began equipping the items.

You have equipped 6 rings. Net effect: +8 Strength, + 8 Dexterity, +6 Magic, +4 Perception, +8 Constitution, and +4 Mind.

There had been a plethora of rings and other trinkets to choose from on the dead Marauders, but sadly, the stat-increasing items did not stack—only legendary gear could, of course. Still, I was able to replace all my old rings and add new ones for attributes I'd not boosted yet.

The bombs and crystals were another welcome surprise and provided me with a host of new buffs and area-of-effect devices. After the encounter with the blood flies, I'd been meaning to do something about my lack of area damage but hadn't gotten around to it yet. So, it was without hesitation that I replaced my slotted-potion belt with the bomber's variant.

You have unequipped a slotted-potion belt.
You have equipped the bomber's belt. Stored devices: 20 / 20.

The shortsword, faithful, was... nice. It was a step up from my rank three stygian blade, and the recall ability would definitely prove useful in battle, but it was not the super weapon I'd been hoping for.

You have equipped the sword, <u>faithful blade</u>, gaining the recall ability and increasing the damage you deal with your offhand by +40%.

The same applied to the ranger's kit. It, too, was an upgrade over my existing armor—something that was long overdue—but that was about all it was.

You have equipped the <u>ranger's kit</u>, gaining +40% physical damage reduction and +4 ranks in stealth.

The magister's cloak was intriguing.

It had belonged to Yzark and was formed from a single piece of supple black cloth. Like the wayfarer's boots, the cloak was a legendary item and worth its weight in gold just for the additional Magic boost it provided.

Surprisingly, the cloak also protected its user against physical attacks—not something that garments usually did—and was obviously designed with mages in mind. But given that the item's damage reduction stacked with armor, it was of use to fighters like me, too.

Sadly, though, because both the wayfarer and magister sets were clothing collections, I suspected I would have to choose between them in the long run. But for now, there was no reason not to use the cloak.

You have equipped the <u>Magister's Cloak</u>, gaining +8% physical damage reduction and +4 Magic.

The most fascinating item, by far, was the aetherstone bracelet. It was made from a thin band of metal—copper, I thought—and studded with five colorless gems, three of which seemed to burn with an inner light. The bracelet, too, had belonged to Yzark and was likely as valuable as the two legendary items I possessed—if not more so.

The item was rank five, and from my prior conversations with Kesh, I already knew how expensive those were. But more importantly, the bracelet granted me mobility. With it, I could teleport from sector to sector on my own.

Sure, I could only do so from a safe zone and then only to go to known key points—and now I knew why my player profile kept track of those—but that was a limitation I could live with. I also needed to figure out how to etch coordinates into the aetherstones. I knew who to ask about that, though.

Nearly as interesting as the bracelet itself were the coordinates already etched in it. I recognized two of them as the safe zones of Nexus and the valley. The third, though...

"Sector 24,401," I murmured. "Now, what could be there?"

The Marauders' home sector was my guess. It bore investigating, but not today or even this month. I snorted. I had far too much to do already. Equipping the aetherstone bracelet, I turned to the next pile: the gear I'd earmarked for selling.

It consisted of a mix of crafting gear, player kits, and alchemy reagents. Altogether, they made for a nice-sized heap and would earn me a tidy sum. Opening my bags of holding, I dumped the equipment inside, set by set.

You have acquired 170 caches of miscellaneous items.
You have acquired 500 alchemy ingredients.
You have acquired 32 sets of crafting gear.

My looting completed, I rose to my feet.

My bags were stuffed to the bursting, but thankfully due to their enchantments, they were weightless. Forlornly, I eyed the last pile—the monstrous mountain of gear I *couldn't* take.

All that is probably worth another few thousand golds.

I sighed. As tempting as it was to take more, I couldn't afford to weigh myself down. *Although...* I paused as something occurred to me.

After considering the notion a bit further, I scrounged through the discard pile and dug up two additional sets of equipment. They would do nicely for a pair of twins I knew.

You have acquired 2 caches of basic items.

Storing away the gear, I straightened. *That's it. I'm done—no more.* Striding back to the gate, I set myself to await the arrival of the last of the Marauders.

✳ ✳ ✳

Dawn came and went, and the sun edged towards noon, and still, the remaining two teams did not return.

Beginning to question the wisdom of waiting, I reflected on the already-dead Marauders. It had not escaped my notice that none of the revived players had returned to their base. More than twelve hours had passed since I'd slain my initial victims—ample time to resurrect and rush back to camp—yet none had shown up.

Either they were too afraid to do so—I snorted, not thinking that likely—or Beorin had actually done as I asked.

I'd not expected the degree of success I'd had when I made the request of the dwarf, and I couldn't imagine how the bounty hunters were keeping over a hundred Marauders under wraps, but what other explanation was there?

I'll find out soon enough, I imagine. Things in the village should be—

Someone banged on the gate.

I stepped closer. "Who's there?" I asked in the dead guard's voice through the closed gate.

"Justin, thank the Powers, you're alive!" came the response. "We've heard all sorts of rumors. I knew they couldn't be true, though. But then... our replacements didn't show up. Is everything alright?"

"Of course, it is," I said jovially and drew back the gate. "Come on in."

It was time to kill again.

$$* \quad * \quad *$$

You have reached level 154!
Your Dexterity has increased to rank 55. Other modifiers: +12 from items.

I dispatched the Marauder team cleanly—and the one after that. Both groups had come in separately, and while they'd known something was wrong, their commanders had found the rumors too outrageous to believe.

In the end, neither team managed to put up much of a fight, and after tallying my gains and investing my new attribute points, I set about my last chore: burning the camp.

With my new fire and acid bombs, it was simplicity itself. After drenching the tents, stores, and abandoned equipment in acid, I set them alight with the firebombs.

You have ignited 5 acid bombs and 5 firebombs!

It's been a productive night's work, I reflected as I swept my gaze over the burning camp. The fire would burn out soon enough, but by the time it was done, I expected nothing would remain of the Marauders' base but ash and debris.

I'd played my hand, and perhaps I'd gone overboard—just a little—but I'd made sure there was no doubt in the Marauders' mind that their presence in the sector was unwanted and would be contested, even if I hadn't spelled-out by whom or why.

Now it was Kalin's turn to act.

How will he react? I wondered. Would he cut his losses and retreat, or double down on his bid for the sector? Whatever response the Marauders chose, though, I was prepared.

Whistling tunelessly, I strolled out the open gate and headed back to the safe zone.

CHAPTER 283: THE FATE OF THE DEFEATED

The trip back to the safe zone was undisturbed and surprisingly pleasant for the most part. The woods near the Marauder base were quiet, and I ran across no foes—players or monsters.

But as I drew closer to the village, the forest grew busier. Spotting a squad of soldiers in the distance, I was reminded that the valley was still a warzone, and no matter my success against the Marauders, the larger three factions in the sector would not hesitate to crush me.

Spurred to greater caution, I took to the treetops and, for good measure, concealed myself in the shadows. Three more Force companies crossed my path, one passing within spitting distance. Perched in a tree, I waited for them to pass.

"... why didn't we attack?" I heard a soldier ask. "They weren't a Light company."

"Didn't you recognize their banner?" the soldier marching beside him replied.

"I know it wasn't from a Light faction," the first voice pointed out.

The second player sighed. "Must I teach you everything? They're bounty hunters."

"Oh." The confused soldier scratched his chin. "And we don't kill those?"

His companion chuckled. "No, we don't, you idiot. The guild is neutral, mercenaries for hire and as likely to work for us as they are for—"

"Quiet in the ranks!" a voice shouted from further up.

The two players promptly fell silent, but I'd heard enough. By the sounds of it, the Light soldiers had run across the bounty hunters. Looking back along the company's line of march, I judged they had emerged from the northern end of the village.

Letting the soldiers pass, I altered my own course to approach the village from the north.

✳ ✳ ✳

A few minutes later, I came across a strange scene.

Fifty bounty hunters stood at attention in the clearing below me, and arrayed before them were over a dozen lines of players in newbie shorts and shirts.

My murder victims.

An unknown entity has detected you! You are no longer hidden.

"Beorin!" someone shouted from ten yards away. "We have company."

My head jerked in the direction of the cry. It looked like I'd been spotted already. *Beorin's people are good,* I thought in admiration and began rising to my feet.

"Don't move," a voice hissed in my ear.

I froze.

There were no mindglows closer than ten yards to me, but the voice... it had come from less than two yards away. Turning my head minutely, I glanced over my shoulder.

My pulse calmed as I recognized the player. It was Snake, Beorin's weirdly dressed squad mate.

"Don't you recognize me?" I whispered.

"I do," he replied equably. "Which is the only reason you're alive."

Huh. I had no response to that.

"Why are you skulking here?" Snake asked.

"I'm not skulking," I replied. "I'm *scouting,* and I didn't know who was down there—until now."

"Well, now you know. Get down," he ordered.

My gaze drifted towards the Marauder prisoners. They were lined up in neat little rows and had been made to kneel. How had Beorin managed to capture so many of them?

"Move," Snake repeated.

"Uhm, I prefer they don't see my face."

The bounty hunter looked at me blankly. "Who?"

Silently, I gestured to the kneeling captives.

Snake's eyebrows drew down in consternation. "Didn't you kill that lot?"

I nodded. "I did, but they don't know it was *me* who killed them, and I'd like to keep it that way. Just give me a second to put on my disguise, then I'll go down."

"Alright," Snake agreed grumpily.

"Thanks," I replied. "Oh, and make sure Beorin knows it's me."

✳   ✳   ✳

You have cast facial disguise. Duration: 3 hours.

Wearing a plain, forgettable face, I strode out of the trees. Standing in the center of the clearing with his arms crossed, Beorin watched my approach. Only a few seconds ago, Snake had informed him of my true identity, and the dwarf's face was alive with speculation.

You have passed a mental resistance check! Multiple unknown entities have failed to pierce your disguise.

I noted most of the prisoners were also studying me curiously but without any spark of recognition. The face I wore now was not one any of them had seen. One kneeling figure, though, was glaring at me furiously.

Yzark.

He, at least, suspected something.

I waved cheerfully at the orc before turning my back on him and heading toward Beorin.

The dwarf raised one bushy eyebrow as I came to a halt. "I don't know whether to be amazed by your daring or... agog at your stupidity."

"What? For waving?" I asked innocently.

He glared at me, not fooled. "For this," he said, pointing to the neat rows of prisoners. "You intend on starting a war, lad?"

The bounty hunter had not lowered his voice, and his words attracted the attention of every Marauder in the glade. The captives' hands had been restrained, I noted. Not with ordinary cuffs but in something that bore the sheen of magic. *Interesting.*

"No," I said lightly, feeling the many stares upon me. "Just delivering a message." I ran my gaze deliberately over the kneeling prisoners. "I trust it's been received."

Yzark glowered at me, his expression rebellious and promising of violence to come.

"If not," I said, holding the Marauder boss' gaze, "perhaps a second lesson is in order."

For a moment longer, the orc continued to stare mulishly; then he looked away.

Beorin snorted, no doubt amused by my theatrics. I turned back to him. "You've done well, bounty hunter," I pronounced in the manner I imagined a client would. "You've fulfilled your end of the job and earned your fee."

"I have, have I?" he asked, playing along. "That's good, then."

I laid a hand on the dwarf, drawing him away from listening ears. "Come, let's talk more in private."

*　*　*

"I'll give it to you, lad," the dwarf said when we were out of earshot, "you don't do anything by half-measures. How many did you leave alive?"

"Not many," I replied evasively.

"That so? But you know, things could've gone more smoothly had you told me you had a second team."

I threw him a puzzled look. "What?"

"The ones who helped you do all that," Beorin said, pointing irritably at the Marauders. "Quite impressive for a few hours of work. The lads and I've tried convincing them to tell us how they died, but no one wants to talk."

"Ah," I said noncommittally.

"So, where are they?" the dwarf persisted.

I glanced at him, wondering how much of the truth I should share. "There is no second team."

"Sure, right," he retorted. "I'm no fool, but keep your secrets if you must."

I shrugged, not caring if he believed me, and turned to study the prisoners. "I'm curious about your own part. You've taken more of the

Marauders prisoners than I expected. How did you do it?" I gestured to the fifty bounty hunters. "And when did they get here?"

"One question answers the other, actually," Beorin replied, still shooting me sidelong looks. Was he still wondering about the 'second team?'

"Oh?" I prompted.

"After our chat last night, I posted one of my men at the rebirth well. So, we were ready when the first group of nine came in." He glared at me from beneath bushy brows. "Though not as ready as we could've been had we known what numbers to expect."

I shrugged apologetically. "Sorry, matters sort of snowballed."

"Uh-huh," Beorin said. "Anyway, capturing the nine scouts was a bit of a challenge for the four of us. They did *not* cooperate. But with Snake on our side, they couldn't hide for long, and we managed to get the job done." He paused. "We had to kill a few again in the process, though."

"Understandable," I murmured.

"After that, I realized we needed reinforcements, so I asked Hannah to expedite things further—which she did—and by the time the bigger group came in, we had the town ringed with bounty hunters." He chuckled. "Hardly any of them got away after that."

"How are you keeping them subdued?" I asked.

He held up a cuff. "With this."

Squinting, I inspected the item he held.

The target is the rank 3 item: <u>manacles of null</u>. This item bears an enchantment that suppresses all abilities of tier 3 and lower.

"I see," I said, drawing back from the cuffs. "And none of the Marauders thought to get reinforcements from the teams blockading the taverns?"

Beorin tugged at his beard. "Not that any of my men saw. Perhaps they didn't think they needed the help." He chuckled suddenly. "Or perhaps they were in too much of a hurry to get their stuff back." He looked pointedly at my backpack. "Where *is* all their gear?"

I ignored the question. "Thank you, Beorin. You've performed outstandingly." I paused. "Just how much is all this costing me, by the way?"

"Five thousand gold," the dwarf replied, his eyes gleaming. "One hundred per bounty hunter."

I winced at the cost but didn't quibble.

"So, what now?" Beorin asked after a moment.

"Let them go, I suppose."

The dwarf blinked. "Just like that? You don't want us to hold them longer? For a few weeks at least?"

I stared at the dwarf. "That can be done?"

Beorin nodded. "Yeah. The guild runs a prison colony in one of the dungeons we own. Inmates are kept in a null field for the duration of the sentence." He jerked his thumb at the Marauders. "This lot will only require tier three containment. Nothing we can't handle."

"A prison colony," I muttered, having flashbacks of my time in Erebus' clutches.

Dungeons, I realized, were ideally suited to holding players. If you controlled the exit portals, you wouldn't even need the null field Beorin described to keep them in. But the idea of imprisoning the Marauders had not occurred to me before, and I wanted to examine the notion more closely before acting on it.

"How much will it cost?" I asked, not for a second believing it would be free.

"Nothing," Beorin said, smiling expansively. "Think of it as a favor... in exchange for a future mission the guild *may* ask you to perform."

I narrowed my eyes. "You mean like Hannah's mysterious task?"

He grinned. "Maybe."

I frowned. Committing myself before I even knew what the guild wanted from me was not wise, and I was under no illusions. By accepting Beorin's *favor*, I would be doing just that—unless I wished to make an enemy of the guild, which I most emphatically did not want.

But what was the alternative?

My gaze slid to Yzark, who was still glaring daggers at me. Killing the Marauders had taught them a lesson—I hoped—but in the long run, it didn't solve the tavern's problems. "This prison, is it a place of evil repute?"

Beorin chuckled darkly. "Oh, definitely. No one *wants* to go there."

"What's it called?" I asked.

"Hell's Breath," he replied.

"Huh, interesting name."

"So, you'll accept?" Beorin asked, making no attempt anymore to pretend it was a favor—and not a bribe—he was offering.

"No."

"What!" Beorin exclaimed, his face a picture of confusion.

"Hold them for a few hours more, then let them go." I cast him a mild look. "I trust the fee you've been paid already will cover that much."

Beorin's eyes narrowed to slits. "You mind telling me why in the seven hells you want to do that? After all the trouble we've gone through to capture them, why—"

"You were right."

The dwarf's brows furrowed. "I was?"

I nodded. "It's foolish to start a war with the Marauders, and imprisoning over two hundred of Kalin's people will certainly accomplish that."

"But having killed them won't?" Beorin asked sarcastically.

"It might," I admitted. "But this is the Game, and dying is... not unusual. The Marauders' deaths will hurt Kalin—enrage him, even—but they won't escalate matters the way imprisoning his followers will." What I did not say, but thought, was that holding the Marauders in a guild prison might set Kalin down a path I didn't want him to go.

Right now, the Power didn't know who I was, and if he leaped to the same conclusions Yzark had, he would believe I worked for Loken. Kalin discovering my real identity—something he might do if he started digging into my connection with the guild—would jeopardize all that and undo everything I'd accomplished with the Marauders so far.

"Hmm," the dwarf said, not disagreeing but not approving either. "So, you've made up your mind?"

"I have."

"And you sure you want to let them go?"

"I am.

Beorin sighed. "On your head be it then." Swinging around, he turned to go.

"One more thing, Beorin," I said, stopping him.

He glanced over his shoulder.

"I know the guild controls its own sectors. But I've been wondering: how can that be?"

The dwarf blinked, perplexed by the seeming randomness of my query. "What are you on about now, boy?"

"The bounty hunters guild is not a Game-faction, right?"

He nodded.

"How can it *own* a sector, then? I thought only factions could do that."

"Ah, I see the source of your confusion now." Beorin turned around to face me fully. "You're right: only Powers can create factions, and only factions can own sectors. But there are Powers, and *then* there are Powers."

I frowned. "What does that mean?"

He grinned, seeming to take delight in my confusion. "Oh, only that some Powers are as mercenary as the guild. More so, in fact."

I stared at him blankly, then caught on. "The guild has made a deal with one of the Powers," I breathed.

He nodded. "Smart boy."

"A Pact," I said. "It must be a Pact you've formed. The guild gets all the rights of a faction while retaining its autonomy, and in exchange, the Power gets..." My brows crinkled. "What does the Power get?"

"Money," Beorin added succinctly. "Money and artifacts."

I nodded slowly. "Which Power has the guild formed its Pact with?"

Beorin shrugged. "No idea. You'll have to speak to Hannah if you want to know that. Or perhaps the guildmaster." He paused. "Now, are we done here?"

I nodded absently. "Thanks for everything, Beorin."

"I won't say it's been a pleasure," he replied. "But it's been... interesting. Goodbye, lad."

I left the bounty hunters' glade deep in thought.

Matters with the Marauders were far from resolved, and I was certain my actions would have repercussions. But the situation had also revealed an unforeseen opportunity.

I'd spent most of last night pondering what the Marauders were doing in the sector, their goals, and how they hoped to achieve them.

Cara and Shael had called the Marauders power brokers, and therein, I knew, lay the answer. The tavern was just the start. A means to an end for Kalin and his people. The Power had his eyes on the *entire* sector.

He wanted to own it.

Kalin must believe he could gain control of the valley, and whatever his strategy, it couldn't depend on might of arms—how could it when the three major Powers in the sector outnumbered him significantly?

No, Kalin had to be relying on something else: be it subtlety, duplicity, or just plain-old diplomacy. Coming to that realization sparked an interesting question: *if the Marauders can do it, why can't I?*

At first glance, the idea appeared ludicrous.

There was one very large and obvious hurdle to me owning any sector: I had no faction. Thinking of sectors and factions is what had spurred the questions I'd put to Beorin.

I had been peripherally aware that the guild owned dungeons—Hannah had told me so ages ago—but until today, I'd never had occasion to wonder how they managed that feat.

Now, I knew.

And it sent my mind into overdrive.

Can it be done? I wondered. Could *I* control the sector? *Maybe.* It would not be easy, though. I laughed. That was an understatement. But the pieces were all in place, or nearly so.

It would require only a little... finesse.

And time. Lots of time. I smiled, daydreaming of what it would mean to rule the valley.

*　*　*

I was still lost in my plotting when I entered the safe zone.

As I strolled down the tavern's street, I noted that the Marauders' blockades were gone. A pair of bounty hunters stood watchful guard in their place.

Nodding to them in greeting, I entered the tavern.

It was lunchtime, and the common room was packed. The players inside were mainly from the smaller factions in the valley, and I didn't spot anyone bearing Muriel's, Tartar's, or Loken's Marks. From what Saya told me, the bigger factions' soldiers didn't frequent the tavern much, having their own private drinking rooms.

Still, there was no denying the room was *full*. I smiled in pleasure. This, I thought, eyeing the boisterous crowd, was the direct result of my efforts last night.

Scanning the room, I spotted Saya sitting at one of the tables with Cara. Shael was on the stage, entertaining the crowd. The twins were about, too, looking harried as they attended to the patrons. Near simultaneously, both turned in the direction of the open door—and scowled on catching sight of me.

My brows drew down. *Now, what's gotten into them?*

"You promised," Teresa mouthed from across the room.

Oh, right. I was supposed to take the pair out hunting this morning. *Oops.*

But I had come bearing gifts, so maybe that would cheer them up. They looked awfully busy right now, though. *I'll talk to them later*, I decided. Striding through the room, I made my way to Cara and Saya's table.

"Morning," I said cheerfully. I glanced out the open door. "Or is it afternoon?"

The pair looked up, and Cara inclined her cowled head. "Welcome back," she said.

Saya's greeting was more exuberant. "Michael! Thank the Powers. I thought something happened. I've been waiting to hear back from you all morning." She lowered her voice. "It went well, I take it?"

In the act of sitting, I paused. "What did?"

"You know," the gnome said, gesturing impatiently to the crowded room. "Whatever you did to cause this."

I sat down. "Ah. Yes, it did. Although, I can't promise my... fix will hold."

Saya waved aside my warning. "Tell me everything," she demanded, practically bouncing in her chair from excitement.

"Perhaps some food and drink are in order first?" Cara interjected, sounding amused. Turning to me, she ran her gaze over me. "Long night?"

"Very," I said, slumping back in my chair.

"Oh, I'm sorry," Saya apologized, finally noticing my bedraggled state. "I didn't realize. Let me get you something." Before I could say anything, she rose to her feet and dashed away.

Cara followed the departing gnome with her eyes. "We've been chatting."

"Hmm? What about?"

"You made a wise choice in choosing her for this. Saya loves the tavern and has a natural knack for business." She laughed suddenly. "Something I have no flair for myself."

I cocked my head, finding the comment strange. "Oh? I thought that was a prerequisite for the job," I joked. "Don't *all* merchants love business?"

In the act of reaching for her mug, Cara froze.

"Sorry," I said, sensing something amiss. "Did something I say offend?"

"No..."

"Whatever it is, I apologize."

"It's not that," Cara said and took a long sip from her mug. "You didn't offend me. Your words reminded me of… things I would rather not remember." She fell silent again.

"I didn't mean to pry," I assured her. "Whatever it is, you don't have to explain."

"It's no secret." She sighed. "It's just that I've spent so long trying to forget it's hard to talk about."

Saying nothing, I waited. If Cara wanted to tell me what was bothering her, she would.

"I'm not a merchant," she said eventually.

I frowned. "Of course you are."

Cara shook her head. "No. I have aether magic. But I'm not a civilian. Nor do I belong to the merchant Class."

I didn't know what to say. Cara wasn't a merchant? That made no sense.

Cara noticed my confusion. "A long time ago, I did something… Something that caused me to become forsworn." I felt her eyes on me again. "Do you know what that means?"

I shook my head mutely.

"Not surprising," she whispered. "Few do. I'm a sworn who betrayed her goddess."

I stared at her, hardly able to comprehend what that meant. Cara's past and the air of mystery her agent's robes gave her had always intrigued me, but I hadn't expected *this*. "I didn't think that was possible," I said solemnly.

Cara laughed hollowly. "Oh, it's possible, if exceedingly rare." She paused. "It's even rarer to survive such a betrayal."

"What did you do?" I asked quietly.

Cara sighed. "Perhaps, one day I'll tell you. But not today."

Respecting her answer, I didn't pursue the matter further. "But… how did you go from being forsworn to becoming Kesh's agent?"

"Kesh bought my debt."

"Bought?" I asked sharply.

Cara nodded absently, her thoughts far away. "I'm indebted to her until the end of my days."

Shock lashed me. "Kesh *enslaved* you?"

Cara refocused on me. "No, she saved me."

Her words threw me again. "What?"

"Do you know what it means to be a forsworn?" she asked rhetorically. "It's like being a criminal, except you don't just bear the shame of your misdeeds in one sector. They follow you wherever you go. Without my robe, I would be revealed as a forsworn." She shivered. "We are hunted wherever we go and considered fair game by everyone. It's another reason why few of us exist."

"Except those who become Kesh's agents?" I asked.

She nodded. "Exactly."

"Are the rest of Kesh's agents forsworn too?"

"Most are," Cara replied.

"What about the safe zones? Can't you take refuge in them?"

"The safe zones offer no sanctuary to the likes of us. Nor does the Adjudicator. The Game considers us oath breakers and no longer protects us. We've broken our Pacts, and the Powers are free to enact their wrath on us as they please."

My lips tightened in a grim line, finally comprehending the enormity of Cara's predicament. "The last time we spoke, Kesh mentioned your term was ending. What did she mean?"

Cara laughed darkly and gestured to her red robe. "The Triumvirate safeguard us. This robe is as much a symbol of their protection as are the enchantments woven in it. But neither comes cheaply. Nor do they last forever. At the end of our terms of service, Kesh must repurchase the Triumvirate's goodwill."

"I see. So, you're a fugitive." I paused. "Just like me."

Tilting her head to the side, Cara studied me. "You may have more than your fair share of enemies, Michael, but you're no fugitive."

"Oh, but I am. I, too, have done something that the Powers despise. Only in my case, they don't know the truth yet. If they did, I suspect I would be hunted as fanatically as the forsworn."

"You?" Cara asked doubtfully. "What could you have possibly done to cause the Powers to hate you?"

I smiled wryly. "Perhaps, one day I'll tell you," I replied, deliberately echoing her words from earlier.

Before Cara could respond, Saya returned, bearing a tray overburdened with food and drink.

✳ ✳ ✳

The moment Saya sat down, Cara shifted the conversation to matters of little consequence. Wolfing down my food under Saya's watchful eye, I didn't object to the change, but I made a silent promise to myself to help Cara if I could.

"Now," Saya said, leaning forward when I was done eating. "Tell us. How did it go with the Marauders?"

"I managed to dissuade them for a time," I replied. "The bounty hunters helped. You should keep a few around, even after the present troubles with the Marauders end."

The gnome nodded, acknowledging my suggestion. "Dissuade how?"

I grimaced. "Better you don't know the details. But it will take Yzark's people at least a few days to reestablish themselves."

Saya sat back and bit her nails. "A few days... that's good." She shot me a glance. "I hate to ask, but do you have a more permanent solution in mind?"

I nodded. "I do, but it may take a while to pull off. A few months, even."

Saya's lips turned down, but she didn't protest. "We'll manage until then." Reaching across the table, she gripped my hands in wordless thanks.

I squeezed back and glanced around the room. "Things seemed to have gone back to normal pretty quickly. You had no problems last night?"

"None," Saya replied.

"That's good." I turned to Cara. "How did the hunt for a premises go?"

Cara sighed. "Poorly."

"Oh?"

"As you can imagine, all the best shops have already been taken. But no one wants to sell even the fringe locations, no matter the price." She shook her head. "I fear they've decided to band together against the competition."

"What about that abandoned cottage you were telling me about?" Saya asked. "Did you manage to find the owner yet?"

I glanced at Saya. "What's this?"

It was Cara who answered. "There's an unoccupied cabin at the southern edge of the safe zone. It's poorly situated, true, but at this point, anything will do. Unfortunately, no one has been able to track down the owner."

I pursed my lips, having a suspicion as to which building she referred to. "What's the owner's name?"

"Mariga," Cara answered. "A single name is not much to go on, but Kesh has her people on it." She shrugged. "They will trace the player's whereabouts eventually. It will take time, though."

I leaned back in my chair. I knew who Mariga was, of course, and why Cara couldn't find her, but while my pact with Arinna's envoy was over, I didn't think it prudent to reveal the Light player's identity. "I think I may have a way of reaching her."

Cara and Saya looked at me curiously, but they didn't ask how, and for a time, the conversation lapsed.

"So, what's next for you?" Saya asked.

"I have a few other things to attend to in the valley," I replied, thinking of the wolves, "then I will see about acting on the second part of my plan for the Marauders..." Retrieving my alchemy stone and bags of holding from my backpack, I plopped them down before Cara. "Which reminds me, how much do you think I can get for all this?"

"Really, Michael? You couldn't wait until *after* lunch?" Saya asked wryly.

I started guiltily in belated recognition that this was perhaps not the most opportune moment to conduct business. "Sorry," I said, reaching for the bags again, "we can talk—

Cara stopped me. "No, it's alright." Laying her hands over the bags, she interrogated the contents. "There is a lot here," Cara murmured.

I nodded.

"It will take a while to offload all of this," Cara continued, "but I believe Kesh will be able to give you... twenty-five thousand for everything."

Saya gasped.

My lips turned down. "That's all?"

Twenty-five thousand equated to about one hundred gold for each Marauder's gear. Granted, I'd kept the choicest items for myself and had been forced to leave a fair amount behind, but I'd expected a better return.

"M-more?" Saya whispered, her voice sounding strangled. "You want... more?"

"You know Kesh's policy on high-ranked items," Cara chided me. "Some of this equipment will be resold to the original owners at a discount." She paused. "But you could always set those pieces aside and sell them through another merchant if that's what you want?"

Sighing, I waved aside her suggestion. I didn't have the time for that, nor did I want to attract the attention that selling the Marauders' gear would bring. "Twenty-five thousand will do. Split the funds between my account and the tavern's."

I glanced at Saya apologetically. "I was forced to drain the tavern's funds to equip myself, but with what's there now and assuming the Marauders resume their antics, will you be able to keep the tavern going for the next few months?"

Saya nodded faintly, her eyes still round.

"Good." I slid the bags into Cara's keeping, and she completed the transaction.

You have lost 240 caches of miscellaneous items and 32 sets of crafting gear.

You have gained 12,500 golds. Money remaining in your bank account: 15,455 gold coins.

The tavern has gained 12,500 golds. Money remaining in the Sleepy Inn's bank account: 14,850 gold coins.

I rubbed my chin on seeing the last Game alert, reminded of something. "You know, Saya... we still haven't gotten around to changing the tavern's name. You have anything in mind?"

She hesitated, then nodded. "What do you think about Wyvern's Roost? I figured it would be appropriate since, you know, that's where—"

"—we met," I finished. "I like it." Best of all, it contained no hint of Wolf. "Wyvern's Roost it is."

By rights of your bill of ownership, you have renamed the tavern 'Sleepy Inn' in the safe zone of sector 12,560 to 'Wyvern's Roost.'

After I renamed the inn, Saya hurried away to change the tavern's signage, leaving me and Cara alone again.

"Do you have anything else to sell or buy?" she asked neutrally.

From her tone and question, I gathered she didn't want to revisit our previous conversation, and I nodded easily. "I do, actually."

The time had come to reap the benefits of my improved thieving. My traps had served me well against opponents who outranked me and in circumstances where the weight of numbers lay against me. They had also proven especially devastating against unwary opponents and in situations where I'd had time to prepare the ground.

Unequipping my wristband, I pushed it across the table. "I need a rank four replacement for this and tier two and three set trap ability tomes."

"Hmm," Cara said. "Give me a moment." A few seconds later, she materialized the items I requested.

You have acquired an <u>improved set trap</u> ability tome. Governing attribute: Dexterity. Tier: advanced. Cost: 25 gold. Requirement: rank 5 thieving skill.

You have acquired a <u>superior set trap</u> ability tome. Governing attribute: Dexterity. Tier: expert. Cost: 50 gold. Requirement: rank 10 thieving skill.

You have lost a simple trapper's wristband.

You have acquired the rank 4 item: the <u>veteran trapper's wristband</u>. Cost: 800 gold. This item can be used to configure traps of expert tier and below. Each trap can consist of a maximum of 4 components, using any combination of triggers, elements, and guides.

As with its simpler variants, the veteran trapper's wristband does not store components but holds trap-making crystals. Each crystal can be transformed into the desired part as and when required.

Currently stored trap-making crystals: 200 / 200.

Available <u>triggers</u>: pressure plates (for use on floors), sound glasses (omnidirectional), tripwires (between two points), motion pins (cone), and remote control (manual activation).

Available <u>elements</u>: lightning, poison clouds, fire, spring-coiled daggers, bear-trap clamps, small explosives, blots of darkness, and ice.

Available <u>guides</u>: reflect (redirects an element in the desired direction), split (divide and reflect an element), and funnel (concentrates and directs an element in the desired direction). Note, guides only stay materialized for 5 seconds.

Money remaining in your bank account: 14,655 gold coins.

My jaw dropped open in shock. The veteran wristband was a *significant* upgrade from the one I'd been using.

For one, the number of stored trap-crystals had increased fivefold. For another, there were two more element effects to employ—blot of darkness and ice—both of which intrigued me.

The biggest differences, though, were the addition of trap guides and the ability to combine *four* trap components in every trap. Together, they would allow me to create traps of greater complexity.

With this, I can shoot lightning bolts around corners, I thought gleefully. *Or funnel an explosion into a single victim.*

"Nice, isn't it?" Cara said, chuckling at my expression.

"Oh, it's far more than that," I murmured. Picking up the two tomes, I wasted no time learning what they had to teach before equipping my new wristband.

You have upgraded your set trap ability to <u>superior set trap</u>. This tier 3 ability increases the effectiveness of any trap you deploy, enhancing its range and strength and making it harder to spot.

You have 14 of 55 Dexterity ability slots remaining.

You have equipped a trapper's wristband. Stored trap-making crystals: 200 / 200.

"That's it?" Cara asked. "You don't need anything else?"

I nodded absently, still inspecting my new toy.

"Your shopping spree is smaller than I've come to expect," she observed.

"I've realized I need to be more circumspect with my ability slots."

Cara nodded, seeming to understand what I meant.

Rolling down my sleeve to hide the wristband, I glanced at her. "I do have two other matters to discuss with you, actually."

"Oh?" Cara asked, sounding wary.

I smiled to reassure her. "The first is with regards to the wayfarer's gloves. Kesh has found a buyer. Can you tell her to go ahead and complete the purchase?"

"Of course. What's the other matter?"

"The second is more in nature of a question." I paused, taking a moment to gather my thoughts. "What do you know about aetherstones?"

"Aetherstones?" Cara asked, sitting back in surprise. "They're colorless gems and not all that pretty to look at, but they do have a curious ability to record aether coordinates. That makes the stones highly prized." She peered at me. "Where did you hear about them?"

"When we left Nexus, I saw a player leave without employing a portal." I shrugged. "One second, she was fidgeting with something on her arm; the next, she was gone. There was no scroll nor any spell cast that I could see."

"Ah, and you're wondering how she did it," Cara said. "The player you observed likely used an aetherstone artifact. With the right enchantments, the gems can teleport someone between sectors."

"That's what I thought." Removing the bracelet I'd looted from Yzark, I placed it before Cara. "I've managed to acquire one for myself."

Cara drew in a sharp breath. "Where did you get that?"

I smiled wryly. "I'm sure you'd rather not know."

Not questioning me further on the bracelet's origins, Cara picked it up and inspected it minutely. "Don't tell me you intend on selling it?"

I blinked at her. "No, of course not!"

"Good because items like these are greatly sought after. Few have them, and even fewer are willing to part with them. They usually only change hands after death."

She eyed me for a moment. *Wondering who I had killed to get it?*

"In fact," Cara continued, "I've rarely spotted an aetherstone artifact in the hands of any but an elite." She pushed the bracelet back to me. "Most tier five players will kill you just to loot that off your corpse. Keep it hidden."

I nodded and covered the bracelet with my hand. "What makes them so rare?"

"The aetherstones, for one. They are hard to find, and this one has five. But the bracelet's value resides in more than its gems. The enchantments required to make such an artifact are difficult, and few possess the required patience or skill."

"How do I use it?"

The question seemed to puzzle Cara. "The same way you would any other enchanted device, of course."

I waved aside her response. "Not to teleport—I expect that will be easy enough—no, what I want to know is how do I etch a location into an aetherstone."

"Ah. That's easy, too. Simply channel mana into a gem. The process can take anywhere between an hour and a day, depending on how much magic you can control. Once the aetherstone is fully charged, you can imprint any of your known key points onto it."

I frowned. "How will I know when the stone is charged?"

Cara tapped my hand covering the bracelet. "Have you noticed that difference between the artifact's aetherstones?"

I nodded. "I have. Three seem to shine with life. The other two are dull."

"There you go. When you charge one of the empty stones, it will burn with the same inner fire as the other three. Then you may imprint it."

"And that's it?"

"That's it," Cara confirmed. "A word of warning, though. After you've teleported to a location, the aetherstone's stored coordinates will be erased and will have to be re-etched."

"I see," I murmured, thinking that to be more of an advantage than a feature of concern. It meant I wouldn't have to worry about anyone stealing the bracelet and learning the coordinates of the nether-infested sector once I etched them. "Thank you, Cara. That was enlightening."

"You're welcome. Is that all?"

I hesitated, then broached the topic she seemed determined to avoid. "I haven't forgotten our earlier conversation, you know. We will speak of it again—soon."

Cara sighed. "That's old history, and I shouldn't have dredged it up, to begin with. Best you forget about what I said."

"I won't." I stopped myself from saying more. There was no point in making promises I wasn't sure I could keep—yet. "I'll see you tomorrow," I said, rising to my feet.

"Bye, Michael," Cara replied, only a hint of sadness in her voice as she watched me leave.

✳ ✳ ✳

I made my way up the stairs and to my room. Slipping into the chamber, I locked the door behind me. It had been a long night, and all I wanted to do was sink into the bed and sleep.

But time was a commodity in shorter supply than gold.

For one, I still had to find the dire wolves, and for another, I had to flesh out my plans for the valley. At this stage, all I truly had was an idea. If I was going to pursue it, I needed to determine how viable the entire notion was— that meant learning how to create a faction and speaking to the representatives of the three major Powers in the sector. If they weren't amenable, my plan was sunk already.

I will have to find Loken and Muriel's envoys and secure a meeting.

I already knew Tartar's envoy, but approaching Talon was more problematic than finding the other two—he had threatened to kill me, after all. I sighed, realizing I would have to risk a meeting with the good captain anyway.

So, prioritize, Michael. Sitting down on the bed, I ran through what I had to do and when.

Visit Captain Talon tomorrow. Find the wolves tonight. Sleep out the rest of the day. I closed my fist around the aetherstone bracelet. *But first, I need to learn how to use this.*

The artifact was my ticket to reaching the arctic wolves. Sure, I couldn't teleport directly into the guardian tower, but the bracelet would take me to the nether-infested sector, and from there, Snow and the others were only one short portal hop away.

For just an instant, I was tempted to go to them immediately. But checking on the dire wolves came first, if only because their circumstances were less certain. It had been nearly two years since I'd seen Duggar's pack, and the surge in the valley's player numbers had to have taken a toll on them.

Bending over the bracelet, I focused on one of its empty aetherstones and slipped mana into it. The stone sucked eagerly at the magic, craving more. I let it have it, and in nearly no time, a torrent of mana gushed out from me and into the gem.

Your mana has been depleted.
Void armor inoperative. Current charge: 0%.

Well, that was easy. I glanced at the stone, expecting a change, but it looked just as dull as before. I frowned. *Perhaps, it just needs time,* I thought and waited anxiously for the stone to light up.

It didn't.

Urgh. Now what? I drummed my fingers on the bed. Cara had said to channel mana into it. *Alright, let's do that.*

Closing my eyes, I spread my awareness. The channeling skill was similar to meditation but, where restoring psi required turning my focus inward, mana was recouped from the surroundings. The world of the Forever Kingdom was saturated with magic, and to regain my mana, I only had to direct some of that mana to seep into *me.*

Which I did now.

You have replenished 1% of your mana.
You have failed to advance your channeling: skills cannot be gained in a safe zone.

Ignoring the Game message, I guided the incoming stream of magic into the aetherstone. It drank it in just as easily as my body had.

I kept channeling, feeding more mana from the surroundings into the dull gem. Cara had been right. The process was simple.

But how long would it take?

✳   ✳   ✳

It was close to midnight before the aetherstone was sated.

By that time, my limbs were shaky and my eyes heavy. I had, in fact, nodded off several times over the course of the afternoon and had contemplated stopping no few times, but each time, I'd shaken myself out of my lethargy and kept going.

And now, finally, I was done.

Blinking blearily, I stared down at the gem that had been the object of my focus for the last twelve hours. It was shining as brightly as the other three on the bracelet and, for the last few seconds, had refused more mana.

Huh, I thought, my thoughts stupid with sleep. *I guess it's charged.* Too tired to move further, I flopped down on the bed. *I'll rest, just for an hour or two, then I'll set out,* I thought drowsily. *The wolves shouldn't be too hard to find.*

Closing my eyes, I let sleep claim me.

Chapter 286: The Strength of a Promise

A mailed fist banged on my door, and my eyes jerked open. What time was it? Two hours couldn't have passed already, surely? It felt like only moments ago that I'd lain my head on the pillow.

"Michael! Are you in there?"

I groaned. It was Terence. "Go away and come back in the morning," I yelled back.

There was a pause. "It *is* morning," Teresa said. "The sun has been up for ages!"

I didn't respond. She had to be lying. There was no way I'd slept for that long.

The pair resumed banging. Covering my head with the pillow, I tried to muffle the sound. No such luck. At times like this, it didn't pay to have sharp hearing.

"You promised to take us hunting yesterday," Teresa shouted reproachfully.

I had, hadn't I? What had made me do a fool thing like that? Now, I was paying for that moment of carelessness.

"Yeah, we're not going to let you back out on your word and sneak out again," Terence added.

Damnation... these two were relentless. "Come back later, then we can—"

"No," Teresa said firmly. "You promised us a full day!"

I'd done no such thing, but succumbing to the inevitable, I sat up nonetheless. I doubted I was going to be able to sleep again anyway. Glancing at the closed shutter, I saw, to my surprise, that soft light was filtering through. So, Teresa hadn't been lying entirely. It *was* morning—if an ungodly hour.

The twins pounded in tandem on the door again.

"All right," I grumbled. "I'm coming."

Marching up to the door, I yanked it open to glare at their smiling faces. "Breakfast first," I pronounced.

✳ ✳ ✳

The common room was nearly empty, not surprising given the early hour. Shael sat alone at the only occupied table. While the twins scampered away to fetch breakfast, I sat opposite the bard.

"Morning," I said. "You're awake early."

The half-elf looked up from the cup he was nursing. "Up late, actually," he corrected, greeting me with tired eyes. He cocked his head as he took in my own appearance. "You look like you've been dragged out of bed."

"That's because I was," I replied grouchily, my gaze drifting to the twins who were already hurrying back with a platter of food.

The bard grinned as he followed my gaze. "By them?"

I nodded as the twins arrived with the food. "Thank you," I said. Retrieving one of my bags of holding from my backpack, I set it down on the table. "You two should eat too. And while you're at it, look at what's in there."

Naturally, the pair didn't take the hint. "What's inside?" Teresa asked, making no effort to leave or take the bag.

I rolled my eyes. "It's the gear I acquired for you and Terence. If we're going to leave the safe zone, you two better be properly equipped. Contrary to what you believe, I didn't forget my promise. I'm just running a bit behind schedule, that's all." I pointed to the bag neither had touched yet. "Now," I said more forcefully, "go and re-equip yourselves with that, and let me have a private word with Shael."

Wordlessly, Terence snatched the bag and yanked Teresa away. She went, but only reluctantly, still seeming disinclined to leave.

Shael chuckled as the twins disappeared again. "You're really going to take them out hunting?"

I glanced at him. "You know about that?"

He smiled. "They tried to convince *me* to take them." He held a hand to his chest. "I pleaded tiredness."

I grunted. "You have a better way with words than I do, then. My own excuses fell flat."

Shael laughed and sipped from his mug again.

Sighing, I dug into my food. I wasn't as mad at the twins as I made out to be. I *had* given them my word, and it was past time I began the day, anyway.

But taking the pair out hunting did complicate matters. How was I going to search for the dire wolves with them in tow? I'd delayed my visit to the pack long enough, and now it seemed I would have to put it off again. I blew out a troubled breath.

"Problems?" Shael inquired.

"Nothing out of the ordinary," I replied, then eyed him. "How are you finding the tavern?"

"A pleasant change from Nexus," he admitted. "I actually have a bed to sleep in, and yesterday I even earned some decent coin."

I swallowed another mouthful. "You have any plans for the future yet?"

Shael's face grew serious. "Why? Do you need me for something?"

I nodded. "I'd like you to stay at the tavern a while longer. I'm not sure how long I will be able to remain in the valley and matters with the Marauders are far from resolved. I would feel comfortable if Saya had someone to call on if things turn ugly again."

"Whatever you need," Shael said. "I will stay as long as necessary."

"I will pay you for your troubles, of course."

The bard shook his head. "Not necessary. Saya is already paying me *and* providing free lodgings, too. More is not required."

I studied him for a moment. "You sure?"

He nodded.

"Thank you, Shael," I said gravely.

"You're welcome, my friend."

I stared at the bard thoughtfully. Was Shael that—a friend? My instincts said yes, but I had to be careful who I trusted and how far.

"Oh, I spoke to that merchant," Shael said, interrupting my musings. "The one Saya was angry about."

"Ah, and what did you find out?" I asked, already having an inkling of what he would say from the Marauder conversation I'd overheard.

"He was bribed, but interestingly enough, by two separate parties."

"Oh?" I asked, sitting up in sudden interest.

Shael nodded. "One, as we suspected, was the Marauders. They wanted the tavern cut off from outside help and paid the merchant to stop the flow of messages. The second party was more interesting. She asked for a copy of the messages to be redirected to her without Kesh or Saya ever knowing. The merchant took both parties' monies but delivered only partially on each request."

"She?" I asked sharply.

The bard nodded solemnly. "The lady never showed her face or gave her name, but the merchant suspects her to be Loken's envoy."

"Of course." Bowing my head, I rubbed my temples as I felt the onslaught of another headache coming.

It made sense. Loken had known about the tavern and Saya, and he'd quite openly warned me he'd be watching. The question was, had he learned anything?

Unlikely.

Neither Kesh nor Saya knew about my bloodline or the wolves. At best, Loken had only learned how wealthy I'd become, which was perhaps not a bad thing either. During our last meeting, the trickster had seemed convinced some mysterious faction or group had recruited me. Maybe, whatever his envoy saw in the letters would allay his fears.

My tension had eased. I had nothing to fear from the letters Loken and his followers had intercepted. But the fact they had gone to all the trouble of doing so reinforced the need for caution.

"What are you involved in?" Shael asked suddenly. "Do you belong to Loken? Is that why you asked me to deliver that message to the Shadow Keep?"

"I'm not." I hesitated, then added reluctantly. "But Loken has taken an interest in me."

Shael inhaled sharply. "The trickster is dangerous. You should stay far away from him."

I grimaced. "I know, but I have little choice in the matter." I studied him anew. "Do you want to reconsider your offer to stay? I'll understand if you want to have no further part in this."

"No," he said firmly. "I will not run away."

I nodded and refrained from asking him again if he was sure. "How did you manage to get all that from the merchant, anyway?"

Shael smiled. "I used a deception ability called guile. It wouldn't work on someone like you, but it works wonders against a player with low Perception."

"Interesting," I mused. It was a pity I didn't have more Perception slots available myself. The ability sounded useful, but before I could ask Shael for a rundown on it, the twins re-entered the room wearing their new gear.

I rose to my feet. "See you later," I said in farewell to the bard and guided the pair outside.

*　*　*

"Where did you get all this stuff?" Teresa asked the moment we exited the tavern.

Not checking my stride to answer her, I turned north along the street. Glancing over my shoulder, I saw the twins were following if more slowly than I liked. Teresa looked the more unhappy of the pair and was peering at me suspiciously.

"Why? Don't you want it?" I asked mildly.

"Don't get us wrong," Terence said, laying a restraining hand on Teresa before she could speak. "This stuff is great and all, but we can't help but wonder what you want in return. We've received 'free gifts' before that turned out to be not all that free."

I nodded, appreciating his explanation, and scrutinized them again.

I'd not been entirely sure of the pair's skill mix, so I'd stored a variety of armor and sword pieces in the bag. In addition, I'd thrown in a tidy number of stat-boosting items. Terence, I observed, had equipped himself in plate armor and had a broadsword and shield strapped across his back.

Teresa had gone for chainmail and had a pair of longswords on her hips. I raised an eyebrow at the blades but didn't comment. Wielding two longswords was infinitely harder than doing the same with smaller blades like mine. But both youths were taller than me, and Teresa looked like she had the height and reach to wield her chosen weapons expertly.

"I expect nothing in exchange," I said finally. "I marked all the stuff you're wearing for trash before realizing you two may find them handy. I assure you it costs me nothing to pass the gear on." That was not quite true but was close enough.

"Trash? That means you didn't buy the equipment," Teresa said, not letting the matter go. "Where did you get it?"

I glanced at her. "From the Marauders, if you must know."

Almost in sync, both twins' gazes darted to the abandoned blockades on the street. The Marauders had still not returned.

"Is that where you were yesterday?" the girl asked. "Killing Marauders?" I nodded.

"That doesn't explain the empty barricades," she pointed out. "No matter how many you killed, they would've returned." Her eyes narrowed. "Did you make some sort of deal with them?"

I laughed. "Hardly. But right now, they're likely reconsidering their strategy."

"How many did you kill?" Terence asked curiously.

"All of them."

He stared at me blankly, thinking I was joking. But when I said nothing further, he blurted, "You can't be serious."

"I am."

"But–but..." he began before running aground.

"How did you do it?" Teresa asked. She seemed less stunned than her twin.

"I slew them in their sleep," I replied, seeing no reason to hide the truth. The Marauders must have figured out that much by now, and as brash as the youths appeared, instilling a little fear in them would not go amiss.

Maybe, it will even be enough to make them stop asking questions.

But if anything, my answer only piqued Teresa's interest further. "How did you catch them unawares?" she asked. "They wouldn't have left themselves unprotected unless—" She broke off. "You snuck into their camp," she concluded.

The girl was smarter than she looked. "I did."

"How did you manage that?" Terence asked. "Wasn't it warded?"

I smiled. "It was."

That seemed to stump him for a moment, but not for long. Turning to his twin, he whispered, "Told you he was an assassin."

"He's more than that," Teresa hissed back. "Now, shush. He's looking this way."

Smiling contentedly, I said nothing more as we left the village.

Chapter 287: A Day in the Life of a Mentor

You have left a safe zone.

"Alright," I said, stopping the twins at the edge of the village. "Time to decide where we're going."

I looked at the two questioningly.

"Don't look at us," Terence said. "We've died every time we left the village."

"I've been out of the sector for over a year," I said patiently. "You two must know the valley better than me by now."

The pair exchanged glances. "We know the location of a few lairs," Teresa began hesitantly, "but nothing with monsters we're up to fighting." She glanced down at her new gear. "Even in this."

"Don't worry about the creatures' levels," I said. "I'll do the tanking."

That earned me skeptical looks.

I laughed. "Don't worry, you'll see. Now tell me."

The two started speaking, cautiously at first, then more confidently, describing all the monster dens and lairs they'd been to or heard tell off from the tavern's patrons.

It made for a long list, but not one minute into their recital, I knew where we were going. I didn't stop them, though. I listened attentively throughout but heard no mention of dire wolves. It boded well, and I began to feel better about the pack's chances.

"So where should we go?" Terence asked as they ran down.

"East," I responded laconically. Turning in that direction, I headed for the treeline.

"*Where* east?" Teresa asked as the twins hurried to catch up.

"East east," I said, not above exacting a small measure of revenge for the pair's early morning obstinance.

"That's not an answer," Teresa snapped.

Ignoring the girl's glower and betraying no sign of my amusement, I kept walking. I noticed, though, that Terence had lost interest in the conversation and was eyeing the nearing treeline with visible concern. Casually, I let my gaze slide to Teresa. She, too, was shooting the approaching forest unhappy glances.

They're afraid, I realized.

"We're heading to the valley's eastern mountain slopes," I said, taking pity on them.

The twins' gazes jerked back to me.

"But there is nothing there except..." Terence's brows drew down.

"... the fire lizards' lair," Teresa finished, her eyes growing round. "We can't fight those things!"

"You can," I said firmly. "And you will."

I had two reasons for my choice of hunting grounds. The eastern mountain range was where the pack had taken refuge from the wyvern mother the last time, and I expected if the dire wolves were to be found anywhere in the valley, it was there. *No harm in doing a little scouting while I help these two.*

The second reason, of course, was that if I was going to spend the day shepherding the pair, there was no reason why *I* couldn't get in some training too. And the fire lizards sounded like the ideal creatures with which to build up my elemental resistance.

Teresa opened her mouth—to lodge another protest, I expected—but fell silent as a squad of players exited the treeline. I tensed before realizing they were not Marauders.

The soldiers, dressed in unrelieved black, walked—no, marched—in a disciplined column and wore a recognizable insignia on their arms: the raging bull of Tartar.

Legionnaires, I thought.

At the head of the column of nearly one hundred soldiers was a half-orc, also familiar. *Ultack.* Did that mean Cecilia was around too? I couldn't spot any sign of her, though, and I returned my attention to the company commander. By the look of it, Ultack was doing well. Not only was he a full member of the legion, but he was also an officer by all appearances.

I wonder if he still remembers me.

Ducking my head, I watched the soldiers draw closer. They wouldn't get near enough to recognize me if they kept on their current trajectory. Still, I wasn't reassured.

"You know them?" Teresa asked in a worried whisper.

"Quiet," I ordered in a low voice, and for a wonder, she fell silent as we maintained our heading.

I needn't have worried about being recognized, though. No one in the legionnaire company spared us a glance, and in hindsight, I understood why. Three lone players posed no threat to a group one hundred strong—at least not on the face of it.

The tartans passed us by, and I relaxed. "I knew some of them," I said, finally answering Teresa's question, "from when I was in the valley before."

"You think they'll recruit us?" Terence asked hopefully.

I rolled my eyes at the boy's obsession with joining a faction. "No, and before you ask, I will *not* put in a good word for you."

Before either twin could think of how to respond, I hurried my steps and slipped beyond the treeline.

✳   ✳   ✳

The village's immediate surroundings were quieter than expected, and while more than one group of soldiers drew close to our small party, I successfully steered us past without being spotted.

After we put a few miles between us and the safe zone, we ran into no other groups, and I began to relax. The valley's southeastern side seemed as abandoned as its southwestern one.

"You sure we're heading the right way?" Terence asked me for what felt like the hundredth time.

I nodded easily.

Both youths had grown unusually tight-lipped once we entered the trees—not that I minded the silence—and I could tell they were tense. The dense underbrush, the looming trees, and the constant cries of predators and prey had them on edge.

"What are you looking for?" I asked after Terence stared too-long stare at an inoffensive piece of shrubbery.

"Threats," he said, not looking away from the bush.

"There's nothing there," I told him mildly.

"You can't be sure of that," he retorted.

"Actually, I can," I said, tapping my head. "My hearing is better than yours, and on top of that, I have other abilities to detect the approach of hostiles. We're safe."

Despite my words, Terence did not look reassured.

"Trust me," I said gently. "There was a reason you asked *me* to accompany you on this trip. I know what I'm doing."

Reluctantly, Terence broke his standoff with the bush, and we continued on our way. The exchange kicked off another flurry of whispers between the twins, and this time, I declined to listen in.

After a moment, Teresa spoke up. "I'm sorry, Michael, we're not normally this jumpy. It's just..." She exhaled mightily. "The forest has not been kind to us."

"I understand. Having your entire company wiped out would give anyone cause for nerves." I smiled reassuringly. "Just try to keep it together a little longer, and we'll be out of these woods."

"I hope so," Terence said fervently.

Cutting short further conversation, we resumed our hike east.

✳   ✳   ✳

Nearly an hour later, we reached our destination. Both twins exhaled audibly as we broke out of the trees.

"We're here," I said.

"We are?" Terence asked, studying the empty mountainside.

"The lair is about half a mile north, but yes, we are." I pointed out a shadowed cavity in the mountainside. "There. That looks exactly like the cave entrance your tavern patron described."

The twins squinted in the direction I pointed. "I don't see anything," Teresa complained.

"It's there," I assured them.

"Are you sure about this?" Terence asked. "The fire lizards are rumored to be rank six creatures. We're nowhere near ready to face that."

"Don't worry. That's what I'm here for."

"You still planning on tanking them?" he asked, nonplussed.

I nodded.

"But how?" Teresa asked. "They do as much fire damage as physical damage, and you're no mage." She made a show of peering behind me. "Unless you're hiding a magic shield somewhere I don't see."

I chuckled. But despite my amusement, I realized I would have to reassure the pair. Otherwise, they would be too on edge in the coming skirmish, and instead of focusing on their own roles would be worrying if *I* was doing my part.

"I have a type of fire resistance skill that I plan on training. I will draw the lizards' attacks and hold their attention while you two strike from the flanks, scoring the kills. How does that sound?"

"Sounds easier said than done," Terence muttered. Teresa nodded in agreement.

Ignoring their ambivalence, I led the pair up the mountain slope. "It will be fine," I assured them again.

It seemed like I was doing a lot of that today.

✳   ✳   ✳

It was a short walk to the cave mouth, although more correctly, it was a tunnel entrance. The fire lizards were nesting inside the mountain itself, and the cave we'd spotted was only the start of a long, dark winding tunnel to get there.

Predictably, the twins were not enthused by the idea of exploring inside.

"Won't it be better to draw the creatures out?" Teresa asked. "That's what Hengis' party did." Hengis was a former tavern patron and the twins' source. He was how they'd known about the lair in the first place.

I shook my head. "That won't work." I gestured to the wide-open mountainside. "Out here, the creatures can come at us from multiple directions. We'll be overrun in no time, and I won't be able to protect you two."

"But it's dark in there," Terence protested. "How will we even be able to see?"

"I can see well enough in the dark, and there is plenty of brush and kindling lying about. Create some torches if you must," I said, striving to be patient. The pair were young and had seen more death than they should have. Understandably they were fearful, and they knew little of my abilities. "Besides," I said, grinning, "once the fire lizards start attacking, there will be enough light to see by."

That did not earn me any answering smiles. I sighed. *I don't think I'm cut out for this mentoring business.*

"Hengis said it was too dangerous to enter the lair," Teresa said. "Are you sure about this strategy?"

I didn't roll my eyes, but I wanted to. Hengis and his party had fled the valley before they ever returned to the lair, which is why no one but the twins knew about the fire lizards. Still, from everything I'd heard about the 'great' Hengis, I doubted his party had been up to the task of clearing the lair. I said none of that, though.

Deciding the time for talking was done, I drew ebonheart and faithful. "I'm going in. Follow me if you wish."

I stepped into the tunnel. After only a few feet, it turned sharply, cutting off the light from the entrance. I paused to listen. The twins were still talking, the sounds of their furious whispering at the cave mouth carrying clearly to me. Leaving them to it, I advanced farther.

Finally, I heard a match strike behind me, marking the sound of two torches being lit. I snorted softly. For all the pair's complaints, they'd come well prepared. Drawing to a halt, I waited for them to catch up.

The twins took their time, alertly scanning their surroundings before taking each step. I did not admonish them for their slowness. With danger so close, their caution was warranted.

Both moved in lockstep with one another. Terence held his shield in his offhand and Teresa, one of her blades. *They function well as a unit,* I thought.

"Good. You came," I said as they drew to a halt before me. "Now, you two hang back. I don't want the lizards to be alerted to our presence before we are ready for them. Understood?"

Curt nods were my only response.

Even better, I thought. Now that the fight was nearly upon us, the pair had given up on their incessant questions and arguments. *This might just work, after all.*

Opening my mindsight and wrapping myself in shadows, I resumed my careful advance.

Chapter 288: Building Resistance

A few minutes later, the tunnel opened into a large cavern reminiscent of the first level of the guardian tower.

Multiple hostile entities have failed to detect you! You are hidden.

Dropping into a crouch, I scanned the chamber. While the cavern contained no lava, the rock floor glowed a dull red, courtesy of the heat generated by the dozens of fire lizards lazing in its depths.

The creatures themselves were man-sized and built low to the ground. Their bodies were covered by a roughened hide with cruelly tipped spikes that, despite their seeming thickness, failed to hide the gleaming crimson of the lizards' innards. Most of the creatures appeared asleep, but now and again, one would emit a small plume of fire through its elongated snout.

Flaming snores? I wondered inanely.

Letting my gaze rove over the cavern, I took count of the creatures' numbers. *Fivescore,* I concluded. It was a sizable lair. The closest lizards were more than ten yards away, but even in the cavern's soft red light, they failed to spot me.

Reaching out with my will, I analyzed all the creatures within range.

The target is a level 61 fire lizard.
The target is a level 63 fire lizard.
The target is …

...

The fire lizards' levels were exactly as the twins had described, and the tactics I'd devised should suffice. *But damn, if it isn't hotter than I expected,* I thought as I wiped away the sweat running down my face.

Behind me, I heard the twins approaching. Retreating from the chamber, I headed back to let them know what I'd found.

✳   ✳   ✳

"This is it," I told the youths after describing what we faced. "Are you ready?"

Tense nods.

Whatever doubts the twins had—and I was sure they still had plenty— they hid them well now that our course was decided. "Good. Cast any buffs you have while I do the same."

Your Dexterity has increased by +8 ranks for 20 minutes.
You have gained an encumbrance aura for 10 minutes.
You have trigger-cast quick mend.

Extracting four healing potions from my backpack, I handed them to the twins. "Use those and heal yourself if it becomes necessary. Now, do you remember the plan?"

"We do," Teresa replied. "Strike from the sides, and don't get in front of you."

I nodded. The three of us had retreated to the tightest stretch of the tunnel. It was barely wide enough for me to swing my swords, and I judged that no more than one of the fire lizards would be able to come at me at a time.

Terence stood a step behind me and held his shield and broadsword at the ready. Teresa was on my left, also a step behind and with her longswords drawn.

"There is just one more thing to do." Walking a few steps forward, I crouched down and, rubbing my thumb across the blue rune on the trapper's wristband, activated the item.

You have passed a thieving skill check!
You have removed 2 trap-making crystals from your trapper's wristband.
Remaining trap-making crystals: 198 of 200.

One of the nice things about my new veteran trapper's wristband was that it did not force me to use four components for every trap. For less complicated traps or when I needed a less powerful effect, I could use a minimum of two parts, thereby rationing my trap-making crystals.

As the enchanted crystals fell into my waiting hands, I cast set trap and configured the device I had in mind.

You have concealed an ice trap element.
You have connected a trap element to a remote-control trigger.
An ice trap has been successfully configured!

Rising to my feet, I pocketed the trigger.

"What did you do?" Teresa asked, studying the empty ground in confusion. The ice trap, of course, was hidden from her eyes.

"I laid a trap."

"A trap? Why would you do that?" Terence asked.

"As a failsafe." I smiled and tapped my pocket. "I don't think we'll need it, but if things start to go wrong, I'll activate the trap, and we'll get the hell out of here while the lizards are frozen."

The twins brightened immediately. "A backup," Teresa marveled. "Clever."

I grinned. "I thought so." Turning around, I faced down the tunnel. "Alright, here goes."

Drawing in a deep breath, I raised my head and howled.

Behind me, I heard both youths start at the sound, and I felt my own measure of surprise, too. What I'd intended as a generic war cry had come out sounding uncannily like a wolf's howl.

I'd yelled to attract the lizards' attention, and I could have chosen any noise, of course. In hindsight, the sound I'd opted for was perhaps not the wisest choice, but it was the battle cry that came most naturally.

"Are they coming?" Terence asked, gripping his weapons tightly.

Holding up one hand for patience, I cocked my head and listened. There was a faint tremor to the floor and what I thought sounded like the tramp of many webbed feet drawing closer. "Yes," I replied, somewhat unnecessarily, as the forefront of the lizard wave rounded a bend in the tunnel.

Catching sight of us, the mass of flickering shapes hissed in displeasure and slithered forward faster.

"There's so many," Teresa whispered in dismay.

Ignoring her, I bent my knees and readied myself. There would be no fancy footwork to this fight and minimal dodging. I would have to rely solely on my swordplay to keep the snapping jaws at bay, my void skills to minimize the fire damage I sustained, and chi heal to restore myself.

No biggie, I thought, yet I couldn't help but wonder if I'd overestimated my ability to hold back the creatures. *A fine time for second thoughts, Michael,* I thought dryly.

Narrowing my eyes, I focused on the lizard in the fore. It was wider than I was and longer than I was tall—which was good, it would keep the others out of reach—and was already emitting short bursts of flame—not so good.

The flares of flames were contained, though. While they would undoubtedly wash over me, the twins were far enough back not to feel the fire's touch. The other bit of good news was that, weighed down by their armored hides, the lizards were slow, increasing my chances of avoiding their attacks.

The lead lizard reached striking distance.

Beating its tail against the ground in anger, the creature opened its mouth, and a small flame ballooned out.

I saw the attack coming but stayed where I was. *This is going to—*

You have failed a magical resistance check!
A breath of fire has injured you!

Raging hot flames bathed me, scorching hair, blistering skin, and charring armor. I clamped my jaw shut, holding in the scream that threatened to burst free, but as much as the flames hurt, the level of pain was nothing like what I'd experienced at the touch of Inga's self-immolation spell.

I was fully aware of the avidly watching twins too. This was the most critical moment. If I cried out now or showed the least sign of fear, the pair would bolt.

Swallowing the agony, I kept my eyes open and focused on my foe. The lizard's jaws were darting forward, reaching for the meaty mass of my thigh. Swinging ebonheart downward, I pushed away the creature's snout.

You have blocked a fire lizard's attack.

I chanced a look behind me.

The twins were staring at my ravaged face in horror. "Attack," I croaked from a throat burnt, blackened, raw, and parched.

"He's crazy," Terence whispered in awe.

"But right," Teresa whispered back.

Jerking into motion, the two struck in tandem from my flanks, doing nearly no damage to the lizard. But that didn't matter. The two were engaged. The battle had kicked off, and everything was going according to plan—so far. I smiled grimly.

Now, all I have to do is stay in the fight.

The lizard's jaw opened again. Bracing myself for another douse of flames, I summoned psi.

✳   ✳   ✳

You have restored yourself with quick mend. Your health is at 100%.

In a fraction of a second, my hair grew back, and my skin took on a new sheen of health.

Of course, in the *next* second, I was engulfed in flames again, and the cycle began anew. I was unfazed, though. Now that the first brush of contact had passed, the battle had settled into a steady exchange of blows.

I had judged the width of the tunnel correctly, and despite frantic attempts by the lizards behind my foe, none of them were able to join their fellow in striking me, leaving them to rage impotently at nothing.

Teresa and Terence had fallen into their own rhythm. Their swords rising and falling, the twins chopped into my foe and, slowly but surely, hacked away bits of its hide armor.

For my part, I kept my maneuvers defensive, fending off every attempt of the fire lizard to clamp its jaws around my ankles, shins, and thighs. Its bout of flames, I ignored.

Most of my attention was not on the physical contest, though. Turning my focus inwards, I concentrated on the Game messages scrolling through my mind.

You have failed a magical resistance check!
A breath of fire has injured you! Your health has decreased to 96%.
Your void armor has reduced the elemental damage incurred by 10%. Void armor charge remaining: 98%.
Your elemental absorption has increased to level 26.

Unlike in previous battles, I kept a close watch on the performance of my void armor. My elemental absorption skill was still too low for me to fully resist the fire lizard's breath attacks. However, the mana shell encasing me still absorbed a decent portion of the damage I incurred, and ever so slowly, my skill was advancing.

Your elemental absorption has increased to level 30 and reached rank 3, increasing your chances of resisting harmful elemental effects by 7.5% and decreasing the damage you suffer from them by 15%.

Given the relative ease of the physical combat, I was able to split my focus as I'd learned to do in guardian tower and cast quick mend when my health dropped too low. Taking matters a step further, I also meditated and channeled mana while in the thick of battle.

You have restored your psi to 100%.
You have replenished 1% of your mana. Void armor charge remaining: 99%.
Your channeling has increased to level 27.

My multitasking was not without consequences, and I missed parrying more than a few blows, but even when the fire lizard clamped its jaws around my leg, it was unable to inflict grievous damage before I recovered and beat it back for the cycle to begin anew.

✳　✳　✳

Thirty minutes went past, then an hour, before the twins finally killed their first fire lizard.

A level 65 fire lizard has died.

Terence whooped, and Teresa laughed. My attention fixed on the rest of the fire lizards still swarming behind the dead beast, I didn't turn to look at them.

"Congratulations," I called over my shoulder. "How many levels did you two gain?" Not unexpectedly, I'd gained no levels.

"One level each!" Terence shouted excitedly.

I frowned. "Only one level?"

"It's because you're helping us," Teresa said. "You can't fool the Adjudicator, you know."

I nodded, realizing she was correct. I glanced at the remaining fire lizards. They were still milling behind the dead creature and making no attempt to advance. My frown deepened. "Why aren't they attacking?" I wondered aloud.

"It's because their underbellies are soft," Terence explained.

I shot him a puzzled look. "What does that mean?"

"The fire lizards know better than to try climbing over each other," Teresa said. "The spiked armor covering the dead beast's back will tear open the bellies of whichever one tried."

"Ah," I muttered in understanding, then gestured at the corpse. "Then, what are you two waiting for? Drag that away, and let's have at the next one."

✳　✳　✳

Six hours later, we still labored on.

The twins had gradually become more efficient at slaying the fire lizards, gaining levels and skills with each kill. My own elemental absorption and channeling skills increased apace, but after six hours, I was thoroughly bored with my routine and decided to add another wrinkle: charging the remaining aetherstone on my bracelet.

As expected, the stone eagerly sucked at the mana I provided, and I was stretched to my very limits to simultaneously tank the fire lizards, restore my psi, keep my void armor operational, heal myself, *and* charge the gem.

It made for an interesting afternoon.

As night fell, after nearly thirteen straight hours of fighting, our small party was exhausted. Behind us was a pile of fifteen corpses. We'd slain close to a fifth of the fire lizards, and though that was nothing to shout about, the twins had gained fifteen levels and multiple ranks in their weapon skills.

My own player level had not advanced at all, and while my skill improvements did not match the twins' gains, they were impressive nonetheless.

Your elemental absorption has increased to level 81 and reached rank 8, increasing your chances of resisting harmful elemental effects by 20% and decreasing the damage you suffer from them by 40%.

Your dodging has increased to level 119. Your shortswords has increased to level 137. Your two weapon fighting has increased to level 119. Your light armor has increased to level 126.

Your chi has increased to level 121. Your meditation has increased to level 143. Your channeling has increased to level 101.

I glanced at my companions. Both their faces were masks of concentration, and none of the fear they'd shown earlier in the day was in evidence. *They're enjoying themselves,* I thought, pleased for the pair.

Still, it was time to cut things short.

I had a long night ahead of me. First, I had to escort the pair back to the village, and then, I had to return to the mountains. I had not, as I'd hoped, been able to scout the area for the pack while training the twins, but I would do so after they were back in the safe zone.

"This is the last one," I said. "Then we retreat."

A perspiring Teresa nodded weary agreement. All three of us were soaked through from the ambient heat generated by the fire lizards.

"Will we return tomorrow?" Terence asked.

I hesitated. I'd only committed to taking the twins on a single hunting expedition, but after my own skill improvements over the course of the day, I knew I would benefit from another day too. "Perhaps," I allowed eventually. It would depend on what I discovered tonight. "I will let you know—"

"*GGGRRRR...*"

I froze as the snarl cut across my mind. Loud. Abrasive. Angry.

"What's wrong?" Teresa asked, sensing my distress. She didn't stop hacking at the fire lizard attacking me, though, and neither did Terence. They had not heard what I had.

The growl was all in my mind. But real. Very real.

Ignoring the question, I fixed on the source of the sound. It had come from a dire wolf—an unhappy dire wolf who, at this very instant, was stalking closer.

Chapter 289: Visitors

"Go away."

The words were hurled in my mind with such force, I was almost pitched forward and into my foe—the fire lizard had not stopped attacking.

"Easy there," I said to the other. *"I'm a friend of the Pack."*

I hadn't recognized the speaker's voice, and my mindsight was empty. Whoever the wolf was, he was intent on hiding himself. Urged to caution, I erected a half-shield of psi around my mind. If nothing else, it would hide my thoughts.

My words drew no verbal response from the wolf, but I sensed him pad closer. *Why the anger, and why the games?* I wondered.

You have failed to detect a hidden entity!

"Leave, prey!" the unknown wolf snapped again.

My brows drew down. *Now, what does that mean?*

"Michael?" Terence yelled. It sounded as if he'd been calling me for a while.

Wrenching my attention away from the strange wolf, I focused on the twins and gestured to the half-dead fire lizard still attacking me. "See to this. There is something else I have to deal with."

"On it," the twins replied in unison, thankfully not questioning me further.

I glanced over my shoulder and snapped, *"Identify yourself!"* I had no target for my mental shout, but I had broadcast my sending wide enough that my visitor could not fail to hear, and this time, there had been nothing polite about my tone. I'd flung my words as forcefully back at the wolf as he had his own at me.

The snap of command in my voice gave the interloper pause and I sensed him draw back a moment. *"I... am... pack,"* he half-whined.

"No, you're not," I retorted.

The wolf's thoughts were shielded, hiding much of his nature—but not everything. His mind felt almost... feral and strangely different from the dire wolves I remembered.

"I AM," the wolf asserted. *"You are not."*

You have detected a hidden entity!

A growl sounded from almost beneath my eyes, this time in the real.

"GO. NOW," my angry visitor demanded.

My gaze drifted downwards to witness two yellow eyes emerge from the darkness as the wolf stalked forward.

The twins gasped. They, too, had spotted our visitor.

"Dire wolf!" Terence wheezed and began to swing his broadsword around. Teresa's stance shifted, too, as she tried to keep lizard and wolf in her line of sight.

I didn't recognize the beast. His fur was torn, scars riddled his muzzle, and three deep claw marks ran down his torso. His eyes were the most disturbing of all. They swam with hate and rage. Barring yellow teeth, the wolf coiled back on his haunches.

He was getting ready to leap.

Damnit. Things were spinning out of control. "STOP!" I roared.

Wolf and twins froze.

Ignoring the trio for a second, I turned back around and plunged my shortswords downward.

You have killed a level 61 fire lizard.

Retracting the bloody blades, I slapped the trigger in my pocket.

You have activated a trap. Twelve fire lizards have been frozen for 5 seconds.

"Lower your swords," I ordered the twins. "He's not a threat." Sheathing my own blades, I advanced on the interloper. The wolf bared his teeth again, but I could see he was struggling not to shrink away.

My own anger was mounting. I was unhappy with the unknown beast, not just because of his ludicrous demands but for revealing himself. How was I going to explain his appearance to the twins?

"Follow," I demanded peremptorily to all three as I brushed past the wolf. My trap would not hold the fire lizards for long.

"*I do not answer to you,*" he said defiantly, sounding sane for once. We were about the same height, but my visitor's size did not daunt me. Despite his denials, I knew he recognized me and, more importantly, the Wolf Mark I bore.

"*I will not ask again,*" I growled. "*Follow.*"

The strange wolf did not respond, but I sensed him swing around, however unwillingly, and stalk in my wake. The twins came behind him, their unease at the looming wolf between us plain to see.

I didn't have time to reassure them, though. There were still the fire lizards to attend to. Spinning psi, I flung a casting at the creatures who were beginning to thaw.

You have charmed 10 of 10 targets for 20 seconds.

Reaching into the minds of my minions, I sent them into battle against the rest of the lair. I wouldn't have bothered, but we needed time to exit the tunnel and escape the nest's awareness.

Chaos erupted as the fire lizards turned on one another, jaws snapping and tails swishing. Both twins spun around at the sound.

"Leave it," I ordered. "I've bought us more time. Now, let's get out of here."

Saying no more, I led our odd party out of the lair.

✳   ✳   ✳

The moment I stepped back onto the mountainside, I spun around to confront the wolf. *"Your name,"* I demanded.

"Cantur," he answered reluctantly.

I nodded. We were finally getting somewhere. *"Where is Duggar?"*

At the mention of the dire wolf alpha's name, a whine of unease escaped the beast. Saying nothing, he crouched submissively.

Mute witnesses, the twins watched on. They surely found all of this more than passing strange, but I had little attention to spare them and would have to deal with the fallout later.

"Don't you recognize me?" I asked, looming over the wolf. *"Don't you recognize my Mark?"*

"Y-y-ess," he whispered.

"Then why?" I growled harshly. *"Why the threats and cryptic demands?"*

The beast hung his head, and I sensed shame and fear, but only a heartbeat later, both were washed away by rage.

"You human. Player. Not true wolf. Player hurt wolves." Hate blossomed in Cantur's mind so thick I could taste it. *"I kill player. You danger."*

I stared at the wolf in shock. *"I'm not—"*

More mindglows brightened in my awareness. Breaking off, I whipped around. We were about to have more visitors.

A second wolf stepped into sight. Then a third and a fourth.

Nervously, the twins edged back toward the lair. Glancing at them, I shook my head, and they stopped their retreat. I didn't recognize two of the newcomers. But the last, I knew.

It was Oursk.

✳ ✳ ✳

Mutely, I watched Aira's mate approach.

He was in nearly as bad a state as Cantur, and my mind flashed back to when I'd first found him and his family in the clutches of the Fangtooths.

Some disaster has befallen the pack, I thought.

It was the only explanation that made sense. My gaze drifted to the other two wolves. They were smaller than Oursk and Cantur, but they were just as thin, the lines of their ribs visible beneath skin that hung loose.

They're starving.

Oursk remained silent as he drew nearer, and my apprehension grew that he, too, would be filled with the same hate I sensed in Cantur.

"Oursk…?" I began, then stopped, unable to go on as he halted before me.

"Michael," the dire wolf greeted, his mindvoice weary but otherwise no different from the wolf I remembered.

I exhaled in relief. Whatever was going on, I still had friends amongst the pack. *"It is good to see you."*

"I wish I could say the same," Oursk replied sadly.

His response put me on edge again. *"What has happened?"*

"Too much," Oursk said, hanging his head. *"I will tell you all later, but for now, I must ask—"*

"*Food,*" one of Oursk's companions interjected. His snout raised, the wolf was tasting the air wafting out of the tunnel.

Oursk's own nose wrinkled, and I could tell he also smelled the lizards' spilled blood, but despite his quite obvious hunger, the big dire wolf turned away from the cave mouth. "*Not now,*" he said, addressing the speaker. "*Later. First, we deliver him.*"

Deliver?

The other wolf licked his muzzle. "*Food. Now,*" he insisted.

"*This is not the time, pup,*" Oursk growled. "*Nor are we scavengers. The kills are the scion's.*"

"*It's alright,*" I said, stepping in. "*Go on. Eat your fill. Then we talk.*"

Oursk glanced at me, visibly torn. Not so the two unknown wolves. As one, the pair rushed into the cave.

Cantur padded forward and nudged me. "*Leave,*" he growled insistently. "*You go. Now.*"

I glanced at the scarred wolf, realizing something was not quite right with him. "*What's happened to him?*"

"*He is mad,*" Oursk said bluntly. "*His mind could not survive the suffering it endured and broke.*"

"*Why is he out here, then? Shouldn't he be safe with the rest of the pack?*"

"*Safe?*" Oursk repeated hollowly. "*There is nowhere safe anymore.*" Before I could ask what he meant, Oursk turned towards the cave mouth. "*You will wait?*"

I nodded. "*Of course. Go.*"

"*Come, Cantur. We eat,*" Oursk said, and the two wolves streaked after their pack mates, leaving me alone with the twins, both of whom were staring expectantly at me.

I sighed. "I guess it's time we spoke."

They nodded vigorously. "Talk about strange," Terence murmured, staring in fascination at the cave mouth into which the wolves had disappeared.

"*Talk* is right. You were speaking to them, weren't you?" Even though Teresa had voiced her deduction as a question, there was no hint of doubt in her tone.

"I was," I said, not dissembling. The twins had already seen too much for me to obscure the truth entirely. "What do you know about dire wolves?"

"Not much," Terence said. "Only that they are big." He paused. "And scary."

My lips twitched. "That they are. They are also sentient and natural telepaths."

"And you're a psionic, which is why you can speak to them," Teresa concluded. "Mind-to-mind."

"Not quite. Early in the Game, after completing a task to help a family of dire wolves, I earned the beast tongue trait. It's the trait that lets me converse with them, not my telepathy skill."

The pair exchanged glances.

"What is it?" I asked, noticing their sidelong looks.

Terence shifted. "It's only... we've got a quest to help the pack."

"The pack? You mean the dire wolves?"

He nodded.

"When did you receive it?" I asked sharply. "And from whom?"

Teresa frowned. "What do you mean from whom? The Adjudicator, of course. As for when: only just now."

I relaxed, but only slightly. Why had the pair received the task but not me? "What is your task called? And what are the objectives?"

"It's titled, 'Aid the Pack,'" Terence said, his gaze turning inwards as he read aloud from the Adjudicator's message. "And it requires us to help feed the dire wolves."

"I see," I said. 'Aid the Pack' was the exact name of the task I'd received after meeting Duggar, even if my own objectives had been different.

"Does that mean we will also receive the beast tongue trait after completing our quest?" Teresa asked, looking enthused at the idea.

I began to shake my head, then shrugged. "Who knows? That's up to the Adjudicator."

Terence was staring in the direction of the lair again. "Where did the wolves go?"

I looked at him. "To eat."

He frowned, then brightened as realization dawned. "Does that mean our quest will be finished soon?"

I smiled. "Probably not. The pack consists of more than those wolves, you know. If you're going to complete the task, I suspect you will have to work much harder."

"Oh," Terence said, deflating. "So, what now?"

I shrugged again. "Those four came here for a reason, and they'll tell us about it once they're done. In the meantime, we wait." Retrieving a bag from my backpack, I threw it at Terence. "Or at least, *I* do."

You have lost a small bag of holding.

Teresa looked at the item in her brother's hands. "What's that for?"

"Well, if you two intend on completing your task, you best get started."

They stared at me blankly.

I rolled my eyes. "There is no way four wolves—however hungry—are going to eat through fifteen dead lizards. Take your knives to the corpses, strip the carcasses of everything edible, and store it in the bag. I'm sure the rest of the pack will appreciate your efforts."

"You want us to go in *there*?" Terence asked. "Alone?"

"It's your task," I pointed out. Sitting down and pretending at a calm I didn't feel, I closed my eyes.

For a minute, the twins didn't move, then their desire to advance their task overcame their fear of the wolves, and they rushed into the tunnel.

I smiled. Oursk knew the twins were with me, and he would see that they came to no harm. Only a moment later, though, my smile died as I recalled the words that had been troubling me ever since Oursk had uttered them.

The dire wolf had said 'deliver him,' and by 'him,' I was sure he'd meant me. It was a strange choice of words and worried me on more levels than one.

I was certain Oursk and his fellows had not happened upon the lizard lair by accident. They'd been *sent* to find me. But it was not how they had located me that bothered me. It was *who* had sent them that had me wondering.

The circumstances seemed... suspicious.

I sighed. But no matter how questionable matters appeared, Oursk was Pack, and I trusted the Pack. Reining in my misgivings, I resolved to hear what the dire wolf had to say.

Chapter 290: Delivery

The wolves and the twins exited the lair an hour later.

The wolves looked sated, and the twins were covered in blood, filth, and offal. I hid a smile. Sometimes, it was nice having minions to do the dirty work. *Especially two motivated minions.*

Rising to my feet, I dusted myself off. "All done?" I asked, addressing the twins.

They both nodded mutely, too weary to speak.

I turned to Oursk. *"Thank you for your generous gift,"* he said.

I nodded. "You're welcome." I glanced at the twins. *"They were no trouble?"*

"Not at all." He gazed at me, his eyes opaque. *"Are they your pack?"*

I shook my head. *"No. But they wish to aid the pack if you will allow it."*

The dire wolf seemed to shrug. *"That will be for Duggar to decide."*

"He is alive, then? Where can I find him and the others?"

"We'll get to that," Oursk said, not meeting my gaze. *"First, let me introduce my pups."*

My eyebrows rose. Earlier, Oursk had been intent on completing whatever task he'd been given. Now, it almost seemed as if he was delaying. *"You brought them with you? Where are—"*

Realizing who he must mean, my eyes drifted to the two still-nameless wolves.

"This is Stormdark," Oursk said, pointing to the darker wolf, *"and this is Shadetooth."*

My eyes widened. I recognized the names, of course. I just hadn't expected the pair to be so big, but then again, it had been two years. One pup was missing, though. *"Where's Moonstalker?"*

"Dead," Shadetooth replied curtly, his mindvoice joyless. The playful pup I remembered was gone. My gaze slid to his sibling. His eyes, too, were dark.

"I'm sorry," I said helplessly. I felt their grief keenly but was at a loss on how to comfort them. *"What happened?"* I asked Oursk.

The older wolf lowered his head. *"A sad tale for another day. Suffice to say, he's gone."* He sighed. *"But it is not because of the past we're here, but the future."*

"What do you mean?" I asked slowly.

"The pack is once more at a crossroads, and I have a favor to request," he said.

"Go on."

"There is somewhere I must take you. I ask that you come willingly and without questions. I've been ordered not to reveal anything."

"Ordered?" I asked, sharply. "Why would Duggar—"

"It wasn't Duggar."

"Sulan, then. How did—"

"It wasn't the elder either."

I stared at the dire wolf; he seemed intent on not answering me. He and Aira were among my oldest companions in the Game. Who could I trust if not them? But he asked too much. "Tell me," I said softly.

Oursk finally met my gaze, his thoughts churning with sorrow and shame. *"As you wish. It was—"*

The dire wolf's mindglow flickered.

The change was so abrupt it caught me by surprise. One moment, Oursk's mind had the bright glow of a healthy mind, the next, it was dull and weak. It was almost as if...

...he'd been attacked.

It was the only thing that made sense. Whatever had befallen the dire wolf, it had occurred too suddenly to be natural. Fearing a follow-up attack, I expanded my mindsight and searched the vicinity for hostiles. But other than for our small party, the mountainside was empty.

A wolf whined.

My eyes flickered back to Oursk. Tremors wracked the dire wolf's body, blood gushed out of his nose, and more leaked out of his eyes. Stormdark and Shadetooth rushed to their sire's side, propping up the weakened older wolf.

"Don't fight it," Stormdark whined.

"Stop." Shadetooth pleaded. *"Let it go."*

Shuddering, Oursk collapsed to the ground, his sides heaving. *"You must go,"* Cantur said, nudging me again.

Shoving aside the half-mad wolf, I knelt beside Oursk. Even if I wanted to leave, there was no way I would abandon Oursk.

"What's happening, Michael?" Teresa asked in concern.

"Stay alert and keep watch," I ordered. Withdrawing a health potion from my pack, I dribbled it into the trembling wolf's mouth.

It made no difference.

I couldn't believe it. The health potion had failed to work.

Bewildered, I sat back. Oursk's condition remained unaltered. My concern mounting, I reached out with my will and analyzed him.

The target is Oursk. His health is at 100%.

The Adjudicator's response deepened my confusion. Game messages were never wrong. So, what was plaguing Oursk that it didn't affect his health?

"This is your fault." Stormdark's words broke through my musings.

"He told you: no questions," Shadetooth growled. *"But you had to ask."*

I stared at the pair. They were right; I should have trusted the dire wolf. If Oursk hadn't tried to answer me, he—

That's it.

The assault on the dire wolf had only occurred *after* he'd tried to respond to my question. In fact, given his earlier cryptic comments, it was likely the mere act of trying to answer me that had triggered Oursk's convulsions.

He has been compelled.

Leaning down, I placed my mouth against Oursk's ear. "You don't have to tell me," I said urgently, hoping he could still hear me. "I understand the reason for your silence now."

The dire wolf's spasms stopped.

I exhaled in sharp relief. Stormdark and Shadetooth prodded their sire, and Oursk climbed back to his feet. But he kept his head low, refusing to look at me, his shame palpable.

Gripping Oursk's muzzle, I forced him to stare at me. "It's alright, my friend. I understand. I will come. No more questions, I promise."

"*Thank you,*" he whispered.

I climbed back to my feet, my expression grim.

A snarl sounded behind me, and I swung around. It was Cantur. "*Player do this. Player do to you, too.*"

I stared at him, finally understanding his earlier mutterings. Cantur had been trying to warn me all along.

"*Thank you,*" I said gravely to the big wolf, projecting my words tightly into his mind alone. "*But I cannot leave, even if it is into a trap that I walk. I will deal with the player, I promise.*"

He studied me a second longer, then, turning about, lay down a few feet away. "*Alpha,*" he pronounced.

I returned my attention to Oursk. Remarkably, he seemed to have made a full recovery already. "Lead on," I ordered.

Like I'd told Cantur, I couldn't leave. Someone had compelled Oursk, which meant that wherever the dire wolves were taking me, it was likely into an ambush.

It didn't matter, though. The pack was in danger, and I would not abandon them.

✳   ✳   ✳

Before we set out, I called the twins over. "You two should head back to the village," I said.

"What about you?" Terence asked.

"I have to go with them," I said, gesturing to the wolves. "I know I promised to escort you back to the safe zone, but I can't anymore. I spoke to Oursk, and he's agreed to allow Shadetooth and Stormdark to accompany you as far as the village's outer limits."

"Why do you have to go with them?" Teresa asked, ignoring everything else I'd said.

I eyed the girl for a beat. *They deserve the truth,* I thought. "Players are threatening the pack," I said quietly. "Somehow, they've learned about my ties to the wolves and are using them to lure me somewhere."

"You're *knowingly* walking into a trap?" Terence asked.

I nodded.

"Why?" he asked, aghast.

"Because he cares for them," Teresa said before I could answer. She stared at me piercingly. "Don't you?"

I sighed. "I do. Now, head back to the village. This is my fight, and you two have already become more entangled in matters than is safe for you." I turned away. "I'll find you at the tavern."

"No," they said in unison.

I swung back. "Excuse me?"

"We're not leaving," Teresa said. "We'll help however we can."

Terence grinned. "And besides, if we don't go with you, how will we finish our task?"

"It's dangerous—" I began.

"We know," Terence said, speaking for the duo. "But Saya was right about you. She said if we stick with you, you won't lead us astray."

I stared measuringly at the twins. "I'm not so sure about that, but if you really wish to accompany us, I won't stop you." I strode toward the waiting wolves. "Welcome to the Pack."

And House Wolf.

Oursk pushed our small company hard, taking us farther east and higher up into the mountains. I didn't try questioning him or any of the other wolves again but kept my senses trained for danger and urged the twins to do likewise.

As we headed deeper into the mountains, we crossed the snow line, and the temperature plummeted. During my time on the tundra, I had endured much worse and barely felt the cold. Not so the twins. But despite their chattering teeth and shivering limbs, they refused to turn back.

Several times, Oursk trotted back to tell me I could leave whenever I wished. He said it so often that I believed he wanted me to go, but I, too, steadfastly refused to retreat, and eventually, we reached an icy clearing atop a windswept plateau.

I slowed to a halt. The clearing was occupied.

Standing in the center of the snowfield, and ignoring the falling sleet and howling wind, was a cloaked figure. Turning my gaze left and right, I swept the area but spotted no one else. Mindsight reported nothing. As did the spectacles of warding.

The stranger was alone.

As far as I could tell, at least. All my buffs were cast, and I was as ready as I could be for battle. But... who planned an ambush in an open clearing and gave me a clear target?

"W-what's g-going on?" Teresa stuttered. "Are w-we there y-yet?"

Glancing over my shoulder, I took stock of the twins. The pair had their arms tightly wrapped around their torsos in a futile attempt to keep warm and were almost certainly suffering from frostbite.

"We've arrived," Oursk announced.

I nodded, having suspected that to be the case. *"Is there shelter nearby?"*

Oursk bobbed his head at a distant pile of rocks on the plateau's northern edge. *"The pack has taken refuge there."*

"Good. I will go on alone from here," I said aloud for Teresa and Terence's benefit. *"Oursk, take the twins to the pack and ensure they stay warm."* I paused, then added, *"And safe."*

Terence glanced at the silently waiting figure. "W-who is t-that?"

"I don't know, but I expect whoever it is, they are the one who orchestrated all this."

"W-we come w-with y-you," Teresa said stubbornly.

"You can barely move," I said sharply. "Go with Oursk and get warm. The pack will inform you if I need help."

"We will," Oursk affirmed and gestured to his companions to escort the youths away. The twins didn't argue further and went willingly, which I suppose said much about their condition.

Oursk hung back, his gaze swinging between me and the waiting figure. *"I'm sorry, Michael. All the pack are. If we could have, we—"*

"Stop, Oursk," I said, raising my hand. *"Whatever is going on here, it's not your doing or the Pack's."* I gestured to the departing wolves. *"Go with the others."*

"Are you sure?"

"I am. I will join you later," I said, even though I was sure of no such thing.

"Good luck, alpha," he said and padded away.

Blowing out a frosty breath, I cast mind shield, causing the entire pool of psi at the pit of my subconsciousness to rise up and reform into steel-like bands around my mind.

Your psi pool has been transformed into a mind shield. Psi abilities are unavailable.

As evidenced by the compulsion spell cast on Oursk, my foe was a master psi-caster. I didn't know if my psi shield would keep me safe, but it was the only defense I had against someone with mental abilities similar—but superior—to my own.

My mind fortified, I turned back to the waiting stranger. The figure had not reacted to my arrival on the plateau nor the departure of the twins and the wolves—even though we'd been in clear sight the entire time.

Reaching out with my will, I cast analyze.

You have failed a Perception check and are unable to analyze your target. This entity is a player, and her Marks are hidden.

I frowned. My failure did not bode well, nor did the fact that my foe's Marks were concealed. I'd not even known such was possible. But at least I now had confirmation that the one who awaited me was a player. With no other choice, I padded across the snow to meet her.

Motionless, the stranger watched my approach.

As I drew closer, I tried to take her measure, but shadows swirled thick about her—magical shadows, not any trick of the light—hiding her face and clothing. It was only her shape that was revealed, and by it, I could tell she was a woman of slim build and near my own size.

Unless that too was an illusion.

I drew to a halt ten yards from the figure.

"You move well across the snow," the stranger said, her voice melodious and carrying clearly over the wind. "It's almost as if you were born to it."

"Who are you?" I demanded, ignoring her comment.

She tilted her head to the side. "You disappoint me. I thought you were more perceptive than that."

I ran through the possibilities in my mind. I'd only run across one player with the level of deception my foe seemed to possess—two if you counted Loken. But while I did not doubt the trickster could seamlessly imitate a female player, nothing about the figure opposite me smelled of his unique... peculiarities.

Nor did I think it was Mariga—or Amgira as was her proper name. I couldn't see the so-called dark druid compelling the wolves. For one, she hadn't known about them, and for another, I'd pegged Mariga as a magic user, not a psi-caster.

Which left...

"You're Loken's envoy."

The stranger clapped her hands. "Bravo. You're not that slow, after all."

Things were beginning to make sense. My gaze slid in the direction of the receding wolves. "What did you do to them?"

"Really? That's the first thing you ask? Not why am I here?"

"Tell me," I growled, taking a step forward.

Now that I knew the identity of the mysterious player, much of my fear dissipated. In its stead, rage took hold. Loken was meddling... again.

"Careful," the envoy said casually. "Or I might be forced to kill you."

Sneering, I took another step. "You wouldn't dare."

"Oh? And why's that."

"Your master needs me."

The envoy threw back her head and laughed. "You really believe that? Loken doesn't need anyone, boy. Much less a lowly tier four player."

Perhaps it was just my imagination, but her words rang false to my ears, and I thought I detected an undercurrent of jealousy in her tone. I strode forward again, my hands dropping to my swords.

"Stay back," the envoy ordered in a clipped tone.

"No." I took another step.

"Oh, very well. I'll tell you." The words were said lightly, but I noticed the shadows about the envoy were spinning more furiously.

Leashing my anger, I stopped. I needed to keep the encounter from devolving into violence if I could.

"I haven't hurt any of your precious wolves—yet," the envoy went on. Her voice went cold. "But make no mistake, I will if I must, wolf-boy."

Wolf-boy? Was that a chanced-upon insult, or did she know more about my origins than she should? Would Loken have shared such information with his envoys? I didn't think so.

"A compulsion spell is hardly harmless," I snarled.

"Is that what you're calling it? It's as good a name as any, I suppose. But my spell did no lasting harm—for which you should be thankful. At worst, the beasts suffered a touch of pain. Nothing irreversible." She pressed a finger against her chin. "Unless, of course, one of them was fool enough to try fighting the compulsion." She shrugged. "Then the damage would've been more... pervasive."

I ground my teeth at her cavalier attitude. "Did your master put you up to this?" I demanded. Would Loken dare use the wolves against me?

He would.

Loken, no doubt, saw my ties to the pack as a weakness, and if there was one thing I'd learned about the trickster, it was that he excelled at exploiting weaknesses.

"Whether he did or did not is no concern of yours," the envoy snapped. "Now, if we're done with this pointless chatter, can we get down to the business of *why* I'm here? You might find these dreary conditions comfortable, but I assure you, I don't."

Folding my arms, I waited for her to go on. Why *was* she here?

"Loken is not happy with you," the envoy began.

"Oh? Fancy that."

The envoy ignored my interruption. "You're interfering with his plans for this sector, which Loken does not take lightly."

I feigned a yawn. "I have no idea what you're going on about."

"Really? I know it was you who slaughtered the Marauders, no matter what you convinced those idiots, Yzark and Kalin, to believe."

I grinned, but there was nothing friendly about my smile. *The Marauders.* So, that's what this was about. "I'm still not following you."

"Drop the act, boy. You're fooling no one. You will desist in your vendetta against Kalin's people. Immediately."

"I will not," I retorted.

The envoy turned to look pointedly in the direction the wolves had disappeared. She said nothing, but the threat was clear.

My grin faded. "I'm beginning to believe your master knows nothing of what you do here."

She turned back to me. "And why's that?"

"Because Loken would never be so foolish to threaten me in such an obvious fashion. He knows how well I react to threats." I narrowed my eyes. "He doesn't know about this little chat, does he?"

"You will break off your attacks against the Marauders," the envoy said, disregarding my question entirely.

But her avoidance was a mistake and only cemented my suspicions.

"If you fail to heed me," she continued, "I will purge this valley of every living wolf."

On the tail end of the envoy's words, I felt a tug on my mind. It was as if a clammy hand had reached out and tried to smear away my resistance.

You have passed a mental resistance check! Your mind shield has repelled the subversive influence of an unknown entity.

Stifling the urge to shudder, I said with pretended calm, "Your mental tricks will not work on me. And if you move against the wolves again, my vendetta will not be with the Marauders but with Loken. The day a single dire wolf in this valley dies at Shadow's hand is the day I make it my sole mission in the Game to foil the trickster's plots and murder his followers wherever I find them."

For a moment, the envoy was stunned speechless. "Who do you think you are to believe you can threaten a Power—or his envoy, for that matter—and get away with it?"

The question was rhetorical, but I answered, nonetheless. "Why don't you ask your master that? *Maybe* he will tell you. And while you're at it, make sure you find out how he feels about your actions costing him the chalice he so desperately wants me to steal."

There was another drawn-out moment of silence.

My response seemed to have confounded the envoy again. I didn't know to what extent Loken shared information with his sworn, but I thought it a safe bet that the envoy didn't know the whole truth of how things stood between me and the trickster, and by her silence, I suspected she was coming to the same realization.

The lull in the conversation stretched out.

Feeling the envoy's eyes resting on me, I remained tightlipped while she weighed my words. Instinctively, I sensed saying more would be a mistake.

"Perhaps, I will," she said finally and turned around. "But we are not done. I *will* be back. And when I return, for your sake, I hope I have the answers you expect."

The shadows about her contracted, and I realized she was about to teleport out.

"Wait!" I shouted.

Pausing, the envoy turned back to me.

"I have a proposition for you."

The silence was palpable.

"A... proposition? After all that?"

I nodded.

The envoy giggled, the sound incongruous with the rest of her demeanor, and I suspected it was her first genuine reaction. "Truly, you are audacious, wolf-boy. Go on. I can't wait to hear it."

CHAPTER 292: A DARING PROPOSITION

"What bargain did Loken strike with the Marauders?" I asked.

"What makes you think there is one?" the envoy asked, her composure in place once more.

I snorted. "I *know* Loken. Whatever ploy he has to get control of this sector—and more importantly, Erebus' dungeons—it will not be his only stratagem. He will have a backup plan, and I'm guessing it's tied to the Marauders' strategy for taking over the valley."

I gestured to her. "By your own admission, that's why you're here. That's why you've threatened the wolves. To stop me from ruining Loken's deal with the Marauders." I paused. "But if you accept my proposition, there will be no need for such a bargain."

The envoy cocked her head. "Assuming what you say is true, what are you proposing?"

"Just this: whatever Loken's bargain with the Marauders, I'm willing to consider the same terms if he gets the Marauders to back down and if he supports my bid to control the valley."

"*Your bid?*" The envoy laughed. "You think you can take over the sector?"

"Why not?" I challenged. Raising my left hand, I ticked off points on my fingers. "I'm more truly neutral than the Marauders—who are, after all, a Shadow faction that Dark and Light will be less inclined to trust."

I raised my second finger. "I already have a relationship with Tartar and his envoy—as Loken well knows." I did not elaborate on what my exact relationship with Captain Talon was; *that* wouldn't do my cause any good.

I lifted another finger. "I've also earned Arinna's favor." Although, the Light Power might not see it that way. "It gives me an in with Muriel."

I held up the last finger. "And finally: Loken owes me."

The envoy stroked her chin. "As... interesting as all that is, it doesn't overcome the fact that you have no faction."

"I'm working on it," I replied.

"So, you have the one thousand soldiers sworn to your cause and ready to claim the safe zone?" she asked skeptically.

"I will," I said.

"Where will you get them from?" the envoy asked, intrigued.

"I have a plan for that," I lied, "but I won't reveal it."

"I see," the envoy said. "And how precisely do you expect me to get the Marauders to—how did you put it?—back down?"

"Kalin already thinks Loken ordered the attacks against his people. I want you to maintain that deception and stop the Marauders from re-establishing themselves in the sector."

"Keeping away the Marauders indefinitely is too big an ask," the envoy replied automatically. Despite this, she seemed to be considering my words. "I can give you one month."

I shook my head. "That's not enough time. I still need to form a faction *and* contact Tartar and Muriel. Six months."

"Three."

"Four. And not a day less." I paused. "I will not enter into a Pact either. Loken must trust in my word or accept the consequence of my ongoing vendetta with the Marauders."

The envoy studied me for a second longer. "What of our bargain with the Marauders? Will you honor it?"

"You will have to tell me the terms first," I pointed out. "I will not commit blindly."

The envoy bowed her head, thinking. "The Marauders pledged access to the dungeon for ten days every month."

"I can promise one week out of four," I replied quickly, and before she could say anything else, added, "What you're asking requires me to do more than take control of the sector. You also need the Awakened Dead pushed back from the dungeon. Right?"

She nodded. "How would you do it?" she asked curiously. "You don't have the strength to take on Erebus and Ishita."

"Neither do the Marauders," I said, which was pure guesswork on my part. "But Tartar does."

"You will use the legion to do your dirty work?"

"Why not? Captain Talon has his own bone to pick with the Awakened Dead. He will be glad to do it." I was making more than a few sweeping promises that I wasn't sure I could honor, but I couldn't afford to appear uncertain before the envoy. "But," I conceded, "I will have to provide him something in return."

"Like time in the dungeon?"

I nodded.

"And you trust Captain Talon to relinquish control of the dungeon after he clears out the Awakened Dead for you?"

"He *is* the honorable sort. He will not betray his word." Assuming he ever entertained the notion of another bargain with me.

The envoy studied me quizzically. "You realize you're constructing a house of cards. If it comes tumbling down, it will be *you* who is left with contracts you cannot fulfill. Whatever deal you strike with Muriel and Tartar, neither will accept excuses if you are not able to live up to your end." She paused. "Nor will Loken."

"You let me worry about that," I said blandly. Seeing that the envoy's mood had mellowed somewhat, I risked a question. "Out of interest, how *did* the Marauders intend on securing Tartar and Muriel's corporation?"

"Muriel was no problem. The Marauders have dealt successfully with her in the past." She sighed. "Tartar was always the weak link in their plans. The Bull considers it beneath himself to deal with the Marauders' likes."

My eyes narrowed. "So, the Marauders bid for the sector was a non-starter?"

"A long shot, perhaps," she allowed.

"Then... you lose nothing in making this deal."

The envoy chuckled. "I wouldn't say *that*. There will be a lot of angry Powers in the Shadow Coalition after this." She eyed me speculatively. "But Loken knows how to deal with them, and strange as it seems, your chances of negotiating a truce in the sector are better than Kalin's. Perhaps, you will succeed where he could not. Tartar is the biggest hurdle to overcome, and for some reason, the Bull seems to like you."

I pasted a smile on my face. "That's me. Likable as hell."

That surprised a snort out of her. "Very well. We have a deal. I will keep the Marauders at bay, and in return, you will take ownership of this sector in four months. By then, I expect you to be ready to grant our people access to the dungeon once every four weeks."

Loken has allocated you a new task: <u>Brokering Peace</u>! The Power's envoy has tasked you with establishing peace in the wolves' valley within 4 months. Objective 1: Negotiate a truce between Muriel, Tartar, and Loken in sector 12,560. Objective 2: Take ownership of the sector. Objective 3: Control access to the sector's dungeon. Note, this task is time sensitive and will be failed if you do not complete it in the allotted time.

I raised an eyebrow. "You don't need to take the matter back to your master?"

"I am his envoy," she replied, a hint of scorn in her voice. "Loken trusts me to run this sector as I see fit."

I nodded thoughtfully. So, was the ruse with the Marauders hers? Was that why she'd been so upset by my interference?

"But if you play me false," the envoy continued, "you can rest assured no amount of bandying Loken's name around will save you. I will end you *and* your allies. Do we understand each other?"

I nodded grimly. "Perfectly."

"Good," she said, "then I look forward to hearing from you in four months."

"Wait!" I said before she could turn around.

"Now what?" she asked, sounding exasperated.

"The compulsion on the dire wolves, when will it end?"

"I've unraveled the spell already," she said. "Their will is their own again." Not waiting for my reply, the envoy contracted the shadows around her and vanished from sight.

✴   ✴   ✴

Only after I was certain the envoy was gone—I hadn't even learned her name—did I let any hint of my true feelings show.

Striking a deal with Loken's lackey had left me feeling unclean. After the manner in which she'd toyed with the pack's minds, the wolf in me cried for vengeance. I'd wanted to rend her flesh, but not only would that have been shortsighted, I doubted I would have been able to pull it off.

In raw power, the envoy was as far above me as I was over the twins.

The unfortunate truth was that to protect the pack, I had to forgive the envoy's misdeeds against them. But I would not forget, and someday there would be a reckoning.

Sighing, I turned around and hiked across the plateau toward the pile of rocks sheltering the pack. A Game notice buzzed for attention, and suspecting what it was, I let it unfurl in my mind.

Congratulations, Michael! You have completed the task: <u>Tavern Trouble!</u> Through force of arms and wiles of mind, you have dealt with the trouble plaguing the tavern. Wolf is pleased, and your Mark has deepened. But be careful, scion, the path you tread is a tricky one. Lies and manipulation will only take you so far.

I snorted morosely.

Even the Adjudicator seemed leery of my plans. There was no disguising it: I played a dangerous game. Partly, I did so to shield the dire wolves and partly to protect the tavern, but a large part also stemmed from a desire to gather power.

Without power, there would be no raising House Wolf, and without House Wolf, there would be no protecting those who depended on me beyond my own death.

If I wanted to leave a lasting legacy in the Kingdom, I had to grasp the opportunities before me. The prospect of controlling a sector as rich as the valley was too enticing to ignore.

Yes, events were moving faster than I anticipated, and yes, I was not as ready as I liked, but if I let this chance pass by, another might not come for years. Not to mention, it would mean abandoning my allies to those who would prey on them.

To shield the dire wolves and to protect the tavern, I had committed myself to chartering a delicate course between three juggernauts of the Game—Loken, Tartar, and Muriel. Not only would I have to forge a lasting peace in the sector between the trio, I would also have to force the Awakened Dead out of the dungeon they were entrenched in, and I would have to do it in four short months.

All in a day's work. Right, Michael?

I laughed in gentle mockery of my own ambitions. One day, I was going to get myself in a bind I couldn't escape, but until that day, I would continue to play the Game boldly and fearlessly.

Raising my head, I saw a small party of wolves approaching. It was Duggar, Sulan, Aira, and Leta. My spirits rose at the sight of the four, and waving, I hurried forward to greet them.

Chapter 293: Back Home

The four wolves came to a stop in a half-circle around me, their minds shuttered and their gazes inscrutable.

My legs suddenly shaky, I drew to a halt and knelt in the snow. "It is good to see you again," I said, unable to help the wide grin that split my face. "I'd begun to fear..." Emotion choked my throat, and I started again. "I thought I would never return, that the pack was lost to me forever."

Aira stepped forward while the others hung back.

Lowering her head, Aira brushed her muzzle against my face. *"Michael,"* she greeted, her mindvoice ringing with warmth, *"I never doubted your return. But stand. It is not right you kneel before us."*

Rising to my feet, I ruffled the dire wolf's fur. "Oursk told me about Moonstalker," I said, projecting my words to her alone. "I'm sorry."

"Thank you," she said, her voice tinged with remembered sorrow. *"He died defending his pack, as brave a death as a mother could wish."* Aira glanced over her shoulder, and Sulan padded forward.

"Welcome home, pup," she said, her voice as acerbic as ever.

"It is good to see you, too, Sulan." I smiled. "You haven't changed a bit."

Snorting, the white wolf nudged me hard enough to topple. *"Nor have you. Still the same insolent pup, I see."* Lowering her head, she held my gaze for a second. *"But you do not disappoint."*

From the old white wolf, that was high praise indeed, I thought, recalling her parting words to me in Besina's lair.

Turning about, Sulan stepped back, and Leta took her place. Finally recognizing the ritualized nature of their greetings, I held myself stiff under the brown wolf's inspection. She scrutinized me for a beat longer, then bowed. *"Well met, scion."*

I inclined my head in return. "And you too, pack elder."

Leta limped back, her mangled leg evidence of the hard times the pack had endured. And where was the rest of the pack council? I wondered.

There had been six the first time I'd visited. My gaze slid to Aira. I didn't think it was an accident that she had been included in their assemblage today. *"Are you an elder now?"* I sent to her on a whisper-thin thread.

"Yes," she replied just as softly.

Before I could congratulate her, Duggar stepped forward. The pack leader took his time inspecting me, his winter gray eyes as inscrutable as when we'd first met. *"Alpha,"* he greeted finally, acknowledging my new status.

"Duggar," I replied.

The black wolf's jaws parted in what I interpreted as a smile. *"You have grown into your own, I see. Welcome back."* Turning around, he padded towards the pile of rocks. *"Come. The rest of the pack is eager to greet you."*

✳   ✳   ✳

The five of us made our way to the pack's den in silence. While I strode in the wolves' wake, I studied the four elders.

Like Oursk and the hunting party, their coats were bedraggled, and their bodies were lean. Given the barrenness of the surroundings, it was no wonder. Food had to be in short supply in the mountains. I bit my lip. It was clear the intervening years had not been kind to the pack, but just how bad had things gotten?

Was I in for more shock?

Before I could work up the courage to enquire, wolves streamed out of hiding and onto the plateau. At the same time, I was bombarded. Words of welcome—exuberant and unfettered—assaulted me, both in the real and in my mind. My ears ringing with the sounds of their greetings, I drew to a halt in stunned shock.

Duggar glanced over his shoulder and seemed to smile. *"I told you. The pack is eager to greet you."*

"Why?" I asked, at loss to understand their welcome.

By my own reckoning, I'd done nothing to deserve it, and truthfully, I'd expected the pack to resent my return, bringing, as it did, the attention of Loken's envoy.

"Why, he asks," Sulan said, sounding amused. *"Perhaps they remember who saved them from the goblin tribes and who stuck out his neck for them— foolishly, I may add—by going up against the wyvern mother."*

"Or maybe," Leta added more solemnly, *"they recognize the Wolf in you and pay tribute to him as much as you."*

"Or it could be," Aira said, rolling her eyes at the other elder, *"that they are simply welcoming a lost brother home."*

Absently acknowledging their replies, I dropped to my knees to greet the wolves streaming across the snow. Their joy was unrestrained and unabashed. Dropping my mind shield, I let them see my own delight. The dire wolves were as much my pack as the arctic wolves and as dear to me as Snow and his brethren.

Letting the big wolves engulf me in their celebration, one thought rang deep in my mind.

I am home.

✳ ✳ ✳

The pack had grown in my absence.

Not significantly, but enough for me to be certain the dire wolves had reversed their previous slow decline. Sitting cross-legged in the shallow caves where they had taken refuge, I counted the wolves milling about.

By my reckoning, the pack numbered six scores. True, all the wolves bore the telltale signs of hunger, and some, like Cantur, seemed of unsound mind, but they had turned a corner, I felt. My thoughts drifted to Loken's envoy and her threats.

I can't let them be imperiled again.

"What are you thinking?" Sulan asked from where she and the other elders lounged across from me.

Beyond them, the pack rested, too, feeding on the piles of lizard meat the twins had gathered. It was no feast by any means, but I suspected it was more food than the pack had seen in months.

"Can't you tell?" I quipped.

"Your mental walls have grown stronger," Aira said approvingly. *"None of us can pry into your thoughts anymore."*

I nodded. "I was thinking of what the pack must have undergone in my absence." I gestured to the cold stone rock surrounding us. "This is not the most hospitable of locations. Why shelter here?"

"The valley is no longer safe," Duggar said, confirming my fears. *"Even the tunnels where we normally hide are often frequented by players."*

"They're like a plague," Leta growled. *"Spreading fast and far."*

"It is only here, in the coldest peaks of the mountain, that few players bother coming," Aira added.

"Few, but not all," I murmured. "How did Loken's envoy find you?"

Duggar exhaled noisily. *"I do not know."*

I met his gaze. "The pack cannot stay here."

The alpha did not reply, but I could see that what I said was not news to him. Duggar had reached the same conclusion himself.

"And where would you have us go?" Leta demanded. *"There is nowhere left in the valley for us."*

I turned to the elder, not blaming her for her anger. "Then it is time to leave the valley," I said equably.

She snorted. *"We are not players. We cannot leave as you do."*

"You cannot create portals," I corrected, "but you can pass through one." I turned to Duggar. "I have a sector in mind that can serve as a new home for the pack."

"That's preposterous!" Leta scoffed. *"The pack can't—"*

"Where?" Duggar asked, cutting across the other wolf.

"It is easier if I show you," I murmured and lowered my psi shield.

Four minds delved into my own, tasting the thoughts I offered. I didn't attempt to sway their thinking and let them see my true, unvarnished memories and plans. Relocating the pack would be hard and not without risk, but it was a step I felt necessary to take.

Loken's envoy had convinced me of that.

The envoy had enacted her entire charade with the dire wolves with one purpose in mind: strongarming me into doing what she wanted. She'd believed—rightly so—that in the pack, she'd found the means to force me to do her bidding. I had convinced her otherwise—barely—and for now, things had turned out alright.

But what about the next time?

And there would be a next time, I was sure of it.

Whether it was the envoy again—with Loken's blessing the second time around—or Loken himself, someone would try using the pack against me, which was why I needed to get them to safety without delay.

My plans for the sector notwithstanding, the valley was no longer a safe refuge for the dire wolves. Even assuming I gained control of the sector, four months was too long to leave the pack unprotected. And besides, now that Loken—and possibly others—knew that the wolves were in the valley, they could always get to them. Me owning the sector would not stop that.

No, the pack had to find a new hiding spot, and there was only one possible place they could go: the arctic tundra.

And the key to getting them there was sector 18,240.

I would have to accelerate my plans for the nether-infested region. Ever since discovering it, the hidden sector had become central to my plans for raising House Wolf. It had been my intent to purge the sector of nether, secure its location with a shield generator—similar to what the Ishita had used in the valley—and only then gather my allies within.

But all that was out the window now.

Now, I would have to move before I was truly ready and use the arctic tundra instead of sector 18,240 to shelter the pack. It could still be done. But not without risk.

"Necessary risk," I thought, projecting the thought to the listening elders.

"Arctic wolves," Aira breathed as she finished reading my memories. *"I've never heard of their like before."* Her thoughts swam with excitement. *"I would dearly love to see them."*

"You've grown a solid pack," Sulan said appreciatively. *"I like your Snow already. I vote, we go."*

"It looks cold there," Leta grumbled. But despite the complaint, I sensed no dissent from the elder.

I turned to Duggar, waiting to hear his opinion.

"I agree," the alpha said. *"But cold is better than dead. The pack shall relocate."* He inclined his head in my direction. *"Thank you, scion."*

On behalf of Wolf, the Adjudicator has allocated you a new task: <u>Resettlement</u>! Loken's envoy has discovered the pack's hideout in the valley. Realizing how this endangers them, you have convinced Duggar to relocate the pack to another sector. Objective: Safely transport the dire wolves to the new home you've chosen for them.

I swallowed relief.

I hadn't been sure the pack would agree to abandon the only home they'd known for centuries, but once again, Duggar and the elders had surprised me. "Good," I said, "then let us solidify our plans." I glanced at Duggar. "How soon can the pack be ready to leave?"

But before the alpha could speak, another did.

"Wolf-man?"

I didn't recognize the speaker. Jerking upright, I slammed my mind shut and swept my gaze across the cave. Where was the intruder?

The elders noticed my sudden alertness and rose smoothly to their feet, hackles raised. I kept searching the darkness, trying to pick out the interloper that was surely hiding close by. The strange mindvoice had been high and sweet, and unlike any wolf I had ever met.

Someone else is here—someone not of the pack.

Was it the envoy?

Duggar growled, and I glanced in his direction to find all four elders staring at me. It took me a moment to realize why. With my mind fully shuttered, I couldn't hear them.

I lowered my mind shields to half-height.

"Finally!" Sulan growled. *"It took you long enough!"*

"There's an intruder nearby," I replied, ignoring her tone.

"Are you sure?" Duggar asked. The big wolf scanned the cave himself. *"I sense no one."*

I nodded. *"I am. He—she?—spoke in my mind."*

Strangely enough, my words caused the wolves to relax. Leta even snorted in amusement.

"What? Whoever it was, they were in my mind!"

"And here I thought you were an alpha," Sulan said as she flopped back down. *"All full-grown and mature, only to find you're still afraid of ghosts."*

My eyes narrowed as I stared at the white wolf. She couldn't be serious, and from the undercurrent of laughter I sensed in her voice, I didn't think she was.

Is Sulan... poking fun at me?

"Stop toying with him," Aira chided. *"There's only the one."* She turned her head nearly flat to stare at me. *"Ghost, that is."*

I blinked. *Aira too?*

"There is no such thing as ghosts," I refuted, but even to my own ears, my denial sounded weak.

"Not ghosts. Ghost." Duggar said. He, too, sounded amused.

"Sit back down," Leta ordered. *"You're making me strain my neck."*

I sat. I still couldn't make sense of what they were on about, but it couldn't be anything threatening if it amused the elders this much.

"Man-wolf?"

There was the strange voice again. This time, it was accompanied by a picture of Anriq and a keen sense of interest.

My alarm grew, realizing that whoever the speaker was, she had riffled through memories I'd not shown the elders. "Who or what is Ghost?" I asked, striving not to react.

"Ghost is a pup," Aira said.

"Not anymore," Sulan retorted. *"The girl must be nearly two years old now."*

"I don't like Sulan," the voice whispered. *"She's nasty."*

"I heard that, you wretched girl!" the white wolf said primly.

Ignoring the exchange, I let my gaze drift to where the pack's young played. The entire contingent romped around the twins, and none seemed remotely interested in the elders or me. The mysterious Ghost was not one of them, I was sure.

"You will not find her amongst the younglings," Aira said softly, her voice serious once more.

My confusion grew. "Meaning?"

"The girl has no body," Sulan answered.

I glanced at her. This time, I sensed grief—ruthlessly contained—lurking beneath her words. "How did that happen?" I asked quietly.

"It was the rings," Leta answered. She looked at me. *"You remember the rings?"*

"The Ring of Astral Walking?" I asked cautiously. It was the artifact the elders had used to send me to the first Wolf Trial.

"That's the one." Leta sighed heavily. *"We didn't know it then, but while we were keeping the spirit portal open for your trial, a pup strayed into the first ring. She was three months old at the time."*

I winced. The first ring, I recalled, was the one responsible for corporeal separation. It severed the ties between the spirit and the body. "What happened to her body?"

"It died," Sulan said morosely.

"Lost..." Ghost echoed.

I shuddered, recalling my own time as a pure spirit in the Mind Trial. It had been a strange experience, to say the least. Worse yet, an unclothed spirit was vulnerable, and as far as I knew, there was no way to mend the damage a spirit sustained without the safe harbor a body provided. "How did the pup survive the loss of her body?"

"We don't know," Aira said. *"It should not have been possible."*

"But Ghost was always an odd pup," Sulan added. *"Unusually powerful for one so young and with an unhealthy dose of curiosity, too. The strangest things caught her interest."* The white wolf's eyes fixed on a spot a few feet from me. *"As they still do."*

I tracked her gaze but saw nothing.

"Look with your mind," Duggar suggested.

Doing as he bid, I opened my mindsight, revealing the mindglows of the four elders and one more—Ghost. Sulan was right. The pup's mind burned brighter than a sun. Reaching out with my will, I analyzed her.

The target is Ghost, a level 1 spirit wolf.

Death is often considered the greatest equalizer. After death, we all pass on. But some spirits are too strong to fade away and remain in the Forever Kingdom even beyond final death. Usually, these entities become wraiths and phantoms—half-mad ethereal beings that are only a shadow of their former selves. But a rare few, those of exceptional mind and will, retain their memories and intelligence, becoming fully-fledged spirit entities.

I pursed my lips thoughtfully at the Adjudicator's explanation, understanding now, at least in part, how the unfortunate pup's strange state had come about.

"Wolf-becoming-man?" Ghost asked, feeling my attention and showing me another stolen image of Anriq. *"Or man-becoming-wolf?"*

"Werewolf," I replied.

"Ooow," she exclaimed, her mindvoice quivering with excitement.

"What's a werewolf?" Duggar asked curiously.

I turned to the alpha. I hadn't deliberately concealed the existence of the werewolves from the elders. Not wanting to burden them with unnecessary information, I had only shown them what they needed to see to make their decision.

"*Look for yourself,*" I said and lowered my mind shield again.

Five mindglows drew closer.

"*Not you,*" I scolded Ghost. She'd taken enough liberties with my memories already.

The spirit wolf shied back, not concealing her hurt.

Immediately, I felt guilty.

While Ghost was technically an adult, in many ways she was still a three-month-old pup. What must it have been like to spend two whole years in spiritform, without any of the normal physical interactions the other wolves enjoyed?

It couldn't have been easy for Ghost, and her differences had likely isolated her from the rest of the pack even if, as telepaths, they could still communicate with her.

She must be lonely.

"*I'm sorry,*" I said, speaking to Ghost alone. "*That was rude of me. You can have a peek, too.*"

Like a frightened bird, she hesitated. "*You won't be angry if I look? I want to see more of the shadow man. He's funny.*"

I bit back a sigh. She was talking about the Loken. How much had Ghost managed to see of my memories in her first foray into my mind? Too much, by the sound of it.

She was still waiting for my answer though. "*No, I won't,*" I promised. "*But whatever you see, you can't tell anyone. Understood?*"

Her mindglow pulsed happily, and not needing to be told again, she dived into my mind. "*Of course, Prime!*" she called out in passing. "*It'll be our secret!*"

This time, I did sigh.

✳　✳　✳

A few minutes later, the five visitors in my mind withdrew.

"*Werewolves,*" Sulan muttered. "*Now, I've seen everything.*"

"*A wolf turning himself into a man?*" Leta wondered. "*Why would any wolf want that?*"

My lips twitched. "Or, for that matter, what sane man transforms himself into a wolf?"

The elder glowered at me, and I chuckled. "Only joking."

"*These werewolves, they guard another Wolf trial?*" Duggar asked.

I nodded. "I'm certain of it."

"*Then you intend on finding them?*" the alpha asked.

"I must."

"*I don't trust them,*" the alpha growled. "*Be careful.*"

"I will," I assured him. "But locating the werewolves is a task for another day. Today, we must see to the pack's safety." My gaze drifted to where the twins still played with a pack's pups under Oursk's watchful eye. "Although, before we get into that, there is another matter we must discuss."

Aira followed my gaze. *"Who are they?"*

"They're my... students."

Duggar tilted his head to the side to study the youngsters. *"They are not Wolf."*

"They're not," I agreed. "But maybe after they awaken their blood, they might—"

The alpha shook his head. *"You mistake me. Their bloodlines are different. They are* not *of Wolf."* This time, I took his meaning.

"Oh," I murmured. Given the task they had received, I'd been hoping the twins bore strains of Wolf blood. It would've made things easier.

Duggar glanced at Sulan, and the white wolf rose to her feet. Trotting to Teresa's side, she lowered her head and sniffed.

Startled, the girl looked over her shoulder at the white wolf looming above her. "Michael..." she called worriedly.

"No need to be scared," I assured her. "Sulan is just..."

I paused. What *was* Sulan doing?

"Calm the girl," the white wolf said wryly. *"I'm not trying to eat her, only ascertain her bloodline."*

"... inspecting you," I finished.

"Cat," Sulan pronounced. *"These two are of Cat. But their blood is weak."* Turning around, she rejoined me and the other elders.

Terence and Teresa were still staring at me. "It's alright. I'll explain later," I said, not sure that I would.

Reluctantly, the pair turned back to the pups vying for their attention.

"What made you bring them here?" Duggar asked.

I shrugged. "Circumstances. I'd not planned on it." I met his gaze. "But having two other friendly players around can still be advantageous to the pack."

Duggar gazed back at me steadily. *"What are you asking?"*

I glanced at the twins again. They'd already forgotten their momentary unease and looked very much like pups themselves as they played with the pack's young.

I closed my eyes. Was it fair to involve the pair further in my troubles? I wondered. They'd been willing, eager even, to learn more about the pack. There was still a chance, though, that they could disentangle themselves from me and choose a safer path.

I won't tell them anything of the Primes or the ancients just yet, I decided. But I couldn't let the twins go their own way either, not until I'd resettled the pack. It was too dangerous—both for them and the wolves.

Opening my eyes, I answered the patiently waiting alpha, "Can you shelter the two here? They can help the pack hunt and build up its reserves of food."

"We will do as you ask," Duggar said.

"Thank you."

"Have you told them they will be staying?" Aira asked.

I shook my head. "Not yet, but I will before I leave. Now, let's discuss what else needs to be done before the pack can depart the valley."

Hours later, the pack council and I finished our planning. The challenge was twofold: one getting the pack to their destination, and two, *surviving* the destination.

I'd spent much of the time making sure the elders understood what to expect. The tundra was not just cold, its snow storms could kill, and the dire wolves were less prepared than the arctic wolves for such weather.

Then, there was my worry about how Snow and the others would react to what they might perceive as an invasion of their territory. It fell to the elders to reassure me. Sulan, Duggar, and the others were certain they would be able to handle any... disagreements that arose.

When everything was settled, I rose to my feet and, accompanied by Aira and Sulan, went in search of the twins. I found them whispering excitedly to each other. "What are you two so happy about?"

Teresa turned around, a cheerful grin on her face. "Oh, nothing important," she said lightly.

"Besides how good it feels to have completed our first task," Terence chipped in. "Which reminds me." Reaching into his vest, he pulled out an item and threw it my way.

You have acquired a small bag of holding.

"Thanks," I said, catching the bag. "And congratulations. Did you get the beast tongue trait?"

Terence's lips turned down. "Sadly, no."

"But we're not letting that get us down," Teresa added. "We've just been discussing what secondary Classes to choose."

"Oh?" I prompted. Teresa's words confirmed what I had suspected: the pair had not progressed beyond their primary Classes .

"We're going to become druids," Terence announced.

My eyebrows rose, and I sensed Aira and Sulan's amusement from beside me.

"Really?" I remarked. "Is that so you two can get the beast tongue trait?"

"Amongst other things," Teresa said defensively. Her amusement faded. "Aiding the dire wolves has made us realize there may be more creatures out there that need help. What better way to spend our time than by serving others?"

"A noble inclination," I agreed solemnly.

Teresa's gaze flickered to the silent wolves. "But you didn't just come over for an idle chat, did you?" she asked shrewdly.

I shook my head. "I'm leaving." The pair rose to their feet. "Alone."

"What?" Terence asked, sitting back down. "Where are you going?"

"Back to the safe zone," I replied.

Teresa's brows drew down. "You're leaving us here? Why?"

I sighed. "By now, you two must've realized that the pack's presence in the valley is not widely known. I want to keep it that way."

"You don't trust us?" Terence asked, looking disappointed.

"It's not that," I assured him. "But there are ways of getting information out of unwilling subjects that you two are helpless to resist," I said, thinking of Shael's abilities. "I'm sorry, I can't risk the pack's safety."

"We understand," Teresa said.

Terence looked at her. "We do?"

"We do," she said, not looking away from me. "Then we are to stay with the pack?"

"Yes." I gestured to my companions. "This is Sulan and Aira. Both are elders amongst the dire wolves. They will teach you to hunt and communicate with the pack." I shrugged. "It will not be the same as talking with beast tongue, but it will allow you to get by."

"Oh," Terence said, brightening. "That's alright, then."

"How long will you be gone?" Teresa asked.

"Hopefully, I'll be back in a couple of days," I replied. "And when I return, you can go your own way." I studied them consideringly. "Or choose to stay with the pack."

The pair exchanged glances, looking intrigued at the possibility.

Clamping hands with each in farewell, I turned around and headed out of the cave. I had already said my goodbyes to the wolves and had a hard night's journey ahead of me. "*Take care of them,*" I said.

"*Rest assured, we will,*" Aira replied.

✻　✻　✻

I was halfway across the icy plateau when I sensed an anomaly.

There were no wolves in sight, but a consciousness burned bright in my mindsight, and I ground to a halt. "*What are you doing, Ghost?*"

"*Accompanying you,*" the spirit wolf replied.

That was what I was afraid of. "*You can't.*"

I was certain most players wouldn't be able to sense the spirit wolf. I, myself, could only see her using my mindsight. But the creatures in the Mind trial had detected my spiritform easily, and it would be foolish to assume that there were no players with similar abilities.

And that would endanger Ghost.

As a curiosity, she would be attacked on sight, either in search of experience or unique loot. "*It will be safer for you with the pack,*" I added.

"*But I want to see the wolf-man,*" she complained.

Her reply gave me pause. "*How do you know I'm going to visit him?*"

"*I saw it in your mind, of course.*"

I rubbed at my temples. The spirit wolf seemed frightfully adept at reading my thoughts and memories. *Perhaps, allowing her that second dip in my mind had not been wise.*

"*You can't,*" I said. "*Not only is Nexus too dangerous for you, if you've seen that deeply into my thoughts, you already know you can't enter a safe zone.*"

Ghost was silent for a moment. "*Will you come back?*" she asked forlornly.

"*I have every intent of returning,*" I reassured her.

She brightened. *"With the wolf-man?"*

"Call him Anriq," I said. *"And yes, I will do my best to bring him, too."*

"Oh. Alright then."

I sensed her retreat to the wolves' hideout.

"Goodbye, Prime," the spirit wolf said.

"Don't call me that!" I yelled back.

A mischievous giggle was my only reply.

I sighed in exasperation. Despite this, I felt my lips twitch upward in a smile. Ghost, I suspected, was going to be trouble. I waited a full minute, and only after I was certain she'd left, did I turn around and begin the slow journey back down the mountain.

There was a certain red-robed player I needed to speak to again.

✳   ✳   ✳

I slipped into the village just as dawn broke.

My immediate plans for the future were coalescing, and despite traveling all night, I felt energized. There were only a few more hurdles to cross before I could get the pack to safety, and until then, I couldn't rest.

The tavern was quiet as I strode in. A barkeep I didn't recognize was on duty, but neither Shael, Cara, nor Saya was anywhere to be seen. They had to be asleep, but I couldn't wait. Rushing up the stairs, I headed, not to my room as would be prudent, but to Cara's. What I had to chat to her about couldn't wait.

I hesitated outside her door, hand raised to knock.

You sure this is the best time to speak to her, Michael? About this of all things?

I wasn't, but on this matter, there was no ideal time.

It would be better if I spoke to her now. If Cara refused, I would have to move on to my second plan, which was infinitely more tricky. Taking the plunge, I knocked.

There was no response.

I banged harder.

"Who is it?" a sleepy voice called.

"Michael," I replied.

A pause. Then, "Give me a moment."

It was longer than that. A full five minutes later, the door peeked open to reveal Cara's faceless hood.

"Can we talk?" I asked, too wound up to comment on the delay. "It's urgent."

"I gathered so," Cara replied drily. She opened the door wider. "Come in."

I stepped in slowly, feeling uneasy about invading her privacy. The room was sparsely furnished and absent of mementos, but then Cara had only been here a few days. Pulling out the room's only chair, I offered it to her.

She shook her head and sat on the bed. "You know, in Nexus, I had resigned myself to being woken at the oddest hours, but here, I expected to get more sleep." Her hood turned in my direction, and I could almost sense her smile. "I should have known better."

I ducked my head. "Sorry, but this won't wait."

Cara laughed. "Business never does. What do you need to sell?" She tilted her head. "Or have you come to buy this time?"

"Neither. Nor is this business," I shifted uncomfortably. "I have a favor to ask. And one to offer."

Cara grew still. "Michael, if this concerns what we spoke about the other day, I told you: it's best forgotten. Those days are—"

"Hear me out. Please."

Cara studied me for a second, then motioned to the empty chair. "Sit."

I sat.

"If I allow you to say whatever you feel you must," Cara continued, "do you promise this will be the last we speak of it?"

Forcing myself to a calm I didn't quite feel, I folded my hands in my lap. "Only if you accept my offer."

Cara sighed. "You are relentless, you know that, right?"

"So, I've been told," I murmured, tension easing.

She snorted. "I didn't mean it as a compliment. I could have chosen a harsher epithet, but I was striving to be kind."

My lips twitched. "Thank you."

Cara shook her head—in despair?—amusement?—both? Without seeing her face, I couldn't be sure, but I thought that the banter had eased some of her own stiffness.

"Go on, then," she said. "Tell me. What is it you need?"

I rubbed my palms along the top of my pants. Now that the moment had arrived, I found the topic harder to broach than I thought. Telling Cara what I planned would be one more irreversible step along a path that would put me in direct conflict with the new Powers.

And it could all go horribly wrong if I'd judged Cara incorrectly.

I trust her, I told myself for the hundredth time. *She won't betray me.* There was no way to be certain of that beforehand, though.

My bout of nerves didn't go unnoticed. "Don't worry," Cara said lightly, the last of her humor seemingly restored. "I won't bite."

"Very funny," I said drolly and took a deep breath. "First, a few questions."

She waited expectantly.

"Do you know the spell, purifying dome?"

I felt her stare.

However she'd expected me to start the conversation, it was not like that. "I do," she said when I said no more. "It's a casting often used by mages in hazardous environments to keep their parties safe. The emporium always keeps a few dozen scrolls of the spell in stock." She paused. "Are you sure you're not here to buy something?"

I shook my head. "Positive. Can you cast the spell yourself? With or without the aid of a scroll?"

"I can't. Purifying dome is considered a combat casting, and my robe prevents me from using any such," Cara replied, sounding confused.

I frowned. I hadn't known that. It was an interesting twist but didn't affect my plans.

"What is this about?" Cara asked. "When you started this conversation, I thought—"

"What about without your robe?" I cut in. "Could you cast the spell then?"

The discussion had entered dangerous territory, and understandably, Cara didn't reply immediately. "I could," she replied quietly. "But so could thousands of other mages. You don't need me for that."

I held up my hand for patience. "You'll understand soon enough. Will the spell work in a nether-infested sector?"

"Of course." She paused. "But only if the nether toxicity in the region is below tier five. Purifying dome only offers protection against tier four and lower hazards."

I nodded. Cara had only confirmed what I'd known. I'd seen Moonshadow employ the spell in the rift we'd entered and knew it worked against the nether, but I had to be certain. The dire wolves' lives depended on it.

"Could you cast purifying dome *while* holding a portal open?"

"Hmm, that's infinitely harder but not necessary. Purifying dome is not a channeling spell. It would be simpler to set up the dome *then* open the portal."

"I see," I said. "And could you open a portal to somewhere you've never been?"

"I couldn't, not normally."

"Oh," I said, disappointed. That did complicate things. It meant I would have to escort Cara to both the portal's exit and entrance locations before she could do what I needed. And how long was that going to take?

Unexpectedly, Cara laughed. "Weren't you paying attention, Michael? I said, not *normally*. I'm reading between the lines here, but I'm guessing you want me to open a portal to somewhere you've already been to?"

I nodded. "Essentially, yes."

"Then, in that case, it's easy enough for any mage to help you. You already have the solution on hand."

I blinked. "I do?"

"Of course. Or have you forgotten about the aetherstone bracelet? The gems are also used to transfer aether coordinates between players. If you etch one of the aetherstones with the location you have in mind, a mage can use the stone to anchor the portal's far end."

"That's... brilliant news," I said, grinning.

"Are you going to tell me what this is all about now?"

My smile faded. "I am. One last question first."

"Go on."

I leaned forward in my chair. "What do you know about the Primes?"

"Primes? Never heard of them," Cara replied offhandedly.

I nodded. "I'm not surprised. Few have."

I'd come to Cara mainly because I needed a mage—someone to open a portal to the hidden sector and keep the nether at bay while the wolves transitioned to the guardian tower's tundra.

There were other options besides Cara—namely Moonshadow or a BHG mage—but those choices were fraught with peril too, and while I'd met my fair share of players in the Game, there weren't many who I thought I could trust with a secret this dangerous.

I didn't have to tell Cara about the ancients or my bloodline, of course. But I couldn't very well expect her to abandon Kesh and the Triumvirate's protection without understanding the consequences of her choice.

Yes, she was forsworn, so the consequences likely mattered less to her than most. But that did not automatically mean she cared for the Primes or a return to the old ways. She had been sworn once and had believed enough in the new Powers to bind herself closely to one, and perhaps still did. In fact, unlike Anriq, Cara had far less reason to look favorably on House Wolf.

But it didn't matter.

Telling Cara the truth was the right thing to do.

It might be easier to spin a tale and convince her to join my cause with lies, but while I had no scruples about lying to my foes, I would not do the same to my allies.

I inhaled deeply before beginning. "I'd hoped to have this discussion with you much later, but now, I'm out of time. The Primes—some call them ancients—are those who came before. They were the original rulers of the Forever Kingdom, and each had their own House populated by players—only they called them scions."

I paused and glanced at Cara. By her stillness, I gathered she was listening avidly. "The new Powers overthrew the Primes, but despite their victory, the Powers still fear the ancients' return—so much so that they've wiped all traces of the Primes' existence from history. However, there are still hidden pockets of ancient lore scattered across the world. I... stumbled across one and it has set me on a different path."

"What path?" Cara asked.

I glanced at her. "You must know I'm neither Light, Dark, nor Shadowsworn."

She nodded. "It's unusual but hardly criminal."

"True," I conceded. "But it hides a deeper truth. I'm... you could say, sworn to Wolf."

"Wolf? As in the animal?"

My lips quirked. "I'm not sure why, but the Primes modeled themselves after beasts. I am a scion of House Wolf, and if I continue evolving in the manner I have, I will eventually become Wolf Prime. That is by no means guaranteed, though."

Cara tilted her head. "Did you say evolve?"

"That's right, and I suspect you know what that means. I've undergone a few evolutions already. Each time my Classes have grown stronger, or I have gained powerful new traits."

"Evolution is the same means by which players transform into Powers," Cara said.

I nodded. Sulan had told me much the same thing before I'd awakened my blood.

"It is a topic much discussed amongst the sworn," Cara added. "Those who have experienced an evolution are marked for greatness and are always carefully—if jealously—watched. Only they have the potential to become Powers."

"What about those who don't evolve?"

She shrugged. "The best they can hope for is to become envoys." She looked at me. "Are you sure it's a... Prime you're becoming, not another Power?"

"I am," I replied and went on to explain about my awakened bloodline, the blood memories, the Wolf trials, and the fallen scions. I even relayed my plans for the future and what I hoped to make of House Wolf. I refrained from relating any specifics, though, and made no mention of Anriq, the dire wolves, or Ceruvax.

The truth was that there was a second more calculating motive behind my honesty. Telling Cara about the Primes and my path was a test. If she wanted to betray me, the information I had given her was in itself ample reason to do so. And at the back of my mind was the thought: *if she is so inclined, better she does so now.*

The fallout would be less.

If Cara ran to the Triumvirate with what I told her today, the new Powers would learn I was a scion, but they would *not* discover the location of the hidden sector. And right now, as the chosen site of House Wolf, it was the more important secret to protect.

"Thank you for sharing that," Cara said when I finished. "I finally understand what you meant about being a fugitive." She paused. "Still, I'm not sure why you've told me all this."

I leaned forward again. "I want you to join me."

Cara appeared startled. "Join you? I'm not sure I understand. From everything you said, my own path is sealed. I'm still bound to Light, even if I'm no longer sworn to the goddess. How can I become a scion of House Wolf?"

"You can't," I admitted. "But that does not mean there won't be a place for you. A place where you are neither forsworn nor hunted."

"What are you saying?" Cara asked carefully.

"I want you to relinquish the Triumvirate's protection. I want you to join me as the combat player you originally were and help me build House Wolf into a refuge, not just for scions of the old ways, but *all* fugitives from the new Powers' so-called justice."

Cara stayed silent so long that I began to worry. "That's a tall ask," she said finally.

I opened my mouth, more arguments at the ready.

"But a worthy cause," she finished before I could voice any of them. She raised her head to look at me. "I think... I think I will join you."

✳   ✳   ✳

"Are you sure?" I asked after I overcame my shock. "That seems awfully..."

"... fast?" Cara finished for me, amusement tracing her voice.

I nodded. "You mind if I ask why you've agreed so readily?"

Rising to her feet, Cara began to pace. "The truth? Ever since I met you, I've been restless. Don't get me wrong. Being Kesh's agent has earned me a nice, quiet life. I've been content. But watching you level, growing in leaps and bounds each time you returned to the shop, it reminded me of... the old days. When *I* was the one doing the leveling."

She laughed. "In hindsight, that is likely why I slipped up the other day—too much time spent daydreaming of my old dungeoning days." Her stride quickened. "When I first became forsworn, I was scared. Lost. Terrified. My fate seemed certain and without hope of escape. So, I grabbed the lifeline Kesh offered." She spun to face me. "Now, after years of reflection, death—even final death—doesn't seem so bad."

"I'm not proposing a suicide run!" I objected.

Cara laughed again, sounding happier than I'd ever heard. "I didn't think you were. But what I'm trying to say is that it wouldn't matter. A life not lived is not a life worth living."

I nodded slowly, understanding her.

"I have one request, though," Cara said, resuming her pacing.

I eyed her carefully. This was a different Cara from the one I knew. She had always seemed so... contained before. Now, she appeared revitalized and possessed of boundless energy. "Go on. I'm listening."

"We must tell Kesh," she said, coming to a halt before me.

"Absolutely not," I replied immediately. "The more people who know, the greater—"

"Not about you," she said, stopping me. "About me. That I'm leaving the emporium."

"Ah." I rubbed my lips, contemplating her request. "Are you sure that's wise?"

"I don't want to remove my robe without Kesh's blessing," Cara said. "Doing so would feel like a betrayal. She saved me when no one else was willing, and I will not repay her kindness without so much as a farewell."

I sighed. Cara didn't seem like she was going to budge on this point. "Alright, I have to head back to Nexus, anyway. How soon can you be ready to leave?"

An errant thought snuck up on me. If Cara did want to betray me, Nexus would be the best place to do it. I squashed the suspicion. It did not do her justice.

"I'm ready right now," she said, surprising me.

"Then let's go," I said, turning towards the door.

CHAPTER 297: A NEGOTIATED PRICE

You have entered sector 1 of the Forever Kingdom.
A shield generator is in place around the city, preventing portals from opening anywhere except in the designated teleportation zones.
You have entered a safe zone.

I kept walking even as I exited Cara's portal, deftly weaving through the players crowding the teleportation dais and stepping off before the knight on duty could accost me.

Cara and I had not left the tavern immediately, after all.

I'd shared a bit more of what I planned with her, but I'd not told her everything. Once we were safely in the tundra, there would be enough time for that.

Glancing over my shoulder, I saw she was right behind me. Gesturing to her to follow, I mapped a path to the emporium. The safe zone was as busy as usual, and I felt like an old hand navigating the streets this time around.

We reached the emporium's walled compound without incident, and the giants on duty waved us through the moment they caught sight of Cara's red robes. It was not soon after that that we were ushered into the old merchant's office.

Kesh looked up, her brows rising as she saw my companion. "Agent, what are you doing here?"

"We must talk," Cara said soberly.

Kesh's eyebrows rose higher, sensing something in her tone. "In private?"

Cara hesitated, then glanced at me, and I nodded. "Yes," she replied.

Kesh's eyes narrowed fractionally, catching the exchange. "I see. Can it wait until after business?"

Cara shrugged, and the merchant turned to me, her features smooth and unruffled. "You're back as well. I assume this doesn't bode well for the tavern?"

I smiled. "On the contrary, matters have been resolved."

"Permanently?" she asked sharply.

"Not yet, but I have a plan. For now, things should return to normal, and your communication with Saya can resume when you... uhm, send another agent there."

Kesh's eyes tightened again, not missing the subtext. She didn't remark on it, though. "What about the merchant who acted as our intermediary?"

"He was bribed," I said and filled her in on the details with the Marauders.

"Marauders," Kesh muttered when I was done. "I never liked them." She frowned at me. "But I don't see how you will stop them from resuming their blockades. Kalin won't give up easily."

"I'm working on it," I said, not yet ready to share my plans.

She didn't push further. "It's your tavern." She reached beneath her desk. "I have something for you. Two somethings, actually."

"The wayfarer gloves?" I asked, stepping forward.

"And something else almost as good," she said with a half-smile.

Leaning over the table, I inspected both items.

The target is the legendary item: the Wayfarer's Gloves. This item is indestructible. Find more pieces in the set to increase the benefits received. The gloves increase the Dexterity of the wearer by +4 ranks and allow him to handle even the most toxic and hazardous of materials without incurring damage. Cost: 12,000 gold.

The target is a nether absorption skillbook. Governing attribute: Magic. Tier: master. Cost: 1,000 gold.

My eyes widened. "You got it!" I exclaimed, my gaze jerking back to Kesh. "How did you pull that off?"

"The brotherhood took some persuading," Kesh allowed, her smile growing. "But in the end, I convinced them it was wise to sell you the tome."

"How?" I asked, still not able to believe she'd manage the feat.

"Your notoriety helped."

It took me a moment to work out what she meant. "You told the stygian brotherhood about the mantis hunts?"

"I certainly did," Kesh said. "I convinced them, too, that they would benefit from having a player like you by their side when they ventured into the nether."

"Well, I'm just glad my fame was good for something." Stretching out my hand, I reached for the skillbook.

Kesh got there first. "Not so fast," she said, covering the book with her hand.

"I don't mind the cost," I said, thinking that's why she had stopped me. "It's expensive, but I expect it will be worth it."

Kesh shook her head. "You might want to hear the brotherhood's terms first."

I looked at her sharply. "Terms? What terms? I thought this was a purely monetary transaction?"

"It isn't," she replied. "The brotherhood desires more than money. They want *you*."

I stared at her. "Me?"

"I may have oversold your worth as a player during the negotiations," she admitted. "Now, they seem fixated on the idea of you participating in their hunts. Specifically, Huntmistress Kartara—that's the brotherhood's leader—wants you to join them on three nether expeditions at a time that is mutually acceptable to both parties."

Stepping back, I folded my arms across my chest. "Request different terms. I will pay more if necessary."

Kesh shook her head ruefully. "I tried. I managed to negotiate the huntmistress down on everything else, but on the matter of the expeditions, she will not budge. I'm afraid these are the best terms you will get."

Before I could say anything else, Kesh pointed to the book. "As a gesture of good faith, Kartara is willing to sell you the tome *before* you fulfill your end of the bargain so you can complete your Class configuration, but she has left strict instructions with every merchant the brotherhood deals with not to sell you any other stygian gear until her say so."

I pinched the bridge of my nose, thinking hard. None of this sounded good. "What's to stop me from buying the book and not complying with the rest of their 'requests?'"

"I wouldn't advise it," Cara said, finally speaking up.

I glanced at her.

"The brotherhood has ties with every major merchant house in the Game, and if they blacklist you... well, at the very least, it will be problematic."

Kesh was nodding. "Not to mention, I gave the huntmistress my word."

I took her meaning at once. Kesh was standing guarantor for the deal. Breaking the terms of her bargain with the brotherhood would effectively mean getting blacklisted by the emporium too. The question was, how badly did I want the skillbook?

I sighed. Too badly to pass up this opportunity.

"Very well, I will accept their terms. But I can't go running to the brotherhood anytime soon. I have other more important matters to attend to first. The huntmistress will have to wait."

Kesh eyed me. "For how long?"

"Four months," I said, without having to give the matter much thought. Until I brokered peace in the valley, I was not going to shackle myself to the brotherhood.

"I can negotiate that," Kesh said and lifted her hand. "Go ahead. It's all yours."

"Thank you," I said and retrieved both items.

You have acquired a nether absorption skillbook.
You have acquired the wayfarer's gloves.
You have lost 13,000 gold. Money remaining in your bank account: 1,655 gold coins.

The Adjudicator has allocated you a new task: <u>Brotherhood Obligations</u>. You have accepted Huntmistress Kartara's terms concerning the sale of the nether absorption skillbook and are duty-bound to join the brotherhood on 3 expeditions into the nether.
Objective: Report ready for duty to Huntmistress Kartara after 4 months.

"Excellent," Kesh said, sitting back. "Now, is there anything else I can do for you?"

"Yes," I said, laying down a piece of paper with scribbled notes. "I require this equipment as well."

Kesh's eyebrows rose as she inspected the sheet. "This is a long list—and a strange one too."

"It is," I said. "Cara has already prepared the items, but she wanted you to approve the transaction. The funds will have to be taken from the tavern's account." On cue, Cara set down a bag and a few other items on the table.

Kesh's eyes darted from the list to the bag, and a moment later, she grunted, "Approved."

"Thanks," I said, taking the bag and items.

You have acquired a <u>large bag of holding</u> containing 29 sets of winter gear, 470 caches of cold weather supplies, and 1 cache of advanced items.

You have acquired 5 x rank 4 nether protection crystals, 5 x rank 4 disease protection crystals, 5 x scent concealment crystals, and 5 x mental concealment crystals.

Money remaining in the Wyvern's Roost bank account: 9,850 gold coins.

Now that Loken's envoy had agreed to keep the Marauders away, I didn't think Saya would need as large a surplus of funds, and I didn't feel bad about drawing from the tavern's account again.

Kesh eyed me speculatively. "I don't suppose you want to tell me what all that is for?"

"You're better off not knowing," I said with a smile.

She disdained to reply.

I glanced at Cara. "I'll meet you at the Wanderer's Delight as agreed?"

She nodded.

Inclining my head, I backed out of the room. "It's time I let you two ladies chat."

✳   ✳   ✳

After leaving the emporium, I headed straight to the safe zone's only hotel and secured a room. Locking myself in the chamber, I pulled out my new purchases and laid them on the desk. It was time to see if they were everything I had expected.

Sitting down, I planted my elbows on the table and studied the two items. The skillbook was no different from any other tome I'd encountered, and at first glance, the wayfarer gloves didn't appear remarkable either.

Like the wayfarer's boots, they were made from supple black leather that did not look anything as indestructible as the Game claimed. Still, I did not doubt the Adjudicator and drew them on without further ado.

You have equipped the <u>Wayfarer's Gloves</u>, gaining +4 Dexterity.

I smiled, pleased by the additional Dexterity. *Twelve thousand gold is a lot to pay for a mere four Dexterity, but—*

I broke off. Another Game message was unfurling in my mind.

Congratulations, Michael! You have equipped a second item from the legendary set: <u>Wayfarer's Suit</u>, and have unlocked the synergies inherent between the two pieces. Tier 1 bonus activated.

Wayfarer's Suit tier 1 bonus: the Dexterity boost provided by each piece of the legendary set is doubled.

Total Dexterity gained from equipped wayfarer items: +16.

"Wow," I exclaimed, nearly falling off my chair.

Sixteen ranks in Dexterity. *That* was certainly worth twelve thousand gold. Naturally, it led me to wonder about the next tier of bonuses and what it would be like to wear the completed legendary set. I would definitely have to keep searching for more pieces, no matter how expensive or hard to acquire each proved. But consideration of the wayfarer suit and its promised benefits did not hold my attention for much longer.

Something far more enticing called to me.

Flexing my fingers, I turned to the second item on the desk. It had taken real willpower not to open the skillbook in Kesh's office, and even now, I could barely curb my excitement. This was the moment I'd been working towards for months, and I wanted to savor it.

Slowly, Michael.

Flipping open the tome's cover, I began to read.

You have gained the master skill: <u>nether absorption</u>.

Nether absorption attunes your void armor to the black void, allowing you to repel or absorb the nether's harmful effects. Note the benefits provided by this skill are only active so long as you have mana remaining.

You have 0 of 6 void mage Class skill slots remaining.

New knowledge seeped into my mind, and I closed my eyes, letting it settle. My Class configuration was finally complete. Knowing what came next, I sat back in my chair and waited, nearly quivering with anticipation.

A Game alert beeped for attention.

Here goes, I thought and willed the Adjudicator's message open.

You have fully configured your third Class.

Congratulations, Michael! Multiple synergies exist between your mindslayer and void mage Classes. You now have the option of combining your base Classes into a tri-blend.

My eyes snapped open. *Options?* I was being given options?

I was nearly giddy with delight at the thought, but Game messages were still scrolling through my mind, and I refocused avidly on them.

Three new paths lie before you.

Each focuses on a different aspect of the constituent Classes and, over time, will evolve further to provide improved benefits. None of your existing skills or characteristics will be lost through any of the offered paths.

The first path is that of the <u>spectral assassin</u>. This path will change your Class ability from void armor to <u>void shift</u>. Void shift performs the same basic functions as void armor, but in addition, it uses the mana absorbed from incoming attacks to phase your body out of the physical plane, temporarily turning you into a being of spirit. Void shift is an activated ability that does not preclude you from attacking while in spiritform.

The second path is that of the <u>voidstealer</u>. This path will change your Class ability from void armor to <u>void thief</u>. Void thief decodes and temporarily retains the signatures of spells absorbed by your void armor,

granting you use of the castings. The theft cannot be resisted, and spells of any tier can be stolen.

The third path is that of the <u>witch hunter</u>. This path will change your Class ability from void armor to <u>void blade</u>. Void blade redirects mana siphoned by your void armor into your weapons, temporarily imbuing them with magic damage. You may apply any of the damage types you absorbed in the past day to your weapons.

Which tri-blend Class do you wish to meld your original Classes into: spectral assassin, voidstealer, or witch hunter?

For a drawn-out moment, I stared off into space, dumbstruck by the options the Adjudicator had presented me with. Then, my thoughts started churning, and I began analyzing the choices on offer from the—albeit meager—information the Game had provided.

The similarities between the paths were obvious. All three modified my void armor ability and worked using the damage it absorbed from incoming attacks. In the process, they added an offensive element to void armor, which had served me only in a defensive capacity up to this point.

But the new abilities would only come into play *after* I was attacked. They would not benefit me against foes who inflicted physical or psi damage—my void armor not being keyed to those damage types.

The limitations were concerning and made the new Classes more reactive than I liked. How much of a problem that proved to be, though, depended on what the Game meant by 'temporarily.' It had applied the term equally to all three Classes.

If 'temporarily' meant something in the order of seconds, then the buffs I received would have to be used immediately, but if it meant minutes or even hours... then I could employ them more aggressively in the *next* encounter—assuming there was one.

I bit my lip. Which Class suited me best, though?

Witch hunter was the simplest. The Class looked like it provided a direct damage boost to my blades and would barely affect my fighting style—regardless of whether the buff lasted seconds or hours.

Voidstealer seemed inordinately complex. Stealing and applying an unknown spell during a fight sounded fraught with peril. Then, too, the benefits I derived from the Class would depend less on me and more on the caliber of my foes. My lips twitched. *It's a good thing, then, that I am usually heavily outranked in combat.*

Spectral assassin was intriguing. If I was interpreting the Class properly, it would let me astral walk and attack my foes while disembodied. This time I did grin. *I wonder what Ghost would think of me becoming an unclothed spirit like her?*

Of the three choices on offer, it was no surprise that spectral assassin drew me the most. I already had a host of abilities—astral blades, slaysight, charm, and so on—to engage my foes while in spiritform.

Void shift also sounded like an excellent escape ability. With it, I could disengage and reposition at will. There was no doubt about it, I was well-suited to the role of spectral assassin.

But...

For some reason, my gaze kept drifting back to the voidstealer Class, and it took me a moment to identify why.

What was bothering me, I realized, were the repeated warnings I'd received about reaching tier five. Morin had mentioned it, and so had Moonshadow. Even Kesh had alluded to it. Then, too, there was what I'd witnessed myself. Despite all the time I'd spent in Nexus, I'd encountered few players over rank twenty.

All the evidence suggested reaching player level two hundred would be... difficult and, worse yet, time-consuming. It would take years of battling tier four foes before I obtained any tier five abilities and was ready for bigger challenges.

But with void thief... I could bridge the gap instantly.

With void thief, I could face a tier five foe *today* and win.

Undoubtedly, the chances of such a victory were slim, and sure, voidstealer was a heavily situational Class—it would only benefit me against certain foes—but that did not change the fact that, of the three Class abilities, void thief was the one with the most potential to shift the course of any given encounter.

Stealing a tier five monster's spells *might* give me a greater chance of defeating it than my own lower-tiered abilities. I rubbed my chin thoughtfully. If I chose the voidstealer path and it proved unusable in battle, then I lost... little. My void armor would still work to repel damage, and instead of investing my Class points in it, I would develop my other Class ability—slaysight.

But if I *did* manage to employ void thief to good effect, my leveling could continue apace—despite the purportedly vast gap between tier four and five.

Voidstealer is the right choice.

There were more than a few downsides, of course. A big one being that before I could steal a spell, I would have to incur damage, and a single attack from a tier five foe could prove fatal in and of itself.

I will find a way to make it work, though.

My decision made, I closed my eyes and willed my choice to the Adjudicator. In a flash, knowledge downloaded into my mind, and my vision exploded with Game messages.

Your Classes have melded!
You have retained your existing rank, abilities, and traits and are now a rank 6 voidstealer.

Legion are the players in the Game, and many are the paths to Power. Some paths are sure and well-traversed, others are dangerous and risky, yet others are hidden behind twisted and convoluted turns that leave their destinations shrouded. You have stepped onto one such path.

The mantle of a voidstealer is one that no one has dared take on before and wearing it will be as much a journey of discovery as of growth. The Class is available only to those with awakened Wolf blood and blends the Wolf's talent for telepathy with the Void's capacity to absorb, granting you a powerful, if select, set of abilities.

Your Class base traits, slayer's heritage and void touched, have melded together to form the new trait: <u>void heritage</u>. It increases your Dexterity by +2, Strength by +2, Mind by +4, Perception by +4, and Magic by +6.

Your Class ability has changed from basic void armor to <u>basic void thief</u>.

The mana pool of a voidstealer is trained not only to absorb his foes' attacks but also to decode and remember their spell signatures, allowing the voidstealer to employ his enemy's casting as his own. However, since the stolen knowledge is not actually learned but stored in the voidstealer's mana, it will, in time, fade away.

The <u>void thief</u> ability is an improvement of void armor in every way. Where all tiers of the void armor ability provide only defensive benefits, void thief allows the caster to enact progressively more powerful 'thefts' against his foes with every tier the ability is advanced.

Basic void thief allows your mana pool to record a single <u>direct-damage</u> hostile spell; this excludes damage-over-time, channeled and area-of-effect spells. The spell is automatically learned once a foe inflicts damage equal to 50% of your void armor. The theft cannot be resisted. The stolen spell is a mirror copy of your target's specific casting and is based on his mix of skills and attributes.

When you employ the stolen spell, it will manifest with the same power as your foe's own casting. Your mana will retain memory of the stolen knowledge for 4 hours. This ability can be upgraded with Class points.

Your secret blood trait has triggered!
To conceal your bloodline, your Class will be reported as being that of a voidstalker to other players and Powers.

For long moments, I didn't move as I read and then re-read my new Class's description.

"Unique," I murmured. My Class was unique. I was the Game's first-ever voidstealer. That made my choice of Class rather valuable or... especially foolish. *Only time would tell,* I thought, turning my attention to the new ability itself.

It was both less and more than I expected.

For one, it had no dependence on my own skills and attributes. I grinned. Theoretically, I could steal even a Power's abilities and use it to the same effect as they did. On the other hand, the fifty percent void armor damage requirement was... harsh.

I suppose that was a reflection of how long it took for my mana pool to decode the hostile casting. Still, it meant I would have to take a pounding first—not my forte at all. Then again, retaining knowledge of the stolen spell for a whole *four hours* made it worth it.

Correctly applied, I realized, void thief would make the ideal dungeoneering tool.

I rose to my feet, cutting short my daydreaming. I'd finished what I'd come to the hotel room for, and as pleasing as my new Class was, it was not the reason I'd returned to Nexus.

Before I took a step toward the door, though, I yawned. Then yawned again.

I sighed, realizing, last night's exertions were finally catching up to me. I glanced at the bed—it looked too inviting to resist. *A short nap wouldn't hurt,* I thought. *After that, I'll head south into the plague quarter.*

Laying down on the bed, I closed my eyes and, before I knew it, was fast asleep.

✳   ✳   ✳

I awoke in the middle of the night.

"Damn," I muttered, gazing at the stars visible through the window. I hadn't meant to sleep as long as I had, but perhaps this was better.

I'd planned on visiting Anriq around midday, then spending the rest of the day in one of the dungeons before returning to him. This way, at least, I would only need to make a single trip to the saltmarsh. And better yet, I would be well-rested for whatever followed tomorrow.

Rising to my feet, I exited the room, intent on hurrying through the hotel's foyer and out of the safe zone. But to my surprise, I spotted two distinctive red-robed figures idling nearby.

I made a beeline for the pair, and they turned my way.

"Ah, I'd feared we missed you," one said.

"Cara," I greeted, recognizing her voice. "Is everything alright?" She was early. We'd planned on meeting first thing in the morning. Why was she here already?

"Everything is fine," she assured me. "Kesh was more amenable to the idea of me leaving than I expected."

"Really?" I asked, my eyebrows rising.

"Really," Cara confirmed. She gestured to the other figure next to her. "This agent will take my place in the valley." She paused. "She is ready to leave. If it's alright with you, I was thinking of making an early start."

I pursed my lips. Cara had told me that the Triumvirate robe would have to be left in the safe zone. She didn't know the full extent of the enchantments the garment bore—no one did—and it was a distinct possibility the Triumvirate could use it to track her.

I'd agreed with her, of course. Whether or not the Triumvirate could track Kesh's agents by the robes they wore, it wouldn't do to take the artifacts of any Power into what I hoped would become our secret base.

But that meant Cara would have to travel across the sector with her forsworn Marks exposed, and while night was certainly the quietest time to cross the valley, I hadn't told Cara where to find the wolves yet. Nor was I comfortable with her making the journey alone, which she would have to if she left now.

My eyes darted to the second agent before returning to Cara. "Hmm, can we have a word in private."

The unknown agent said nothing, but Cara nodded, and turning around, I led her a few steps away. "Are you sure everything is fine?" I asked in a whisper. "Kesh didn't say *anything*?"

"On the contrary, she had lots of questions, but it seems I am not the first agent to leave the emporium's service." Cara shook her head sadly. "There have been others, who after decades of hiding, also grew restless and relinquished their robes. Kesh only wanted to be certain I had thought matters through."

I frowned.

"She had lots of... practical advice, too," Cara added, her hands tightening about the pack she clutched in her hands.

"What's that?"

"My old gear," Cara said, wonder in her voice. "Kesh kept it safe all this time." She laughed self-deprecatingly. "It seems the old lady was better prepared for this moment than I was."

I nodded slowly. There was more to Kesh than I'd suspected. Given all she had done for Cara and other forsworn like her, perhaps the old woman was not as tightly bound to the Triumvirate as I had been assuming. One day, Kesh and I would need to have a franker discussion. But not today. "You didn't tell her...?"

"I told her nothing about your own part," Cara said, allaying my worries. "In fact, Kesh was careful not to ask for any details about where I was going with you." She shrugged. "As I said, I am not the first soon-to-be-fugitive to leave her service."

I nodded again. That was becoming abundantly clear.

"So, are you finally going to tell me who exactly I'm meant to take and where?" Cara asked pointedly.

I studied her faceless hood, wishing I could see her face. "The where is not important for now. The who—" I bent closer—"is a pack of dire wolves."

"Wolves! How did—" Cara began, then stopped herself. "Never mind, stupid question. They are in sector 12,560?"

"They're hiding in the mountains bordering the valley. Head dead east from the safe zone, and you will find them—or rather, they will find you." I eyed her. "But I'm not sure you should be traveling alone through the valley, especially considering—"

"I'm not helpless," she said primly. "I have my gear, and I have the skills I honed over the course of a lifetime. No matter how long it has been, I've not forgotten how to use them." She patted her pack. "Besides, Kesh has gifted me with a few enchantments that will see to it that no one short of a Power can find me. Don't worry. I will reach the mountains unseen."

"You're sure?"

Cara nodded. "I'm more worried about the wolves. How will they know I'm a friend?"

I grinned. "Oh, I've told them all about you, don't worry." My smile faded. "But they will have questions of their own for you and will require you to bare your thoughts to them."

Sulan and Duggar had insisted on being allowed to inspect Cara's mind before they trusted her with the pack's safety. She would be met by a delegation and rigorously interrogated before being allowed near the pack. And while I was certain—mostly certain—of Cara's loyalty, I found the pack's precautions reassuring.

"Dire wolves are telepaths, right?" she asked.

"They are."

"Good. That will make it easier," Cara said, not sounding fazed by the promised questioning. She turned around to rejoin her companion. "I will see you in the mountains?" she asked over her shoulder.

I nodded. "Once I'm finished here, I will head there straightaway."

Not saying anything further, Cara strode away, and I turned to the hotel's exit.

It was time to visit Anriq.

Chapter 299: The Responsibilities of an Alpha

Head down, and with my hands in my pocket, I left the safe zone at a fast walk. Anriq was my last bit of unfinished business in the city, and once I'd seen to him, I would be free to return to the valley and shepherd the dire wolves to safety.

The streets of the plague quarter were as deserted as I'd come to expect, and no one accosted me as I made my way to the saltmarsh district. Pausing on its watery banks, I cracked open an enchantment crystal.

You have activated a single-use enchantment, casting a ward of disease protection around yourself. For the next 4 hours, you will be shielded from tier 6 and lower infections.

Right, I thought, wading into the marsh, *let's hope this visit goes better than the last one.*

* * *

I found Anriq exactly where he said to meet. He was asleep in the hollow beneath the tree, and at my approach, I sensed him wake.

"You're sleeping here?" I asked in surprise as he emerged from his hidey-hole.

The werewolf rubbed eyes still heavy with sleep. "You came back," he said, his voice dull.

"Of course I did," I said. "Why? Did you think I wouldn't?"

Anriq ignored the question. "I suppose you're here for Dathe?"

I stared at him, nonplussed by his reaction. The youth was a wreck. He still wore the sealskin robe I'd given him—now tattered and torn—but his boots were missing, his hair was unkempt, and his beard was overgrown.

"How are you?" I asked, deciding to back up the conversation a bit.

"Terrible," he replied listlessly. His eyes bore into mine, and though he did not voice it, I thought I could read the question in his eyes: *how could I not be when you left me here to rot?*

I winced. I *had* abandoned Anriq in the marsh, even if it had been with the best of intentions and his idea to begin with. And while it had only been four days since I'd gone, four days in the saltmarsh could feel like a lifetime. "I'm sorry," I said quietly.

The werewolf scratched beneath an armpit and glared up at the sky. "What time is it even?"

"Close to midnight," I replied.

"You're here for Dathe?" he asked again.

"No."

The werewolf said nothing, just stood with arms hanging loosely and staring at me with lifeless eyes.

I sighed. "I'm here for *you*."

"Oh?"

"It's time we got you out."

A spark lit in Anriq's eyes, but I couldn't tell if it was born of anger or hope.

"Like you did the last time?"

Anger then. I shook my head. "I have a plan."

Once more, Anriq said nothing, but I waited him out this time.

"Go on then," he said finally. "Tell me."

I shook my head. "Not until you clean up first and eat something." I threw him the bag I had brought.

You have lost 1 cache of advanced items.

"What's this?" Anriq asked, catching it by reflex.

"Your new gear. Now go. Get dressed and eat."

✳   ✳   ✳

It took the werewolf an hour.

I waited patiently the entire time, my thoughts morose. More and more, I was beginning to realize leadership was not without some heavy burdens. My first instinct had been to yell at Anriq, to ask him what the hell was wrong with him, and if it were anyone else, I probably would've.

But I was honor-bound to protect the young werewolf.

It was my duty as an alpha and a scion of House Wolf, a duty I had accepted when I allowed him to follow me. I sighed. And it was a duty I would continue to fail at—as I had with Saya and the dire wolves—if I could not provide him with a safe haven.

Once more, I felt my goals shift.

Cleansing the hidden sector and fortifying it took priority. It would become not just Anriq's home but the wolves and Cara's. Mine too.

But I couldn't afford to ignore my promise to Loken's envoy either. Establishing a faction would allow me to claim not just the valley—assuming I could jump through all the necessary hoops—but also the hidden sector once I'd rid it of the void tree.

Still so much to do, I mused. At this rate, I was never going to get around to searching for Ceruvax.

"I'm ready," Anriq said, interrupting my thoughts as he rejoined me.

I took a long look at the werewolf. Anriq had cleaned himself up and had equipped the armor and other gear I'd brought, although he didn't appear comfortable wearing them.

"Much better," I said. "Everything fit?"

In response, Anriq tugged at his chainmail vest. The finely-woven steel mesh covered him from head to foot, leaving only his taloned fingertips and face exposed.

The chainmail was not regular armor, of course, but had been especially designed for shapeshifters. It would expand and contract as needed when Anriq shifted, not losing integrity in the process.

"It's too... tight," he complained. "And why do I even need it?"

I did not roll my eyes. "We discussed this, didn't we? I know your pack—former pack—doesn't like using armor and weapons, but your rampager Class already has the skills for both." I glared at him. "And it's foolish leaving them undeveloped."

"You expect me to run around the saltmarsh wearing all this?" he protested. "It will slow me down unnecessarily, and besides, there is—"

"No," I said patiently. "Like I told you, we're leaving."

"Huh-uh."

He still didn't believe me. "Swing that axe," I said, ignoring his skepticism. "Let's see if you're any good with it."

"And hit what?" he asked, glancing at the nearby tree. "You want me to whack that?"

Tugging a tuft of marsh reeds free from the water, I squashed them together in a ball and flung it aloft. "Hit this rather."

Anriq swung the big two-handed axe I'd bought him. Once. Twice. Thrice. Each blow was blisteringly fast, but each blow *also* missed the reed ball by miles.

I sighed. "Right, looks like you've got a lot of work ahead of you."

He scowled at me. "So what, you're going to train me now?"

I shook my head. "I wish I could, but I can't. You're going to have to tackle the dungeon by yourself."

"You're abandoning me then," he accused. "Why am I not surprised? Just like the last— Wait. What dungeon?"

"The guardian tower," I replied mildly.

"That's the public dungeon in the plague quarter you mentioned the last time, right? Why would I ever go there?"

"Because it's the only way you're going to get to the arctic wolves."

"Arctic wolves?" the youth repeated, and for the first time, something other than anger and scorn filled his voice. "Are they your pack?" he whispered.

"They are."

A frown lit his face as he put two and two together. "And you make them live in a dungeon?"

"Not by choice," I said stiffly. "The guardian tower is unusual. The third level—which is where you'll be going—is huge. You could wander there for years and still not explore its entirety."

"So, you're sending me to your pack?" Anriq asked, still full of disbelief.

I nodded.

"But you're not coming yourself?"

"I can't."

"Why not?" he demanded.

"It's going to take you weeks to reach the arctic wolves."

"So what? You have matters more important than your pack to attend to?" he asked, sarcasm back in full force.

"Unfortunately, yes," I replied, my own voice bland. "There is another pack I must usher to safety."

Renewed consternation flickered across Anriq's face.

I smiled at his confusion. "Make yourself comfortable. I have a lot to tell you, and there is little time..."

✳ ✳ ✳

An hour later, I finished filling Anriq in.

I'd told him about Snow, the dire wolves, and the trouble in the valley, leaving out little except for the existence of the hidden sector. That no one needed to know about yet.

"So, you have a choice, Anriq," I said when I was done. "You can wait in the saltmarsh until I return from my errand, or you can tackle the guardian tower yourself and escape Nexus on your own."

I'd spent the better part of the past hour detailing the layout of the dungeon and relaying potential strategies for Anriq to get through the first two sectors and reach the arctic wolves.

"You spent an entire year on that tundra?" Anriq asked, still flummoxed by that aspect of my tale. "That's how you became the arctic wolves' alpha?"

"Essentially, yes," I said, not elaborating.

"And you're sure I can find the pack in—what did you say?—a few weeks?"

"I'm not. That's why I've provided you with winter gear and enough food to survive for months on the tundra. What I am sure of, though, is that Snow and the others will find you. When I get there, I will direct the pack to look for you. If you stick to the markers I mentioned, we will find you easily enough."

"You still haven't told me how you will get there before me," he pointed out.

"And I won't," I replied calmly. "Us being pack does not mean I will share everything with you. There are many things I will not tell you, both for your own good and the safety of the others who depend on me. You understand?"

Surprisingly, he nodded.

"Good. So what will it be?"

Anriq hefted his axe and rose to his feet. "Well, I'm not staying here, that's for sure."

✳ ✳ ✳

This time around, with darkness for cover and me scouting the way, Anriq and I reached the entrance of the guardian tower without incident.

The werewolf was as prepared for his dungeon dive as I could make him. I had loaded him up with a small cache of enchantments and other supplies—everything I'd deemed necessary to see him past the savants, ratmen, and tundra.

But in the end, it would depend on Anriq himself.

"You ready?" I asked as we stood outside the portal.

His gaze fixed on the glowing gateway, Anriq nodded. "I think I am."

"I hope you don't think this means I'm abandoning you again," I said quietly.

He glanced at me. "I shouldn't have said that."

I inclined my head in acknowledgment of his apology and clasped his hand. "Good luck. I'll see you on the other side."

"Wait," Anriq said before I could turn around to go. Reaching into his pocket, he held out something to me. "Take it."

I studied the item in his hand. It was a key—Dathe's key.

"Why?"

"Just in case I don't make it."

I shook my head. "You'll make it. Keep the key, and if you still feel like giving it to me when we meet on the tundra, then I'll gladly accept."

Anriq straightened, my refusal fueling his confidence and increasing his determination just as I had hoped. "See you in the tundra, then." Turning around, he ducked into the portal.

✳ ✳ ✳

After seeing Anriq off, I hurried back to the Nexus teleportation platform and, despite the lateness of the hour, found it still busy.

I hurried onto the dais and closed my right hand around my left without pulling up my sleeve to expose the aetherstone bracelet. My tasks were completed, and it was time to go.

Finding the right gem, I willed myself to its stored location.

Aetherstone bracelet activated. Connection to the ley line network formed. Selected exit: safe zone of sector 12,560.

Transfer commencing...

...

...

Passage completed!

Leaving sector 1. Entering sector 12,560 of the Forever Kingdom.

Chapter 300: The Bridge to Nowhere

You have entered a safe zone.

Aetherstone bracelet deactivated. Remaining stored locations: 2. Charged and unetched gems: 2. Uncharged gems: 1.

I emerged not in the center of the village as I expected but on its northern edge. *Hmm*, I thought, studying my surroundings with interest. No one was about to witness my arrival.

The aetherstone gem I'd used had been etched before I had acquired it—presumably by Yzark. I'd not thought about it earlier, but I supposed there was no reason to always use the middle of a safe zone as an exit spot for a portal. There were no restrictions on this sector, not like in Nexus. In fact, a mage like Cara could teleport directly to wherever she wanted in the valley, but unfortunately, the aetherstones were more limited in scope.

Turning east, I headed out of the safe zone, not bothering to stop by the tavern. Shael and Saya were likely sleeping, and there was no point worrying them. I didn't expect to be gone for long, anyway.

I reached the trees without incident and took to the treetops, leaping from branch to branch without pause. The journey passed swiftly, and the sky was only beginning to brighten when I reached the mountain plateau with the wolves' den.

As I stepped into the icy clearing, I found a delegation waiting: a dozen dire wolves and three humans. My gaze leaped immediately to the 'stranger.'

It had to be Cara.

Cara proved to be a black-haired and brown-eyed woman who, if appearances could be trusted—which they couldn't in the Game—was no older than twenty-five.

She wore a silver shirt, form-fitting white pants, knee-high boots, and a heavy gold overcoat. Her hair was pinned up and fastened with a pair of golden clasps that glittered with as many enchantments as the rest of her gear. A brace of wands was sheathed at her hip, and soft white gloves covered her hands.

As much as I wanted to gape, I kept my expression studiously blank while I drew closer. Whoever or whatever Cara had been in her previous life, she had clearly been a player of means.

No wonder she'd seemed amused by my worry about her crossing the valley.

I doubted anyone in the valley except the envoys posed a threat to her—one-on-one, at least. I drew to a halt in front of the large welcoming party. Before I could say anything, words dropped unbidden into my mind.

"I like her."

My gaze tracked to my right, to where I sensed Ghost lurking. Cara, I noticed, was already looking that way.

"Who?" I asked unnecessarily.

"The nice lady. She glows prettily. And she has the most fascinating tales to tell."

"You can speak to her?" I asked in surprise.

"No, but she can see me, and she has let me peek into her mind," Ghost said, sounding pleased. *"Do you want to know what she thinks of you?"*

"No!" I said quickly.

"Oh." She paused. *"Then, can I show her what you think of her?"*

"A definite no to that too!"

"Aw, you're no fun."

Everyone stared at me, and I realized I'd spoken aloud.

"Problems?" Aira asked.

"Just Ghost being meddlesome," I sent to her privately.

"Ah. I'll speak to her."

"Thank you," I whispered back and ran my gaze over the gathering. That Cara was here meant she must've passed the elders' tests, which pleased me, but I was surprised at the presence of the twins. *"What are they doing here?"* I asked Sulan. *"I thought we agreed not to involve them just yet."*

"Still questioning me, pup?" she retorted. *"I changed my mind. They are trustworthy and wish to stay with the pack."*

"But the risk—"

"They understand the risks."

I paused. "You told them where we're going?" I asked, deliberately speaking aloud this time.

"Safyre did. But I asked her to," Sulan replied.

"Safyre?" I wondered aloud.

"That would be me," Cara said, smiling at me.

Of course. I'd forgotten Cara was not her real name. *Idiot!*

"Can you believe it?" Terence asked, looking awed. "When she told us she was Cara—the *same* Cara you'd brought to the tavern—I nearly fell over."

Teresa nudged her brother. "That wasn't from disbelief. You were overcome by her beauty. Admit it, you think she's pretty."

Terence turned bright red. "I do not!" Realizing what he'd said, he spun hastily to address Cara. "I didn't mean—"

Cara—it was Safyre now, I supposed—laughed. "No offense taken." Her gaze drifted to me. "I guess I *should* introduce myself properly." Her tone, as familiar and soothing as usual, immediately put me at ease.

I nodded. "That would be nice," I murmured.

"I'm Safyre, a level two hundred and one aetherist." Her smile faded. "And a forsworn as well."

The twins didn't so much as blink, by which I gathered Cara—Safyre—had already explained to them what that meant. Her level didn't surprise me, not after seeing her gear, but her Class did. "What's an aetherist?"

"Exactly what it sounds like," she replied. "I specialize in manipulating the aether and summons from the gray void."

"There are creatures in the aether?"

Safyre smiled—the new name would take some getting used to. "Not as many as in the nether, but certainly. Primarily, they are lost spirits." Her eyes shifted to Ghost. "Like your friend there, if of less sound mind."

Which explained how she could see Ghost. I nodded. "Have the wolves filled you in?"

Safyre's lips turned down momentarily. "With some difficulty, yes. Communicating without words was not easy. I gather we're going to a nether-infested sector, one whose location is... hidden?"

"Correct." I turned towards the twins. "Are you two sure you want to come along?"

"We are," they replied in unison.

"Once you leave the valley, there will be no coming back," I warned.

"We're aware," Teresa assured me.

I sighed. The pair made for two more for whose well-being I was responsible. I glanced at Duggar, and he answered my unspoken question. *"The pack is ready to depart and, like we agreed, are waiting in the den. The moment the portal is open, and you pronounce it safe, we will pass through."*

I nodded. "Perfect. Then, let's begin."

✳   ✳   ✳

The plan was simple.

Safyre would open the portal to the hidden sector using my logged key point for the tundra's nether portal. I would pop through, scout the area, and ensure there were no stygians nearby. Cara would follow after, cast purifying dome, and then reopen a portal for the wolves.

If all went well, each dire wolf would spend no more than a few seconds in the nether-infested sector as they ran *out* of one portal and into the next.

If all went well.

"Stay back," I told the others. Accompanied only by Safyre, I strode towards the center of the icy clearing, heading to the same spot where I'd met Loken's envoy.

"Last chance to back out," I told Safyre, only half-joking.

She threw me a dry look. "The die has been cast already; there is no going back for me. And I must admit I am curious about this hidden sector you've found. How did you ever manage to locate it?"

"That's a story all of its own. I will tell you about it once we reach the tundra."

"You better," she said, coming to a stop. "This looks far enough?"

I glanced back at the waiting wolves and twins. They were a few dozen yards away and far enough not to be endangered. "It is."

Focusing on one of the charged but unetched stones in the aetherstone bracelet, I willed the location of the tundra's nether portal into it.

You have etched an aetherstone with the aether coordinates of nether portal 1 in Kingdom sector 18,240.

Currently stored aether locations: 3. Charged and unetched gems: 1. Uncharged gems: 1.

Removing the bracelet, I handed it to Safyre. "Here you go. It's ready for you."

"Thank you." She handed me something in exchange.
"What's this?" I asked, looking at the thin band of gold in my hand.
"Communication device," she replied.

This is a farspeaker bracelet. It is item 1 of 4 in a matched set of devices and will allow you to communicate through the aether with the other bearer(s) while you both occupy the same sector.

"I've used one of these before," I said and drew it over my right arm.
"Great, then you know how it works," Safyre replied. "Should I cast my buffs now?"
I nodded. "I'll do the same." Closing my eyes, I turned my focus inwards.

Your Dexterity has increased by +8 ranks for 20 minutes.
You have gained an encumbrance aura for 10 minutes.
You have trigger-cast quick mend.

Opening my eyes, I saw that Safyre was surrounded by a shimmering bubble of silver—a mage's shield. She was still chanting, though. After debating with myself for a beat, I withdrew an enchanted crystal and cracked it open.

You have activated a nether protection crystal. For the next hour, you will be shielded from the ill effects of the nether at tier 4 and lower concentrations.

I was eager to train my nether absorption skill, but with an entire infested sector at my beck, there was no need to rush, and truly, I was not going to chance anything going wrong on this venture.

Safyre has cast aether grace on you, granting you the buff: <u>phantom</u> (50% chance of all physical attacks passing through your body). Duration: 5 minutes.

"Wow!" I exclaimed, turning towards her. "That's some—"
I broke off, staring at the five identical Safyre copies smiling back at me. "Mirror images?" I guessed.
"Aether projections," one of the Safyres corrected. "They have limited autonomy but do real damage."
I whistled. "Impressive."
She eyed me critically. "I have more buffs that I can cast. Should I?"
"Please do," I said, more than a little curious to see what she could do.

Safyre has cast aether protection on you (+50% reduced nether damage). Duration: 5 minutes.
Safyre has cast warrior's boon on you (+10 to all physical attributes). Duration: 5 minutes.
Safyre has summoned a level 188 drow phantom.
Safyre has summoned 3 level 150 feral specters.
Safyre has summoned a level 199 aether saint.

"Wohoo," Ghost remarked, padding around the five spirits Safyre had summoned. *"They're a little frightening."*

I agreed. In fact, Safyre was more than a little frightening, too. Judging by her buffs and summons, defeating her in battle would be... uhm, difficult. Were all elites this strong? *I may have my work cut out for me.*

I turned to the spirit wolf. *"You shouldn't be here,"* I chided. *"Join the others."*

"But how am I going to see what's going on from back there?" she complained.

Before I could reply, Safyre opened her eyes. "All done," she said, eyeing the results of her work in satisfaction.

I shook my head ruefully as I studied the aetherist anew. She shone so brightly from the enchantments wrapped about her that I had to slit my eyes when looking at her. "I feel... redundant."

Safyre laughed. "I might have gone a bit overboard," she admitted. "But you did say you wanted to be as prepared as possible, and it has been so long since I cast any of these spells that I couldn't resist." She shook a finger at me. "But don't sell yourself short. I *know* what you're capable of."

I raised my hands, palms out. "Alright, I'll say no more. You ready to begin?"

She nodded. "Opening the portal now."

Taking a dozen steps back, I crouched in the snow and let myself fade into the background, then checked my blades. For the upcoming encounter, I'd swapped out faithful for my old stygian shortsword.

The chances of danger—on this side of the portal at least—were slim, but I'd not forgotten my last, truncated visit to the nether-infested realm. The moment I passed through the gateway, I expected things to get hairy.

Safyre has cast greater portal. A ley line to sector 18,240 has begun forming...

   ...

   ...

Chapter 301: A Fatal Impulse

A portal has opened.

I rose to my feet. *"I'm going in,"* I said through the farspeaker bracelet. I padded forward, eyes trained on the luminous curtain before me, but around the corner of my eye, I noticed Safyre's summons stiffen.

I paused and swung towards the caster. *"What's—"*

"Something is coming through!" Safyre yelled. "Get back!"

My head whipped back towards the portal. She was right. A dark miasma was pouring through.

A stygian.

I drew my swords in a flash, but for a heartbeat, I was torn between advancing on the emerging foe or withdrawing. Temporizing, I unfurled my mindsight.

"What is it?" Duggar asked tersely.

"Danger," I said. *"Withdraw to the cave and make sure the twins go with you. Safyre and I will handle this."*

"Understood," the alpha replied, not voicing any arguments.

Leaving Duggar to see to the pack's safety, I reached out with my will to the stygian. It still hadn't passed fully through the gateway. Whatever it was, it was big.

The target is a level 158 stygian shambling horror.

The tension eased from me. For all its size, the approaching enemy was no great threat, and even without Safyre's help, I was certain I could handle it. With her buffs and summons thrown in the mix… it wouldn't be much of a fight.

"It's only a rank fifteen shambling horror," I yelled to Safyre. "I'm going to engage."

"Wait!" she cried. "I can sense more enemies crowding behind this one. The horror is blocking the portal, but the others look set to follow on its heels."

More? "How many?" I demanded.

"I can't tell," she replied, sounding frustrated. "Can't you look through the portal with your mindsight?"

Could I? The notion had never occurred to me.

"Send your summons forward," I instructed, "and hold the horror at the gate. I'm going to try and do as you ask."

She nodded curtly.

Trusting her to protect me, I closed my eyes and concentrated solely on my mindsight. Only nine mindglows were in range.

Safyre and her five pets. The stygian. Me. And Ghost—*what is she still doing here?*

"Get back, Ghost!" I snapped.

The spirit wolf didn't reply, but I had little attention to spare her. Safyre's summons had engaged the shambling horror, and I didn't expect the battle to last long. I couldn't see past the portal, but I knew where it was. Concentrating hard, I tried to push my awareness through and 'see' beyond.

To no avail.

I deflated. "I can't do it," I yelled. "I can't extend my awareness past the edge of the portal."

"Damn. We have to close the gateway, then," Safyre said.

"Agreed. Go ahead."

"I'll go look!"

My head snapped to the left, only now noticing the bright mindglow racing towards the tear in the air. "Ghost, no!" I shouted.

"Don't worry, I won't be long," she replied brightly. Then she was gone.

"Michael, what's happened?"

"Ghost—the spirit wolf, I mean—she has gone through. Hold the portal open." I took a step forward.

"Euww, there are hundreds of nasty creatures here, Prime," Ghost sent, her mindvoice hushed. *"I don't like them."*

I froze. The spirit wolf was speaking to me from beyond the gate. *"Get back now!"* I ordered.

"In a second. Oww. This one is even bigger than the others. He's huuuge."

I ground my teeth in frustration. *"Ghost, come back. Please!"*

A stygian shambling horror has died.

"Michael!"

At Safyre's cry, my gaze whipped back to the gate. Three other stygians were flying through the gate. Smaller than the shambling horror, they fit through easily.

Another came through. Then another.

Ghost had said hundreds were waiting to enter on the other side. Dread curdled in my stomach, realizing what had to be done. "Close the portal," I ordered.

"Are you—"

"Now!" I ground out harshly, eyes tracking the seven other stygians that had come through in the interim.

Safyre has cast dispel greater portal. A ley line to sector 18,240 has begun closing...

...

"Prime?" Ghost called, her voice sounding small. *"I don't like it here. Can I come back now?"*

"Yes! Quickly, before—"

A portal has closed.

My mental projection cut off midway. The gateway was shut, leaving Ghost stranded on the other side and out of reach. *Hold on, Ghost,* I thought.

I'm coming—I turned to the nearest stygian—*just as soon as we deal with these.*

Even the twenty stygians that had made it through were no match for Safyre. Partially, that was because most were under rank fifteen. Smaller than the shambling horror, they wheeled and dived through the air, attempting to strike at us from above.

None came close to landing a blow.

Safyre and her copies—each with two wands apiece—blasted fifteen stygians out of the sky all on their own. Unable to withstand the concentrated firepower, the creatures quickly succumbed.

I took care of the rest, if in a less flamboyant fashion. Shadow blinking from stygian and stygian, I dealt death while airborne. None of the nether beasts managed to land a blow, and my new Class did not come into play at all.

As the last stygian died, I alighted softly on the ground, my thoughts mired in rage. I was furious, but I was not sure with whom.

Myself. Ghost. Even Duggar.

The spirit wolf shouldn't have been anywhere near the portal, and that was on Duggar and me. But she should also have listened when I'd called her back. I shoved my swords back into their sheaths. There was plenty of blame to go around.

"What happened?" Safyre asked quietly from behind.

I turned around. "Ghost saw a few hundred more stygians waiting on the other side of the portal. That's why I made you close it."

"Ghost... that's the spirit wolf?"

"She is that, and a member of the pack too." I paused. "I have to go after her."

Safyre nodded, saying nothing of the risk. If I died in the nether-infested sector, there was no coming back. "If there are that many stygians near the portal's coordinates, we can't open another gateway. They will be waiting for that. You will be spotted and overrun the moment you step through."

I nodded. "I will have to use the bracelet." Unlike a traditional mage's spell, the aetherstone did not create a luminescent gateway.

"That might work," Safyre said, handing the artifact over.

"What happened?" Aira asked.

I glanced over my shoulder. The wolves had re-emerged from the den, and this time it was not just the elders but every adult in the pack from what I could see. The twins, thankfully, were not among them.

I exhaled heavily. *"I can't say for certain, but I think we just got unlucky. A horde of stygians was close enough to the portal to sense its opening, and they tried to rush through."*

I remembered the stygian shambling horror from my last trip into the hidden sector. Was it only simple misfortune, as I had told Aira? Or had the beast and its fellows been waiting for my return all this time? I shuddered. If the latter was true, then it was more than a little disturbing.

The elders were still looking at me, seeming to sense there was more I was not saying.

Sighing, I delivered the bad news I was avoiding. *"Ghost went through. I told her not to..."* I shrugged. *"But she wouldn't listen,"* I finished lamely.

The wolves exchanged glances, and behind their shuttered minds, I was sure they were conversing furiously.

"Is she dead?" Duggar asked finally.

I shook my head. *"I don't think so. Ghost has no physical form, so the nether won't affect her. There is also no reason any of the stygians would be able to detect—much less harm—her. But she is alone, likely scared, and without a way back."*

"Won't she go into the dungeon?" Oursk asked. *"Its entrance is but a few steps away.*

I shrugged. *"I don't know. You likely know the answer to that better than me. Would she?"*

He looked away. *"I'm not... sure."*

"What are you planning?" Aira asked.

The pack were more philosophical about death and loss than I was, and I was sure the elders would not approve of what I intended, but I didn't shirk from Aira's gaze. *"I am going after her."*

Sulan stepped forward. I braced myself, expecting a blistering scolding for my brashness, but she surprised me. *"This is my fault,"* she said, going down on all fours. *"I should have kept the pup in the den. I'm sorry, scion."*

I stared at the white wolf. Shame and guilt rolled off her in waves. Sulan, I realized, cared more for Ghost than she let on. *"It's as much my fault as yours,"* I assured her. *"I saw her hanging about the portal. I should have suspected... something."*

Leta snorted. *"You're both behaving like fools. I'm not sure what's gotten in Sulan, but she's wrong."* The elder stared at her companion. *"You've been coddling that wolf for too long, Sulan, and this is what it's got you. Ghost is no pup. She should know better than to disobey a battle leader in the midst of a fight."* She turned to me. *"The pack comes first. Ghost is lost. Accept it."*

Sulan growled at Leta but didn't contradict her, and all eyes turned to Duggar, whose own inscrutable gaze rested on me.

"Tell me, alpha," he said, stressing the title. *"Truthfully. If you went after Ghost, do you think you can retrieve her without dying?"*

I hesitated. There was no way to know that for certain, and I didn't want to lie to Duggar, but I could not give the elders more reason to argue. And Leta was wrong. Despite her 'age,' Ghost *was* a pup in every way that counted.

"Yes," I said firmly.

"Then you must go," he said, sitting on his haunches.

Leta growled in disagreement, but the alpha disdained to look at her.

I inclined my head at Duggar, appreciating his support. "I have a plan, not just to get Ghost back, but to finish what we came here to do. The pack will travel to the tundra today." I met Leta's angry eyes. "And if I have my way, no one will die today."

✳   ✳   ✳

There was no time to debate matters further.

We'd wasted enough time already, and every second longer that I delayed, the greater were the chances that Ghost would wander out of range.

I pulled Safyre aside. My plan had one potential hiccup, and I had to check with her first. "Do you need the aetherstone bracelet to open the portal again?"

"I don't." She tapped her temple. "Now that I've already opened one portal, I have the location logged."

My shoulders eased. That was the answer I'd been hoping for. "Take this," I said, handing her a pack.

She took it without question.

You have lost a <u>large bag of holding</u> containing 29 sets of winter gear and 470 caches of cold weather supplies.

"If something happens to me, it's up to you to get the pack to safety." I gestured to the bag she held. "And build a future for them, the twins, and yourself on the tundra with that. Can I count on you?

She nodded solemnly.

"Thank you." I closed my eyes and sucked in a breath. I'd not been wrong about Cara—Safyre. She had proven trustworthy in every respect, and I knew I could depend on her to see things through.

Looking at her, I told her what I planned. "I'm going to teleport to the sector alone." I held up my hand, stilling the questions I could see bubbling behind her eyes. "Fighting the stygians there is suicide, I know. But I don't intend on fighting. I plan on doing what I do best—running and hiding."

I grinned, and so what if my expression was a touch more maniacal than was comfortable? "I will draw the stygians away. *All of them.* Give me five minutes, then you can open a gateway and let the wolves through."

Safyre squeezed my arm but refrained from pointing out the multitude of flaws in my plan, for which I was grateful. "I will need to send you to the valley's safe zone first, of course, so you can use the aetherstone bracelet. Once you reach the hidden sector, though, how will you find Ghost?"

"I will call to her with mindspeech as I draw the stygians away. I don't think the beasts will be able to hear. Hopefully, Ghost will answer." I tapped the farspeaker bracelet. "Contact me the moment you open the portal and when the last wolf reaches the tundra." I held her gaze. "Do not delay or linger in the sector for *any* reason. Once I have Ghost in tow, I will circle around the stygians and rejoin you in the tundra."

Safyre nodded. "Do what you must. I will see to it that the pack reaches the tundra safely."

She had not released my arm, and I squeezed hers in return. "Good luck, Cara."

She smiled, pleased by my use of her old name. "Don't die," she replied. "That would make me... cross."

Eased by her words and feeling more relaxed than I had any right to be, I retreated a few steps and waited while Safyre closed her eyes and summoned a portal into being.

Safyre has cast lesser portal.

The curtain of light materialized, and I ducked through without hesitation, transitioning, between one second and the next, from mountain to village.

✱   ✱   ✱

You have entered a safe zone.

The tear in the air vanished behind me, and I glanced around. Safyre had sent me to a secluded area of the village, one I immediately recognized. I was outside Mariga's cottage, and best of all, no one was around to observe me.
This is perfect.
Dropping into a crouch, I wrapped myself in shadows and reached out with my will to the bracelet on my wrist.

Aetherstone bracelet activated. Connection to the ley line network formed. Selected exit: nether portal 1 of sector 18,240.

I was on my way. *I'm coming, Ghost.*

Transfer commencing...
...

...
Passage completed!
Leaving sector 12,560. Entering sector 18,240 of the Forever Kingdom.

CHAPTER 302: SUCCESS AND FAILURE

You have entered sector 18,240 of the Forever Kingdom. Reminder: This region is under assault by a young void tree that has taken root in the heart of the sector. Remaining time until the sector is pulled into the Nethersphere: unknown.

Warning: You have entered the nether! The nether toxicity at your current location is at tier 2. The dark miasma infecting the region is unconducive to life and will cause your health, psi, stamina, and mana to degenerate by 15% per minute. Current status: Protected. Remaining duration: 45 minutes.

Your farspeaker bracelet has been deactivated. The matching device(s) are not present in this sector.

I reappeared in the same position—crouched, hidden, and with my mindsight unfurled.

Heavy banks of smog that I'd known to expect roiled all around me, transforming everything beyond a few yards into a wall of gray. I wasn't about to complain, though. While the free-floating nether reduced visibility, it concealed me, too.

Multiple hostile entities have failed to detect you! You are hidden.

The Game message came as no surprise.

Mindsight reported the area to be thick with hostiles. Dozens upon dozens of them, closely packed atop one another. I glanced upward. Even though I could not see them, I knew most of the stygians had to be flying above me. Were they like the ones that had come through the portal—rank fifteen creatures?

I suspected so but didn't dare attempt an analyze to confirm. The last time I'd done that in this sector, my target had detected me, and this time around, retreating into the tundra was not an option.

I lowered my head, aware of the ticking clock but knowing I couldn't act hastily. There were perhaps two dozen ground-bound stygians around me, but I couldn't see them. Now and again, one would come close enough to penetrate the wall of gray, and I would get a glimpse of a body part—a scaled tail, a glistening tusk, or an armored torso.

But again, despite temptation, I didn't try analyzing the beasts.

Unbending slowly and readying myself to flee if it became necessary, I called out softly with my mind, *"Ghost?"*

There was no response, neither from the spirit wolf nor the milling stygians. Emboldened, I projected my mindvoice further. *"Ghost, where are you?"*

Still no response.

I tried again, broadcasting my mindvoice as far as it would go. *"GHOST! ANSWER ME!"*

"Prime?" came a faint response. *"Is that you?"*

Sharp relief sang through me. *"Yes! Come to me."*

"Where are you?"

"The same spot where the portal opened."

"I don't know where that is," Ghost replied, her voice small. *"I got turned around following a slug-thing, and now, I don't know where I am. I'm sorry. I should have listened to—"*

"Shh, none of that now," I ordered. *"Follow the sound of my voice."* Raising my head, I howled. Not in the real, but with my mindvoice.

AhhhooOOOOOooowhoooo...AhhhooOOOOOooowhoooo...

I howled over and over, one long, undulating cry that never let up. Ghost didn't reply again, but I knew that wherever she was, she couldn't fail to hear me.

A minute went by, and I began to get edgy, but I kept going. Another passed, and I knew I was nearly out of time. I didn't let up, though.

Seconds later, a blinding star appeared at the edges of my mindsight. *Ghost.* I broke off my howl, chest heaving from the mental exertion.

"Prime! I found you!" the spirit wolf cried, dancing around me in delight.

I smiled and, unshuttering my mind, let her see my joy that she was safe.

"What's going on?" Ghost asked, suddenly anxious.

She'd sensed more than my surface thoughts, I realized. She had felt the mix of emotions beneath too.

"The others are coming through soon," I said, not attempting to disguise the truth—or my own worry—from her. *"I have to draw the stygians away before that happens."* I fixed my gaze on the spirit wolf's mindglow. *"Ghost, this is serious. Can I trust you? To follow my lead and all my instructions—to the letter?"*

"I'm sorry," she said contritely. *"I should not have disobeyed you before. I will do as you ask. Promise."*

"Good. Then stick close to me and don't wander off. Things are about to get complicated."

Lifting my head, I howled again. This time in the real.

*　　*　　*

The response was instantaneous.

Multiple hostile entities have detected you! You are no longer hidden.

I didn't hesitate. Cutting left, I raced into the nearly impenetrable cloud of gray, adjusting my stride as the terrain revealed itself. The stygians gave chase.

My legs pumped, and my feet pounded, both threatening to give way with each step as the ground rose or fell in unexpected ways. But my agility proved equal to the challenge, and I caught myself every time, averting disaster.

A shape burst through the mist.

I threw myself out of the way, weaving psi.

You have evaded an unknown hostile's attack.

I bounced across the hard ground, my tumble nowhere near as controlled as I liked, and scraped hands and knees in the process. Two dark minds rushed up from my rear.

But my spell was complete, and I was ready for them.

You have cast windborne.

Spell-manifested wind formed at my back, and in the next instant, I flew up a ramp of air and out of the reach of my pursuers' snapping jaws.

You have evaded the attacks of 2 unknown hostiles.

I rocketed off the windslide and went into freefall. Mid-air and without clear sight of the ground, I did the only thing I could. I shadow blinked behind a lone stygian twenty yards ahead.

You have teleported into the shadow of an unknown hostile.

I lurched, finding uneven ground underfoot, but once more, I managed to retain my balance and evade my foe's lashing tail. Putting my head down, I resumed my flight and howled again.

My deft maneuvers had caught my landbound enemies flatfooted, and the distance between me and the nearest one was opening fast. Sadly, the same did not hold for my airborne foes, and a few seconds later, the sky turned black with dark minds.

The flying horde from the nether portal had caught up.

My jaws tightened. Escaping so many was not going to be easy. I drew psi in anticipation.

"Turn left, turn left," Ghost sang.

I stumbled and almost lost the threads of my spell at her unexpected cry. *"Ghost,"* I rasped in reproach. *"You told me you were going to—"*

"There's a river ahead. Can't you see it? You'll run straight into it if you don't change direction." She giggled. *"Or do you want to get wet?"*

I blinked. Was she right? But it didn't matter, one direction was as good as another. Swerving left, I kept running.

Five shapes hurtled down from the sky, but before they could strike at me, I flung the spell I held ready.

You have cast mass charm. You have charmed 5 of 5 targets for 20 seconds.

"Oh, I like that spell," Ghost said.

A grin slipped on my face. The spirit wolf sounded like her old self again, and even amidst the deadly chase, I found her mood infectious. My thoughts circled back to her earlier warning. Ghost might appear a naïve child at times, but she was not stupid. *Was* there a river?

Deciding to put her words to the test, I sent one of my new minions diving into the ground to the right; the other four I ordered to attack their former fellows.

Continuing my flight, I listened for the moment of impact.

The splash was audible even over the sound of my feet slapping against the ground, and my mouth dropped open. The spirit wolf had been right.

"Ghost, can you see through the nether?"

"Nether?" she asked. *"What nether?"*

I smiled, her surprise was answer enough. *"Listen closely. I want you to describe the surrounding terrain in as much detail as possible. Leave nothing out."*

"The ground, you mean?"

"Yes."

"Alright... but can't you see it yourself?"

I shook my head. *"My vision is obscured by a gray mist—we call it nether."*

"Oh. Is that why you nearly ran off that cliff?"

My grin turned sickly. *"Probably. Now go on. Tell me what you see."*

I listened intently as the spirit wolf relayed what she saw. Her detailed description confirmed my suspicion: Ghost had no notion of the nether at all. It was completely invisible to her spirit sight.

Which raised an interesting question: if Ghost could not see the free-floating nether, did it mean it was not of the physical world? Not real? *Is it purely magical?*

A thought worth pondering—but later.

Maintaining my steady jog, I kept my senses trained for danger while I led the stygians on a merry chase.

✶　✶　✶

Five minutes later, and only a few minutes late by my reckoning, a Game message flashed for attention.

Your farspeaker bracelet has been activated. The matching devices have entered the sector.

A heartbeat later, Safyre's voice rang sharp and clear in my mind. *"Michael, the portal is open."*

"Any stygians about?" I asked, dreading her response.

"A handful still lingered," she replied crisply, *"but they've been put down already."*

"That's the best news I've heard all day," I panted, ducking low to avoid a diving stygian. *"And the pack?"*

"Passing through as we speak. A dozen adults have already entered the dungeon portal and are in the tundra. Two—the big black one and the old white one—are sticking by my side."

"That's Duggar and Sulan," I huffed. *"So everything is going smoothly?"*

"It is." A pause. *"What about you?"*

"All good. I found Ghost. We have our hands full with the stygians, but we're managing," I replied.

The spirit wolf's sight was proving to be an unlooked-for boon. Her guidance had sped my flight and, just as importantly, ensured I hugged the river, which in turn, kept my right flank protected from the landbound stygians. And so far, I was managing to outrun those on my left.

The flying beasts, though, were an ongoing problem. I'd avoided being tagged, but it was only a matter of time.

"Let me know if anything changes on your end," I said to Safyre.

"I will," she replied and fell silent.

"Nine beasts—the flying kind—approaching from over the water," Ghost sang out.

The spirit wolf was enjoying this, I realized. *"How much time do I have?"* Ghost was also acting as my spotter, warning me of incoming danger before it entered the range of my mindsight. Sometimes, though, I still had to remind her what information was necessary to relay.

"Fifteen seconds," she said cheerfully.

I grunted in acknowledgment and held back the charm spell I'd been readying for use against the two stygians swooping from above. Screeching to a sudden halt, I let them overfly me.

You have evaded the attacks of 2 flying serpents.

My maneuver slowed me down, but that couldn't be helped. Keeping a wary eye on the stygians behind me that were drawing closer, I resumed running.

A few seconds later, just as Ghost had predicted, nine fast-moving shapes zipped into my mindsight, and I wasted no time releasing my prepared casting against them.

You have cast mass charm. You have charmed 9 of 9 targets for 20 seconds.

To my immense relief, my charm spell had yet to fail me since entering the sector. After the horde was alerted to my presence, I'd not been afraid to inspect my foes and had analyzed more than a few of them.

I had learned that the majority of the stygians in the region were serpents like those I'd run across in the rift with Simone's party and, like them, were usually below rank fifteen. As a result, I'd come to depend heavily on my charm spell. Focusing on my new minions, I ordered them to attack the stygians at my rear.

"Uh-oh."

"What's wrong?" I wheezed.

"The big one is back," Ghost replied.

'Big ones' was the term Ghost applied to the more powerful stygians. Unfortunately, despite repeated attempts, I'd failed to analyze any of those so-labeled. None had entered my sight range yet—the spirit wolf had successfully steered me clear of every 'big one'—but I suspected I would not relish encountering one.

"Which one is it?"

Ghost didn't reply immediately, and when she did, her voice was unusually subdued. *"This one hasn't chased you yet."*

I frowned. *"But you said it's 'back.' When did you see it before?"*

"Near the portal, before it closed."

"And where is it now?"

"Flying above you."

My gaze jerked up involuntarily, but of course, I saw nothing. My trepidation grew. None of the other big ones had been flying creatures. *"Am I able to outrun it?"*

"I don't think so," Ghost whispered.

That did not bode well. More than Ghost's words themselves, her muted responses worried me. She was scared. And that was unusual. But it was more than the spirit wolf's fear that I found disconcerting.

The skies above me were clearer than they had been since the first flying serpent had caught up to me. *"Where are the rest of the stygians? Has the big one chased them away?"*

"No. I think..." A long pause. *"I think he is gathering them."*

"Gathering them?" I asked, trying not to let my alarm show. *"Where?"*

"Above you. The smaller beasts are circling the big one."

That was definitely not good news. *"How many do you see?"*

"Fifty that I can make out. More are arriving every second."

What Ghost described was not typical stygian behavior, not as I understood it. So far, the beasts had attacked in fits and starts as soon as they entered striking range. There had been *no* attempts at coordination.

Until now.

Was the big one controlling the others? It sure sounded like it. *Damnation!* I cursed, my pulse quickening. Things looked like they were about to go from mildly bad to impossibly bad.

"Is something wrong?" Duggar asked suddenly, his mental voice made faint by distance. *"I can sense your unease."*

I hesitated, then spoke truthfully. *"I'm not sure. The stygians look like they are gathering for a concentrated assault. I may not be able to—"*

"They're diving," Ghost broke in tersely. *"All of them."* She paused. *"You have twenty seconds."*

My heart lurched. *All of them?*

"Scion?" Duggar called.

"No time to talk," I wheezed, my thoughts preoccupied with the incoming assault. There would be no dodging a wave that big.

Do I fight? I wondered. My steps faltered, and I drew psi. If I could get amongst the flying serpents before they finished their dive, then perhaps I could...

Could what?

There was no fighting fifty stygians. The very idea was ludicrous. Beads of sweat broke out across my brow. I was staring final death in the face, I realized. And the best plan I'd come up with was... one last stand? *Damnit, Michael, think! There must be a—*

Duggar's presence grew in my mind until he was like a rock for me to lean against. I calmed immediately. *"Thank you,"* I panted, not knowing what the alpha had done but grateful, nonetheless.

For one fatal second, fear had nearly overtaken me, but now I saw more clearly. Fighting was not the answer, I realized. More running was.

My steps firming, I altered my course and made a beeline for the river. According to Ghost, its waters were deep and the current swift, but right now, the river offered the only hope of escape.

It was a slim hope, but I clung to it.

I couldn't die here—in a blaze of glory or otherwise—too many depended on me. Reminded of my responsibilities, I reached out to the dire wolf alpha again. *"Don't wait for me, Duggar. I don't know how long it will take me to get back to the portal. And one more thing—"*

I broke off to swerve around a large ditch.

"Yes?"

"The werewolf, Anriq, the one I told you about, do you remember him?"

"I do."

"He is on his way to the tundra. Tell Snow to find him. He, too, is pack now."

Before Duggar could respond, a hundred mindglows crossed the border of my mindsight—the flying serpents diving in attack. Ghost's estimate had been on the low side.

I was out of time, but the river was finally in sight.

"I will see it done," Duggar promised. *"Stay safe, scion."*

"I'll do my best," I replied. Leaping forward, I dove into the water.

The river was a raging torrent.

The moment my body hit the water, I was swept away, and the hundred dark minds swooping down on me disappeared from awareness.

Limbs windmilling, I tried to right myself, but the current was too strong, and I was pushed beneath the frothing surface. Icy water gushed into my eyes, mouth, and nose. Kicking frantically, I tried to lift my head clear.

It was useless.

Squeezing my eyes shut, I closed my mouth. *Calm, Michael,* I admonished. I could no more fight the river than the stygians, I realized, and ceased struggling.

Obligingly, the river pulled me under.

But the first blush of my panic had subsided, and I stayed relaxed. Letting my limbs hang loose, I tried to get a feel for the raging currents and take stock of the situation.

The nether creatures—both airborne and landbound variants—had vanished from my mindsight. But one other mindglow still stuck close. *"Ghost, are you alright?"*

"I am," she said, sounding distracted. *"This is the first time I've dived into a river, you know. Who knew it would be so strange?"*

By happenstance, the currents flung me up, and not wasting the opportunity, I gulped in a deep lungful of air.

"What's strange about it?" I asked, resuming my conversation with the spirit wolf, which in itself was more than a little odd.

Ghost sounded as if the river didn't bother her at all, which on reflection, it likely didn't. Being without a body was not without some benefits, after all.

"The current is carrying me downriver as fast as it is you," Ghost said, *"but I don't feel as if I am moving."*

"That does sound weird," I agreed. It was an inane conversation to have while the river was trying to drown me, but it kept me from dwelling on how dire my situation was.

The turbulent waters wrenched at my body again, this time pulling it downwards, and I dropped like a stone, sinking for what felt like an eternity. *How deep is this river, anyway?*

A mindglow appeared below me.

For a moment, I almost tensed and fought the river's pull, but then forced myself to relax. Were there stygians lurking beneath as well?

That could be problematic.

A dry understatement but much better than panic. Reaching out with my will, I analyzed the creature swimming below.

The target is a level 15 river turtle.

Huh. Imagine that.

The river still contained ordinary wildlife. I wasn't sure why that surprised me, but I found the discovery unexpectedly heartening despite my circumstances. Even as nether-infested as this sector was, it was not irredeemable.

I opened my eyes, and another surprising realization followed in the wake of the first: the river's waters were clear and unclouded, bearing no taint of nether whatsoever. I wanted to explore the implications of that more closely, but a less happy thought intruded: my lungs were near-bursting. It was time to get some air. *"Ghost, are you on the surface?"*

"Yes, Prime."

"Perfect." Weaving psi, I shadow blinked to her.

You have teleported to Ghost.

For a brief instant, I was free of the water. Then predictably, the river pulled me back, but not before I drew in a deep breath of air.

Once more, I sank to the bottom. A second turtle had joined the first, and perhaps curious about the interloper in their realm, they swam closer to inspect me. But as fascinating as the river's wildlife was, I turned my focus upwards. It was time to get a better handle on the situation.

"Tell me what you see, Ghost. Are the flying serpents still around?"

"Yes. They've caught up again."

"Are they trying to get into the river?"

"No. They're hanging back."

That almost made me smile. *I should have jumped into the river earlier.* But who knew that all it took was a little water to escape the stygians?

Now, though, it was time to leave.

The pack's exodus should be nearly complete. And every second longer that I spent in the river lengthened the trip back. By now, the raging current must have carried me miles from the portal to the guardian tower.

"The big one is still around," Ghost added.

Urgh. *"Where is it?"*

"Flying directly above you."

Damn. The unpleasant news didn't change matters, though, even if it complicated them. I still had to get out of the river, and cloaked in shadows, I could make the journey back in some measure of safety.

"Alright, Ghost, here is what I want you to do..."

✳ ✳ ✳

You are hidden.
You have teleported to Ghost.
You have cast windborne.

With the spirit wolf's help and one perfectly executed sequence of psi spells, I escaped the river's clutches. I had instructed Ghost to reposition herself along one of the riverbanks, then teleported to her and surfed my way to the shore on a windslide.

Wet and bedraggled, I crouched on the riverbank and scanned the surroundings.

The area was thankfully free of stygians. *"Follow me,"* I ordered Ghost. Ignoring the water dripping from my clothes, I turned northeast and crept through the mists, heading toward the guardian tower's nether portal.

Without landmarks, navigating the nether-infested sector would have been impossible if not for one thing: my budding explorer trait.

Thanks to the trait, the location of each of the sector's key points shone unerringly in my mind. Even blind, I knew in which direction to head.

Unbidden, a Game message scrolled through my vision.

Congratulations, Michael! You have completed the task: <u>Resettlement!</u> The dire wolf pack has been transported to their new home in sector 107 of the guardian tower. Wolf is pleased, and your Mark has deepened.

I rocked to a halt, a contented smile on my face. It was done. Safyre had come through, and the pack was safe. Now, all that was left was for me to join them.

"Michael?" Safyre called, speaking through the farspeaker bracelet.

"Here," I replied and resumed my journey through the haze of nether.

"The pack is through, and I'm about to close the portal."

"Thank you," I said, nearly choking with emotion.

"Are you safe?" she asked, sensing something in my voice.

"I'm not in immediate danger if that counts," I replied.

"It does," she said, and I could hear the smile in her voice. *"Can you make it back to the portal on your own?"* she asked.

"I think so," I said, then added, reluctantly, *"But it will take time. I'm miles away."* Not to mention that anything could happen between now and then. Safyre would know that, though.

"How did that happen?"

"I fell into a river."

A pause. *"You're joking?"*

My lips twitched. *"I'm not."* Recalling the turtle, I realized Safyre might be able to satisfy my curiosity about them. *"I discovered something surprising in the water. There was this—"*

"Incoming!" Ghost sang.

I froze. *"Where?"*

"From up above. The big one is coming down from the sky, as are the other beasts with him."

"Can they see me?"

"I'm not sure," Ghost admitted. *"But the serpents have not begun an attack dive. They are gliding around the big one. Does that help?"*

It did. I pursed my lips. Why *were* the flying stygians descending? Did they know I'd left the river? And would my stealth hold once they got closer?

"Is everything alright?" Safyre asked. She couldn't hear Ghost, of course.

"I have incoming," I replied absently, still puzzling over how to respond to the approaching stygians.

"I'll leave you to deal with them, then," Safyre said. *"Speak to me when you can."*

"You should go through the portal," I said, realizing she intended to wait for me. *"The stygians could ambush you at any moment."*

"I'm safe enough for now," she responded, unconcerned. "Their last assault was nothing to shout about. If more come at me than I can handle, I will retreat. Promise."

Their last assault? How many attacks had she fended off already? *Safyre can take care of herself*, I reminded myself. *Probably better than you can.*

I turned back to Ghost. "How long until our guests arrive?"

"A minute, maybe? The big one flies slowly, and the other beasts are keeping pace with him."

I frowned. "Did the big one descend before?"

"No," she said emphatically. "He is scary. I would have noticed if he'd come closer."

"Describe him for me."

"He's big."

I didn't roll my eyes. "How big?"

Ghost had to think about that for a while. "Bigger than all the other beasts put together? Bigger than a thousand Duggars?"

That was big, alright. "What else can you tell me about him?" I asked, struggling to contain my rising worry. A monstrosity that size—even if it was slow—couldn't be taken lightly.

"Uhm... he's round like a ball and has hundreds of long gray things extending below him."

"Tentacles?"

"Yes!"

My frown deepened. I could not make sense of the creature Ghost had described, but someone else might. "Safyre, how much do you know about stygians?"

"I'm not an expert," she replied, "but I've been on my fair share of rift dives. Why?"

I fed her Ghost's description of the big one. "Do you know what that is?"

Palpable silence.

"Safyre?" I prompted.

"Are you sure that's what's after you?" she asked, her tone unwontedly serious.

"That's what Ghost has described seeing, and I have no reason to doubt her."

"Then you better run," Safyre said bleakly. "The creature you describe is a stygian overlord, and I've not heard of one below level three hundred."

My eyes widened. "Did you say—?"

"Yes. They're slow and can normally be outrun, but in a sector like this, already teeming with stygians, that might not be so easy. When the nether gains a foothold in a new sector, the overlords are usually the ones to smash down the defenses of any fortified settlements in the region."

"Prime!" Ghost said excitedly. "The big one is doing something."

"What?" I asked tersely.

"I don't know, but a dark light is forming between his tentacles."

Was the overlord readying a magical projectile? That seemed like a reasonable assumption. Doubling my pace, I moved as fast as I could while still retaining my stealth.

"What sort of attacks do the overlords have?" I asked Safyre.

"They use blobs of nether primarily," she said, speaking rapidly as she sensed my urgency. *"The projectiles move only slightly faster than the overlords themselves, but what they lack in speed, they make up for in spread. A single blob can drench an area over a hundred yards in diameter."* She paused. *"You won't escape it on your own, not with all those other stygians around. Tell me where you are, and I'll come to you."*

That was patently impossible. I was too far away for Safyre to reach in time, even if she could navigate through the mist. Besides, I was not about to endanger her. All I said, though, was, *"I don't think that's a good idea. I'll handle it."*

"But—"

"Please, Cara," I said, stopping her. *"Go, while you can. And look after the wolves for me."* Since I can't.

Even through the farspeaker bracelet, I heard her unhappy sigh. *"As you wish. Take care, Michael."*

"The dark light is moving," Ghost reported, interrupting before I could reply to Safyre. *"It's heading this way!"*

I cut back toward the river. I had no idea if the water would shield me from whatever casting the overlord had thrown my way, but once more, it was my best hope of escape.

Only hope.

Banishing the pessimistic thought, I dived into the water again.

Chapter 304: The River to Somewhere

Multiple hostile entities have failed to detect you! You are hidden.

In the wake of the stygian overlord's attack, the flying serpents launched their own assault, streaming before, behind, and even *through* the descending magical projectile.

I was safely hidden beneath the water, though, and with no target against which to direct their fury, the serpents aborted their dives to skim along the river in search of me.

Your farspeaker bracelet has been deactivated.

The Game alert was a relief. Safyre was gone. And out of danger. Which left only me to get to safety. I was not certain how I was going to accomplish that, though. Making the river my new home was not an option.

"What's happening?" I asked Ghost from the river bottom.

"The big one's magic is about to hit the water, and more stygians are approaching the riverbanks," she reported.

"Call it an overlord," I said absently. *"More? What type?"*

"Crawlies," she replied.

Landbound stygians. *Hells.* The overlord must have summoned them. I couldn't do anything about them, though. Staying submerged, I waited for the overlord's spell to hit.

It took longer than I expected, but when the casting finally landed, its impact was unmistakable.

The water turned bright yellow.

"Oow, golden water!"

I waited to see what else happened. Whatever had turned the water yellow, I was sure it was nothing good. Just swimming in the stuff might be deadly. I glanced around in sudden trepidation.

Only to relax a heartbeat later.

The surrounding water was crystal clear. In fact, most of the river's depths remained unchanged. It was only the surface that had turned yellow. Unfortunately, that did not help me much.

My lungs were crying for air.

Damnation. I would have to rise to the top soon. *But not yet,* I thought stubbornly. Eyes riveted to the surface, I waited for the river to carry me past the yellow taint or for it to dissipate.

"Is the overlord leaving?" I rasped, searching for a distraction from the burning sensation in my chest.

"No." A pause. *"He's coming closer."*

Well, that's just… great.

Deciding not to ask any more questions, I waited. A second passed. Then another. Was the yellowness of the water above lessening?

I couldn't tell.

Finally, feeling myself turning blue, I accepted the inevitable and shadow blinked.

You have teleported to Ghost.
A hostile entity has detected you! You are no longer hidden.

I gulped in air and my eyes darted sideways. Yellow scum—so thick it was nearly solid—floated atop the river. No wonder it hadn't affected the water below.

Warning: the nether toxicity in this vicinity has increased to tier 12! Your health, psi, stamina, and mana are degenerating at a rate of 45% per minute (reduced by 4 tiers due to existing protections).

Urgh. So that was what the yellow stuff was: raw nether.

I sank through tainted water quickly again, but the single second I'd been in it was enough to convince me I didn't want to face the overlord on land.

"It's firing again," Ghost reported.

I didn't have to ask her who she meant. Drawing on the shadows, I cloaked myself—or tried to.

A hostile entity has detected you! You have failed to conceal yourself.

Hells. What now?

✳   ✳   ✳

An hour later, I was still in the river.

The overlord had not ceased its bombardment or moved away. A silent sentinel, it kept pace with the current to remain above me. According to Ghost, the stygian hovered a mere sixty yards above the river's surface, but that still put it beyond the reach of my mindsight.

The train of landbound stygians following along the riverbanks had grown too. And worse yet, despite repeated attempts, I had failed to conceal myself again.

I knew the reason, of course.

The overlord hanging in the sky was to blame. The beast seemed intent on catching me, and each time I resurfaced for air, it launched another nether blob into the river.

My straits were dire, no doubt about it.

The only thing I had going for me was the river itself. For some reason, the stygians appeared reluctant to enter the water. And as powerful as the overlord's blobs were, after close observation, I was able to discern that their effect dissipated after five minutes.

The hour had seen me cycle endlessly between the river surface—to steal breaths of air—and the river bottom—to hide from the overlord's blobs. The only upside to all the strenuous activity was that I had advanced my nether absorption skill at a record-breaking pace.

Your nether absorption has increased to level 41 and reached rank 4, increasing your chance of resisting harmful nether effects by 10% and decreasing the damage you suffer from them by 20%.

I'd gained four skill ranks in less than an hour, a phenomenal achievement—if only it weren't in such deadly circumstances.

But the Game alert also served to remind me of something else. It was time to renew my defenses. Removing an enchantment crystal from my belt—not easy to do when submerged in a river—I ground it in my fist.

You have activated a nether protection crystal. For the next hour, you will be shielded from the ill effects of the nether at tier 4 and lower concentrations.

The enchantment did not protect me from the nether blobs, but it did lessen the detrimental effects of the spell somewhat. Protections seen to, I turned my attention inwards and focused on my mental compass.

I'd resigned myself to not returning to the guardian tower, at least not by the most direct route. By now, its nether portal was a few dozen miles away and well out of reach.

There was only one other possible means of escape.

Draven's Reach.

It was the sector's second dungeon, and while I knew nothing about the dungeon, its rank, creatures, or layout, its gateway offered hope for Ghost and me. The Game's nether portals were specifically warded against the stygians, and the pursuing horde would not be able to follow us through one.

All we had to do was reach it.

Draven's reach portal shone just as brightly in my mind as the one to the guardian tower. Crucially, though, the river was leading me *towards* it, not away.

In fact, given how rapidly the portal's direction was changing in my mental compass—shifting from dead south to east—the time to leave the river was quickly approaching. Every instinct was telling me the dungeon's entrance was close to the river shore. And for both Ghost's sake and my own, I hoped I was not wrong.

"Almost time," I told Ghost. *"Ready?"*

"Yes, Prime."

I had just a few more preparations to make myself. Crushing the other enchantment crystal I held ready, I turned my attention inwards and cast my buffs.

You have activated a rank 4 Dexterity enhancement crystal. For the next hour, your Dexterity has been increased by +8.

You have cast heightened reflexes, increasing your Dexterity by +8 ranks for 20 minutes.

You have cast load controller, granting you a 10-minute encumbrance aura that slows any armor-wearing foe within 2 yards by 20%.

You have trigger-cast quick mend. When your overall health falls below 30%, it will instantly heal you for 20%.

For what I planned next, speed was vital.

With all my gear and buffs, my Dexterity was almost one hundred. I was undoubtedly quick, and most of the stygians would have difficulty catching me. I only were I was faster.

While you're at it, why not wish Safyre was here? I thought dryly. *Or better yet, that you were both safe in the tavern?*

My mental compass swung dead east.

Breaking off from my musings, I focused on the here and now. It was time. *"Go,"* I ordered.

At the command, I sensed Ghost climb up the eastern riverbank and race past the nearby stygian beasts who could not see her. I waited, giving her time to draw ahead. Then, spinning psi, I formed a windslide and hopped on.

Windborne flung me upwards and towards the river's eastern shore. Breaking through the river's frothing surface, I gulped in air—the response near automatic now—but unlike on previous occasions, I did not fall beneath again.

Windborne kept pushing me higher, and when the spelled ramp finally came to an end, I was two yards above the water and my upward trajectory continued in a graceful arc.

I had only seconds to act.

My senses extended, I scanned the area. Mindsight reported nothing over me, but I did not doubt that the flying serpents circling in the hazy mists above had started their dives. Or that the equally-unseen-overlord was readying a nether blob. The river's western shore was out of range. But on the eastern bank, I sensed a dense mass of mindglows.

Focusing on the farthest I could see, I shadow blinked.

You have teleported 20 yards.

I re-emerged in the real with my blades sheathed and poised to flee. It took me only a split-second to adjust to the sudden shift in terrain, then my feet were pounding hard against the ground as I raced eastward.

The stygian I'd targeted whirled around to nip at me, but I had already passed beyond its reach. Drawing in more psi, I prepared another casting. My teleport hadn't carried me clear of the gathered mass of landbound stygians—as I'd known it wouldn't—and those still ahead were turning to confront me.

"Overlord firing!" Ghost sang from ahead.

"Got it," I replied grimly, beginning another mental clock in my head. If my escape went perfectly, I would be able to outrun the descending blob. But if it didn't...

No point worrying about that now.

Two stygians converged on me. Sidestepping the striking jaws of the first, I leaped over the taloned paw of the second to land lightly behind the creature. Not looking back, I kept running.

The gap between Ghost and me was closing fast, and she was already too close. *"Run faster,"* I panted.

A shape hurtled towards me from the left. Dropping into a roll, I let it sail over and regained my feet without missing a stride. Five more beasts approached from the fore, but my spell was ready, and I released it without hesitating.

You have cast mass charm. You have charmed 5 of 5 targets for 20 seconds.

I grimaced. I'd been saving the spell for the aerial assault, which I expected to arrive at any moment. But done was done, and I would have to adjust my tactics accordingly. Weaving through the now-docile shapes ahead, I sent them to guard my rear.

The way ahead was almost clear. Only two more stygians lay between me and open ground, and I could pass them with a single leap of shadow blink, but I didn't. I glanced upward.

C'mon, what's the holdup?

Right on cue, a mass of shapes rocketed through the upper edges of my mindsight—the anticipated wave of flying serpents. Hopefully, it was all of them. But there was no time to count.

Weaving psi, I slipped out of the real...

You have teleported to Ghost.

... and back into it twenty yards away.

A second later, the foiled serpents' outraged shrieks filled the air. *Music to my ears.* Grinning, I surged past Ghost. Buffed as I was, I was faster than her. Turning my focus inwards for a brief moment, I readjusted the course of our flight according to my mental compass.

The portal was so close now I could almost taste it.

"Five seconds until blob impact!"

Damn. Damn, and damn.

We were almost there. And windborne was not ready yet. Knowing there was nothing else I could do, I kept running. The ground sloped downwards— we were on some sort of grassy knoll—and my pace increased a touch.

"I see it!" Ghost exclaimed.

"How far?" I panted.

"Close," she said eagerly.

"Don't wait for me. When the spell hits, keep going until you reach the portal."

"Why? Will the blob hurt you this time?" she asked in confusion.

I didn't get a chance to explain.

An enormous plume of dense yellow jettisoned down from above, turning everything sickly yellow before obscuring my vision entirely.

An unknown entity has cast the composite spell, <u>blob of nether,</u> over an area you currently occupy. The first spell-stage has been activated, spreading <u>noxious fumes</u> over the targeted area.

Warning: your surroundings have been contaminated with a concentrated dose of nether. The nether toxicity has increased to tier 24! Your health, psi, stamina, and mana are degenerating at a rate of 105% per minute (reduced by 4 tiers due to existing protections).

The nether the overlord had discharged was so concentrated it was clumping together to form a semi-solid sludge. Nor was it filtered, as before, by the river's fast-moving water.

The net effect was something altogether different—and twice as bad.

You have failed a magical resistance check!

Your void armor has reduced the nether damage incurred by 10%. Void armor charge remaining: 99%.

Your health has decreased to 99%.

Your stamina has decreased to 81%.

Your psi has decreased to 87%.

The yellow goo clogged my nose. My eyes burned, and I coughed, almost gagging as I inhaled more of the wretched stuff. Blinded and disorientated, I tripped over my feet and rolled down the hill.

You have failed a magical resistance check! Your health has decreased to 98%.

"Prime!" Ghost cried.

"Keep going," I ground out as I bounced down the slope. *"I won't be able to see at all in this mess. Wait at the portal, and I will teleport to you."*

You have failed a magical resistance check! Your health has decreased to 96%.

But despite the horrid feel of the nether, I was relieved. As debilitating as the effects of the overlord's spell were, they would not prevent me from reaching the portal. In only a few more seconds, I would escape the free-floating nether's clutches.

The noxious fumes have reached maximum dispersion. The first spell-stage is complete. Second stage spell(s) released.

I bounced to a stop at the bottom of the knoll, the Game alert still flashing before me.

Uhm, really? I wasn't sure which stunned me more—the roll down the hill or the contents of the Game message. Spells within a spell? Staggering back to my feet, I took a stumbling step in the direction I knew the portal to be. *What the hell is stage two?*

I didn't have to wonder for long.

As my left foot pressed down, biting agony shot up my leg.

You have failed a magical resistance check! A <u>necrotic spike</u> has been activated, inflicting nether damage upon you.

Void armor charge remaining: 89%.

Your health has decreased to 90%.

Ouch! That had hurt.

Leaning down, I felt along the top of my left foot and touched something sharp and elongated. It had gone through the wayfarer boot as if it didn't exist. Wrenching the thing out, I brought it close for inspection, and only when it was inches from my face could I make out what it was.

The shard in my hand was about half a foot long and formed from a glistening ebony substance—the very same material I had found in the stygian's nest during the rift dive with Simone's people.

Why am I not surprised? I thought and threw the shard away. I glanced at the ground, certain more spikes awaited ahead. That one little spike had cost me five percent of my void armor and only slightly less health, and I didn't fancy walking over more.

"I'm here!" Ghost reported.

I checked my mindsight, but the spirit wolf was out of range. That didn't matter, though. I knew in which direction to head. Spinning psi, I cast windborne.

For a short, blissful stretch of ten yards, I flew through the yellow plumes of nether, but by the time the spell came to an end, I was no nearer to seeing Ghost.

Damn, I thought and jumped blindly off the windslide. My leap carried me a few yards further, after which I crashed ignominiously into another trio of waiting shards.

Necrotic spike activated. You have sustained nether damage.
Necrotic spike activated. You have sustained nether damage.
Necrotic spike activated. You have sustained nether damage.
Void armor charge remaining: 70%.
Your health has decreased to 74%.

"Hurry," Ghost urged. *"The serpents are gathering for another dive."*

More good news, I groused as I picked myself up. I couldn't wait for windborne to be ready again, and I was still taking damage from the nether. There was no help for it. I would have to risk walking across the spelled ground. *"How far am I from you?"*

Ghost hesitated. I knew she wasn't good at measuring distances, never having needed to do it before. *"Sixty yards, maybe?"*

My heart sank.

"Is that too far?"

It was. But I didn't say so. My mindsight extended only twenty yards, which was how close I needed to be to Ghost before I could shadow blink to her. That meant covering the remaining forty yards on foot.

If I move in a leaping-run, I can clear more ground with each step. I didn't hesitate, even knowing the cost. From a standing start, I jumped.

My left foot crunched down.

Necrotic spike activated. You have sustained nether damage.

Ignoring the shooting pain, I leaped off the injured foot and forded another four yards.

Necrotic spike activated. You have sustained nether damage.

I came down on my right foot and sprang forward again. Then again and again.

Necrotic spike activated. You have sustained nether damage.
Necrotic spike activated...

...

"Keep coming, Prime! You're almost here."

Too focused on my agonizing leaps, I didn't respond to Ghost's encouragement, but it kept me going.

Necrotic spike activated. You have sustained nether damage.

Void thief triggered! You have acquired the spell, <u>necrotic spike (stolen)</u>, from an unknown entity and will retain memory of it for the next 4 hours.

Necrotic spike (stolen) is a tier 6 spell that, when triggered by a hostile, will drain 5% of the target's health. The damage inflicted is magical in nature and will bypass all physical defenses and armor. The spikes will remain manifested for 5 minutes before dissipating.

Note, stolen spells are spells that have already been modified with the original owner's skills and attributes. Their power is not determined by your own characteristics, and there are no attribute or skill prerequisites for you to meet. You will, however, have to expend the same amount of mana as the original owner to cast the spell.

Even the surprising Game alert did not break my concentration, and I kept jumping trying to eke out as much distance as I could between leaps.

Necrotic spike activated. You have sustained nether damage.
Necrotic spike activated...

...

Void armor depleted.
Your health has decreased to 32%.
Your stamina has decreased to 7%.
Your psi has decreased to 13%.

Finally, Ghost's mindglow came into sight—as bright and welcoming as the sun. Almost shuddering with relief, I shadow blinked to her while still mid-leap.

You have teleported to Ghost.

"You made it!" the spirit wolf sang.

"Only thanks to you," I rasped tiredly as I crashed to the ground besides her. The overlord's noxious fumes had sapped much of my energy, and I was circling the drain in more ways than one. Heaving myself to my feet, and steadfastly ignoring the many ebony shards buried in my boots, I glanced behind me. I couldn't make out any of the approaching stygians through the yellow mess, though.

"Ten seconds to flying serpents' arrival," Ghost reported.

I turned back to the portal. Even this close-up, the luminous curtain of magic was barely visible through the nether haze. I had no idea what the dungeon held in store for Ghost and me, but it couldn't be worse than what awaited us here.

"Then, let's not hang around to greet them," I huffed. Inhaling deeply, I limped into the dungeon.

Transfer through portal commencing...

...
...
Leaving sector 18,240. Entering the Endless Dungeon.

* * *

The End.

Here ends Book 4 of the Grand Game.
Michael's adventures will continue in **Wolf in the Void**.
<u>Get it here</u>!

I hope you enjoyed the story! If you did, please leave a <u>review</u> and let other
readers know what you think.
<u>Click here to leave a review</u>.
Happy reading!
Tom Elliot.

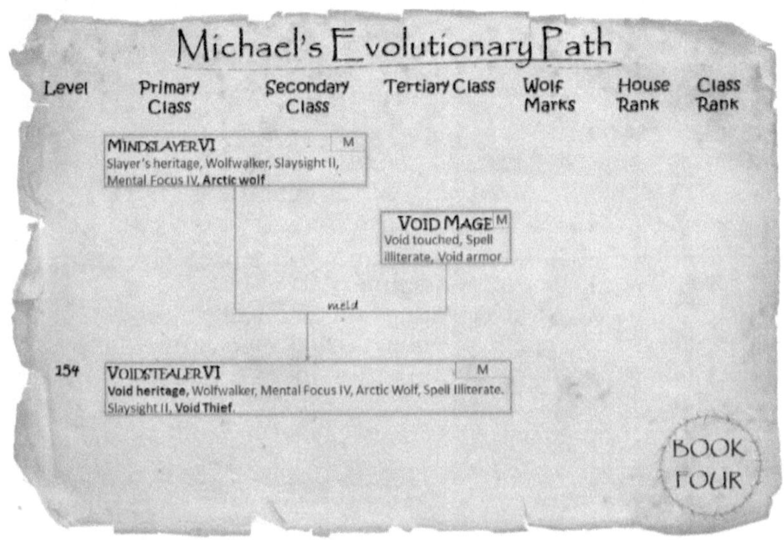

Player Profile: Michael

Level: 154. Rank: 15. Current Health: 32%.
Stamina: 7%. Mana: 0%. Psi: 13%.
Species: Human. Lives Remaining: 2.
True Marks (hidden): Pack-alpha.
False Marks (fabricated): Lesser Shadow, Lesser Light, Lesser Dark.

Active Buffs

Damage reduction: Life: 0%. Death: 5%. Air: 40%. Earth: 40%. Fire: 40%. Water: 40%.
Shadow: 5%. Light: 5%. Dark: 5%. Nether: 20%. Physical: 54%*.

Additional resistance (excluding inherent resistance provided attributes):
Life: 0%. Death: 2.5%. Air: 20%. Earth: 20%. Fire: 20%. Water: 20%.
Shadow: 2.5%. Light: 2.5%. Dark: 2.5%. Nether: 10%. Physical: 0%.

Immunities: Entanglement: tier 2 spells*. Mind spells: tier 2 spells*.
** denotes buffs affected by items.*

Attributes

Available: 0 points.
Strength: 21 (13)*. Constitution: 27 (19)*. Dexterity: 79 (55)*. Perception: 35 (31)*. Mind: 75 (71)*. Magic: 31 (21)*. Faith: 0.
** denotes attributes affected by items.*

Classes

Available: 2 points.
Primary-Secondary-Tertiary tri-blend: voidstalker (fabricated). voidstealer VI (hidden).

Traits

void heritage (hidden): +2 Dexterity, +2 Strength, +4 Mind, +4 Perception, +6 Magic.
beast tongue: can speak to beastkin.
Marked: can see spirit signatures.
wolfwalker (hidden): improved senses in all conditions.
anointed scion (hidden): bound to House Wolf.
inscrutable mind: +8 Mind.
secret blood (hidden): conceals bloodline.
mental focus IV: increases effectiveness of Mind skills by 40%.
budding explorer: all key points in newly discovered sectors logged.
arctic wolf (hidden): +5 Constitution, +2 Mind, +3 Strength.
spell illiterate: cannot cast mana-based spells.
potion resistance II: potency of potions reduced by 2 ranks.

Skills

Available skill slots: 0.
dodging (current: 125. max: 550. Dexterity, basic).
sneaking (current: 127. max: 550. Dexterity, basic).
shortswords (current: 139. max: 550. Dexterity, basic).
two weapon fighting (current: 121. max: 550. Dexterity, advanced).
light armor (current: 126. max: 190. Constitution, basic).
thieving (current: 102. max: 550. Dexterity, basic).
chi (current: 124. max: 710. Mind, advanced).
meditation (current: 143. max: 710. Mind, basic).
telekinesis (current: 127. max: 710. Mind, advanced).
telepathy (current: 116. max: 710. Mind, advanced).
insight (current: 147. max: 310. Perception, basic).
deception (current: 111. max: 310. Perception, master).
channeling (current: 101. max: 210. Magic, basic).
elemental absorption (current: 81. max: 210. Magic, master).
null force (current: 15. max: 210. Magic, master).
null life (current: 4. max: 210. Magic, master).
null death (current: 11. max: 210. Magic, master).
nether absorption (current: 48. max: 210. Magic, master).

Abilities

<u>**Constitution ability slots used:** 10 / 19.</u>
load controller (10 Constitution, expert, light armor).

<u>**Dexterity ability slots used:** 41 / 55.</u>
crippling blow (Dexterity, basic, shortswords).
minor piercing strike (5 Dexterity, advanced, shortswords).

improved backstab (10 Dexterity, expert, sneaking).
improved trap disarm (5 Dexterity, advanced, thieving).
superior lockpicking (5 Dexterity, advanced, thieving).
superior set trap (10 Dexterity, expert, thieving).
whirlwind (5 Dexterity, advanced, two weapon fighting).

<u>Mind ability slots used:</u> **57 / 71.**
superior mass charm (10 Mind, expert, telepathy).
stunning slap (Mind, basic, chi).
windborne (10 Mind, expert, telekinesis).
heightened reflexes (10 Mind, expert, chi).
twin astral blades (5 Mind, advanced, telepathy).
long shadow blink (10 Mind, expert, telekinesis).
quick mend (10 Mind, expert, chi).
simple mind shield (Mind, basic, meditation).

<u>Perception ability slots used:</u> **31 / 31.**
improved analyze (5 Perception, advanced, insight).
improved trap detect (5 Perception, advanced, thieving).
conceal small weapon (Perception, basic, deception).
superior facial disguise (10 Perception, expert, deception).
superior ventro (5 Perception, advanced, deception).
lesser imitate (5 Perception, advanced, deception).

<u>Other abilities:</u>
improved slaysight (hidden) (Class, advanced, telepathy).
basic void thief (hidden) (Class, basic, any void skill and telepathy).

<u>**Known Key Points**</u>

Dungeon Sector 14,913 (candidate's dungeon) exit portal and safe zone.
Kingdom Sector 12,560 (wolves' valley) nether portal and safe zone.
Kingdom Sector 1 (Nexus) safe zone.
Dungeon Sector 101 (scorching dunes) exit portal and safe zone.
Dungeon Sectors 102, 103, and 104 (haunted catacombs) exit portals and safe zones.
Dungeon Sector 105, 106, 107, 108, and 109 (guardian tower) exit portals.
Kingdom Sector 18,240 nether portal 1 (guardian tower), and nether portal 2 (Draven's reach).

<u>**Equipped**</u>

<u>**Weapons**</u>
stygian shortsword, +3.
ebonheart (+30% damage).

<u>**Armor & Clothes**</u>
ranger's kit (+40% damage reduction, +4 ranks stealth).
bomber's belt (5 x acid bombs, 5 x smoke bombs, 5 x ice bombs, and 5 x fire bombs).

belt of the chameleon (11 x rank 4 nether protection crystals, 11 x rank 4 disease protection crystals, 10 scent concealment crystals, 5 x mental concealment crystals, 4 x rank 6 disease protection crystals, 2 x rank 5 poison protection crystals, 2 x rank 4 strength enhancement crystals, 1 x rank 4 dexterity enhancement crystals, and 3 x rank 4 magic enhancement crystals).
wayfarer's boots (legendary item, +8 Dexterity, move soundlessly).
wayfarer's gloves (legendary item, +8 Dexterity, hands immune to hazardous substances).
magister's cloak (legendary item, +4 Magic, +8% physical damage reduction).

Rings & Accessories

adept's ring (+6 Magic).
goliath's ring (+8 Strength).
acrobat's ring (+8 Dexterity).
sharpshooter's band (+4 Perception).
hale stone (+8 Constitution).
savant's ring (+4 Mind).
troll's talisman bracelet (+6% damage reduction).
gift of the unbound ring (immunity to tier 1 and 2 entanglement spells).
band of stillness ring (immunity to tier 1 and 2 Mind spells).
aetherstone bracelet (2 / 5 stored locations, 0 stones charged).
simple potion bracelet (3 / 3 full heal potions).
veteran's trapper's wristband (198 / 200 trap-making crystals).

Other

backpack, small bag of holding (50 slots), large bag of holding (200 slots), hunter's alchemy stone.

Backpack Contents

Money: 73 golds, 5 silvers, and 3 coppers.
20 x field rations.
2 x flasks of water.
2 x iron daggers.
1 x bedroll.
bounty letter authorization.
1 x coil of rope.
tavern bill of ownership.
Tartan token.
2 x full mana potions.
3 major mana potions.
2 x minor mana potions.
Viviane token.
Kesh Emporium access card.
cat claws.
spectacles of ward seeing (detect tier 4 wards).
BHG ID (junior member, 1 / 10 active jobs).

simple map of Nexus.
1 x rank 6 cure disease potions.
commune rod.
superior analyze, greater trap detect, ability tomes.
enchanted leather armor set (+20% damage reduction, -35% Dexterity and Magic).
10 x acid bombs, 14 x smoke bombs, 10 x ice bombs, and 10 x fire bombs.
slotted-potion belt (2 x rank 4 cure poison, 1 moderate heal, 2 full heal, 2 full mana potion, 3 major mana potions).
faithful (+40% damage).

Miscellaneous Loot

None.

Alchemy Stone Contents

None.

Bank Contents

<u>Money</u>: 1,655 gold, 0 silvers, and 0 coppers.
2 x full healing potions.
2 x full mana potions.

<u>Tavern Money</u>: 9,850 gold, 0 silvers, and 0 coppers.

Open Tasks

Find the Last Wolf Envoy (hidden) (find Ceruvax).
Heist in the Dark (steal chalice from the Power, Paya).
Silent Brethren (find out what has happened to the guardians).
A Perverted Trial (stop the Triumvirate abuse of the Combat Trial).
Brokering Peace (establish peace in sector 12,560 within 4 months).
Brotherhood Obligations (report to the brotherhood after 4 months).

BOOKS BY THE AUTHOR

BY TOM ELLIOT

The Grand Game (series page)
Book 1: The Grand Game: ebook | audiobook
Book 2: Way of the Wolf: ebook | audiobook
Book 3: World Nexus: ebook | audiobook
Book 4: House Wolf: ebook | audiobook
Book 5: Wolf in the Void: ebook | audiobook
Book 6: A Scion's Duty: ebook | audiobook
Book 7: Ancient Debts: ebook | audiobook
Book 8: The Lost Reclaimed: ebook (coming soon)

The Grand Game Box Set (series page)
Book 1-3: Birth of a Player: ebook
Book 4-6: Rise of an Elite: ebook
Book 7-9: The Making of a Power: ebook (coming soon)

The Grand Game, Elana (series page)
Book 1: Empyrean's Rise: ebook
Book 2: Empyrean's Flight: ebook

Annals of the Runeguard (series page)
Book 1: Proving Grounds: ebook

BY ROHAN M. VIDER

The Dragon Mage Saga (series page)
Book 1: Overworld: ebook | audiobook
Book 2: Dungeons: ebook | audiobook
Book 3: Sponsors: ebook (coming soon)

The Gods' Game (series page)
Crota, the Gods' Game Volume I
The Labyrinth, the Gods' Game Volume II
Sovereign Rising, the Gods' Game Volume III
Sovereign, the Gods' Game, Volume IV
Sovereign's Choice, the Gods' Game Volume V

Tales from the Gods' Game
Dungeon Dive (Tales from the Gods' Game, Book 1)

AFTERWORD

Thank you for reading the Grand Game!

If you enjoyed the book, please consider leaving a review on Amazon [click here]. I'm already working on Michael's next adventure.

If you have any questions, comments, or want to support my writing, please feel free to contact me through my site, TomLitRPG.com or Discord.

Alternatively, if you wish to learn more about the world of the Forever Kingdom, understand the system of the Grand Game better, or are just looking for the latest news on the Grand Game, please visit my site at TomLitRPG.com or signup up here for my: Newsletter.

Regards,
Tom
Support my writing on **PATREON**
Amazon Author page | Goodreads | Facebook | Reddit | Discord |

Definitions

Accord: old agreement between new Powers ceding control of Nexus to the Triumvirate.

Adjudicator: controller and arbitrator of the Grand Game.

alchemy stone: a device used to store alchemical components.

ancient: old Power.

anointed scion: a scion who has bound himself to a bloodline.

ascendant undead: term the Adjudicator used to describe Stayne, meaning unknown.

blended Class: a combined Class.

blood awakening: the process of recalling blood memories.

blood infusion: the absorption of the essences from former scions.

blood memories: gifts from your forebears containing the power of the ancients themselves.

bi-blend: a combination of two melded Classes.

bloodline: reference to the ancient from which the player is a descendant.

civilian player: a player without a class or combat abilities. Civilians do not have a player level.

class-unique skill: a skill that is unique to a Class and can only be acquired through a Class stone.

closed sector: a landmass that does not physically border another, making the area inaccessible except by portal.

composite spell: a multi-stage spell made up of two or more individual spells.

controlled sector: a sector owned by a faction. Ownership of a sector gives the faction's players increased privileges in the region.

Class: a defined path or vocation that gives a player access to specific skills.

Class evolution: the advancement of a Class, generally to a better-ranked one, due to particular traits, skills, or Marks acquired by the player.

Dark: one of the three Forces.

Darksworn: a player pledged to the Dark who values the self over the collective.

Elite: a tier five player, i.e. someone above level two hundred.

ebonblade: soulbound weapons found in the Twilight Dungeon.

envoy: a trusted representative of a Power authorized to speak on their behalf.

Endless Dungeon: A section of the Nethersphere where dungeon mechanics are active.

evolution: the advancement of a player's core characteristics.

follower: a player that has pledged themself in a binding vow to a Force or Power.

Force: Light, Dark, Shadow. The building blocks of the cosmos and energy in its rawest form.

Forever Kingdom: the world of the Nethersphere and Kingdom.

forsworn: a sworn who has betrayed their Power.

Game: refers to the Grand Game.

gatekeepers: holders of ancient lore, guardians of the ancients' trials.

House: House of the Ancient.

House of the Ancient: a grouping of followers pledged to one Prime.

Kingdoms: the collective name given to sectors located in the aether.

lycan: werewolf.

ley line: magic threads connecting nether sectors.

Light: one of the three Forces.

Lightsworn: a player that champions the cause of the many, even to his own detriment.

marshmen: mysterious dwellers in the saltmarsh district.

meld: the process of combining multiple Classes into one.

mindglow: the visible signature of a mind as seen with mindsight.

neutral sector: a sector unowned and unclaimed by any faction or Force.

Nethersphere: collective name given to the sectors in the nether.

new Power: one of the Powers that usurped the ancients.

oath breaker: one who has broken a Pact.

Pact: a binding enacted between a Power and player, overseen by the Adjudicator.

Power: an evolved player.

Prime: head of ancient bloodline. An ancient.

Prime Conclave: a gathering of Primes referred to by Kolath.

Primehood: the act of becoming a Prime.

rift: unstable portal from the nether. Ley line created by stygian seed.

scav: short for scavenger. A player who loots kills not his own.

scion: one bearing the blood of an ancient.

scion abilities: the abilities Michael had earned during the Wolf trials: astral blade, chi heal, mind shield, shadow blink.

seeking spell: spell that distinguishes friend from foe.

stolen spell: a spell acquired from another and cast using their skills and attributes.

soulbound: an item that remains with the player after death.

sworn: as in sworn servant. A sworn is a follower of a Power who has sufficiently deepened their binding Mark.

the real: reference to the physical realm.

trap-making crystal: crystal in trapper's wristband. Can be manifested as different trap components.

trials of the ancients: tests created by the Primes for their successors.

tri-blend: a combination of three melded Classes.

trigger-cast: a spell held in readiness and invoked under specific conditions.

upgrade gem: a game item used to advance an ability a single tier.

voids: informal term used to reference players who possess a void Class.

void Classes: a rare subset of Classes that specialize in damage reduction.

windslide: ramp of air formed by windborne spell.

were-trait: a trait carried by all were-players, fueling their ability to shapeshift.

weres: short for werewolves and other were-players.

wolf trials: ancient trials created by Wolf Prime.

wolfkind: used interchangeably with wolfkin.

FACTIONS

Albion Bank: major non-aligned bank in the Forever Kingdom.
Awakened Dead: A Dark faction.
Axis of Evil: An alliance of Dark factions.
blackguards: Policing force in the Dark quarter.
dawn brigade: Policing force in the Light quarter.
gray watch: Policing force in the Shadow quarter.
Mantises: A Dark faction of assassins.
Marauders: small Shadow faction.
Shadow Coalition: A power bloc of Shadow, made up of like-minded Shadow Powers.
Tartan: the faction of Tartar, the god-emperor.
Tartan legion: the military forces of Tartar.
Triumvirate: A unique faction composed of Light, Dark, and Shadow that control Nexus.
Unity Council: the governing body of Light, made up of all Light-affiliated Powers.

GUARDIANS

Kolath: mysterious construct in the Guardian Tower.

GUILDS AND NON-FACTIONS

Bounty Hunters Guild (BHG): headquartered in the plague quarter, mercenaries.
Information Brokers: A gnomish organization in the plague quarter.
Kesh Emporium: merchant company owned by Kesh.
Stygian Brotherhood: headquartered in the plague quarter, experts in all-things-nether.

HOUSE WOLF

Atiras: Dead Prime Wolf.
Ceruvax: Last envoy.

NON-PLAYERS

Arden: Gnome information broker.
Cyren: Gnome senior information broker.

PLAYERS

Anriq: werewolf criminal.

Barac: crusader, male centaur.
Beorin: senior BHG member, dwarf.
Bornholm: Michael's companion from Erebus' dungeon, dwarf.
Cara: alias given to Kesh's agent in plague quarter by Michael.
Dathe: unknown werewolf player.
Devlin: Viviane's guard, unknown aquatic species.
Ent: guard outside emporium, armsmaster, giant.
Eyes: The BHG HQ doorkeeper, species unknown.
Jasiah: duelist, human male.
Genmark: ward architect, gnome male.
Gintalush: mantis assassin, insectoid.
Hannah: BHG client liaison officer, human female.
Kartara: huntmistress at Stygian Brotherhood Chapterhouse.
Kesh: master merchant, owner of the emporium, human woman.
Lake: guard outside emporium, berserker, giant.
Michael: protagonist.
Misha: Marauder tracker, aka the Hound.
Moonshadow: aeromancer, male elf.
Morin: Michael's companion from Erebus' dungeon, the painted woman.
Orlon: Triumvirate knight-captain in the plague quarter, human.
Pitor: rank 15 warrior, Kalin sworn, human, Marauder sub-boss.
Richter: constable in Triumvirate citadel, human civilian.
Saya: apprentice alchemist, tavernkeeper in wolves' valley, gnome.
Shael: red minstrel, half-elf.
Simone: sharpshooter, half-elf female.
Stayne: Erebus' henchman.
Stonebeard: Triumvirate captain, dwarf.
Talon: the captain, Tartar's envoy.
Tantor: Michael's companion from Erebus' dungeon, high elf male.
Teg: Michael's escort in citadel, human.
Terence: rank 2 human fighter, swordsman.
Teresa: rank 2 human fighter, blade devotee.
Tevin: Marauder knight.
Toff: player outside haunted catacombs, ogre
Trion: Triumvirate holy knight, Herat sworn, human.
Trexton: herbalist in Triumvirate citadel, Simone's contact, dark elf.
Wengulax: mantis assassin, blade dancer, human.
Wilsh: Blackguard captain, human.
Yzark: Marauder boss.

POWERS

Arinna: Light Power.
Artem: Shadow Power. Goddess of nature.
Erebus: Dark Power, leader of the Awakened Dead faction.
Herat: Light Power, member of the Triumvirate.
Ishita: Spider goddess, Dark Power, member of the Awakened Dead.
Loken: Shadow Power.
Kalin: Minor Shadow Power, faction leader of the Marauders.

Menaq: Dark Power, leader of the Mantis faction.
Muriel: Light Power contesting Wolf Valley.
Mydas: Shadow Power, member of the Triumvirate.
Paya: Dark Power, junior member of the Awakened Dead ruling council.
Rampel: Dark Power, member of the Triumvirate.
Tartar: Dark Power, also known as the God-Emperor.
Viviane: Power owning the Albion Bank.

WOLFKIN

Aira: dire wolf dame.
Barak: dire wolf elder.
Cantur: half-mad wolf.
Duggar: dire wolf alpha.
Oursk: dire wolf sire.
Leta: dire wolf elder.
Monac: dire wolf elder and former alpha.
Moonstalker: Oursk's pup.
Shadetooth: Oursk's pup.
Snow: arctic wolf pack alpha.
Star: Snow's mate.
Stormdark: Oursk's pup.
Sulan: dire wolf healer.
Suva: dire wolf elder.

Locations